Praise for *Hush*

"A brilliant debut from a very talented author—a guaranteed page-turner that will keep the reader riveted from beginning to end."
—Katherine Sutcliffe

"With *Hush,* Anne Frasier slams into the fast lane and goes to the head of the pack. This one has Guaranteed Winner written all over it."
—Jayne Ann Krentz

"Warning: Don't read this book if you are home alone."
—Lisa Gardner

HUSH

Anne Frasier

AN ONYX BOOK

ONYX
Published by New American Library, a division of
Penguin Putnam Inc., 375 Hudson Street,
New York, New York 10014, U.S.A.
Penguin Books Ltd, 80 Strand,
London WC2R 0RL, England
Penguin Books Australia Ltd, Ringwood,
Victoria, Australia
Penguin Books Canada Ltd, 10 Alcorn Avenue,
Toronto, Ontario, Canada M4V 3B2
Penguin Books (N.Z.) Ltd, 182–190 Wairau Road,
Auckland 10, New Zealand

Penguin Books Ltd, Registered Offices:
Harmondsworth, Middlesex, England

First published by Onyx, an imprint of New American Library,
a division of Penguin Putnam Inc.

First Printing, May 2002
10 9 8 7 6 5 4 3 2 1

Printed in the United States of America

PUBLISHER'S NOTE
This is a work of fiction. Names, characters, places, and incidents either
are the product of the author's imagination or are used fictitiously,
and any resemblance to actual persons, living or dead, business
establishments, events, or locales is entirely coincidental.

For Neil and Martha

*A very special thanks to my editor, Ellen Edwards,
and agent, Steve Axelrod*

Prologue

He spun the dial on the combination lock—quickly because he'd done it so many times. Clockwise to twenty-six, counterclockwise one revolution, stopping at ten, clockwise to eighteen. He heard the familiar click and pulled down on the lock, watching with an almost sexual excitement as it fell open. He slid the catch through the holes in the handle, then opened the locker, the door rattling with a satisfying metallic resonance.

The locker was where he kept his souvenirs. He'd gotten it at an auction, from the physical education department of a high school that had closed. It was tall, with hooks to hang things and shelves to put smaller objects.

Using both hands, he reached in and pulled out his scrapbook.

Scrapbook wasn't really a good word for it, because *scrap* had a negative connotation. For one thing, *scrap* implied something torn, something leftover, like table scraps, or scrap metal. For another thing, if you took away the *s,* you'd have *crap.*

And the book he held with both hands was more than crap, much more. It was his treasure book, his *life.*

He walked in reverse until the backs of his legs came in contact with the metal springs of his bed, the soft edge of the mattress. He sat down with his treasure book on his lap, his knees together to support the book's weight, his feet on the cement floor of the basement.

It was one of the scrapbooks you could get at any discount store. The kind young girls kept hidden under their beds, bringing them out to share with best friends. His scrapbook was an ivory color that had yellowed around the edges because he'd had it so long. Gold letters spelled out SCRAPBOOK.

It bothered him that it had turned yellow. He wished it hadn't. But he couldn't get a new scrapbook. It wouldn't be the same.

He opened the book.

Glued to the first page was a photograph of a young woman sitting in a hospital bed, a baby in her arms, smiling at the camera. He gently ran a finger across the photo, across the woman's face, giving the bundled infant a little caress before turning the page.

Mementos.

The woman's driver's license. Her tiny book of addresses and phone numbers. Discount-store photos of people he didn't know taken in front of fake Christmas backgrounds. Colors that had once been red were now orange, proving that there was really no such thing as a good deal.

People were stupid.

They smelled, and they were stupid.

The next page was a Polaroid of his first kill, taken in the park where he'd left her. She was already dead when he had her pose for the camera. And since she was a whore, he'd pulled up her dress and pulled down her pants to expose the dark pelt of hair that covered her sexual organs. She had a hand on one hip where he'd placed it, another in her hair in a provocative, slutty pose.

He'd tried to make her smile, tried to pull her lips away from her teeth, but her expression just kept slipping back into a sort of grimace. For his next kill, he brought Scotch tape so the mouth would stay where he wanted it.

Around her neck was the opal necklace he'd given to his mother. She wore it all the time. That made him happy and made his crotch tingle. He pressed the spine of the book against himself.

He continued through the book, reading the yellow clippings he'd cut from newspapers. The Madonna Murderer.

Madonna. Mother and child.

The mothers weren't *virgins,* they were *whores.* Whores! *He* was the untouched virgin. *He* was the immaculate birth.

The cow upstairs hadn't given birth to him. He couldn't have come from her womb. Not with her stupidity, her TV game shows, her white-trashiness.

He continued turning pages until he came to a photo he'd cut from a newspaper. A photo the paper had gotten from her high school yearbook.

Her hair was long, blond, and straight, her smile wholesome in a cheerleader kind of way.

Hers hadn't been a satisfying kill. She'd robbed him of his pleasure, and in so doing, she'd confused him, sending him into a dark oblivion of pharmaceuticals.

The mental hospital represented a period of time when his mind was foggy and a veil covered his eyes. When his normally quick mind was as thick as motor oil, his thoughts floating away like balloons. But now his head was clear once again.

Looking at her now, he could almost smell her woman's blood, her mother's blood, her birth blood.

He pressed the spine of the book down harder against him, harder, harder, gasping in pain and pleasure.

His mother had caught him masturbating when he was thirteen.

"Dirty boy," he now whispered in a high-pitched voice. "Dirty, dirty boy. Don't ever touch yourself like that, dirty boy. Dirty, dirty boy."

He heard her stumbling footsteps in the room above his head. His face flushed hot with guilt. His hands shook as he closed the scrapbook but continued to hold it over his throbbing penis.

It was ten o'clock in the morning and she was already on her way to being dead drunk. She was almost always drunk. He actually liked her better drunk because when she was sober she saw too much. She would stare at him with her wild eyes, and he would simultaneously wonder why she hated him and what it would feel like to kill her.

Chapter 1

Outside Ivy Dunlap's bedroom window a woodpecker jackhammered away at the wooden shutters of the stone house.

Damn bird. Damn annoying bird.

Her neighbor, Mrs. Gafney, told her if she put a plastic owl on the corner post it would scare the woodpeckers away. But then Mrs. Gafney also sprinkled salt into the sidewalk cracks to kill the weeds, corroding the cement until it turned to dust. She was the same person who ate packages of cookies after midnight while the crumbs gave her bedsores, all because *The Enquirer* had told her the body burned more calories while a person slept.

Mrs. Gafney lived half a mile away. In winter, Ivy could sometimes see the sun reflecting off the metal roofs of the Gafney house and barn, and on clear nights she could spot the yard light twinkling an uninvasive hello. Sometimes she could even hear Mr. Gafney calling to his milk cows, their bells gently answering as the animals slowly headed for fresh hay and the milking machines. But in summer, when the leaves were on the trees and the air was heavy with dew, Ivy could almost forget the Gafneys existed.

St. Sebastian was a beautiful land of faraway water. Forty miles to the north was Georgian Bay, to the south, Lake Erie. To the west lay Toronto and Lake Huron, to the east, Lake Ontario. Residents of Toronto had summer cottages in St. Sebastian, but few were brave enough to visit in the dead of winter when the wind howled and the roads were closed for days. Not far off, in Bainwood, there were supposed to be men with feet that pointed backward. Ivy had never seen such men, but Mrs. Gafney swore it to be true.

In this part of Ontario, the landscape had been shaped by glaciers that had crawled and creaked patiently across the earth, rolling the stones smooth. Children spent their summers picking up those ice-age remnants from farmers' fields, piling them high until their nails broke and their fingers bled. It was said that there were no rough stones in St. Sebastian, and of that Ivy was certain.

Outside, the woodpecker continued its morning ritual, moving from one shutter to another, testing them all for bugs.

Ivy lay there listening. Perhaps the tone of her breathing changed, telling Jinx that she was awake, because the tomcat pounced on the bed. He was a polite animal, always waiting until her eyes were open before bothering her, before he tiptoed across the bed to finally lie across her stomach, purring while she pet him.

She scratched him under his chin the way he liked it, talking to him all the while, saying things like, "You lazy guy. You just love attention, don't you?"

She hadn't known she was a cat person until Jinx showed up at her door one winter night when the snow was two feet deep and the wind was blowing so hard that the furnace couldn't keep the house warm. He was half-wild, but his hunger had made him temporarily tame. She took him in and fed him, and he let her pet him that first night. But by the next morning, the warm milk and bread had done their work and he had reverted back to the cat he'd been before hunger had taken hold. She tried to catch him to throw him outside—the sun was shining, the wind had stopped—but he was a yellow streak, disappearing under the curio cabinet, where he stayed for three whole days. She tried to coax him out with warm milk, but he wouldn't budge. She offered him a tiny slice of ham, putting it just out of his reach. One stiff, yellow paw appeared from below the antique cabinet, swiped at the ham, and pulled it into the darkness.

"Gotta get up now," Ivy said, gently pushing the cat to the side and flinging back the covers.

In the kitchen, she put milk in his bowl before pouring some over her cereal. After breakfast, she ran three miles on the treadmill, showered, then went outside to the garden. She was gathering strawberries when she heard the far-off ringing of the phone through the open kitchen window.

She got to her feet, moving toward the sound with the bowl of strawberries in one hand. Her sandals, damp with morning dew, took her down the stone path that led from the garden to the kitchen. Inside, the phone was still ringing. She picked up the receiver and answered with a distracted "Hello?"

On the other end was a voice she hadn't heard in years. A voice she'd begun to wonder if she'd ever hear again. It belonged to Abraham Sinclair of the Chicago Police Department, the man who had helped her disappear.

"It's happening again," was all he said. It was all he had to say.

The ceramic bowl she'd picked up at a flea market slid from her nerveless fingers, crashing to the flagstone, shattering. Strawberries rolled across the floor, finally finding darkness in the cobwebs and dust beneath the antique pie safe.

Breathe, Ivy reminded herself. *Breathe.*

The moment she'd feared and dreaded and lived for brought her to her knees.

"Claudia? Are you there?"

Claudia. A name from another life.

"Yes," she said, her voice sounding relatively strong considering the way she was kneeling on the floor, quaking. "I—I'm here."

"It's been a long time."

"Yes."

"We need your help, but I'll understand if you want nothing to do with this."

He would be relieved if she said she had put it all behind her, that she'd moved on with her life, that she was now married with two lovely children. From that imagined life, she would be able to tell him about her safe, secure, mundane yet wonderful existence where she carpooled during the school year and made dandelion crowns in summer.

In a way, she *had* moved on, but not to the extent she would have liked. Because she'd come to find out that no matter how good a person's intentions, it was impossible to forge deep relationships when you harbored secrets that could never be told.

She suddenly saw with an almost spiritual clarity that everything she'd done up to now had been in preparation for this moment. Subconsciously she'd spent the years waiting for a phone call she'd hoped would never come. And all the friends, all the Jinxes and birds and gardens and bowls of strawberries in the world would never be enough. Waiting for this phone call—that's what had driven her.

As the years had passed, she'd begun to believe that her new life was real, her old life over. But now the life she'd worked so hard to build for herself in St. Sebastian faded. In her mind, the friends she'd made and the people she'd met suddenly didn't seem in complete focus.

She would have to make something up, say she was going away for a while, maybe to care for a sick relative. Yes, that should work. The Gafneys could have her strawberries and asparagus, and later, if she was gone that long, her Concord grapes. She was scheduled to teach two summer classes in criminal psychology at the University of Guelph. Those would have to be canceled.

And Jinx. What would she do about Jinx? Mrs. Gafney would be willing to come and feed him, but he'd get so lonely.

She pushed herself to her feet. She straightened. Lately she'd been feeling older than her thirty-nine years. But now, like a soldier preparing for battle, she mentally shook off all things physical. "I'll come."

Chapter 2

Chief Homicide Detective Max Irving took a drink of cold coffee, grimaced, and put the stained cup back down on his desk. He glanced at the clock on the wall, realized he'd missed lunch, then opened up the coroner's report. It was the third time he'd read it in two hours.

Tia Sheppard and infant boy, Timothy Sheppard. The mother's body had ligature marks around the throat, along with twenty-two stab wounds concentrated in the breast and womb—the areas most symbolic of motherhood.

The infant, Timothy Sheppard, died of suffocation. There were no marks of any kind on the body.

Except for the number of stab wounds, the report was almost identical to that of the Madonna Murders of years ago. Max couldn't allow himself to take the obvious path, yet at the same time he had to leave his mind open to all possibilities, no matter how implausible.

The Madonna Murders. It was the name a reporter from the *Chicago Herald* had come up with, and it had stuck even though it wasn't entirely appropriate—the victims being unwed mothers and their infant sons.

Such tag lines were no longer allowed, but that didn't seem to keep them from showing up.

Sixteen years ago the crimes stopped, and the investigation was eventually turned over to CHESS, Chicago's Central Homicide Evaluation Support Squad, a squad that dealt exclusively with cold cases. That was until last week's murder of a mother and son had people whispering in fear.

His gut feeling was that the murders were the work of a copycat. He felt it was highly unlikely that a serial killer would reemerge again after close to two decades. If the killer had been, say, twenty-four at the time of the original murders, that would make him forty-one now, an age much older than the CPD's profiler had come up with. But then profiles weren't foolproof.

He put in a call to the forensic lab even though he knew they wouldn't have any information yet. It never hurt to remind them of the importance of their report.

"Do you know how backed up we are?" the frazzled lab tech asked.

"Prioritize."

"We are."

"Do I need to mention that this could be a serial killer case?" Max couldn't believe he was lending voice to the very kind of media blitz he'd ranted against.

"Join the club. The serial-killer club."

Black humor. They all did it. It was the only way to get through. But the lab technician's next words were serious.

"We have detectives heading two different Chicago serial-killer investigations. One in Area One, one in Area Three, and now this mother-infant business in Area Five. How do I prioritize that?"

Ten years ago it was speculated that there were fifty
serial killers working in the United States at any given
time. Now, even though violent crime was down nationwide, serial killings, spree killings, senseless, random acts of cruelty and violence increased on a daily
basis. "How much longer?" Max asked, trying to keep
his impatience from reflecting in his voice.

"Three, maybe four days."

As soon as Max hung up, the phone rang. It was
Superintendent Abraham Sinclair summoning him to
his office at Chicago Police Department Headquarters
in Area One.

Max pulled his blue Chevrolet Caprice up to the
guardhouse window, flashing his ID and badge. The
guard nodded. The wooden arm lifted and Max shot
through, parking in a lot that was as flat and spread
out as a discount store's—the CPD's contribution to
urban sprawl.

The soles of Max's black leather shoes rang out
against the marble floor as he moved through the re-
volving doors and passed the wall of stars, a memorial
to Chicago police officers killed in the line of duty
dating back to 1872. Max checked in with the officer
at the desk, then moved down the hall, taking a silent
elevator to the fourth floor and Superintendent Sinclair's office.

It was rare for Abraham Sinclair to summon Max
to Headquarters. Their meetings sometimes took place
over the phone, but more likely over a hasty lunch
or dinner.

Preoccupied, Max moved down the hall, mumbling
an apology when he brushed shoulders with a female
officer. She gave him a smile of reassurance, but he

was already past her, his gaze narrowing on the Superintendent's closed door.

Max didn't waste smiles on strangers. He didn't even waste them on coworkers. Occasionally he wasted them on friends, but only occasionally.

Max knocked. Without waiting for an answer, he opened the door and walked in.

Even though the room hadn't been occupied all that long when you consider a policeman's entire career, and even though the flavor of the newly constructed Headquarters was supposed to be that of open airiness, the Superintendent had somehow managed to bring with him the cramped dark feel of his old digs on South State Street. There was a weariness to it, an aura of the taint that eventually became part of the people who dealt with crime and perversion on a daily basis.

The walls were filled with many years' worth of awards. Abraham's navy-blue jacket, which hung over the back of his chair, was adorned with medals, his desk with family photos. He had a lot to be proud of. Superintendent Sinclair was a black man who had worked hard to tear down racial barriers. He'd established the domestic violence program and was the single driving force behind Chicago's drastic drop in homicides. He'd worked hard to open up lines of communication between officers and citizens, blacks and whites, rich and poor. He was a role model for everyone, and other cities looked to him as a shining example.

Sinclair glanced up from his phone conversation, waving Max into a chair, which Max ignored. Not a command, only a suggestion. Max would rather stand. He'd rather pace.

Sinclair swiveled in his chair, turning his back on Max. "I'm going to have to call you later," he said, quickly ending the conversation. He hung up, then swung around and looked Max in the eye, interlacing his fingers together over a thick file folder that Max noted was labeled "Madonna Murders."

"It's my granddaughter's birthday," Abraham announced.

Abraham had always had a way of mixing his two worlds—something Max didn't do. Max didn't chat about his son when he was at work, and he didn't talk about work to his son. In that way he hoped—foolishly, perhaps—to keep Ethan from being touched by bad things.

Max got to the point. "You wanted to talk to me about the mother and son homicide?"

"I wanted to let you know that I'm bringing in somebody else to help on the case."

"FBI?" It was unusual for someone to come in from the outside unless he was FBI.

"No. Her name's Ivy Dunlap."

"Dunlap? What are her qualifications?"

"She has a degree in criminal psychology. Teaches at the University of Guelph—"

"Guelph?"

"Ontario."

When Max thought deeply he didn't make eye contact until the idea formulated somewhere in the room. Then, bang, his eyes locked with Abraham's—the equivalence of snapping his fingers.

"Isn't she the one who came up with some in-depth theory about something she called symbolic murder? Some bullshit about serial killings representing metaphors of the unconscious mind?"

"I wouldn't call it bullshit." Abraham seemed disappointed that Max had remembered.

Max suspected this was someone working on a story, wanting to get the "real, inside picture." But what that kind of person really wanted was a sanitized version of some of the most horrific crimes being committed in the world today. Max didn't want to be a part of it. "I don't want some damn novice screwing up evidence, passing out at crime scenes," Max said. You could be straightforward with Abraham. That's what made him such a good Superintendent. And they'd been friends for years.

"Give her a chance. She's a professional. I think she'll be an asset."

"Why somebody from Canada?" Canada had its share of psychotic homicidal maniacs like the Scarborough killer, who hung his victims on fences, but the country's entire count didn't add up to Chicago's tally. "It doesn't make sense."

Years ago, Max probably would have been given some speech about the world not making sense, and how he just had to obey when given orders. Now Abraham Sinclair, man of the new millennium, pushed himself to his feet and said, "I have to get going. Got to get a birthday present."

The closer Abraham got to retirement, the less interested in work he became. Burnt-out, Max figured, but also mentally moving on, moving away, moving forward to time spent with his granddaughter, winter vacations in Florida.

Max stared at him, suddenly wondering if Abraham and this Dunlap person had something going. If that were the case, why hadn't he mentioned her before? Max had known Abraham a long time. Through his divorce, his battle against the alcoholism that was so much a part of Homicide. As were broken relationships. It was hard to work with the horrors they saw on a daily basis, then go home and watch sitcoms with your wife, or talk about what kind of wallpaper would look best in the bathroom. Even a child's fever seemed trivial in comparison to what they dealt with every day.

"She's flying in tomorrow. I'm picking her up and bringing her to Grand Central," Abraham said. "I want you to let her in on everything pertaining to the case." He picked up the folder and handed it to Max. "See that she gets this."

"Over half the information in this folder is classified."

"She's to have access to it."

"We can't risk having her leak any of it to the press."

"That isn't going to happen. And you know damn well this is no reflection on you. I assigned you to the case because you're the best and I knew you wouldn't need any hand-holding."

Bringing Dunlap in was obviously important to Abraham. He wouldn't stick his neck out if it wasn't. But sometimes when women were involved guys did stupid things. He'd seen it happen over and over. He wouldn't have expected a tough guy like Abraham to fall so hard, but Max knew nobody was immune, especially if mind-blowing sex was involved.

So he came right out and asked. "Are you sleeping with her?"

Abraham sighed, his reaction answer enough. "Let it go, Max. If I could tell you more, I would, but I've told you too much already."

That was enough for Max. He let it go. If Abraham

thought Dunlap should be involved in the case, then she should be involved in the case. Max couldn't help that he didn't have the time or patience to deal with her.

Abraham shut off the fan, grabbed his jacket, and headed for the door. "What should I get her?" he asked.

"Get her?" Was he getting the woman a welcome gift?

"My granddaughter. She's six. What do six-year-olds like?"

"Hell if I know. I have a six*teen*-year-old, and I don't know what he likes."

"Better get it figured out. You're running out of time."

Max was trying to face that ugly reminder when Abraham threw him a new, more harmless one.

"Got your Web page done?"

Not that again. "I don't need a Web page."

"Gotta have a Web page. It's one of the simplest ways to keep the lines of communication open. My page has a smoking gun."

Side by side, they left the building, small-talking to the parking lot, where Max told the older man good-bye before ducking inside his car, dropping the murder file on the passenger seat. He checked his voice mail on his mobile phone, disappointed but not surprised to find that Ethan had failed to leave a check-in message the way he was supposed to. They'd had another blowup last night, and Ethan was never cooperative after a battle.

Instead of heading to Grand Central and his office as he'd originally planned, Max turned in the direction of home.

Ethan was on probation after being caught with beer. The last year hadn't been easy, and Max was afraid this was just the beginning.

Max had hoped Ethan's summer job would have been the answer to their problems. Working twenty hours a week combined with hockey practice and summer-league tournaments should have kept any kid out of trouble. But lately Ethan seemed to be able to find trouble in the most harmless of places.

Max's parents in Florida had offered to take Ethan for the summer, as had his brother in Virginia, but Max was afraid three months away would only make things worse. They needed to spend more time together, not less.

When he was little, Ethan used to love the idea that his dad was a policeman. For Halloween, he always had to wear a blue uniform and badge. And even when it wasn't Halloween, he'd cruise through the house in his little policeman outfit, making siren sounds, pulling over imaginary people and writing out tickets.

But recently everything had changed, and suddenly being a cop was about the uncoolest thing a guy could be. For Ethan, it seemed to represent everything he hated and resented about Max. Max told himself it was just Ethan's age, that in a couple of years everything would be okay, that their relationship would be back to normal. But what if that didn't happen?

When you're young, you keep thinking things are going to change, things are going to get better. But by the time you hit forty, you pretty much know this is it.

When Ethan was hardly more than a baby, they'd lived in the heart of Chicago, but Max had worried that it wasn't a good place to raise a kid, so they'd moved to the suburbs, to a brand-new community northwest of the city that had shot up overnight out of someone's cornfield. It made it a lot harder to get to and from work, but Max had figured it was worth it.

But the pop-up suburb had an incomplete feel to it, like something that just wasn't right, wasn't quite *real,* almost like a movie set. When people raised families in that sterile environment, it produced directionless children who became directionless teenagers, then directionless adults. With no roots, no past to stand on, you got hollow kids.

The United States was full of rootless, empty kids who played video games all day. In between, they skateboarded down immaculate sidewalks past yards that had never known a weed. And if you looked into their eyes, you didn't see a dream of the future there, just a weird emptiness. Max didn't know what the answer was; all he knew was that somewhere along the line, they'd all taken a wrong turn.

Max had been thinking about moving back to the old neighborhood, but just days ago he'd driven by only to find his entire block gone. In its place he found a parking ramp, a store that rented video games, and a Starbucks. Anytown, U.S.A. Did people really want that? Who decided on that sameness? How had it happened? When Thomas Wolfe said you could never go home again, he hadn't meant because the damn place was *gone.* Something like this had never occurred to Wolfe. This *cleansing.*

Sometimes Max just wanted to stop in one of those huge hardware stores, buy some color in gallon cans, and paint his house purple. Not that he was terribly fond of purple, but someone needed to take a stand.

When Max got home Ethan wasn't there and hadn't left a note.

Shit.

Max hoped he wasn't in for a replay of last night's broken curfew.

At 1:30 A.M. the night before, Max had heard the sound of the front door. He'd gotten out of bed and turned on the hall light just as Ethan was tiptoeing to his room. Under the glare of the ceiling light, Max had seen that Ethan's eyes were bloodshot. Smoking dope again.

"You're grounded," Max had said. It was the only thing he knew to say, even though he was fairly sure the words meant nothing, just like Ethan's probation.

Then Ethan had spoken a line that had been said too often in the last fifty years in houses all across the country. "You can't tell me what to do. You're not my *real* father." It was a cliché that actually hurt. It didn't seem possible, but there it was.

God knew he loved the kid more than life itself—but damn, he could be such a pain in the ass.

"I want to find my real father," Ethan had said.

With this whole Madonna Murder case resurfacing, Max felt scattered—and he needed to give the case his full attention.

Max had known the day was coming when Ethan would want to know about his real father. But why now, when everything was so crazy? There were things Max hadn't told him, things he didn't quite know *how* to tell him—but now wasn't the time.

It had just happened to him, this fatherhood thing. A weird cluster of events he'd gotten caught in the middle of. Max had met Ethan's mother when Ethan was three years old. They'd gone out a few times.

Okay, maybe ten, twelve times. It was one of those things where Max was pretty sure they didn't click, but he'd wanted to give it a little longer. One night he'd decided to tell her it just wasn't working, when she told him she was dying. And she was looking for someone to take care of her son.

Max wished he could say he'd jumped right in and started helping her, supporting her, but the truth was, he ran. Three weeks later he went back.

He'd seen quite a bit of death, quite a few dead bodies, by the time he met Cecilia, but nothing he'd seen in any way prepared him for the slow, cruel death of cancer. And after you watch someone die of cancer, you're forever changed. Your view of humanity, of what it means to be a human on this planet Earth, is forever questioned and never answered. Such intimate knowledge of death threatened to weaken Max in ways he didn't want to be weakened.

Cecilia was so brave that he fell in love with her a little in those last few weeks. He took care of her until she died, and he adopted Ethan. Adopting Ethan changed Max's life in ways he'd never imagined, but now the profound love he felt for his son was mixed with confusion and frustration.

So here they were, two hostile men living in a glistening suburb on the edge of nowhere, trying not to kill each other. Now Max had to hone his parenting skills, baby-sit some novice who wanted to play cop, and find a madman who was killing women and their baby boys.

Chapter 3

Ivy Dunlap's flight was scheduled to arrive at Chicago O'Hare at 11:48. That knowledge left Abraham sweating and zipping through heavy Chicago traffic in his ancient BMW with its cracked leather seats, intent on getting to the airport in time to see her step from the walkway because he had to know if she would be recognized. If so, he'd make sure she got back on the next flight out of there.

God knew Abraham no longer looked the way he had all those years ago, but some people change a lot over time, some don't. He'd quit going to high school class reunions because at his twenty-fifth he couldn't recognize half the people there. It was like reminiscing with a bunch of strangers. Some looked so unlike their former selves that fingerprints or dental records would have been the only way to identify them. It had depressed him when he wasn't able to recognize his old buddies, but now he hoped the sixteen years Ivy Dunlap had spent in Canada had drastically changed her appearance. For her sake he hoped to hell she was fat, gray, and ugly.

He was running late because he'd stopped to pick

up a birthday present for his granddaughter. He'd ended up getting her a Tae Kwon Do Barbie, something that wouldn't please his daughter, Marie, who disapproved of Barbie. But Abraham thought a Tae Kwon Do Barbie would be a good role model. Every woman should know how to protect herself. That's what was important here. His granddaughter. Not Marie's misplaced feminist issues.

There were predators out there. People needed to educate their children. People needed to be aware. The general public thought the only serial killers were the ones thrown in their faces by the media. Not true. And most people thought the chances of coming into contact with one of the monsters was so remote that it didn't merit consideration or worry. Not true again. There were monsters everywhere.

Her flight was on time, a Boeing 747. People gushed out of the walkway, some in groups, some by themselves, eyes seeking, then finally finding, the person meeting them.

Abraham recognized her immediately. It wasn't her size that gave her away—she was smaller than he remembered. And it wasn't her shape, she'd lost that almost boyish coltishness—or her hair—which used to be blond but was now red. It wasn't really anything about her except the calm way in which she spotted him, the way she looked at him in a manner that was so direct, so *intimate,* for lack of a better word, that it jolted him.

Her eyes spoke of a recognition that went beyond physical appearance, a recognition that was rooted in Abraham's deep knowledge of her; he was the only living person who knew the full, true story of Ivy Dunlap.

He must not have changed so much, because she spotted him right away. "Abraham!"

Her voice was deeper, older, and it kind of snagged on his name. His own rush of emotion took him by surprise as he welcomed her into his arms, and he briefly felt as if he were embracing a frail bird with delicate, fragile wings.

"It is so good to see you," she said, pulling away just far enough to grab him confidently by both hands. They stared at each other a moment, and he knew they were both thinking of another time, sixteen years ago, at this very airport. He had given her a new ID, a new past.

Claudia Reynolds was no more. Now she was Ivy Dunlap, born in Ottawa, Ontario, the only child of Canadian Thomas Dunlap and French-Canadian Jennifer Roy. Abraham had handed her the plane ticket and money, telling her a trusted friend would be meeting her in Toronto.

"I like the red hair," he said.

"A hundred percent natural," she joked.

Ivy picked up a green canvas backpack she'd dropped. He took it from her. "Luggage?" he asked.

"Yes." She glanced around uncertainly.

"It'll be downstairs."

She fell into step beside him, unconsciously letting him lead the way. He asked her about her flight. No problems. Had she eaten? Yes.

Ivy had expected to find memories crashing down on her the moment she stepped off the plane. When the pilot had announced that they'd be landing in Chicago in ten minutes, her heart had dropped, then began beating rapidly as an overwhelming sense of panic rushed over her. Since then, she'd managed to calm herself. The airport was too generic, too full of the energy of busy travelers, to be any kind of threat.

With slight pressure on her arm, Abraham indicated that they needed to take the escalators. She turned, finding her footing and grabbing the moving rubber handrail at the same time.

Abraham.

The first thing she'd thought when she'd seen him was, *He's old.* His hair was turning gray. But then her own hair had turned gray years ago, almost overnight. He'd put on weight. But she'd recognized him immediately. His stature. His aura of confidence. Even though he was dressed in a dark suit and tie rather than the Chicago Police Department blues, it was easy to see he was a policeman. A superintendent now, head of the CPD. When she'd known him, he was Detective Sinclair.

Sixteen years was a long time, but not long enough to have aged a man as much as Abraham had aged. He was so *worn*. Another of the walking wounded.

The Madonna Murders had been hard on him, he'd confessed to her once. Harder than any other homicide he'd ever handled. They'd been the beginning of a downward spiral that had eventually ended in alcoholism and divorce.

She'd been out of the mental institute two years when the phone had rung in the middle of the night. Phone calls in the middle of the night tended to be serious stuff. Upon recognizing his voice, she'd almost dropped the receiver, thinking the Madonna Murderer had reemerged. But no, Abraham needed to talk to somebody, somebody who would understand what he was going through. He needed to talk to somebody whose life had been touched by a serial killer.

He was drunk. Not sloppy drunk, but sad, weighted-down-by-life drunk. It was one of the few conversations they had during her years of exile, but it had taken only a couple of broken sentences for her to understand just how far-reaching was the madness and damage of a human predator.

Her flight's luggage wasn't yet on the carousel. They waited in the crowd of people. They waited along with a mother and her two tired, whimpering children, businessmen and -women, cowboys in their tight Levi's, pointed boots, and big shiny buckles.

Ivy directed her gaze to the chute where the luggage would soon appear. Deliberately not looking at Abraham, she said, "I want to be the bait."

She heard his quick intake of breath, felt his fingers wrap around her arm as he dragged her away from the crowd. Like loose sand, people quickly filled in their vacated spot.

When they were in their own private huddle, Abraham put his face very close to hers and whispered, "We don't even know if it *is* the Madonna Murderer."

"If you use me for bait we'll find out."

"Absolutely not."

"I'm not afraid."

"I know. That's what worries me."

"Use me. That's why I came."

"That's suicidal."

She shrugged and smiled. "Kamikaze."

"You've changed."

She knew he meant that she no longer did whatever he told her to do, without question. "I've found my calling, that's all."

"I'm beginning to wish I'd never telephoned you."

"What choice did you have? You promised."

"I didn't know you had a death wish."

She was close enough to see fine perspiration collecting at his hairline and steel resolve in his eyes. And she knew there was no use in arguing. Not at this point anyway.

Gone was her friend. Gone was the sad, lonely man who'd drunkenly phoned in the middle of the night. This was Superintendent Abraham Sinclair talking to her, the tough, hard, won't-take-any-shit cop.

"You're much bolder than I remember. If you think you're going to be running the show," he said with conviction, "then you may as well recheck your luggage and get back on a plane to Canada."

Ignoring his threat, she wrapped her hands around his arm. "I never used to be bold enough."

He moved past their argument. "I've arranged for you to stay with someone who used to work for the CPD. Her kids are in college, she has an extra room, and she won't ask questions."

"I appreciate it, but I prefer to have a place to myself. I'm hoping to find something today."

"Are you sure? I thought you might be more comfortable with people around."

"Thanks, but I really prefer my own space."

"Okay, but I'll leave her number with you in case you don't find a place, or you change your mind." He pulled a portable phone out of his pocket and punched in a number. "Max? Abraham. I'm heading in your direction and I wanted to make sure you were going to be around. I've got a meeting with the mayor in forty-five minutes. On my way downtown, I'm going to drop off Ivy Dunlap at your office."

Ivy detected a muffled reply, but couldn't make out

any words. Abraham disconnected and slipped the phone back into his pocket. "Max Irving," he said by way of explanation. "I'll tell you about him on the way."

Chapter 4

The woman sitting on the wooden bench outside Max's office wasn't what he'd expected. Then he decided she had to be someone else entirely until she stood and introduced herself.

"Hi, I'm Ivy Dunlap." She extended her hand.

Now he could see that she was of medium height and was as compact as a ballet dancer. She wore a light skirt that fell neatly over curved hips and flat stomach to flutter in colors of red and black and burgundy around her knees. Her top was a black, slightly fitted T-shirt, on her feet a pair of running shoes. Over her shoulder was a green canvas backpack.

He didn't know why, but for some reason he'd expected her to be on the far side of middle age, rapidly flying toward retirement and winters spent on the Gulf Coast. Turned out she was probably close to his age. Well, according to some—Ethan, for instance—that *could* be considered old. Funny how one's perception of age changed over a life span.

He shook her hand and studied her at the same time. Her hair was red and straight, and she had those kind of short, Audrey Hepburn–waifish bangs. Her cheekbones were dusted with the same pink as her nose, making her look as if she'd been working in a garden all day. She reminded him of somebody. . . . Who? And then it came to him. Ethan. The coloring. Her blue eyes. Her cheekbones, the shape of her face.

He was in control of the handshake. He was *always* in control of the handshake. When meeting a man, his grip was firm and strong, held just long enough to be polite without seeming too chilly. When meeting a woman, his grip was firm but nonthreatening.

He released her hand.

As he looked into her eyes, he felt a weird jolt of surprise, or possibly recognition, even though he was certain he'd never seen her before. Her eyes—they were old. Not old, as in the old he'd expected, but *sad*. When she looked at him, there was no shrinking away, no slow closing of the eyelids, no pretense. Just that bold, straightforward *sorrow*. And yet it was more than sorrow, as if she'd moved past the pain and could now face anything. In his job as a detective, he'd seen such eyes before. Like the faces of concentration camp survivors, they always belonged to someone who had lived through the horrendous.

For some reason he couldn't explain, the sight of her made him all the angrier. Christ, he *was* going to be baby-sitting. He didn't have time for this shit.

He wanted to grab her and shake her and ask her what the hell she was doing there. Instead, he managed to tamp down his reaction, to pull a mask over the most rampant of his feelings. Rather than attacking her directly, he said, "You know, there are people out there being murdered." He wanted to make her understand this wasn't a game.

He'd expected her to recoil at his straightforwardness, at the hostility in his voice.

Her eyebrows lifted slightly. "I know," was all she said.

I know! Didn't she get it? She was in the way! She was in the damn way!

She pulled a file folder from her backpack and handed it to him.

"What's this?"

"A profile."

"I've already seen it."

"Not this one."

He held up the folder, trying even harder to keep his anger in check. "This is *your* profile?" he asked in disbelief. The woman was incredibly brazen. Her putting together a profile and expecting him to take it seriously was like telling him she was a brain surgeon even though she'd never had any schooling or been in an operating room.

"What if we're dealing with a copycat killing? Then your profile doesn't mean shit."

"Do you think it's a copycat?"

"Maybe." He felt no compulsion to fill her in on his theories.

"You need to read my profile. I'm interested in hearing your comments."

He shoved the folder back at her until she was forced to take it. He had to stop this now, before it went any further. And he had to let her know who was calling the shots. "I'm gonna be straight with you," he said. "Because I don't have time for bullshit. You can tag along. It'll be a pain in the ass, but I've got my orders. You can get me coffee, get me newspapers, food. You can do research when I ask you for it. But nobody said I have to play cop with you."

"You're not going to read it?"

"Hell no, I'm not going to read it."

"Then I'll tell you what it says."

She began spouting off the profile. She had the damn thing memorized.

"The killer is male, most likely of European descent, in his early to mid-forties. Graduated from high school. Went to college, most likely intending to major in mathematics, but flunked out due to an inability to focus and excessive time spent in fantasy. He lives with a relative, most likely his mother. As a child, he lacked a male role model and exhibited traits that make up the homicidal triad: bed-wetting past a normal age, fire-starting, and cruelty to animals. As you know, the most common motivators for serial killers are domination, manipulation, and control. This man is a loser who feels society has screwed him. He will come across as extremely confident, but in actuality he feels inadequate. His murdering of women is a redirected hatred of his mother. The babies are simply innocent victims. Killing them makes him feel as if he's not only getting back at her, he's saving himself at the same time. In short, his overriding fantasy is to rid himself of his domineering, abusive mother." She stopped. "There's more, but that's probably enough for now. I can see I'm boring you."

Boring? "Hardly that."

What the hell was Abraham thinking? And the weird way she'd delivered "her profile" only reinforced his idea that he was dealing with some wacko.

Yet he couldn't deny that it bore an uncanny resemblance to the profile put out by their own guy. Had she somehow gotten a copy? That would explain things. That and the fact that ever since retired FBI

Agent John Douglas began writing his profiling books, everybody wanted in on the game, and everybody thought he, or in Dunlap's case, *she* was an expert. But let Ms. Dunlap get a good look at a violent crime scene and she'd be out of his hair.

"And you came by this knowledge . . . how?"

While he spoke to her, Ivy was intensely aware of his presence in the crowded hallway, but also the presence of people she couldn't even see. They filled the building, sitting in offices, riding elevators, flowing out the double glass doors to board buses on the noisy Chicago street.

The city of Chicago housed millions of people. She could feel those people. She could feel their pulsating presence, smothering her, suffocating her. And not only feel the people who were there now, but also the people who had been there before.

"I have a degree in criminal psychology and have been studying psychopathic behavior for the last ten years."

"That doesn't necessarily make you an expert. Have you had any actual field experience?"

She let out a heavy sigh. "Listen, I don't want to argue. I'm tired, and I still need to find a place to stay. A place that allows cats."

Cats?

He looked past her. Now he could see that under the bench where she'd been sitting was a gray plastic animal carrier, the kind people used on airplanes.

She'd brought her damn cat with her.

Ivy knew that coming back to Chicago would be one of the hardest things she'd ever done. She'd mentally prepared herself. She'd pulled in, shut herself off, focusing on her immediate problems—finding a place to stay and dealing with the man in front of her.

Interacting with another human being was the last thing she felt like doing at the moment, especially one as irascible as this one.

"A cat?" he asked, his voice echoing her own disbelief.

Indeed, why *had* she brought poor Jinx here?

"You brought your cat?"

Detective Irving wore black dress pants, a rumpled white dress shirt, and a tie that had been yanked open at the throat. The sleeves of his shirt were rolled up, and he was sweating. Behind her, in a dark corner where the wax on the linoleum had turned a yellow brown, an oscillating fan blew stagnant air in their direction.

Click, half circle, *click,* return.

"I didn't have anybody to leave him with," she said.

One hand at his waist, elbow out, he scratched his head with his free hand, completely at a loss. In that moment, she allowed herself to feel a little sorry for him. For a fraction of a second, she wondered what his home life was like. It could be bad. Really bad. She thought of several combinations of bad scenarios, then let it go.

Abraham hadn't given her any personal information on Max Irving, only saying he was the best at what he did, going so far as to relate a case where Irving had used hypnosis to aid in an investigation.

As she looked at him now, she was surprised to distantly note that some women would probably find him attractive, with his short dark hair that was as boyishly rumpled as his shirt, with his distracted air, piercing brown-green eyes, skin that looked as if it had been dusted with gold.

"Okay," he said, seeming to arrive at some kind of decision. "Come into my office."

Once inside, he grabbed a phone book that was so big she would have had to hold it with two hands. He dropped it on his littered desk and began tearing through the pages.

"What's your price range?"

She mumbled a figure she thought adequate.

"Not in this city," he said as if to further underscore how little she was in touch with the real world.

She knew that the building they were in wasn't all that old, having opened in the early eighties, when Jane Byrne was mayor. But for some reason his cramped office had the feel of all old buildings—of being a little off-center, a little warped by time, a place where eras collided. Chicago had witnessed the rise and fall of Al Capone, who, when compared to the sick, twisted Madonna Murderer, seemed almost a nice man just making a living.

While Ivy was dwelling on Chicago and how much it had seen, Max Irving was barking into the telephone, jotting down numbers and addresses on a yellow tablet. He hung up, tore the top sheet from the tablet, and announced, "Found you a couple of places. Rent by the week. You can have a pet, but it'll cost extra."

She put out her hand for the paper, but he ignored it. "They're not far from here. I'll take you."

"That's totally unnecessary."

He still wouldn't give her the paper with the addresses. Five minutes ago, he'd seemed eager to get

her out of his hair. He would have been ecstatic if
she'd told him she was leaving the country. Now he
was going to help her find an apartment. Why?

"I'll fill you in on the case on the way."

She gathered up poor Jinx, who was still in a highly
sedated state from the drugs the vet had given Ivy.

"Pretty mellow cat," he said, looking at Jinx lolling
in the corner of the cage.

"Isn't that what they always say?" she asked. "He
seemed like a nice guy. Quiet. Kept to himself."

At first she could see that he didn't know she was
kidding. Then he smiled even though it was fairly obvious he didn't want to. "You Canadians think you're
pretty damn funny, don't you?"

She shrugged. "Best comedians come from Canada."

He was thinking about arguing, but then she saw
defeat cross his features.

She smiled back at him. Americans had a hard edge.
Interacting with them was like remembering how to
ride a bike. You might be a little wobbly at first, but
you could pick it up again pretty easily.

Max gathered up the Sheppard case file in its brand-
new, stiff and slick manila folder, complete with eight-
by-ten color photos of the crime scene, then grabbed
the Madonna Murders file in its soft-sided, fingerprint-
stained folder, wound a huge rubber band around
both, latching them together, then tucked the whole
mess under his arm.

"No suitcase?" he asked Dunlap, looking around
the hallway, not seeing anything.

"Left it at the front desk."

"How long have you known Superintendent Sinclair?" he asked as they walked down the hallway. He

should have offered to carry the animal crate, but he'd be damned if he was going to trot around with a cat.

"A long time," she said.

An elusive answer. "Years?"

"Yes."

"Where'd you meet?"

"I can't remember. It seems I've always known him. Have you ever felt that way about someone?"

Max didn't answer. Besides, it was a rhetorical question.

They passed the front desk where phones were ringing, people were conversing, computers were humming. A prostitute in handcuffs was led past them. A street person was crying, begging to be allowed to go home and feed his cats.

"In just a minute, Mr. Van Horn." The clerk looked up at Max and his companion, and shot Max a questioning look. Max just shrugged and rolled his eyes.

"This yours?" Max asked, indicating a black, canvas suitcase with a paper airline tag around the handle.

She nodded, and he picked it up.

His goal was to get Dunlap out of the building before he had to introduce her to anybody. His instincts told him she was too fragile to handle such a difficult investigation, and there was no sense in wasting time introducing her to people she might never see again.

Crime-scene photos used to be black and white, the argument being that they were less disturbing that way. But there were a lot of things that didn't show up in black and white, so now they were always in color. Color was good. Color weeded out the people who couldn't hack it.

The lobby was where the press waited, hoping to get

an unauthorized scoop. So far, the Sheppard murders hadn't been publicly connected with the earlier homicides. There were around four hundred murders a year in Chicago, down from an all-time high of eight hundred. If the victim wasn't famous, the homicide didn't attract attention, and was only given a few lines in the *Herald*. But let somebody make some sort of comparison and the lobby would soon be swarming with camera crews.

Max spotted Alex Martin, a fairly new reporter on the police beat. New reporters had it tough. Most police officers trusted and worked with only a few journalists. The others they ignored, so it was hard for anybody starting out to get a fresh story.

But Alex was young and ambitious, energetic and relentless. He had so much energy it was exhausting to spend five minutes with him. He jumped up from where he'd been sitting scribbling notes.

"Detective Irving!"

Leaving his sandwich and wrapper on the bench, he hurried up to Max, looking like he'd stepped right out of a Gap ad with his khaki pants, his wild tie, his leather sandals. "Detective Irving! May I talk with you a moment?" He glanced in Dunlap's direction, a brief question bringing his dark eyebrows together, quickly dismissed her as nobody important, then focused back on Max.

"About this murder." With the skill of a desperate man, he stepped in front of Max, blocking his path. "The Sheppard case. Any leads?"

Max stopped in his headlong flight for the door. He let out a deep, weary breath, wishing the guy in front of him would vanish, taking the woman and her cat with him.

"Is it true that a baby was murdered too?"

"You know damn well I can't talk about the case right now. When I know more, we'll get you a copy of the report."

"What about a press conference? Do you foresee this being big enough to merit a press conference?"

"We don't hold press conferences for every murder in Chicago."

"Yeah, but I thought this might be different."

"Only if you make it different. You won't do that, will you?"

"You mean pad a story?"

"Exactly."

"Hell no. I mean, no. Of course not."

"Good."

Max glanced to his left, ready to indicate to Dunlap that it was time to go. She wasn't there. He spotted her near the check-in desk, talking to the street person they'd passed earlier. She was holding up the cage so he could look in at her cat. The man was nodding and smiling now—two pet owners comparing notes. Ivy pressed something into the man's hand—money, Max supposed—then quickly caught up with Max.

"What a relief to see you treat everyone with courtesy," she said conversationally once they were outside in the parking lot with the noise of an overhead street ramp, the heat, the people. "And here I thought it was just me."

"Should I be more like you and give every homeless person in Chicago money?"

"The reporter was just doing his job."

"I don't have the time or the inclination to be charming."

Chapter 5

The reality of being back in Chicago was beginning to sink in. A part of Ivy couldn't believe she was here, in the city where such awful things had happened, where her life had changed so drastically.

She could feel her mind slipping.

Don't fall apart. Not in front of him. Not in front of anybody. *Don't fall apart.*

This is what I wanted, she told herself. True, but that didn't mean it didn't scare the hell out of her.

The noise. The chaos. Had it always been this bad? Cars honking, sirens blaring, the shriek of bus brakes, and the smell of diesel when the huge vehicle pulled away from the curb? Construction, wood-planked walkways, jackhammers. How did people stand it? How did they think? Function?

The man beside her seemed oblivious to it all.

It was two o'clock in the afternoon. They were driving through city traffic, Max Irving steering with one light hand on the wheel. There were cars in front, cars behind, to the left, the right. She tried to shut herself off, tried to block out the noise of the traffic, to block out the past that suddenly didn't seem like the past anymore.

Confusion. So much confusion.

"Here." Max startled her by tossing a folder in her lap. She stared at the bold, black print: Sheppard Case.

"Go on. Open it. That's why you're here, isn't it?"

Ivy opened it.

The first thing she saw was an eight-by-ten color glossy of the murdered mother. It was a close-up of her face. Straight, chin-length blond hair, matted with blood, blue eyes open wide. Lividity on the right side. Lividity occurred when the heart stopped mixing plasma. The red cells settled like sediment in wine, turning the skin anywhere from red to purple. From the photo, anyone with a slight knowledge of forensics would be able to see that the victim had been moved several hours after the death. So the head shot, horrific as it was, wasn't taken simply for shock value— although Ivy was fairly certain that's why Irving had not only tossed it to her, but why he'd put it on top. Talk about staging. She refused to play his game. She slammed the folder shut and closed her eyes, resting her head against the headrest.

"Not going to puke, are you?"

"Certainly wouldn't warn you if I was."

She may not have ever profiled an actual case, but she'd spent the last ten years profiling everyone she came in contact with, from bank teller to grocery clerk. Ivy had honed her profiling skills until she'd gotten so good at judging the book by its cover that she'd been in danger of becoming a parlor trick at the psychology department's yearly Christmas party.

Irving was easy. A hotshot detective, burnt-out but unwilling to admit it to himself. Used to have a sense of humor, but didn't have time for such nonsense anymore. Problems on the home front. Looking at him, a layman might conjure up a trophy wife, one he ignored unless they were fighting about his job and his lack of attentiveness. But Ivy had noted his rumpled clothes, his air of distraction—an ongoing state that clung to parents, especially single parents, who were juggling two worlds: the world of work and the world of home.

What she didn't understand was why he had it in for her. "Why do you resent me so much?" She opened her eyes and lifted her head. "Is it because I'm a woman?"

"That has nothing to do with it."

"Because I'm from Canada?"

"Oh, come on. I don't want to get into this."

"I do." Anything to get her mind off the past. Earlier she'd been too tired to fight with him. Now she welcomed it.

"I don't have anything against Canadians. I just think we can handle this without your help."

"You didn't handle it before."

"*I* wasn't on the case before."

Somebody cut him off. He laid on his horn, then missed the light completely. "Shit," he said, slamming his hand against the steering wheel. Apparently he wasn't as oblivious as she'd thought.

In the backseat, right behind his head, Jinx decided it was time to complain by letting out a long, weird, drug-laden meow.

"You wanna know what bothers me?" Irving asked, his voice and demeanor reflecting ever-increasing agitation. "That cat. That damn cat. I don't think somebody who has to haul her damn cat with her is going to know jackshit about a serial killer. I don't think somebody who keeps flinching"—he snapped his fingers in front of her face, she flinched and drew back in the seat—"every damn time a horn honks is going to be able to handle a case like this. I don't think spending ten years with your nose in a book is quite the preparation you need for this job. I worked my ass off to get where I am. I went to George Mason University. I trained at Quantico. Do you know how hard it is to get into Quantico?"

Okay, she could see his point, understand why she was a sudden irritant. She wished she could tell him the truth, tell him why she was every bit as qualified as he was, but she couldn't. And anyway, none of that really mattered. Not Max Irving's opinion of her, or her lack of a satisfactory presentation. Catching the killer, that's what mattered.

Ivy was ready to take the first apartment they looked at, just to get it over with, just to get out of Irving's car, get out of the noise, get Jinx settled, take a couple of aspirin, *be alone*. She needed to be alone so all of this could settle, could soak in. This being in Chicago, a place of unspeakable horrors. Here. Now. All around her.

Memories. She kept holding them back, holding them back. . . . But they were building. She didn't know how much longer she could hang on, how much longer before they came crashing into her mind.

"This place is no good," Irving said halfway into the tour of the prospective apartment.

Ivy opened her mouth to protest when Irving grabbed her arm and dragged her with him down the dimly lit hall that smelled of marijuana, body odor, cooked cabbage, and the rotten smell a building succumbed to when the termites were done with it.

She planted her feet firmly on the floor and wrenched her arm free, feeling true anger for the first time that day, for the first time in maybe . . . years.

"What the hell are you doing?" she demanded.

"Keeping you from making a stupid mistake."

She wanted to slug him. Instead, she pushed at him with both hands while the manager watched from the open doorway of the apartment they'd just exited. "Don't tell me what to do," she said. "Are you always such an ass?"

"Only when I have to be."

"That's reassuring."

He began ticking off the reasons she shouldn't take the apartment. "Bad locks. Bad windows. Cockroaches. And . . . a crackhead living in the hallway."

She followed the direction of his gaze to a dark corner where she could barely make out a human shape curled up on the tile floor.

There were times to hold your ground, and times to let that ground be conquered and taken. Irving could damn well place his flag and take the battle for his own.

His mobile phone rang and he quickly answered it.

"What time do you get off work?" Irving asked the caller. Then, "I'll be there to pick you up. Understand? No catching a ride with anybody, no taking off to Ryan's." A pause. "No excuses. I'll be there at nine o'clock."

When kids were little, you dropped them off at the sitter and didn't worry about them for the rest of the day. When they got older, got to be teenagers, it was a completely different story.

"A teenager?" she asked after Max ended the call.

"Yeah." There was a lot of weight in that single word.

"Ah." She nodded.

"A son," he added, as if by telling her she would understand how much more difficult having a son would be over a daughter. Which told her he didn't have a daughter.

"Ah."

"You have any kids?"

She'd been asked the question so many times in her life that her reply was instant and without emotion. "No, but my friend Helen says having a teenager is like living in a war zone where you have to be hyper-vigilant at all times."

He laughed and tucked his phone away. "Ethan's a good kid. A great kid. We're just going through a rough patch right now. We'll get through it."

It wasn't his words, but rather the emotion and emphasis behind them, that told Ivy he loved his son very much.

The next apartment met with his reluctant approval. It was a turnkey, meaning the basics like sheets, towels, TV, and dishes were supplied. And there was a grocery store a block away.

The place had no living room to speak of. Upon stepping inside, you were immediately in the kitchen. The first thing you smelled was gas from the pilot light. Right there was a small table with two black stools, a few steps more and you were at the white enamel sink. To the left of the kitchen area was the bedroom, with the bathroom off that. Next to the double bed was a window with white paint so thick it would be hard to open or shut. Ivy could tell that the building had once been nice, years and years ago; it still had that hint of past elegance, like beautiful wooden floors and ornate ceiling lights.

Students lived there. And businessmen whose real homes were somewhere else. Construction workers. Displaced people in a transient period of their lives. Some kids. Mothers in the middle of a divorce. Or maybe their husbands had abused them one too many times and they'd moved out.

Not a happy place.

But a real place.

"Get another dead-bolt lock on the door," Max told the landlord.

Ivy collected Jinx from Max's car. Max seemed suddenly more than happy to carry her huge black suitcase up the two flights of stairs. He put it down just inside the door and placed the case files—one thick, one thin—on the narrow kitchen table.

"There's no direct subway line from here to Grand Central Police Station," Max told her. "You'll have to take the Green Line to Central, then catch a metro bus."

"I'm sure I'll get the hang of it." Even though she was in an unfamiliar area of Chicago, she had a good sense of direction.

After Max left, Ivy sweet-talked the still-drugged Jinx, opening his cage so he could come out when he felt like it. She offered him water that he refused to drink and poured dry cat food in a bowl.

While he was still indisposed, she walked down to the corner store and picked up some groceries, along with other necessities like toothpaste, toilet paper, and cleaning supplies.

Back at the apartment, she donned a pair of yellow rubber gloves and cleaned the bathroom—claw-foot tub, sink, medicine cabinet, and toilet—with a disinfectant so strong it made her eyes and throat burn.

When she'd completed the requisite tasks needed to make her new home habitable, when she could no longer put off the inevitable, she sat down at the table and opened the thick case file, the one labeled "Madonna Murders."

Chapter 6

Ivy stared at the glossy black-and-white eight-by-ten. The photo was of a woman murdered in a neighborhood park sixteen years ago, her body dragged into the bushes, her baby discovered not far away, wrapped caringly in a blue blanket.

The way the infant was found was typical of murder by a relative's hand, often a parent. Someone who loved the child. But the Madonna Murderer most likely didn't know any of his victims. If by some chance he did, he probably didn't know them well. But in his confused mind, he *thought* he knew them. In a way, he thought all of the victims belonged to him.

The mothers weren't treated with the same—for lack of a better word—respect. Their bodies were left like so much garbage, stab wounds to the chest and abdomen, ligature marks and blue bruises left by the killer's fingers around the neck. There had been an ongoing debate over what came first, the stabbing or the strangulation. Cause of death was sometimes asphyxiation, sometimes bleeding out.

In the tiny apartment, there were no chairs, only the stools. Nothing to prop under the doorknob. Jinx

meowed, beginning to come out of his drugged stupor.
He stepped from his carrier on uneasy legs, drank a
little of the water Ivy had poured for him, then took
a few more steps and fell over, the bell on his collar
ringing.

"You poor thing."

Ivy picked him up, the heavy limpness of his body
a stark contrast to the wired way he usually felt when
she held him. She wouldn't give him as much of the
tranquilizer on the way home.

It was apparent that he wanted to be left alone. She
removed his stretch collar, sliding it over his head.
Then she showed him the litter box, which he sniffed
suspiciously before getting back in the carrier—a ves-
sel he normally avoided to the extent of hissing and
yowling.

Ivy hung the little red collar with its tiny bell and
silver rabies tag over the doorknob, then sat back
down at the table and took a deep breath.

The smells of the inner city . . . Stale sweat, cooking
grease, moldy wallpaper glued to rotten wood. Plastic
garbage containers overflowing with soiled diapers.
Sour, spit-up milk caked to stained towels.

The sounds of the city. Sirens. The squealing of tires
on hot, sun-softened asphalt. A baby crying. The re-
petitive bass of rap music coming from a chopped blue
Chevy that cruised slowly up and down the narrow
street, its modified engine producing a deep testoster-
one rumble.

The apartment with its air of slight decay . . .

It all took Ivy back to a day she'd hoped to examine
from a great distance. But past and present meshed,
and she realized with dismay that her life had not

moved forward in a linear fashion, but was spiraling backward upon itself until she was one inhalation away from yesterday . . .

They say bad things come in threes. That was certainly true for Claudia Reynolds, the person Ivy had once been. Within a short span of time, she had lost everyone she cared about: her father, her mother, her boyfriend.

Under her photo in her suburban Des Moines high school yearbook was the caption "Girl Most Likely." That could have been taken any number of ways, but in Claudia's case it had meant girl most likely to *succeed.* She'd graduated with so many offers of full scholarships that she had been able to pretty much take her pick of schools, and finally she had decided upon the University of Chicago. At the time, Chicago was known as the murder capital of the world, but that didn't stop her from settling on the school where her boyfriend was going. She'd planned to pursue a degree in fashion design. It seemed so frivolous now, so shallow—and yet she was still drawn to fabrics of rich hues and textures. And really, college hadn't been about a degree, it had been about being near Daniel. She'd imagined their relationship quickly blossoming to the point where they would share an apartment. Share dreams. Share the future.

She became pregnant.

Up until the pregnancy her life had been perfect to the point of embarrassment. Bad things didn't happen to Claudia Reynolds. When she was little, her charm was so great that people would rub her head for luck. On her sixteenth birthday, she bought a lottery ticket and won half a million dollars. But later the money was taken away because she hadn't been old enough to buy a ticket in the first place.

Strange luck.

Once during a school hockey game, the goaltender had her kiss his smelly gloves—and his team won. After that, he would always look for her before he took to the ice. One time, when she wasn't there to kiss his gloves, he broke his arm and had to sit out the rest of the season. The next year he couldn't get the magic back and after a month of bench-warming he quit, taking his wounded pride with him.

It wasn't a good thing to be someone's luck. There was so much pressure, and so many things could go wrong.

Her accidental pregnancy threw something out of balance and suddenly her life went from charmed to cursed. And once the bad stuff started, it didn't stop.

She'd always had weird periods so by the time Claudia realized she was pregnant it was too late to have an abortion—and she wasn't sure she could have gone through with it anyway. Before she could share the news, her boyfriend tearfully told her he'd met someone else.

A week later, her father, a grade-school teacher, had a heart attack and died. After that, Claudia's mother, who'd depended on her husband for everything, seemed to lose the will to live. She mentally drifted away. Her doctor put her on antidepressants and tranquilizers. In that numb state, she stepped off a curb in front of oncoming traffic and was instantly killed. But Claudia knew what had really killed her: sorrow.

And so something in the universe shifted, and Claudia became one of those people she'd always looked at from a distance, never thinking about what the inside of their lives must be like.

In the three years she'd been in the relationship with Daniel, her circle of friends had dwindled to two—herself and Daniel. When it was over and she finally looked back without the happy glasses, she wondered how she'd allowed herself to turn into one of those girls who breathed for one person and one person alone. She had allowed herself to be consumed by someone she hadn't even really known. From that point on, she swore she would never let a man be the most important thing in her life.

Her parents had very little put away toward retirement. Claudia had no recourse but to sell their house, which was ten years away from being paid off. With the equity, she paid for funeral expenses and outstanding bills, then moved back to Chicago to continue her education. If she was careful, the remaining money would last a year, maybe more. And once the baby was born, she would get a full-time job.

She was seven months pregnant when she rented the efficiency apartment on the second floor of a five-story building that stood between a crumbling art-deco theater and the Saint Cristobel Mission where the poor were fed two hot meals a day.

Claudia worked at the mission three days a week. She may have been pregnant, but she was still strong, still able, so she helped out where she could. In return, she received support from strangers.

Later the police would want to know about everyone she'd come in contact with at the mission, everyone she'd ever spoken to, which of course was an impossible request. She saw a lot of the same faces, but there were new ones every day. There were people she saw once and never again. And unfortunately, some people simply didn't stand out. They were poor, they were dirty, they were hungry lost souls. That's what she remembered most about them.

She tried not to dwell on it because the world was made of questions that had no answers, but she would sometimes catch herself wondering how and why her luck had gone from good to bad. Her good fortune, while not exactly making her shallow, had given her an insulated view from a window she didn't care to move past. She had known about poor people, she had even participated in food drives, but she'd never understood the depths of poverty. She'd never looked at it from the inside.

She was afraid of pain so she went to Lamaze classes, clutching a pillow to her growing stomach. She was the only one without a coach in a class of forty women. Jacob, a mission volunteer, offered to be her coach, but she declined. He'd done enough for her already.

Jacob had helped her find the apartment. His mother was a social worker, and he knew the ins and outs of everything available to an unemployed, single expectant mother. He told her about free meals at the mission. He took her to a clinic where she could get prenatal care.

Childbirth was hell.

How could this be natural? There had to be something wrong. She was being ripped in two. And then she had another thought: If she died, nobody would miss her. Nobody would even know she'd ever lived.

No, the midwife told her everything was going along fine. Everything was okay.

At 11:24 P.M., five months after her mother's death, Claudia Reynolds gave birth to a twenty-inch, seven-and-a-half-pound baby boy. Right then and there, when she looked into his sweet little face, into those sweet, unfocused eyes, she was lost, feeling a love so powerful it scared her. And she thought she could endure all the curses in the world for him.

"His eyes," she said in amazement as the nurse settled the wrapped infant into Claudia's waiting arms, "they're so blue."

"Most newborns' eyes are blue. They usually change in a few weeks."

For some inexplicable reason, Claudia felt her baby's eyes wouldn't change. They would stay a deep ocean blue the rest of his life.

The pain she'd felt for the last nine hours was forgotten, replaced by a new kind of pain, the pain of a love so bright it hurt. She could feel it in her throat, in her head, behind her eyes.

With amazement, she touched his tiny, red, wrinkled hands with their miniature fingernails. And later, when he cried and cried, she cried too. And because the love she felt was so monumental, so huge, so empowering, she knew she was going to be the best damn mother in the world.

To say she was unprepared for motherhood would have been an understatement. She'd never been around any babies in her life, and didn't have an older, experienced woman to help her. Those things combined to create a recipe for disaster, because everybody knew that good intentions alone couldn't raise a child.

A woman needed a plan.

A woman needed support.

A woman needed sleep. God, how she needed sleep.

The nurses at the hospital taught her how to bathe her son, being careful to keep the umbilical cord dry. They taught her how to get him to latch onto her nipple, and how to change his diaper. They taught her how to keep him warm, and how to keep him cool.

Still, unsure of herself and her new role, she begged to stay at the hospital one more day, just one more day.

No.

Thirty-five hours after her baby was born, Claudia took a cab home. With her cherished bundle, she climbed the stairs to her apartment.

She never wondered what she had done. She never regretted her decision to keep him. He was a plus, only a plus. Because now her life had purpose, now she had a reason that extended beyond her own aura of wants and needs to incorporate another human being, an innocent, helpless child. Her child. Once again a male was the center of her world—and she allowed herself to be consumed by him.

She would name him Adrian.

Claudia wasn't superstitious, and yet for a brief moment she wondered if she should name him something biblical, just to keep God happy. But she'd had enough of men with biblical names.

The problems started on the second day home. He cried all the time, but when she checked his diaper, it wasn't wet. Her breasts, which by this time were like rocks, only frustrated him when she tried to get him to nurse.

In the middle of the night she slipped into a pair of jogging pants because she still couldn't fit into her jeans. With eyes burning from lack of sleep, she wrapped up her baby, little Adrian, and carried him down the steps to the street below, toward a corner grocery store that was open all night.

At the store, she bought a baby bottle that was shaped like an oblong letter O, two cans of baby formula, and returned home.

When she reached her apartment she found the door ajar. Her negligence frightened her. In her exhaustion and worry, she'd forgotten to close the door.

She closed it now, locking it behind them. She put Adrian in his bassinet, washed and sterilized the baby bottle as quickly as possible, then poured in the rich-smelling formula.

When she dragged the nipple across the infant's mouth, he didn't respond. He just kept crying his openmouthed, toothless, red-faced wail that hurt her like a knife blade. Then, as soon as some of the formula dribbled into his mouth, his breath caught. And caught again.

And then he quit crying and began tugging madly at the nipple, making little animal noises as he sucked.

Claudia let out her breath. The tension in her shoulders relaxed, and she sent up a silent prayer. *Thank You.*

A few moments later, milk from her heavy breasts came down, saturating her shirt and the infant she held in her arms; she'd simply been too tense to nurse.

Baby Adrian drank all four ounces of the formula Claudia had put in the bottle. He still acted hungry but she was afraid to give him any more, afraid he would spit it up or get a stomachache.

She changed his wet, milk-soaked clothes, put a blanket over her own saturated top, and cuddled and hummed to him until he fell asleep. Then, very carefully so she wouldn't wake him, she put him down in the bassinet.

She was changing her top when she heard a sound, like something falling. Like something getting knocked over and falling, hitting the floor.

Her sleep-deprived mind immediately tried to make sense of the sound. She at first dismissed it, then decided that perhaps some of the boxes she'd stacked in the closet had tipped over. Maybe her own footfall, or maybe someone in the apartment upstairs, had caused the floor to tremble just enough. As soon as she thought of the apartment above her head, she immediately dismissed the noise, at last finding a logical place to put it. The sound hadn't come from her apartment at all. It had come from upstairs.

So convinced was she that she didn't even open the closet door to look inside. So convinced was she that she crawled into bed, knowing she had to grab what little sleep she could, glad she'd been able to handle the milk crisis in a calm, nonhysterical manner. She could do this. She could be a mother. She could give her baby what he needed.

Even though sleep deprivation had made all of the muscles in Claudia's body ache, made her eyes bloodshot, she had a feeling of semiconsciousness even after her breathing became rhythmic, even after the bed seemed to swallow her, welcome her. That deep, deep sleep was forever elusive. She was a mother now.

Somehow, a corner of her mind had to remain ever watchful, ever listening for a cry, a whimper that would indicate her baby needed her.

As Claudia slept, the sentinel heard a sound that didn't fit the sounds that a baby would make. The sentinel listened again, wondering if Claudia needed to be alerted.

There it was again.

Something sliding across a wooden floor. A dragging footstep?

The sentinel ran through possibilities. Someone in the hallway, going to another apartment. Someone upstairs. Someone downstairs.

There.

Again.

In the apartment. *In the apartment.*

Claudia came awake with a start. A sound played back in her mind. A scraping. Like a hard-soled shoe sliding across a gritty wooden floor.

Had she dreamed the sound?

But it had seemed so real, as if she'd really heard it.

She lay in the darkness, eyes wide, breathing shallow, not daring to move, ears keen, waiting, waiting, waiting, for a sound that was real, a sound that wasn't part of a dream.

As she lay there, she thought about the Madonna Murderer.

And remembered that her door had been open when she came home from getting the baby formula.

And suddenly she knew there were three people in her apartment, not two.

She reached out and turned on the light next to her bed, hoping it would silence her fears, hoping she would laugh when she realized how foolish she'd been—hoping that the sound had been nothing but a vivid dream after all.

But there in the dim light of a twenty-five-watt bulb was the form of a dark-hooded man leaning over her baby's white wicker bassinet, a form as terrifying as Death.

She screamed loudly, shrilly, her lungs and throat burning with the effort. While she screamed, she lunged at the figure standing above her baby.

He dropped something and it hit the floor, shattering.

Later police would find that it was the snow globe that was his signature, a gift left for the infants.

Unmindful of the glass shards cutting into the soles of her bare feet, Claudia threw the weight of her 120 pounds at the dark figure, continuing to scream as loudly as she could. Footsteps sounded from above.

The man shoved her backward on the bed, one of his arms sweeping the white lamp with its ceramic teddy bear to the floor, shattering the bulb, drenching the room in darkness.

He put a hand to her throat, to stop her screaming, to stop her breathing.

She struggled for air and he spoke to her, his voice high and excited.

"You mustn't raise your hand to me. Have you no respect? You whore. Whore, whore, whore. Pretending a virgin birth. But I know you. I know you're a whore."

Through the lightshow behind her eyes, she was aware that someone was pounding on her apartment door.

"What's going on in there?"

Chicago, she thought fleetingly. Who would have thought someone would come to the aid of a stranger in Chicago?

She fought to pull the fingers from her neck, but the

man was strong, his hands locked to her like talons, all muscles and trembling tendons.

The light in her head flashed one more time, then came darkness, a deep, black darkness that swallowed her, that was beyond dreaming, beyond the deepest sleep. Before she lost consciousness completely, she felt something hot and wet and sticky on her chest, and she smelled the metallic scent of blood.

Ivy shut the Madonna Murders case file. She put a hand to her face and realized she was shaking. Her skin was cold and clammy even though it had to be above eighty degrees in the apartment.

What was she doing here?

Pretending that she had come back to catch the murdering bastard? People spent entire lives fooling themselves. Talking about the things they were going to do, discussing their Big Plans. When all they were really doing was trying to get by day to day. Because the truth was, people had to have something to dream about, to hold as sacred, even if it was something they would never accomplish.

Chapter 7

It was 2:00 A.M. in Shady Oaks. Fake antique street-lamps followed the curve of the sidewalk in perfect symmetry. The sprinkler systems were going, and if Ethan Irving stood in the right spot, lining things up just so, he could see a small rainbow that would never reach the sky. Beneath the rolled-out lawns that had come from a sod farm a hundred miles away lay corn-fields that had once been timberland where Indians had roamed and hunted.

People talked bad about the suburbs, but Ethan liked the comforting murmur of life just beyond his bedroom window, liked where he'd grown up, mostly because it was the only thing he'd ever known, at least the only thing he could really remember. But every once in a while he hated it for its lack of personality. Genericville. He sometimes felt that if he had the guts to get out of there, he'd never come back. Not once he saw the rest of the world. But Genericville was safe. He'd hung around with the same bunch of kids most of his life. Problem was you always had to be the person they expected you to be. And the older you all got, the more you fell into old roles when you were together. Ethan had long suspected that when his friends were with other people they were different. They showed growth—an expanded, wiser version of their former selves.

With his headphones on and Walkman turned up, filling his head with the sound of the Smiths, Ethan moved down the middle of the street, the soles of his sneakers slapping against asphalt that still held the heat of the sun. He slowed when he got to the Carter house. John and Lily Carter. A couple in their mid-twenties. They'd moved in two years ago, and Ethan had had a little crush on Lily ever since. He talked to her sometimes. She must have been lonely, because she always seemed glad to see him. She was support-ing her husband while he went to school and brought women home when Lily was at work.

Lily wanted to have a baby someday. She'd even planted an apple tree in the front yard for the kid.

"Everybody needs an apple tree to climb," she'd explained.

Ethan had helped her plant it. She'd dug deep so the roots wouldn't have to work as hard to take hold, and as she dug, she found a perfect arrowhead. She'd tried to give it to Ethan, but he wouldn't let her. She should save it for the kid—if she had one.

Here she was, planning for the future, while her husband went behind her back, ruining all her plans. She just didn't know it yet. Was that the kind of crap that happened to everybody? Lily was nice. Beautiful. Why wasn't her husband happy? Was *anybody* ever happy? Really?

Ethan thought too much. That was his problem. Words, ideas, eating away at him. He didn't like it, this thinking. He envied his friends who didn't seem to think at all. Or were they faking it too, just like him?

As he approached his house, Ethan turned off his Walkman and removed it. Earlier that day, he'd left his bedroom window unlocked. Now he slid it open, then, after dropping the Walkman inside, he pulled himself up, his belly pressed against the window frame, his head inside the pitch-black room. Headfirst, he wormed his way in, finally rolling to the carpeted floor. He lay there a minute, catching his breath, listening, hoping Max, who had hearing like a wild animal's, didn't wake up. He was thinking he'd gotten away with it when a voice came out of the darkness.

"Four hours past curfew," Max said.

There was no anger there, just a low, smooth tone that sent Ethan's heart racing, that made his stomach tighten.

"But then I guess I should be honored that you came home at all."

Never try to fool a cop. Ethan should have learned that by now.

He didn't know where the idea came from, but Ethan said, "I'm not staying."

He stood up and jerked open the curtain. Light from the street poured into his room. He began grabbing clothes, anything, stuffing them into his backpack, not really thinking, just wanting out of there, away from Max. He'd figure the rest out later. He stuck his Walkman between some clothes, then zipped the pack.

There was enough light for Ethan to see Max sitting in the corner on the floor. He unfolded himself and got to his feet. "You can't leave. You're on probation."

Ethan's heart continued to hammer. He could feel it in his throat, in his head. To hell with Max, Ethan tried to tell himself. Ethan didn't give a shit what he thought. The guy was nothing to him. Nothing.

So why did he have this awful gnawing feeling in his gut?

To hell with Max.

The window was still open. Ethan briefly thought of diving out, but he was afraid Max might grab his legs before he could get away. And if he dove out the window, Max would know what a panic he was in. No, it would be better to walk past him and out the front door, as if he didn't give a shit. There was nothing cool about diving out a window.

He grabbed his backpack and walked.

Past Max.

Down the hallway.

Unlocked the front door.

Out the door.

Down the sidewalk.

He heard a sound behind him.

Ethan dropped his backpack and cut to the right, through the yard, through the sprinklers. He wasn't fast enough. Hands, arms wrapped around his waist as Max tackled him, bringing him to the ground. For a second, Ethan saw black dots. He blinked them away. Water sprayed in his face. His head was shoved against the wet grass.

That pissed him off. That really pissed him off. He let himself go limp. Max released him and was moving away when Ethan rolled over. With a roar of rage, he jumped to his feet and attacked, the top of his head meeting Max's stomach, propelling the man to the ground.

Victory!

Oh, shit. He'd knocked down his old man. And now they were rolling through the grass, water from the sprinklers blasting Ethan in the face. Ethan let go of Max and was ready to haul ass out of there.

"Ethan!" Max's hand lashed out, grabbing him by the ankle, pulling him down. Max had shouted his name, but it now occurred to Ethan that he hadn't sounded mad.

Max's grip on Ethan's ankle relaxed. Ethan scrambled to his feet while Max rolled to his back, one foot on the grass, leg bent, arms spread out. The guy was *laughing*. Trying to catch his breath, but laughing all the same. Lying there on the grass, water soaking him, laughing. And then Ethan became aware of his own clothes, soaked, wet and cold, heavy, aware of a jet of water hitting him in the face, and he began to laugh too. He didn't want to. Didn't want to be sharing a joke with Max, but damn, he couldn't help it. And once he started laughing, he couldn't stop. He laughed until his knees went weak and he had to drop to the ground. He laughed until his stomach burned, until tears ran down his cheeks along with the water.

Somebody called the cops on them.

The cops didn't get there until after Max had extended a hand to help Ethan to his feet. They didn't get there until the two men had gone sloshing into the house, until Ethan had slipped into a pair of gray jogging pants, Max some plaid boxer shorts.

Two cops came to the door. From his room, Ethan could hear Max talking to them in a low voice. Then they left.

This round had turned out okay, but that didn't

mean Ethan was going to cut Max any slack. And he knew it didn't mean their problems were over. Things would cool down for a day or two, but then they'd reach a flash point again. They always did.

Max knocked on the bedroom door and silently handed Ethan his backpack.

After he left, Ethan lit a couple of candles, cut the lights, and threw himself on his bed. Then he grabbed his Walkman from the backpack, put on the headphones, and cranked up the music all the way, so loud it should blow out his eardrums. But he didn't care. The music. He didn't know what he'd do if he didn't have music. Go crazy, maybe. But he *did* have it. Not the crap his friends listened to, but the good stuff, stuff that was too deep, too meaningful for radio, stuff that kind of tore a hole in your soul and left you aching for more.

Ethan was sixteen years old and he didn't have a clue what he wanted to do with his life. Shit. In two more years he would be out of high school. What then? *What then?* He couldn't see past graduation day. He couldn't see himself doing anything but hanging out, playing video games, riding his skateboard, listening to music.

One day not long ago, Max had told him he'd better start thinking about his future, making plans. Didn't the guy know you shouldn't say that to a sixteen-year-old? A real parent wouldn't have said that kind of crap. They'd say things like, "When I was your age, I didn't know what I was going to do either. Don't worry. It'll come. And when it does, you'll know it." But no, Max didn't say anything like that. Instead, he started grilling him, asking him what he was interested in. And Ethan would answer, "Hell no, I don't want to be a cop!" Or, "Hell no, I don't want to join the army!" And then Max would start talking about college, and how Ethan had better start studying for his ACT. And that would make Ethan's heart beat all the faster. He was just a kid. He'd spent his whole life doing nothing, and now, suddenly he was supposed to know exactly what he wanted.

What he wanted was to find his father. All along, he'd had the idea that if he could find his dad everything would fall into place. Because his real dad would know what to say. He and his real dad would sit around in the backyard, drinking beer, shooting the shit. His real dad would show him how to clean a carburetor, and how to tune an engine just like his friend Tyler's dad had done. His real dad wouldn't talk about the importance of noticing details in case you were ever a witness to some kind of crime—which is exactly what had happened to Ethan a couple of years ago. He'd been in the Quick Stop buying some pop when it was robbed.

"What'd they look like?" his dad had asked. "How tall? What kind of clothes?" He didn't say, "I'm glad you're okay." And when Ethan had said he didn't know, Max had gotten this look on his face, a look of confusion, then acceptance. Like he shouldn't have expected anything of Ethan in the first place.

His real dad wouldn't have done that. His real dad would have just been glad he was okay.

His mom . . .

Sometimes he thought he remembered her, but how could that be? He was three years old when she died. Death—the idea of death—scared the hell out of him. First you're there, then you're not.

He could almost remember her voice, and the way

he felt when she spoke to him. Loved. That's how her voice made him feel. But how could he remember that? No, he was only filling in the blanks with his own imagination.

Max. Max was the first person Ethan remembered. It was Christmas, and he and Max had gotten a tree. Max had lifted him up so he could put tinsel on the top. When Ethan remembered those times, he didn't hate Max. But that Max didn't seem like the high-strung Max he knew today.

A person could almost think Max didn't have any feelings, but Ethan knew better. He'd never forget a night, years ago, when Max had picked him up from the baby-sitter's. All the way home, he didn't say a word. Ethan finally asked about the smell—a rotten, sweet, awful odor that seemed to be coming from his dad.

Max didn't say anything for a long time, then asked, "You can smell it too?"

"Yeah," Ethan said.

"Rotten cantaloupe," his dad finally told him.

And when they got home, Max took a long, long shower. When he came out he was wearing a clean pair of jeans, his wet hair smelling of lemons. In the middle of the night, something woke Ethan up. At first he couldn't place the noise, and then, with a sort of awkward embarrassment, he realized his dad was crying.

When he got older, he found out that lemon shampoo was the best way to wash the smell of death from your hair.

Chapter 8

Abraham gripped the wooden podium, pulling his thoughts into coherence while the always solid, always dependable Detective Irving stood to his right. Also present at the press conference were Cook County State Attorney Roger Jacobs, Cook County Board President Jane O'Riley, and Deputy Chief of Area Five Grace Simms.

Abraham had spent the entire morning on the phone. The mayor had called twice in three hours, with Abraham assuring him that this latest homicide could not yet be linked in any way to the homicides of sixteen years ago.

He'd also had several conversations with hospital administrators who were expecting panic to erupt in their maternity wards.

He could have let his assistant handle some of the lighter calls, but that wasn't what Abraham was about. Through his entire career, he'd made it a point to be accessible, even from his position at the top. He wanted the public to know that the murders were high on everyone's priority list, especially the Superintendent's. By the time the conference rolled around, Abraham had put away two pots of coffee and a roll of antacid tablets, and he needed something stronger than aspirin for his headache.

Looking out into the auditorium, he was relieved to see that the majority of the seats were vacant. So far the mother-and-child homicide wasn't big news and wouldn't be unless a connection was made to the Madonna Murderer.

Many of the faces were familiar. Chris Humes, from the *Sun.* Victoria Price-Rand, from the *Trib.*

Abraham quickly gave them the facts.

"What about the Madonna Murderer?"

The question Abraham had hoped to avoid came from a shiny-faced young man Abraham had never seen before.

The good reporters, the ones who didn't screw up a case by leaking information, were, in turn, respected by the police. In exchange for their cooperation, they were sometimes granted starring roles in the investigation process. They were sometimes given exclusive information that could eventually lead to a distinguished career in the newspaper business.

Stalling, Abraham asked, "What's your name?"

The reporter fiddled with the plastic press pass clipped to his shirt, as if Abraham could read the name from thirty feet away. "Alex Martin, sir."

Irritated, weary, Abraham plunged in. "At this point, there's no evidence to draw any kind of connection between this homicide and the homicides of sixteen years ago. Next question." He directed his gaze away from the new reporter.

"B-but, sir," Alex stammered, his hand raised.

Superintendent Sinclair ignored him, choosing instead to call on one of the more established reporters.

The incident made Alex so angry that he sat in his

chair biting his nails and obsessing over it while losing track of his immediate surroundings. Ten minutes later, the room came into focus as Detective Irving eased his way behind the podium.

Alex settled back to listen to more bullshit.

"What about the FBI?" someone asked.

"The FBI's Chicago field office is involved in the case," Max Irving said.

"Any plans to bring in other agents?"

"Not at this point. We have our own excellent profiler, Special Agent David Scott, who has been instrumental in the apprehension of several criminals over the last four years," Irving told them. "He has a remarkable success rate."

"But he's only one man. What about his caseload?"

The reporter, Victoria Price-Rand, had brought up an ongoing problem. Everyone in the police department and FBI was overextended. Last Max heard, Agent Scott was juggling 150 different homicide cases. Max himself was overseeing about the same number. Too much crime, not enough law enforcement, not enough crime labs, not enough manpower. And it was only going to get worse. DNA labs could now process results in as quickly as two weeks, a vast improvement over the time it used to take, but technicians were so backed up that it could still take months to get results.

And to get an FBI agent sent down from Quantico—well, the only way that would happen was if this last case could be linked to the Madonna Murders.

Two hours later, Alex Martin sat in the belly of the newsroom, fingers flying over his keyboard, typing up his condemning piece on Superintendent Sinclair, getting more pissed as he wrote. Around him, other reporters sat in front of computers, keys clicking, phones ringing, printers spewing out stories that were coming in off wire services.

Journalists just getting out of college always imagined themselves doing human-interest stories. Or commentary. Or starring in a column dealing with life, the United States, the world. A column where the person would become famous and readers would wait in anticipation for the next thought-provoking article.

Those were the kind of things journalists dreamed of, that and of course a billion-dollar career writing more than one Great American Novel. Nobody ever said, I'm going to cover high school basketball. I'm going to write obituaries—which were tough as hell to do. Alex knew that for a fact because that's where he'd started out. And nobody said, I'm going to go to college, major in journalism, so I can hang around police stations, so I can sift through daily logs of domestic arguments, public intoxication, traffic arrests, and report it. Day after day after day.

Wouldn't win a Pulitzer that way. No, to win a Pulitzer, you had to dig and dig, you had to uncover everything you could uncover, expose every corner to light.

He was paying his dues, he knew that, but he wanted a story. A real damn story. He also knew that wasn't going to happen either, because cops had their favorite reporters, guys they'd worked with for years. Those were the ones who got the stories, those were the ones who got the exclusives. Not somebody like him. That much was made obvious when Sinclair ignored him in front of his peers. It was hard enough to earn the respect of fellow reporters without someone publicly humiliating you like that.

And so he typed, hitting the keys with hard, angry

strokes, wondering if he'd ever get a decent story, if he'd chosen the right career. But with four years of student loans hanging over his head, he had to stick with it. Even if it wasn't right. Even if he'd made a mistake. That was the heartbreaking thing about college. You had to make a choice—a *guess,* really—about what you wanted to do with the rest of your life. It was a roll of the dice, because there was a big chance you could be wrong, a very big chance. And unless you were independently wealthy, once it was done, it was done.

More and more, Alex was thinking he'd made a mistake. And that was a hard thing to deal with. That feeling of knowing you didn't belong somewhere, that what-the-hell-am-I-doing-here feeling of mounting desperation.

Alex gave his story a file name: Abraham Sinclair.

He was still staring at the article when his desk advisor stopped by.

A few years back, the *Herald* had hired a new CEO and gone through massive restructuring. During that time, some lamebrain had come up with the idea of changing everybody's job title. Gone were the more militant-sounding titles like "chief" and "deputy." Now people were "directors," and "advisors," and "overseers." In effect, they'd edited the *edit* out of *editing.*

His advisor's name was Maude Cunningham. Maude was probably called a broad in her younger days. She could have been anywhere between sixty and seventy. She'd started when the paper was a male-dominated ship and female reporters had to be tough and resilient. She smoked, and Alex suspected she drank fairly heavily because she had that dried-up-prune look peo-

ple got after indulging for decades. Her voice was a
harsh rasp, and the air that came from her lungs was
as stale as a mausoleum's. Alex figured she was one
X ray away from a cancer diagnosis.

"We can't run that." She was perched on the corner
of his desk, tapping a long red fingernail against a
yellow front tooth.

Alex reread it.

It was an out-of-control defamatory piece, full of
adjectives and qualifiers used to describe Sinclair's cal-
lous treatment of Alex. There wasn't a newsworthy
bit of information in the entire thing.

"I was just shitting around." He clicked the cancel
button, then tried to exit the program, but the soft-
ware wouldn't let him off the hook so easily.

Do you want to save file Abraham Sinclair?

The question blinked at him.

He hit the "no" button, deleting his article.

"I'd like to do some research on Sinclair, find out
what he had to do with the Madonna Murders," he
said.

"Are you talking a revenge piece? That's not what
this paper is about. I don't want you using the paper
to carry out a personal vendetta. You have to grow a
thicker skin if you're going to stay in this business.
Every day you're going to run into people who don't
even know you, but hate you because you're a newspaper reporter. That's because writers have power.
Don't abuse it. Go ahead and look in the archives,
but stay off Sinclair's back. I can tell you he was in
charge of the Madonna case years ago. It cost him his
marriage and he ended up having to go to a treatment
center in Minneapolis to dry out. Try to see it from

his side for a moment, and maybe you won't resent him so much."

"So I have your approval to see what I can dig up?"

"I want you to have something ready *in case* we need it. If any more murders occur, or if the police come up with a solid connection between these new cases and the Madonna Murders. In the meantime, just try to stay abreast of the current situation without making enemies of the entire police force." She smiled at him in a tough-broad, I-like-you sort of way. "I realize those two things might be a little hard for you to accomplish, but please make an effort."

Chapter 9

The lady Ethan was trying to serve couldn't decide what she wanted. She stood staring up at the wall menu, waiting for something to hit her in the face, as if expecting the menu to change or start flashing or something. Who knew?

Ethan wished lightning would strike them all.

It was a bagel shop, for chrissake, not some five-star downtown snobbery where Ethan's next step would be to suggest a hundred-dollar wine. Why couldn't people make up their minds?

He waited impatiently while the line behind her grew until it reached the door.

Finally she said, "I'll have a plain bagel with cream cheese."

That's how it was with the people who couldn't decide. They always ended up ordering the most boring thing on the menu.

"Light or regular cream cheese?"

"Huh?"

"Light or regular cream cheese?" He shouldn't have asked, but customers like her were also the ones who would return the bagel to demand a different cream cheese.

He got off in a couple hours, but he wasn't looking forward to it. His dad was picking him up and they were going to a movie. Didn't Max get it? Couldn't he see Ethan didn't want to hang around with him? The phoniness of it all—he couldn't take it anymore. That Max was going out of his way for these father-and-son outings enraged him. When Ethan was little and would see something on TV that scared him, he would chant to himself, *This isn't real. This isn't real.* That's what he did now with Max.

The indecisive woman moved down the counter, where she would probably spend another hour trying to decide if she wanted a latte or an espresso, raspberry or chocolate-almond flavoring.

"Can I help you?" he asked the next customer.

He and his dad had always been close—that's what made the truth sit in his gut like a bunch of mold-covered rocks. One day not long ago, Ethan had a fight with a neighbor. In retaliation, the kid tauntingly told him that the reason Max adopted Ethan was because his dying mother had begged him to take him in and be his father.

Which made Ethan a charity case.

It was hard enough finding out you were adopted, but you could always tell yourself that your dad *wanted* you, wanted a kid, otherwise he wouldn't have done it. Now he couldn't even believe that. . . .

At first Ethan had tried to deny the charity thing, but in the end he couldn't put it from his mind, and he was eventually forced to recognize it as truth. It made perfect sense. He felt stupid for not seeing it before. He knew Max hadn't known his mother long, so why else would he have adopted him? Max was the kind of person who always wanted to do the right thing. "Duty-bound" was the phrase Ethan had come up with to describe him.

But it was hard and depressing knowing his entire childhood had been a sham. That his past was a rug that had been pulled out from under him. That all the times they'd spent together had been done out of duty.

Max was always telling Ethan that people had to look out for the less fortunate. Ever since he could remember, Max had sent money to a girl and boy in Bolivia. Those kids were adults now, and they still sent Christmas cards and letters, and Max now had two new children he supported. Ethan had always thought it was cool of Max until he found out he was just like those kids. At least they knew they were charity cases. At least with them there had been no pretending.

He wanted to talk to somebody about it, but his buddies didn't talk about that kind of stuff. They would feel weird and embarrassed, and they wouldn't have any answers anyway. That's what you realized when you got older. When you were little, you thought you were just too young to understand the answers and that when you got older things would come into focus. Then you had to finally face the truth: There were no answers.

Ethan swung around just as a coworker spit on the plain bagel with light cream cheese.

"What the hell are you doing?" he whispered.

"What's it look like? I'm givin' her my House Special. I hate it when them bitches hold up the line like that. Like they're the only people wanting to eat."

Jarod had been working at Bagels, Bagels only three days, and was a total pain in the ass, one of those rich kids whose parents made them get a summer job so

they wouldn't stay in bed all day watching MTV and
playing video games. He was sour and rude, and the
only time he enjoyed himself was when he was fucking
something up—which was about every two minutes.

Ethan grabbed the bagel and threw it in the trash.
"Fix another one, and do it right."

"You talkin' to me? You tellin' me what to do?"
He was also one of those white kids who liked to
talk black.

"Yeah, I am."

Jarod dropped his arms to his sides, his hands
clenched, his face red. Everything about him was
confrontational.

"Come on, man." Ethan gestured toward the bagel
container. "Just make another one." He couldn't believe they were fighting over a fucking bagel. "It's no
big deal."

Jarod pulled off his green bagel cap and tossed it
on the floor. "Fuck you. Fuck you, man." He
stomped out.

Wearily, Ethan prepared a new bagel and took it to
the cash register where the woman was waiting to pay.

She pushed it back at him. "I don't want it," she
said, her chin raised in indignation. There was no way
she could have heard or seen what Jarod had done
with the original bagel, but she couldn't have missed
his tantrum. "I have no desire to eat in such a hostile
environment. What's your manager's name? I want to
report this." She had a pen out, and now Ethan could
see she'd already noted his badge and written his
name on a napkin.

He stared at her and wondered if he should have
kept his mouth shut about the spit bagel.

Two hours later, Ethan was putting away the last

of the cream cheese when he heard a commotion at the door. Why the hell did people come at closing time? He looked up to see a bunch of his friends piling in, laughing and shoving one another all the way to the order area. Ryan Harrison, a neighbor, hockey teammate, and longtime friend, sprawled partway over the counter.

"You have to buy something," Ethan said. "The manager's in the back office."

The last time his friends had shown up, the manager had kicked them out because they'd overtaken and dirtied two tables, helped themselves to self-serve ice water, straws, and napkins, and left a soggy mess for Ethan to clean up while not purchasing a single item.

"Give me a pizza bagel and medium soda," Ryan said while Heather Green tugged at his arm, pleading with him to buy her a bagel too. He rolled his eyes and ordered a second one. Heather smiled broadly and winked at Ethan. Heather was always laughing and happy. Even though she lived down the street from him and he'd known her forever, Ethan felt a little clumsy around her because he'd heard she was sexually active while he was still a virgin.

"Did you hear about the record show at Navy Pier?" she asked.

"No," Ethan said. She was also one of the only girls—or guys, for that matter—who knew anything about music. Not a lot, but more than his buddies.

"Next month. Tickets are ten bucks for three days."

"You going?" he asked.

"Can't. Family vacation. We're going camping in Colorado."

"Cool." He gave them their bagels and self-serve

drink cup, then totaled their order. "What about you?" he asked Ryan.

"The record show? I don't know." He shrugged. "Maybe. Will your dad let you go?"

"If he doesn't, I'll sneak out." There was no way he would allow his dad to keep him from going to something so important.

"You're so intense at those things," Ryan said. "It's kind of a drag."

"Thanks." Nobody got it. Nobody got Ethan's infatuation with music. Not the radio crap, but *music*. Good music.

He hung out in a few select chat rooms—it was great "talking" to people who loved and revered the same things he did—but why didn't he actually *know* anybody like that?

How could you respect somebody who didn't understand good music? What if he met a girl and fell in love . . . but she listened to crap? Could he marry her? Could he spend the rest of his life with her?

"Right now we're going to an all-ages show at the Quest," one of his other buddies, Brent, said. "Wanna come?"

"Who's playing?"

"I don't know. We just thought it would be something to do. We're going to try to hook up with Pasqual or Donnie Issak to get us some vodka. We have enough money for three fifths."

"I can't."

"Come on, man. Don't you get off work pretty soon? We stopped to get you."

"Yeah, but my dad's picking me up."

Brent laughed. "Oh, yeah, that's right. You're grounded. I forgot. Bummer."

"If it's such a bummer, why are you laughing?"

"I was just thinking about how drunk you were the other night. You were funny as hell. I almost wet my pants. I didn't know you could be so fucking funny."

Ethan had a fuzzy memory of climbing on top of somebody's car. He'd removed his pants and tied the legs around his neck like a cape and was shouting things like, "I'm the king of the world!" Thinking about it made his face hot. The cape thing was bad enough; he hoped he hadn't done anything more embarrassing than that.

Headlights suddenly illuminated the interior of the small shop. When the lights were cut, Ethan could make out the car. "Cool it," he told Brent. "My dad's here."

"Hey everybody," Brent announced. "Ethan's daddy's here to pick him up."

Chapter 10

It used to be that thirteen was his lucky number. But lately the number twenty-two had been showing up with unwavering regularity. Anytime he looked at the clock, it was something twenty-two. 2:22, 5:22, 7:22. Like that. The other day, he bought a sandwich and a Coke and it cost him $6.22. Then he picked up a newspaper and there was a picture of a wrecked bus on the front. The bus's number? Twenty-two. Then it occurred to him that his address was 7852. If you added those, you got twenty-two. . . .

A thud above his head made him jump.

She was awake.

Soon she would begin bellowing at him, making demands.

He could smell her through the floorboards. Her stink permeated the whole house. Did she take a shower at all anymore? He didn't think so. In some ways he liked that, because it meant he was the only person using the shower. He didn't like knowing someone else had been there, that those were *her* body hairs stuck to the soap and the fiberglass shower floor. He couldn't stand knowing that she'd left invisible sluffed-off skin behind, along with her stench. It was much better that it was just him.

Why had she always hated him?

Dirty boy. Dirty, dirty boy.

He remembered the first time he realized she was different from other mothers . . . and that *he* was different from other children.

Kindergarten.

That single word made him break out in a cold sweat.

She'd taken him to the huge brick schoolhouse, her sweaty hand swallowing his as she pulled him along, his short legs trying to keep up, his fear creating an acid taste in the back of his mouth.

His legs were almost too short to make it up the steps, but she didn't slow down. "Come on. Let's get this over with," she said, tugging at him, pulling his arm straight up from the socket. As soon as they stepped inside he felt alien. And that alien feeling never went away.

Women—other mothers—looked at them, then quickly looked away. Some put hands to their faces, covering their nose and mouth. Some moved back to let them pass, as if afraid he or his mother might brush up against them.

He wore little red shorts and a red-and-white-striped T-shirt that didn't cover his belly. His shorts were stained from "shit," as his mother called it, and his feet, in the faded, cracked flip-flops, were crusted with dirt.

His mother was dressed the way she always dressed when she wore clothes, in tight terry-cloth shorts and a tank top with black, coarse hair sticking out from under her armpits. She had always seemed huge to him—she was his mother—but now he saw that she was three times as big as the other women standing in the hallway trying not to look at them.

"Come on," she said, jerking his hand, dragging him into a room where a beautiful woman sat at a desk. She had black hair and red lips, and a warm smile that made everything seem okay.

Other women were sitting at desks, filling out papers. Some children were in the corner, playing with toys.

His mother dropped his hand. The woman behind the desk said hello to him and asked him if he'd like to play with the others.

He looked up at his mother. Would she let him?

"Go on," she said, using her angry face, her angry voice.

So he walked slowly over to where the other children were playing. One boy had a plastic car he rolled along green carpet that had a drawing of streets on it. A girl with blond hair was playing with colored blocks, stacking them higher and higher. He thought she was pretty.

The girl looked at him and said, "You stink."

The boy looked up, then pointed. "You pee-peed." That wasn't enough, he had to announce it to everyone in the room. "He pee-peed," he said in a singsong voice, still pointing. "Teacher, he pee-peed."

He could feel something hot and wet trickling down his leg, his foot, puddling on the carpet. The smell of urine stung his nostrils. Confused, he wondered what he'd done wrong.

The beautiful woman behind the desk stood up. She wasn't smiling anymore. Her red mouth was a straight line, her dark brows drawn together, creating deep

creases between her eyes. "Isn't he toilet trained?"
Her voice held disbelief combined with shock.

"Thought you could take care of that," his mother
said. She waddled across the room, grabbed his hand,
and pulled him after her, his wet feet squishing in his
flip-flops.

But now she wore the opal necklace he'd given her.
And she had something from every mother he'd ever
killed. Seeing her wear his gifts made him feel wonderful because they were the truest symbols of his deep
and profound feelings for her.

From above his head came a crash, followed by a
heavy thud that shook the house.

What now? he wondered. *What now?*

And then she began screaming and moaning.

"My leg! My leg! I broke my leg!"

Chapter 11

In Japanese, *Sachi* means "child of bliss." LaDonna Anderson wasn't Japanese, but she'd traveled to Japan as a high school exchange student. That had been years and years ago. And even though she'd thought about her Japanese parents often, hoping to someday go back there, she never had. She'd married a kind, patient man who developed emphysema from working in a coal mine. They had one child, and LaDonna named her Sachi, child of bliss.

Sachi was a beautiful girl who became a beautiful woman. When her father died and LaDonna was too overcome to speak at the funeral, Sachi delivered a wonderful eulogy. She was that kind of person. Someone who could do anything.

And when she accidentally became pregnant and announced she would keep and raise the baby without the father's help, LaDonna had thought, *Yes, you will.* And she thought, *There are no accidents. Only miracles.*

During Sachi's pregnancy, she and her daughter often talked about going to Japan together someday. It was a dream they'd often shared through the years, and now that dream included a child. They would take Sachi's baby with them. . . .

The baby ended up being a boy. Sachi named him Taro, Japanese for "firstborn son."

It had been expensive to have the special birth announcement put in the paper. Even though LaDonna couldn't afford the forty-dollar fee, she'd done it anyway. She wanted all of her friends to know that she was proud of her new grandson, proud of her beautiful daughter.

LaDonna worked nights at a market only three blocks from where she and Sachi lived. She could pick up a paper that evening when she got to work, but she couldn't wait so long. And sometimes there were no papers left by evening.

She got up early and walked to the market, buying a paper and a cup of flavored decaffeinated coffee for Sachi, caffeinated for herself. Sachi had temporarily given up caffeine and chocolate because she was nursing. Some people said it didn't matter what a mother ate, that it didn't have any effect on her milk, but LaDonna knew better. Food like beans and brussels sprouts made a baby colicky, and caffeine kept an infant awake, and Lord knew a mother needed that baby to sleep as much as possible.

LaDonna hurried home with the paper.

They'd lived in the apartment on Mulberry for more than three years. Enough time so that she no longer saw the carved names on the walls, or noticed that the handrail to the second floor was loose. What was outside their apartment didn't matter. Because inside was their world, their safe, cozy world.

In the kitchen, LaDonna cut out the birth announcement and stuck it to the front of the refrigerator with a magnet. Later, she would take Taro's hospital photo and the birth announcement and have them framed. It would be a surprise for Sachi. Something she could save along with all of her other treasures.

The apartment was still quiet, so she left the white plastic lid on Sachi's coffee, opened her own, and sat down at the small round table in front of the bay window to read the paper. A short time later she heard the sound of a fretful baby, heard Sachi's sleepy voice. Then all was quiet, and LaDonna imagined Sachi nursing her tiny, red-faced baby, smoothing his straight black hair.

Later, Sachi came out in her bathrobe and put the bundled baby in LaDonna's outstretched arms.

"I brought you coffee," LaDonna said, not taking her eyes from the infant who was staring in her direction with crossed eyes. "Raspberry decaffeinated."

"You've been out?" Sachi lifted the lid and inhaled. "Ah, that smells almost as good as caffeinated."

"I wanted to pick up a paper."

Steam swirled up from her cup as Sachi lifted it to her mouth. She took a cautious sip. "Why not wait until tonight?"

"There. Look on the refrigerator."

Sachi took four steps and leaned forward. "A birth announcement?" she asked in a puzzled voice. "Mom, nobody puts birth announcements in the paper anymore. Not unless you live in some small town where everybody knows everybody and they have a weekly paper that tells about things like Cousin Myrtle visiting from a town five miles away. Or a photo of somebody in a goofy hat and glasses with a caption reading 'Lordy, Lordy, Look Who's Forty.' "

LaDonna felt deflated. She'd thought Sachi would be happy about the announcement. "I wanted to put it in the paper," she said stubbornly, frustrated that she would have to explain her actions. She certainly hadn't thought Sachi would question them.

"Why?"

"Because I'm so proud of you both. My Sachi. My Taro."

Sachi sat down at the table across from her mother and smiled in that sweet and wise Madonna-like smile that made her seem so much older than her twenty-two years. She smelled like baby powder and raspberry coffee, and the muted sunlight that fell through the window painted her in a soft, golden patina. "I know that, Mom."

LaDonna wanted to hold that moment, stop that moment, embrace, absorb, understand that moment. The perfect circle of love. Mother and child, mother and child.

That evening, LaDonna headed for work, leaving Sachi curled in the corner of the couch, filling out birth announcements, while Taro slept peacefully beside her. Later, Sachi changed his diaper, nursed him, then put him down for what she hoped would be at least a few hours, giving her a chance to catch up on her sleep.

She was dreaming about driving around and around in a car, desperately looking for her missing baby, when she heard a knock. Thinking it was early morning and her mother had forgotten her key, she shuffled sleepily to the door and opened it.

A dark-hooded man stood in the opening.

Adrenaline surged.

She tried to slam the door. He pushed it open, his hand immediately going for her throat, cutting off her scream before it began.

Chapter 12

City of Big Shoulders. That's what somebody named Carl Sandburg had called it, or so Ronny Ramirez had been told.

It was 2:00 A.M. and Ronny Ramirez was on patrol as one of the rapid response teams implemented by Daley in the late nineties. Ramirez loved Chicago. He loved his job—most of the time.

The son of migrant workers, he'd lived in the United States his whole life. Before he was born, his parents used to come up from Mexico to Missouri every fall to pick tomatoes, then pears. When the season was over, they returned to a little scrap of land that belonged to his grandfather where they grew produce and sold it in Mexico City. But when Ramirez's mother became pregnant with him, they decided to stay where they could take advantage of free hospital care in exchange for agreeing to be poked and prodded by students for two weeks before, during, and after the delivery. Twelve students had been chosen to participate in the birth. One had performed the episiotomy. Another had caught the afterbirth.

I've never had so many strangers looking at my crotch, baby, his mother had told him. But the whole humiliating experience had been worth it, because her son, Ronny Ramirez, was born a citizen of the United States.

Now that one of them was a legal American, the family remained in a small farming community where most people chewed tobacco, drove trucks with huge tires, and talked like they were underwater. There, both of Ronny's parents graduated from fieldwork to factory jobs, and they were soon able to buy all of the things that they'd done without in Mexico, from electronic equipment like 35-millimeter cameras and VCRs to big appliances like washers and dryers. Even more important, Ronny was able to get an American education.

In school he was considered a curiosity. He excelled in sports, so he was accepted into the exalted inner circle made up of the children of rural families.

Ramirez hated it.

He kept thinking there had to be someplace better out there somewhere. There had to be a place that was more than cornfields as far as the eye could see.

His Mexican roots were as foreign to him as they were to the kids he went to school with, yet he never felt he belonged in the farming community where he'd grown up. He was a man without a country.

And then he discovered Chicago.

It embraced him, welcomed him. And for the first time in his life he felt a part of something. He wasn't sure what yet—he'd only been there four years, but the familiarity was comfortable. It felt like home.

The police scanner flashed, the dispatcher announcing a ten-one—a matter of utmost urgency. That was followed by the code for a possible homicide and an address. "Available area units please respond."

Ramirez's reluctant partner for the evening, Regina Hastings, flipped on the lights, then announced to the dispatcher that they were only five minutes away.

Ramirez gunned the patrol car until they were flying down almost deserted streets, Hastings gripping the handle above the door as he took a corner too fast.

"Slow down, will you? Chrissake, Ramirez. What's your fucking hurry?"

But she knew what his hurry was. Ramirez always liked to be the first officer on the scene. It was like a contest with him. A call could be way the hell on the opposite side of Area Five, and he'd haul ass over there like the show couldn't start until his face appeared on the scene.

He shot her a glance over his shoulder, white teeth flashing in his dark, handsome face. He didn't take the next corner any slower.

Tires squealed across dry pavement, and for a brief moment, it seemed that the patrol car might tip up on two wheels.

Prick, she thought. He was one of those pricks who became a cop because he wanted to drive fast and carry a gun, not to mention intimidate people. He had a reputation as a love-'em-and-leave-'em kind of guy. But in all fairness, hers wasn't an unbiased opinion. She'd gone out with Ramirez once—an occurrence she kept trying to scribble out of her mental journal. But no matter how many times she tried to scratch it out, it kept appearing again like the invisible ink she'd played with as a kid, the kind you ran under water to make show up.

She'd been a cop long enough to know she preferred to date cops. They were the only ones who understood the daily stress in an officer's life. Ramirez, on the other hand, wanted to be looked up to. It was apparently an intense need that another cop couldn't satisfy. The only time they had what could be called a conversation, he'd confided that he actually *liked* foot patrol because people could get a good look at him in uniform. She'd laughed, and that had been that.

Nobody laughed at Ronny Ramirez.

The patrol car squealed to a stop in front of a five-story brick apartment building. There were lights on in several of the windows; a cluster of people stood on the cement steps that led to the front door.

"This must be the place," Ramirez said, shoving the gearshift into park and cutting the engine.

"I hope somebody has a sticker to give you for being the first one here," she said sarcastically as she opened her door.

Hastings guessed there were approximately ten people gathered under the porch light. Clinging to wrought-iron railings, rubbing away fingerprints that may or may not have told them something. A compromised crime scene was Homicide's biggest complaint. But cops had no control over what happened before they arrived on the scene, and unfortunately not much control over what happened after they arrived if there wasn't enough manpower to keep the crowd back.

People started talking at once. Words jumped out at Hastings, enough for her to piece together that a young woman was upstairs, and that she was dead.

"Are you sure she's dead?" Hastings asked.

"Dead? No damn foolin' she's dead," a black man told her. "There's blood everywhere."

Ramirez and Hastings waded through the people, telling them to please stay back. Behind them, sirens wailed as an ambulance pulled to a stop in the middle of the street. That was immediately followed by two more police cars.

Hastings relaxed a little, relieved that they had backup to control the crowd.

"The baby," a woman in a pink nylon nightgown said. "Did you tell 'em about the baby?"

Hastings hesitated. In front of her, Ramirez stopped and turned around, their eyes meeting in silent concern. From deep inside the dark heart of the apartment, someone was wailing, a high, keening, anguished sound.

The woman finished her contribution to the story. "Baby's dead too."

Baby's dead too.

That single statement set off a network of phone calls.

Protocol dictated that in the event of an unusual murder—mass shootings, serial killings, execution killings—certain measures were to be implemented. On the night Ronny Ramirez and Regina Hastings got the call that sent them racing to Mulberry Street, several more units were dispatched in hopes that the killer was still in the area. Like a well-oiled machine, everybody did his or her part, with everything falling into place. Within ten minutes, there were six officers strategically stationed around the apartment building, another twenty setting up checkpoints at intersections. When all protocol was initiated, a call was put in to the head of the homicide squad.

"Get a containment perimeter set up," Max Irving said, the portable phone gripped between his ear and neck as he pulled on a pair of jeans. "The perpetrator could still be in the area. And cordon off the crime scene." He buttoned and zipped his pants, then reached for his shoulder holster, slipping it on over a white T-shirt.

"Done," said the officer who'd introduced himself as Ramirez.

"I'll be there in a half hour."

Immediately upon ending the call, Max punched number nine on his speed dial: Chicago's mobile crime lab.

Jeff Ellis was having sex for the third time in one night with the blonde he'd met at Nightlife, a club just off Michigan Avenue where all the cool people hung out. He liked to go there wearing his dark suit, trench coat, and black sunglasses because women got off on that. For some reason, death and a trench coat turned women on.

When he was out, he would have people guess what he did for a living. FBI was what he got most of the time. But when he went on to explain that he was a mobile-crime-lab technician, they usually liked that just as much.

He'd tried to get into Quantico, thinking it would be about the coolest thing to be an FBI agent, but his application was always turned down. Not his fault, he was damn sure of that.

He was beginning to ejaculate when the phone rang near his ear. Without pausing in his stroke, he picked the black portable off the bedside table and put it to his ear.

"Yeah!" he shouted.

The woman under him grabbed his hips and lifted herself to him. Flesh slapped flesh.

"We need the mobile crime lab at—"

"Hang on a second." He pushed *mute*, dropped the phone on the bed, then thrust himself deep into the woman—he couldn't remember her name—his semen finally spilling into the rubber wrapped around his engorged cock. When he was done, he pulled out, rolled to his back, and grabbed his cell phone.

Once again he pushed the *mute* button. "Yeah?" Dead silence. Then he realized the mute button must not have engaged the first time. "Shit." He pushed it again. "A little unfinished business," he said breathlessly into the receiver. "If you know what I mean."

"Get your ass over to 2315 Mulberry Street on the northwest side."

Detective Irving. A pissed-off Detective Irving, but then Irving was always pissed off about something. "What have you got?" Ellis could be called in on anything from a hit-and-run to undetermined death.

"You'll see when you get here."

Which meant it was something Irving didn't want to talk about over the phone, in case the call was intercepted. "Homicide?" Ellis asked, playing dumb.

"Just get your ass over here."

Ellis and Irving had never gotten along. Irving was so damn serious and had an attitude that rubbed Ellis wrong. And Irving had trained at Quantico. He wasn't FBI, but he'd still spent time in the FBI Academy program. It was a tough, eleven-week course for law enforcement officers from all over the world. Ellis had applied too, only to get passed over year after year. He asked Irving to put in a good word for him, but Irving spouted some bullshit about making it on his own merit. Ellis had hated the bastard ever since.

In the bathroom, Ellis flushed the rubber down the toilet, then got dressed. Since it was the middle of the night, most technicians would have shown up at the scene in anything they could throw on. Not Ellis. He always wore his suit and trench coat. No matter what. No matter how hot or how cold the weather, no matter if it was day or night.

He was double-checking the items in his technician's case when he remembered the blonde. He glanced up to see her pouting at him from the bed, the sheet pulled up to her waist, her breasts large and unnaturally round and high.

"You have to leave." He pulled a twenty from his billfold and tossed it on the bed. "Call a cab."

At first it seemed that she was going to say something. Then she pressed her lips together and snatched up the money.

He made a helpless gesture with one hand, shrugging his shoulders at the same time. "Hey baby, that's the way it is."

Reminding her of his important occupation softened her. "Did somebody die?" she whispered.

His eyes were on his open case, mentally cataloging equipment. Powders: white and black metallic. Brushes. Magnetic pencil. Forms. Camera. Film. Flash. Black Magic Markers. Paper evidence bags. Then there were the things that weren't issue, that he'd added himself. Baggies. Flashlight. Measuring tape. Tweezers. Scissors. Extra dress shirt. Black cloth for photo backdrop. Surgical-paper shirt and pants and shoe covers.

He was always adding to his collection.

"Homicide," he said, snapping shut the case, experiencing some satisfaction at passing Irving's veiled information along to a total stranger.

"Oh my God," she said with a mixture of awe and horror, pulling the sheet up over her breasts.

"Get up. Get dressed," he said.

"Why can't I wait here until you come back?"

Now that the sex was over, he wanted her out of there. "You don't want to be here when I get back," he said. "You don't want to see me when I get back."

Her eyes grew big and her collagen lips formed a circle. "Will you have blood on you? The victim's blood? Like on your shoes or something?"

"Maybe. I never know. But it's more my frame of mind," he said, injecting his voice with a touch of pathos, wondering why he bothered when he didn't give a shit about her. "I'm just really . . . *down* after spending a few hours at a crime scene. I need to be alone. You can understand that, can't you?"

The truth was, he didn't feel anything. He never had. Never. No, that wasn't exactly true. He sometimes felt a sense of disgust—not directed toward the killer, but the victim. Somehow, it always seemed they got what they deserved.

Chapter 13

A phone rang out in the darkness, making Ivy's heart race in sleep-drugged panic. At first she thought she was home, in St. Sebastian, and that Abraham was calling to tell her there'd been another murder. But then she remembered where she was: Chicago. Dark, haunted Chicago. And the phone was still ringing.

Disoriented, she fumbled in the dark, stubbing her toe, finally finding the screaming phone.

"Hello . . . ?" she mumbled, bent at the waist to keep from dragging the phone to the floor. The receiver smelled like grease and plastic, and her own voice echoed back at her.

"There's been another murder," Max Irving announced without preamble.

She straightened and the phone slid from the small table, crashing to the floor while she still held the receiver to her ear, the curled, sticky cord stretched taut. Jinx, who'd been sleeping near her pillow, quickly disappeared under the bed.

"Thought you might want to know."

She shut off the ceiling fan, killing all extraneous noise. "Where?"

She listened intently, chest rising and falling, heart

hammering, ears picking up the sound of a far-off siren. Nearer, possibly in the same room with Irving, was the sound of indistinct conversation. Her mind shuffled through various backdrops, finally settling on the homicide, realizing he was already at the murder scene.

"No need for you to come out in the middle of the night," Irving said.

Was she imagining it, or was there a challenge, a dare hidden behind the smoothness of that delivery? Perhaps he wanted to be able to tell Abraham that she couldn't be bothered to leave her bed.

"I'm coming."

She picked up the phone from the floor. With the receiver to her ear, she reached for her backpack on the floor near the bed, finally snagging it with her toe. She dragged it to her, then dropped to her knees, digging until she found her stenographer's notebook and pen.

She uncapped the pen with her teeth. "Give me the address."

Surprisingly, he didn't argue. He gave her the address, then said, "Call a cab. It's not far from you, only a few miles."

With one finger, she ended the call, then quickly put in another to Yellow Cab. After hanging up, she grabbed the clothes she'd taken off just hours earlier—jeans and a T-shirt. Probably not professional crime-scene attire.

Into her canvas backpack, she jammed the notebook and pen. Then, slipping her bare feet into a pair of clunky-heeled leather loafers, she grabbed her apartment keys and headed out the door.

Downstairs, she waited just inside the double doors

that locked automatically whenever someone came in or out of the building, straining to see the street through a narrow strip of beveled glass.

In the distance, she finally spotted distorted head-lights. On the roof was the lighted cab logo. She watched as the vehicle pulled up next to the curb in front of her building.

Fresh, cool air hit her in the face as she stepped outside. The moon was almost full, a few of the brighter stars visible past the glare of light pollution.

She slid into the backseat of the cab and gave the driver the address.

They floated through the surreal cityscape, stopping at traffic signals that continued to function even though most people were in bed asleep. As they drew closer to the crime scene a roadblock consisting of a single police car with a flashing red strobe stopped them. A uniformed policeman shined a powerful flashlight inside the cab, first at the driver, then at Ivy. She lowered her window and pulled out the temporary badge Abraham had issued to her. The policeman took it from her, examined it with his flashlight, handed it back, and let them pass. Two blocks later, they were at the scene.

She paid the driver. Too distracted to mentally compute the tip, she gave him what she thought was adequate. It must have been too much, because his bored-out-of-my-mind attitude vanished and he flashed her a big grin before she stepped away.

It was a poor neighborhood, with converted three-story houses that came almost to the street, all looking alike, with hardly enough room for a person to squeeze between them. Most were shingle-sided with tar-paper roofs, but the apartment building Ivy was looking for turned out to be brick. People gathered on their front steps, watching, whispering. Some of them must have been there awhile, because a few yawned and shuffled back into their homes.

Just another homicide. Go back to bed.

In the yard of an adjoining house, a pit bull barked deeply in its barrel chest and lunged at a chain-link fence, its feet and nails stirring up a cloud of dirt as it continued its display of aggression. Yellow crime-scene tape surrounded what there was of the yard, taking in the entire sidewalk and part of the street where more patrol cars pulled up, lights flashing, strobing off the apartment windows, giving the area an even weirder, unreal carnivalesque feel.

One uniformed policeman stood where the yellow crime tape wound around a streetlight.

He took a step toward her, his expression stern. "No press allowed."

Once again, she pulled out her temporary badge. "I'm not press."

He squinted at the badge, then straightened, his shoulders relaxing. "Oh, yeah. Detective Irving said you might be coming."

She clipped the plastic photo badge to her T-shirt, then lifted the crime-scene tape with one hand as she ducked underneath.

A policewoman was stationed at the door. Other officers were scattered about, tablets in hand, interviewing people, hoping to find an eyewitness.

"Second floor," the policewoman said.

"Thanks."

Even though the building looked to have been built about the same time as Ivy's, it was in much worse condition. Names had been carved into the plaster walls with a sharp knife. Behind a dark-stained door with dripping, yellow varnish, a woman sobbed uncontrollably while someone in a low voice tried to comfort her.

Ivy's heart hammered as she moved up the flight of stairs. She put her hand out to steady herself, grabbing the sticky railing; it shifted precariously and she let it go.

Up, up, her footsteps echoing.

It was eerily quiet inside the building except for the fading sound of muffled crying.

The apartment door stood open, another policeman stationed there. Once again, she gave her name and lifted her badge. The policeman nodded.

Just inside the door was a combined living room and kitchen. The wooden floor was scuffed. It creaked when she moved across it. On the wall above the couch was a watercolor of a Japanese garden, in one corner a small rock fountain flowing with soothing contentment. Next to it, on the floor, was a tiny bonsai tree, spilled, its roots exposed, black dirt in a little pile next to it. From the ceiling hung a beautiful lantern made of rice paper. Letters had been cut in the lantern. They probably meant things like "happiness," "prosperity."

She couldn't quit looking at the objects in the living room, each telling a more personal story about the owner. Origami; more watercolors, these of flowers; a black lacquered box; a silk pillow.

A world of their own. A sweet, safe haven.

God damn it. God, God damn it.

She wanted to reroot the bonsai tree, but she knew she wasn't to touch anything. Normally a crime scene remained a crime scene for two or three days. After that, the plant could be picked up. By then it would probably be too late. It was probably too late already. Roots could only be exposed to the air for a short time before the plant died.

In the kitchen area, on the refrigerator, was a birth announcement.

Years ago, Chicago papers used to routinely publish all the births within Cook County. That was done away with during the reign of the Madonna Murderer, and even though the murders stopped, the announcements never resumed. Most people didn't even think about it. Most people wouldn't have been able to tell you why birth announcements were no longer in the paper. But Ivy knew.

She forced herself to look elsewhere, to move in the direction of the hallway. Low voices could be heard floating from the bedroom. From inside came the click and whir of a camera shutter. A white flash lit the hall again and again and again.

The room was crowded, and it suddenly occurred to her that Irving must have called her as an afterthought. The experts were wrapping things up. All the discussions had taken place. Party's over.

It was a group of professionals doing their job. The medical examiner had apparently been there and gone. One woman was snapping pictures, another running a video camera. Two men, one in a suit, one in a black trench coat—probably officers from the mobile crime-scene lab—were bagging evidence. Around their necks hung white masks used to keep them from inhaling fingerprint powder. Two other men, possibly the coroner and his assistant, seemed to be waiting. Another man, Max Irving, stood over the bed. He had a tablet in his gloved hands, taking notes.

He was wearing jeans.

Well. Thank God she'd dressed appropriately, she thought, squelching a sense of hysteria that had been building in her ever since she'd stepped into the building. Incongruous thoughts come to a person at a time like this.

Because it really wasn't the jeans that concerned her. It was what lay beyond the jeans, still within her field of vision, but blurred. Like peering through the lens of a camera, her depth of field grew and the background slowly came into focus. Past those jeans she saw a woman's bare legs dangling from the side of the bed, one foot almost touching the floor, the other slightly higher.

She thought of the bonsai tree. She thought of the woman crying behind the dark door.

Young legs. Pretty legs. Legs splattered with blood.

The room smelled like a baby, like powder and bath soap. It also smelled like blood, and urine, and feces.

Next to the bed was a white wicker bassinet with a mobile attached.

White wicker.

She moved across the bedroom to the bassinet. She looked inside.

The infant seemed to be sleeping peacefully. Just lying there so sweetly. But upon closer inspection, she could see a tinge of blue around his eyes, his lips, his tiny fingernails.

"A boy?" she asked, knowing the answer.

Max looked up from his notebook, obviously surprised to see that she'd gotten there so quickly. Or gotten there at all.

"Yeah. Born a week ago. The mother is Sachi Anderson. The grandmother, Sachi's mother, is downstairs giving a statement."

The grandmother. So. That's who was sobbing downstairs.

He reached into the back pocket of his jeans, pulled out a pair of white latex gloves, and handed them to her. Without comment, she took them and slipped them on.

Inside the bassinet, tucked near the foot of the mattress, was a snow-globe music box. The killer's signature. He always left a gift for the baby.

"Go ahead. We're done with the baby."

Done with the baby. As if the child were nothing.

She lifted out the music box. Inside the cheap glass globe was a mother holding an infant. Unfortunately there was nothing very unique about it. It was something that would have been mass-produced and sold fairly cheaply.

She found the mechanism at the bottom and wound it just one turn, then released the catch. The tune was familiar:

Hush little baby, don't say a word.
Mamma's gonna buy you a mockingbird . . .

The camera finally stopped clicking. Orbs of light floated in front of her.

"That's that," the photo deputy said. "Let's roll her over."

They rolled the body over, then the camera shutter began clicking again.

Ivy shut off the music box and put it in the bassinet.

When she turned, the dead woman was on her back, and the guy in the trench coat was bent over her. Ivy watched as he cut strands of straight dark hair from the woman's head and put them in an evidence bag. He did the same with her pubic hair. Then he clipped her fingernails and put the clippings in a small envelope, then a larger evidence bag.

"Be thorough, Ellis," Irving said abruptly.

The guy in the trench coat looked up. He was neatly groomed in a high-maintenance, expensive kind of way. Ivy could immediately tell he wasn't used to being bossed around.

"Are you implying that I do half-assed work?" Ellis asked.

"I just want you to know this case is important."

"Haven't you read the rule book? All cases are important." Ellis laughed sarcastically and Ivy caught a glimpse of why Irving might not like him.

Their little altercation had been enough of a distraction for Ivy to let down her guard, and now she could see what she'd been afraid to notice before. The woman was nude, with bruises on her wrists and ankles, and what looked like clothesline cord around her neck. Her face was so swollen that it was impossible to tell if she'd been beautiful. Worse than that, her fixed eyes were open and her mouth had been Scotch taped into a wide grin.

There were several stab wounds; the mattress beneath the body was saturated with blood. The Madonna Murderer always went for the womb. Of that, Ivy could offer proof.

She also knew that he killed the mothers out of hatred—but he killed the infants out of love. A sick, twisted love, but love all the same.

When the coroner pulled out a thermometer, Ivy turned away. She couldn't watch. But it was all still there in her mind, just like a photo. Just like the photos in the case file. The grin. The glazed, pupil-filled eyes.

Time of death would be calculated by taking the normal temperature of 98.6 minus the rectal temperature to come up with the approximate number of hours since the death.

"Time of death, 11:15 P.M.," the coroner announced.

She'd been dead less than three hours.

"11:30 P.M. for the infant."

Which meant the mother had fought to save her baby. That she had fought the killer until she could fight no more.

Irving must have been thinking the same thing, because he looked up at a uniformed officer—a young, dark-skinned policeman standing near the bedroom door. "I want all units to be on the alert for a man with possible fresh scratch marks on his face," he told him.

The body was lifted onto a gurney covered with an unzipped black body bag, ready to be taken to the morgue for autopsy. She was tucked in and the bag was zipped.

"What about the baby? Can't we just put it in with the mother?" the assistant asked.

"It probably won't make any difference," the guy Irving had been arguing with said. He looked at Irving. "But for the sake of possible cross-contamination of evidence, give it its own bag."

Which they did, with everybody there knowing it was ridiculous, that the arrogant guy in the trench coat was just doing it for Irving's sake. All Ivy could think of was that he'd called the baby an "it."

Then they were gone.

The bodies.

The coroner.

The photographer.

The only people left were the two guys from the mobile crime lab, Irving, and Ivy.

Ivy would have left immediately, but she didn't want to have to see the bodies being put in the ambulance.

She really didn't want to be in this bedroom either.

The crime-lab guys continued to prowl around, clipping here, dabbing there.

"Get the drains," Ellis said to his partner. "And the toilet."

His partner straightened. He was young and unremarkable. "Why don't you get the toilet? I got the toilet last time."

Ellis stared at the younger man, whose eyes finally broke contact as he moved away, out of the bedroom to examine the toilet. Sometimes killers tried to flush things away, and sometimes objects were found trapped in the bend of the toilet bowl. Ivy felt a moment of sympathy, knowing that the young technician was going to have to reach into the toilet searching for possible evidence.

With him out of the picture, Ellis stopped in front of her, looked her in the eye, and said, "What are you doing here?" Over his shoulder to Irving he said, "What the hell's she doing here? Every unnecessary person is one more set of footprints closer to a compromised crime scene."

"She's supposed to be here," Irving said wearily, his tone conveying that her presence was out of his hands.

"What's your purpose?" Ellis asked.

There were very few people Ivy hated immediately, but she hated this man. He made Irving look like a damn saint, a damn bleeding heart.

She never broke eye contact, saying, "I'm here to sell popcorn."

From Irving's direction came a snort of laughter. Then again, maybe she was there for comic relief.

The guy continued to stare at her, passing a pink-tipped tongue over his lips. Then he smiled and turned away to continue combing the room for evidence.

Ivy followed him. "He's not an 'it,' " she said.

The guy looked up.

"The baby," she explained firmly. "The baby's not an 'it.' "

"What the hell's your problem?" In one gloved hand, he held an evidence bag, in the other a blood-saturated swab. He looked truly perplexed, unable to figure her out.

"These are real people," she said, gritting her teeth so her lips wouldn't tremble. Words bounced off the walls of her brain as she struggled to package her emotions so she could find something that would make him understand even though she knew it was useless. "You're dehumanizing them," she explained slowly. "Just like the killer."

He continued to stare at her blankly, his mouth slack, his head tilted, his shoulders hunched in a what-did-*I*-do pose.

Recognizing the futility of what she was trying to communicate, she pushed past him and walked out of the bedroom.

As she moved through the living room, she wouldn't let herself look in the direction of the bonsai.

Out. She had to get out.

Soon she was outside, pulling in huge gulps of air, her heart pounding, her mind unable to shut off the images of the grinning mother, the blue-tinged baby.

A camera flash went off in her face, momentarily blinding her. Someone grabbed her arm. "Can you tell me about the murder?" a male voice asked.

Ivy blinked, finally able to make out the young reporter who'd stopped Irving in the lobby that first day. "You'll have to talk to Detective Irving," she said, pulling her arm away.

Suddenly there was a little flurry of activity as an officer realized the reporter was inside the crime-scene tape.

"Get the hell out of there," the female officer yelled, striding over.

The reporter scrambled under the tape, disappearing into the darkness.

Ivy ducked under the tape, walked a few yards, and there he was again, talking fast. Right in front of her, tablet in hand, pen poised. "A female. I know that," he said. "An infant," he said urgently. "I have to know if there was an infant."

"I can't talk about it."

"What about you? What's your involvement in the case?"

She stopped and let out an indignant breath. "I can't tell you that either." A little warning flag went up. *Can't tell.* Poor choice of words. Damn poor choice.

"Listen—" She put a hand to her forehead, then her hair—and realized she hadn't even brushed it before hopping in the cab. Not that it mattered. A woman was dead. A baby was dead. Her hair deserved no thought. If she were Catholic, she would have made herself say one hundred Hail Marys.

"Oh, forget it." She shoved him out of the way, saying as she passed him, "Talk to Irving."

Is this what happened when you lived alone for too long? You found everybody irritating? First Irving, then Ellis, now this reporter. Was her judgement skewed? Or was she seeing people the way they really were? Either way, it was disturbing, unpleasant. In the last hour, she'd had enough reality to last her sixteen more years.

She kept walking, and thank God he didn't follow.

She hadn't thought about how she would get home, otherwise she would have asked her earlier ride to return for her. There were no cabs around, and she had no way to get back to her apartment without one. She kept walking, knowing it wasn't safe and yet also knowing there was enough activity in the area, enough police and gawkers, to make the dangers of walking in a bad area of town late at night not any more dangerous than walking there at noon.

She'd gone possibly two blocks when a siren let out a little squawk. She turned to see a police car gliding beside her. The passenger window silently opened and the young officer she'd seen speaking with Irving earlier leaned across the seat so he could look up at her.

"Detective Irving told me to give you a lift."

"I can find my own ride." She could see lights in the distance—hopefully an all-night gas station where she could use the phone.

"I've got my orders," he said in a half-teasing, half-serious way.

What difference did it make?

She opened the door and got in, giving him her address.

Chapter 14

It was almost light when Alex Martin left the loft he shared with two other guys in the River North district of what was rapidly becoming known as "the" place to be, a trendy area where the rent was high and a lot of people his age lived. It was a place where warehouses had been converted into apartments with huge, curtainless windows, wooden floors, and room for parties of several hundred.

Outside the subway entrance, he grabbed a copy of the *Herald* before catching the Red Line. It wasn't yet rush hour, and there were plenty of places to sit. He took a seat and unfolded the paper, smoothing the center crease. At one time there had been some discussion about the *Herald* going to a more user-friendly tabloid format, but they'd eventually decided against it. No matter how accurate and well written the articles, the tabloid presentation had a tacky stigma that would have been impossible to rise above, and the *Herald* prided itself in its credibility.

Alex quickly skimmed the print, nothing sinking into his brain, his thoughts being pulled in a completely different direction.

To his article on the third page.

He'd been surprised to find that they'd wanted it at all since he'd thrown it together just minutes before the paper went to print. But they'd yanked a wire article and had a spot they were looking to fill.

A lot of readers would probably have passed by it the way they'd passed by his story about the police-mentoring program, and the story he'd done on alcoholism in the police force—an article that had been hidden deep in the body of the paper. He wasn't very good with a camera. In fact, he rarely took pictures. He left that to the photo department, which meant he'd never had a story run with a photo. The photographers were always too busy with bigger stories. But last night, for some inexplicable reason, he'd grabbed a camera. It must have been a five-star day, or the planets were all aligned, or something, because when he got back to the photo lab with the roll of film he'd taken at the homicide scene, he found he'd captured a multitude of elements in one single click of a shutter.

The photo was of the woman with the short red hair, the one who'd refused to talk to him. She was hurrying from the apartment building, caught in mid-flight by the camera, one foot on the top step, the other touching air. Her expression, possibly undetectable to the human eye, captured in a fleeting one-sixteenth of a second, spoke of everything she'd seen, and everything she felt.

Horror.

Anger.

Sorrow.

It was all there, in one powerful image.

The caption wasn't bad either: "Dark At The Top Of The Stairs."

In the early morning hours, an unidentified woman leaves a homicide scene at a northwest-side apartment complex where a mother and her infant son were found dead.

The article itself was one of his best, he thought, something that might get the attention of his bosses. It was nothing like the fiction he'd put aside in order to keep food in his belly, but it was possibly some of the best of his nonfiction career.

The caption was further validated by the article's opening sentence.

The killer among us. He preys on every moth-er's deepest fear—the loss of her child. And if that isn't tragedy enough, the loss of that child under the most horrific of circumstances.

The recent double homicide is the second to have occurred in the Chicago metro area in the last two weeks. There are many questions, but so far no answers. Questions like, Why aren't the police getting information to the public? If the people had been informed, would the latest vic-tims be alive right now? The only thing we know for sure is this: The dark at the top of the stairs is real.

At the paper, he felt like a star.
Walking to his desk, people praised him.
"Great story, Alex."

"Nice going."

Maude caught him before he could sit down. "Great stuff, Alex."

"You didn't think it was too—" He paused, searching for the right word, and finally came up with, "Dramatic?"

"Are you kidding? It was real. That's what we want. Reality."

Superintendent Abraham Sinclair stared at the *Herald*'s black-and-white photo of Ivy Dunlap. She had a fleeing-the-castle expression on her face, the kind you might have seen on the cover of an old paperback.

"This is nothing but a bunch of overwritten, sensationalized crap," Abraham told Max, who'd stopped by his office to assess his reaction to the article. He tossed the paper down on his desk. "You know what it looks like? It looks like an ad for a horror movie, that's what it looks like."

Max picked up the paper. "At least it's on page three, not page one."

Abraham walked to the window and stared down at the traffic in the street below. Had he done the right thing in bringing Ivy here? He normally didn't doubt himself, but when it came to the Madonna Murderer, he doubted himself about everything.

He was tired.

People were always asking him what he was going to do when he retired, telling him he'd be bored out of his mind. That wasn't going to happen.

But what if he couldn't shut off his mind? What if he went to Florida to fish, and all he saw were murdered babies, murdered mothers, floating just below the water's surface?

The guilt. Abraham couldn't get away from the guilt. Eighteen years ago, when the murders first started, he'd been an Area Five detective just like Max. He'd been pretty confident then, and he really thought he could catch the madman. But he didn't catch him, he never caught him, and twelve mothers and their babies had died.

That's why he'd worked so hard to help Claudia Reynolds. To help her get a new identity, a new life in a new country.

He was able to get her Canadian citizenship. For some reason just as inexplicable as everything else they did, serial killers rarely crossed borders. That didn't apply to everyone, of course. There was Christopher Wilder, who killed several people in Australia and then, when things got hot there, moved to the U.S. where he continued his spree before he was brought down by his own gun during an altercation with two officers.

Abraham kept track of Ivy over the years. He knew she'd spent time in a Canadian mental institute, but had come out of that darkness to get a master's degree in criminal psychology. She'd even published a book-length study on the mind of the serial killer.

But the Madonna Murderer was never found.

After the killings stopped, Abraham fell into a deep despair. He started drinking. Then he started taking pills. Then he combined the two until he almost died. His wife couldn't take it anymore and left him.

And now the killer had resurfaced.

Was there a God? That's what he wanted to know. Because sometimes it sure as hell didn't seem like it.

"What about the FBI?" Abraham asked. "Any news from them?"

"The Bureau is swamped, but they're pulling two people off other cases and sending them down," Max told him. "They should arrive this afternoon or evening."

Chapter 15

Max and Ivy stood side by side in Autopsy Suite Four of Cook County Morgue wearing face shields, yellow disposable aprons, and white disposable rubber gloves. There would be blood, there would be splatter, and in this age of AIDS, it was best to take every precaution.

A half hour earlier Max had swung by Ivy's apartment, possibly to gloat, possibly to see if she was still in town after last night's initiation into the ugly, horrifying world of senseless violence. When he'd buzzed her apartment, telling her to come on down if she wanted to get in on the autopsy, he had to wait less than five minutes.

He was reluctantly impressed.

It was common for rigor mortis to set in three hours after death. It began in the muscles of the face and eyelids, then spread slowly to the arms and legs, taking about twelve hours to affect the whole body. In most cases, if the victim hadn't been burned or poisoned, the process reversed itself after thirty-six hours, until the body was soft and supple once again.

Sometimes the medical examiner would wait until rigor mortis was gone and the body was flexible once more. But in such a serious homicide, it was best to move forward as quickly as possible.

The sheet-covered body of the female victim lay on a steel exam table that was concave and funneled to a drain. The floor was concrete, the walls white tile. Almost all equipment was made of stainless steel and would endure years of sterilization. A fume vent hung overhead, with the exam table itself equipped with down-draft ventilation.

Chief Medical Examiner Eileen Bernard clipped a tiny microphone to her liquid-impermeable gown with hands that were covered by the preferred thick surgical purple gloves that offered more protection than the lighter ones. Under her left glove she wore another of wire mesh.

Eileen Bernard had been Cook County Chief Medical Examiner for nine years. Before that, she'd been an assistant, and before that a professor of forensic pathology at the University of Minnesota. Max figured she'd cut open more dead bodies than almost any other person on the planet.

Stranger than that, she actually liked it and didn't try to pretend otherwise. Which took Max to a question that had lingered uncomfortably in the back of his mind for a number of years: Did Eileen Bernard have something in common with serial killers? Did she also have that obsessive need to cut people up, to see what they looked like on the inside? Only, she was doing it legally and getting paid a tidy sum in the process.

She turned on the tape recorder, operating it with the foot switch so her hands could remain free. "This is Dr. Eileen Bernard," she said into the microphone. That was followed by the case number, victim's name, age, weight, length.

Even though Max had already seen the body at the crime scene, he still felt a fresh jab of shock when Bernard uncovered it completely, exposing it to the glare of the blinding overhead spotlights.

The smell wasn't bad, certainly not like other autopsies he'd been to where the victim hadn't been found for days. But it was amazing how quickly the human body began to decompose—just minutes after death, so that even now that sweet-foul odor hung in the room, although the exhaust system fought to suck the stink away. Soon it would creep into his sinuses, cling to his hair. Back at Central, he'd shower and change, but the smell would still be there, no matter how much soap he used, or how hard he scrubbed.

He used to put Vicks up his nose, but after four or five times, he began to associate the smell of menthol with death and now it was just as bad as the real thing. Anytime anybody came at him sucking on a cough drop, Max would recoil, the smell of a half-rotten body gusting into his face. And no way would he ever use it on Ethan when he was little. Instead, he would run a hot shower and wait for the bathroom to steam up. Then he would sit there on the closed toilet, holding Ethan until he stopped coughing and finally fell into a peaceful sleep.

Bernard pulled close the tray containing the tools of her trade—scalpels, forceps, chisels, and rubber mallets. She was systematic and always followed the same procedure she'd taught her students. Conform to routine and get everything the first time. As far as Max knew, there had never been the need for an exhumation on any of her cases—a testimony to her thoroughness.

She began by examining the body from head to toe,

front to back, while her morgue assistant, a huge, sober-faced man, silently and solemnly stepped in when needed. Normally, a coroner used two assistants, but it was apparent this guy could handle it by himself.

After the initial overview, Bernard numbered the stab wounds with a black marker, her assistant helping to roll the body. "The wounds are confined to the chest and abdomen." She rechecked her count. "Twenty-two in all." She stood back while the assistant climbed up on a short ladder to take photographs from above.

She verbally cataloged every wound, its location, depth. "These were all done with the same instrument. A knife that was long and wide." She swung the flex-arm dissecting lamp with its magnifying glass closer. "See this?" With a purple, blood-smeared gloved finger, she pointed to ragged flesh. "Serrated."

"Same as the other victim," Max stated.

"Yes."

"But bigger than, say, a steak knife."

"Yes."

"A heavy bread knife?" Ivy asked.

Her voice rang out hollowly in the room, perhaps coming out louder than anticipated, as many voices did when the owner struggled for bravery.

Max shot her a quick glance, wondering if she'd had enough. Her eyes were focused on the victim. Instead of the fear and revulsion he'd expected to see, he saw what looked like sorrow.

"Sharper," Dr. Bernard said. "More like the kind of knife used by a butcher in order to cut through bone."

She went on examining the body, pointing out the red-and-purple ligature marks around the throat. The victim's mouth was still taped into a wide grin. She peeled the tape away but rigor mortis kept the jaw from going slack. "Hard to tell, but I'll bet she was a beautiful woman." She forced the mouth open and peered inside, then inserted two gloved fingers. "Crushed windpipe."

"Asphyxiation?" Max asked.

"I don't think so," she said slowly, thoughtfully. "It looks to be postmortem. Just to make sure she was dead. As if twenty-two stab wounds wouldn't have done the job."

With the aid of her assistant, Dr. Bernard placed a rubber block beneath the victim's neck, stretching the neck and the tissue of the upper chest. Then she reached for a scalpel. Pausing below the collarbone, she glanced up.

Max Irving stood there, his face, behind the clear acrylic shield, unreadable as always. Next to him, the woman he'd introduced as Ivy Dunlap stared at the body, at the woman's face, her lips parted, her breath creating little puffs of condensation on her face shield.

Bernie hoped to hell she wasn't a fainter. Irving hadn't said anything past the introduction, no explanation as to why the woman was there. It was unusual to have a civilian at an autopsy, but not unheard of. She'd had a couple of reporters before, years ago when rules were a little less stringent. None of them had lasted past the first incision, let alone the cutting open of the skull with the bone saw in order to weigh the brain.

Opinions varied as to what was worse: the smell of hot bone, the sound of the high-pitched whine of metal against cranium, or the sight of a human skull being cracked open like a nutshell.

None of it bothered her. She couldn't remember a

time when it had ever bothered her, not even when she was little and would find a dead animal on the Oklahoma highway that ran just a hundred yards from her home. She used to peel back the hide to see the muscles, the intestines, poking around with an inquisitive finger. The anatomy of anything fascinated her. All her life she'd tried to understand other people's revulsion toward anything dead, but couldn't. For her, looking inside a human body was no different than pulling a flower apart to see how it was put together.

Her parents had never understood her compulsion, and to this day her mother still asked why she didn't practice as a real doctor so that she could use her skills to save people, not cut them up when they were already dead. A hard thing for any parent to get, Bernie supposed.

Starting at one shoulder, just below the clavicle, she began the incision, following a line to the breastbone. The invasion was deep, penetrating skin, fatty tissue, and muscle in one motion. An identical incision was made on the other side. At the meeting place of the sternum, an incision was made down the entire torso, going around the navel and ending at the pubic bone. With shears, she then clipped through the rib cartilage until she was able to remove the rib cage and set it aside, exposing the thoracic organs.

She took samples of skin and tissue, dropping them into containers of formaldehyde. After she was finished collecting samples, she poured water over the remaining organs from a steel pitcher.

"Suction."

The assistant unwrapped a plastic wand, attached it to the hose on the suction machine, then turned the dial to medium. He prodded with the clear plastic tip, suctioning around the heart. Pink, blood-tinged fluid trailed up the tube to be deposited in a quart container.

"Heart intact. Lacerations to the liver and spleen."

Dr. Bernard poked around at various veins and arteries that lay collapsed and as flat as tapeworms. "She bled out completely. Did you notice how there was hardly any lividity? No blood left in her body to settle."

"She bled to death?" Max asked.

"Yep."

"Could she have been saved?" the woman, Ivy, whispered, her voice trembling slightly.

She'd be going down soon, Bernie thought without disdain or criticism. It was simply something that happened. The nature of the beast, just as killing this woman had been an act the killer couldn't control.

"You mean could she have been saved if she'd been found in time?"

"Yes."

"Well, with the damaged liver and spleen, all the wounds, it's doubtful." What did she want to hear? Why did it matter? Bernie never questioned occurrences that had already happened. It was a pointless waste of time. She didn't read fiction. She no longer went to movies. Art and music did nothing for her. She existed in reality, a place she liked to be. She'd wasted a lot of time filtering movies, TV, through everyone else's eyes, trying to understand her fellow humans.

Fake. All of it fake. Especially the portrayal of death. Death was the total absence of spirit—something that no one could emulate, no matter how good the actor.

"Doubtful," she said, continuing to consider the

question. "But maybe," she answered truthfully. "If he hadn't crushed her windpipe. He made sure she wouldn't be crawling anywhere, picking up the telephone, dialing 911." She reached for the bone saw that hung from a pulley above her head. "This next procedure was never a favorite of my students." Nine out of ten passed out the first time they witnessed the dissecting of the throat.

She would be nice and give Dunlap good warning. And she had to give her credit for making it to this point. A lot of people didn't. In fact, she could recall a certain detective who'd all but passed out on her not that many years ago. "All ashore who's going ashore."

Sometimes she didn't say anything. Sometimes she just started cutting. But she didn't feel like being mean today, so she issued the warning. And Dunlap was already looking a little washed out. Bernie looked at Max, raising one eyebrow. But then, maybe he wanted her to faint so he could catch her. Maybe that's what this was all about.

He looked back at her through his face shield, his stone features never changing.

Maybe not.

Ivy shook her head, saying, "I'm okay," even though she was afraid she wasn't okay.

She forced herself to watch as the dissection continued up the trachea, esophagus, and finally the removal of the tongue. It was the tongue that did it.

Ivy spun around and ran, pulling off her face shield and dropping it on a medical cart. Into a nearby trash container went the apron and gloves. Then she was pushing through a door marked EXIT in red, illuminated letters. Outside the building, she sucked in a deep breath, but instead of smelling fresh air, she smelled the sweet-rotten smell of death and formaldehyde. It filled her sinuses, her lungs, her throat. Bile rose, burning her esophagus, and dizziness collected behind her eyes.

She could feel the sunlight on her cold, clammy face. She took a few steps in the direction of Max Irving's faded blue car with the dented side panel, which was parked in the shade of a puny tree where birds were chirping, calling encouragements to her. She moved in the direction of that shade and those gaily singing birds, distantly wondering why they'd chosen to live in Chicago when they could live anywhere. If she were one of them, she'd go to St. Sebastian, where the sun didn't shine so harshly. A place that didn't smell like death.

She needed that shade. Not the shade of a cement building, a morgue, but that cool, tree-cast shade. Before she could reach it, dizziness washed over her again and cold sweat brought her to her knees, small bits of gravel poking through her khaki pants.

"Put your head down."

Mentally, she fought him because she didn't want to collapse in a heap in the middle of the parking lot. But physically she had no more strength than a rag doll as his hand pressed against the back of her scalp, forcing her forehead to her thighs.

Even in her near faint, she understood that another man, a man who had last physically forced his will upon her, was now preying upon other innocent women.

She cursed her own weakness.

She hadn't prayed in years, but she pulled together a semblance of prayer now while darkness danced behind her eyes and the hot, unforgiving surface of the parking lot bit into her knees, and a man for whom she felt no affinity pressed her to the ground.

Those earlier childhood prayers had been sent skyward at the pleading of her mother, and Ivy had cooperated for no other reason than to keep from going to hell. She'd quit praying when she discovered she was already there.

Give me strength, she begged, not of God but of herself. She was the only person who could get her through this, the only person she would trust. Which was a scary thought; she had so many weaknesses, so many doubts.

Coward, she taunted.

She straightened her neck, fighting the hand that was not only there to help her, but to hold her down, to keep her from doing what she'd come here to do.

She pushed him away and got to her feet, staggering to the shade tree, bracing one hip against the car's fender.

Irving followed, dropping to the ground, his back against the narrow trunk of the tree. With arms dangling over bent knees, he said, "I puked my guts out at my first autopsy."

She looked up at him, surprised at that admission.

Earlier, he'd taken off his jacket and tie and rolled up the sleeves of his white dress shirt to just below the elbows.

Ivy rubbed her face and tried to swallow the acidic taste in her mouth. She wished she had some water. "I threw up when I had to dissect an earthworm," she told him, now that they were confessing things.

He laughed and scooped up a piece of gravel, then gave it a toss. "That's pathetic."

"I know."

She was already regretting her admission, that tiny peek she'd given him into her past, another life. She must remember not to talk about herself, not even about earthworms.

"So what are you doing here, Ivy Dunlap?" he asked, voicing a path of questioning her carelessly innocent words had begun. "What road brought you to this point?"

She was saved from reply by the sound of the delivery door being opened. Dr. Bernard's assistant stuck his head out. "We're getting ready to start on the baby." It was the first words the man had spoken.

"Wait here," Irving said, getting to his feet. "This shouldn't take as long."

"I'm going in."

"Nausea is a cumulative thing. It'll happen again."

"I won't let it."

He shook his head, but didn't argue.

Five minutes later, they were back in the autopsy room, dressed in their precautionary gowns and shields. Once again they stood near the stainless-steel exam table, the mother's body replaced by that of her infant son. The table seemed enormous in comparison to the baby's tiny body, a body that looked heart-breakingly small and alone.

Dr. Bernard began the initial cursory exam in much the same way as before, going over the infant, but this time with a softer, gentler voice. The reverent mood broke when she discovered what looked like an injection site on the infant's scalp.

"Could he have been given an IV at the hospital?" Irving asked.

"This is more recent than that. Very little bruising, and what there is hasn't turned."

"What do you think it is?" Ivy asked.

Dr. Bernard looked up at her with impatience. "I don't waste my time on suppositions," she said harshly, then softened her words by adding, "which is one reason I would have made a damn lousy detective."

"If you ask Bernie the color of a car," Irving said conversationally, "she'll tell you what color it is on the side she can see, but you won't get anything more out of her unless she walks around the whole damn thing."

Dr. Bernard grunted. "We'll get a tox screen."

"He's making doubly sure the victims don't survive," Ivy said with conviction. "First there was the mother's crushed trachea, and now the baby injected with something."

"Changing his MO," Max stated.

"Escalating," Ivy replied. "That's not uncommon."

"No, he's perfecting his skills."

She looked at him through her mask. "Getting smarter and more cunning with each victim."

He nodded grimly.

It seemed they could finally agree on something.

Chapter 16

The ringing of the telephone dragged Ivy from a semislumber—the only kind of sleep she'd been getting lately.

It was Max Irving, calling to tell her that he'd scheduled a task-force meeting for 10:00 A.M. Would she be there? he wanted to know.

In the background, she heard music, loud music. Suddenly it stopped, and a youthful male voice said, "I'm ready, Dad."

The trajectory of Max's voice changed, his words directed away from the phone, toward the world he lived in, a world Ivy was subconsciously trying to piece together in her head. "I'm on the phone," he said to the owner of the youthful male voice.

Dad. His son. Max Irving's son.

"I could have slept another fifteen minutes," the boy's voice lamented in the background.

Sleep . . . She remembered that kind of sleep, the kind that came so easily to the young . . .

"You'll live," Max said, humor in his tone. Then back into the mouthpiece, apparently recalling Ivy on the other end of the line, "Task-force meeting," he repeated. "You going?"

Why didn't he just say what he thought? She had no patience for these games. "Don't you mean, Have I had enough after yesterday?"

"Did I say that?"

"Indirectly. Don't treat me like an idiot."

"I didn't call you to start a fight." He sounded annoyed, impatient.

"Who are you talking to?" she heard his son ask, plainly curious to know who had evoked his father's irritation so early in the morning.

"Nobody."

"Thanks," Ivy said dryly.

"Damn. I mean—"

"Don't apologize for finally saying what you think."

"You're reading more into this than is there. I just called to tell you about the task-force meeting. Will you be there?"

As Jinx circled her legs, raising his back with each pass, Ivy assured Irving that she'd be there, then hung up as Jinx continued his curling motion, the yellow hair on his back smooth under her palm. She smiled a little. Call her sick, call her twisted, but she actually enjoyed getting under Irving's skin.

The orange-handled scissors cut out the newspaper article, his hands moving with precision as he turned the clipping first one way, then the other, the scissors making a clean rasping sound that he liked. Finished, he followed with the accompanying photo that had been taken of an unidentified woman leaving the crime scene. He liked the caption, "Dark At The Top Of The Stairs," and he made a mental note of the reporter's name.

He felt a nagging at the back of his mind. Even

though he could identify the cause of his anxiety, that knowledge didn't make the nagging go away. Everybody had a name. Everybody had to have a name— and he didn't know if he could add the photo to his collection without knowing the name of the unidentified woman.

He pulled out a scrapbook from under his bed. This scrapbook was different than the other one. This one contained all the newspaper articles written about the Madonna Murderer. It contained photos of the people who had worked on the case.

Most of it was filled with yellowed clippings. There was Abraham Sinclair, looking thirty years younger and fifty pounds lighter than he did now. His face had been circled with Magic Marker, his name printed in large capital letters in the margin. Back then, Sinclair had been a run-of-the-mill detective. Now he was Superintendent. Head of everything. It made him feel very clever to know he'd outsmarted the Superintendent of the whole Chicago Police Department.

"Poor Abraham," he said, staring almost wistfully at the photo. They shared a lot of history, the two of them.

There were several pages dedicated to Abraham. Small cutout articles about his wife and his children. The kids had been very active in school sports and area theater, so it had been easy to keep up with them. Much later, after getting out of the mental institute, he'd followed Abraham's daughter, anxious for her to get pregnant and have children of her own. But the daughter had given birth to a girl rather than a boy. It would have been thrilling to have killed the mother and son. He'd imagined Abraham showing up at the crime scene to find his dead daughter and grandson.

He'd imagined reading about it in the paper, imagined the grief on poor Abraham's face.

He'd fantasized about killing the mother and son for so long that he'd almost killed the mother and daughter out of sheer disappointment. But the medication he'd been on at the time had a powerful, mind-controlling quality, and it hadn't allowed him to act on the impulse. Killing a female infant would have been murder for the sake of murder. Murder with no purpose. He was above that. Better than that. Killing Abraham's grandchild would have put him on the same level as every other murdering idiot out there, and the last thing he wanted was to be like everybody else. Anyway, the numbers hadn't been right. Not then. And the daughter was married. Unfortunately.

The girl—Kiki was her name—had just turned six and would grow up to be a whore like the rest of them. But she was almost a niece to him, and he'd sent her a birthday card with the picture of a puppy on it.

He turned to a fresh page at the back of the scrapbook. He lifted the clear film, then positioned the photo and article on the heavy white paper. In the margin, with black waterproof Magic Marker, he carefully printed the name of the reporter: ALEX MARTIN. All caps. Then, next to the photo of the woman, he added a question mark. This was done in pencil, so that he could later add the name with permanent ink.

On the opposite page was a photo of Detective Max Irving along with the copy of an article that had been in the paper a week ago, taken at the press conference held after the first new murder.

"Detective Irving has been put in charge of the case,"

Sinclair was quoted as saying. *"And I have every confidence he'll find the killer."*

There had been no accompanying photo of Irving. But that had been easily rectified by a visit to the Police Department's Web site. Irving himself didn't have a page, but basic information was supplied in the overview.

Every name had a face. Every face had a name.

Under the photo of Detective Irving was another one—this of a sweaty, blond-haired young man in a hockey jersey. Number thirty-two. A good number. A nice, round number that rolled off his tongue.

ETHAN IRVING.

The boy was a rising star on his high school's hockey team.

Hockey.

A rough sport. A sport that took an enormous amount of skill.

The high school where Ethan played was called Cascade Hills.

Even though he didn't like hockey, didn't like sports of any kind, he thought he might go watch a game sometime.

There would be a lot of people there, and he didn't relish the thought of putting on his social mask to mingle with the masses. But if Ethan were playing, it would be worth it. If Detective Irving were watching, it would be interesting.

It would be fun.

From upstairs came the sound of his mother banging her wooden cane against the floor—her signal for him to get his ass up there.

His heart hiccuped, then began to thud so loudly that the sound filled his head.

Calm down. It's okay. It's only the bitch upstairs. Only your mother.

"I'm coming!" he shouted.

Now that she'd broken her leg, she was bedridden—which meant he had to personally attend to her every need. Luckily she'd been prescribed heavy-duty pain-killers and sleeping pills, and he'd discovered that if he increased her dosage, she'd sleep for six or seven hours straight. If only he could make her sleep forever . . .

Chapter 17

Sachi Anderson and her infant son had been dead two days when the task force convened for the first time.

A room on the second floor of Headquarters was now home base for everyone involved in the case, and it would remain home until the killer was caught or spending was cut, whichever came first.

Grand Central Station, so named by schoolchildren because it was at the junction of Grand and Central, replaced the old Shakespeare building that had been so old it was said to have horse stalls at ground level. The new building had gone up in the eighties. At that time, standard design and construction dictated small, high windows made of Plexiglas. If you were to combine a flat-roofed grade school and a fortress, you'd come up with Grand Central. It seemed to Ivy that a building couldn't have been any more nondescript.

Chicago could be a dark place, and even on a sunny day the two small windows in the task-force room didn't do much to dispel the gloom. That was taken care of by artificial fluorescent strip lighting.

A room that had been empty at the beginning of the day now contained four desks complete with phones, headsets, and computers. Chicago metro maps hung from the walls. Couches and chairs had been brought in, along with a small refrigerator and coffeemaker.

Home away from home.

Ivy looked at the room with a combined feeling of dread and relief. Dread, because she knew the couches symbolized a future of sleepless nights and more killings; relief because the seriousness of these mother-child homicides had been realized and funds had been allocated—not always an easy thing to pull together so quickly. She suspected Abraham of doing a lot of talking and dancing over the last few days.

Members attending the preliminary task-force meeting began to filter in, their somber faces reflecting the brutality of the crimes they would be dealing with. Two people, a man and a woman in business suits, introduced themselves as FBI agents from the National Center for Analysis of Violent Crime or NCAVC.

"We'll only be here a couple of days," the woman, Mary Cantrell, told Ivy, shaking her hand. "Mainly to leave you with proactive suggestions. You'll be free to use them or disregard them as you see fit."

The words were spoken in a way that implied her and her partner's "suggestions" weren't always received with open arms, or, more important, an open mind.

Accompanying them was a man named David Scott, who turned out to be one of Chicago's local FBI agents. He had the weary, rumpled, out-of-shape look of someone who had spent too many years behind a desk eating unhealthy food and drinking brackish coffee.

He cast a furtive glance at Special Agent Anthony Spence, who so far hadn't spoken a word. Spence's

demeanor fit that of the stereotypical FBI agent—
those frozen-faced men in black suits and shades, except that this agent had no glasses and wore an impec-
cable gray suit that enhanced the gunmetal of his
bloodshot eyes. It occurred to Ivy that the rigid
Spence would make Irving look like a stand-up comic.

Looking at him, his feeling of inferiority obvious,
Chicago Field Office Agent Scott fiddled with his
short, wide, striped, outdated and wrinkled tie, then
dropped it to run his hand around the waistband of
his beige pants, as if to check and see if everything
was in place.

Two police officers joined the growing group, the
smell of fryer grease emanating from a bag balanced
on a cardboard tray. One of the new arrivals was
Ronny Ramirez, the young officer who'd given Ivy a
ride back to her apartment the night of the Anderson
murders. The other she recognized as the female officer who'd been stationed at the door of the apartment
that same night.

The female officer told everybody hello and pointed
to her badge. "Regina Hastings," she said, pulling out
a chair, plopping down, and digging into her breakfast sack.

"I never knew a woman who could put away so
much meat," Ramirez said in what seemed half
amazement, half admiration.

Hastings swiped at her mouth with a big napkin.
"Yeah, and I like my meat cooked and on bread."
She took another bite of her sandwich, big white teeth
sinking into the English muffin, while Ramirez made
a choking sound. If his skin wasn't so dark, everybody
would be able to see him blush.

Hastings laughed and opened the plastic lid of her

Styrofoam container. The smell of coffee wafted upward, galvanizing the group to action as they moved toward the coffee machine where a full carafe was brewed and ready.

Anthony Spence took his black, with a palmful of orange-coated tablets.

"Headache?" Ivy asked, beginning to feel the sympathy she always felt whenever a person took on human attributes.

"Migraine," came the brusque, reluctant admission. He tossed back the pills, following with scalding coffee. Jumping and cussing, he spilled dark liquid on the lapel of his suit and the floor in front of Ivy.

So much for cool.

"He's not used to stimulants," Mary Cantrell said dryly, grabbing a napkin from the table and dabbing it at the stain on his suit. "Depressants are more his thing," she explained, her gaze catching Ivy's with a you-know-what-I-mean look.

No, Ivy didn't know what she meant. That he was an alcoholic? He wouldn't be the first FBI agent to succumb to self-medication. Ivy would guess that almost every person in the Behavioral Science Unit and NCAVC had had a drinking problem at one time or another.

Ivy was sensing an undercurrent between the two agents, a latent hostility or rivalry. These two didn't like each other. That was the only thing Ivy got.

Why did people have to be so damn . . . human? Always fighting. Always backbiting. When Jane Goodall first began her studies of chimpanzees, she thought they were our gentle, more compassionate brothers and sisters. Then years into her research, she sorrowfully discovered they were just like us. Animals plagued by jealousy and hatred. They were gentle, yes.

But they were also capable of horrible atrocities such as violent acts of murder and cannibalism. They too were guilty of crimes against their own kind.

Spence dropped a napkin on the floor, pushed it around with the toe of a black dress shoe until the spilled coffee was soaked up, then bent and retrieved the soiled napkin with a wince.

So, he cleaned up after himself.

Five minutes later, Detective Irving made his appearance, along with Superintendent Sinclair and another man about Abraham's age whom he introduced as a toxicologist.

It was unusual for the Superintendent to personally involve himself in an investigation and Abraham explained that he would only be joining them for the initial meeting. Some in the room may not have known of his responsibility for the case when he was a detective, and it was strange to think that Hastings and Ramirez would have been kids when the Madonna Murderer had first terrorized Chicago.

The initial meeting didn't include the entire task force. Once a plan was mapped out, recruits would be brought in and briefed, those officers consisting of foot cops, beat cops, rovers, fact checkers, information gatherers—people who would be neck deep in the tedious business of records, reports, interviews, and statistics.

Irving passed out folders to everyone present. Inside were abbreviated versions of the original Madonna Murders case file, combined with the two new homicides.

"No one else is to see these files," Irving instructed. "Not your wife, or husband, not any officer outside of this room."

Introductions were made once more, then everybody pulled up a chair and got down to business.

"Okay," Irving said, "this is where we are. No fingerprints found other than those belonging to members of the family and the victim. No DNA found that belonged to anyone other than family members or victims. No saliva from the drinking glass that could be connected to anyone else."

"The bite wound?" Abraham asked.

"Our killer is apparently not a secretor."

Ivy knew that eighty percent of the population were secretors—meaning they left DNA in other bodily fluids. Some criminals would get a drink, leave something on a glass. Use the toilet, not flush, or it didn't flush completely. And some—many—bit their victims. There had been a few cases over the years where bite marks themselves had been as incriminating as a fingerprint—Ted Bundy, for one. But more often, unless the perpetrator had some unusual dental work, saliva was the better way to go.

"What about degraded-DNA tests?" asked Agent Scott.

"The lab is also running tests on evidence pulled from the Cold File—evidence collected from the original Madonna Murder crime scenes," Irving said.

"Testing methods have advanced over the last sixteen years, and we're hoping to find something we didn't have the resources to find before. Unfortunately, the DQA1 involves minute amounts of secretions, and there are very few lab technicians trained to run these tests. They're backed up and haven't even started on our samples."

They moved on.

"Prison release records have been checked, but we're having them rechecked," Irving stated. "We had a couple of suspicious people, brought them in for statements, but they were clean, at least as clean as a former drug dealer and sex offender could be. We're rechecking everybody who is out on parole."

Irving had a straightforward, no-nonsense attitude that went over well in a group of professionals. He was in charge, and yet an equal. There was no room for inflated ego in such a situation.

"There are three known reasons why killings like this stop," he explained. "Number one is suicide. Two is that the killer left the area to kill somewhere else. Three, he was arrested for some other offense and was serving time. It's been long speculated that the Madonna Murders stopped sixteen years ago because the killer was arrested and incarcerated for another crime altogether."

"And now he's out," Ramirez said.

"Right, but again this is speculation. Keep in mind that all ideas are welcome and there is no such thing as a stupid question."

"What about mental hospitals?" Spence asked.

"We've got information brokers on that, but so far they haven't uncovered anything interesting." The question was answered quickly and succinctly, without distracting Irving from his initial path.

"Ramirez and Hastings are to be in charge of interviewing everyone within the grid zones, following up on those interviews if they have to."

Ramirez leaned back in his chair, arms across his chest. "Two people?"

"I said, In charge. We'll pull people from other areas as we need them. We may be able to enlist the help of some retired officers. We'll run television and newspaper announcements asking for citizen involvement. Those announcements will have the number of the direct line to this room. So far we've been getting about twenty calls a day, but with the announcements we can expect that to pick up. Unfortunately, you receive a lot of revenge-driven stories when something like this happens. Relatives and neighbors are quick to turn in somebody they don't like, even if they haven't killed anybody."

"I'm afraid we're getting ahead of ourselves." The words came from Abraham, who was sitting next to Ivy at the long table. "You've both looked at the photos, looked at the case file," he said to Agents Cantrell and Spence. "What's your conclusion?"

"I think it's the same person," Spence said immediately and with total conviction.

"I agree," Cantrell added. "I've based that on these photos."

She spread out six eight-by-tens on the table, two black-and-whites, four color. "These two," she explained, pointing to the black-and-whites with the chewed end of her pen, "were victims of the Madonna Murderer. These," she said, indicating the more vivid color shots, "were taken at the last two crime scenes. The posing is the same. Notice the way the hands are resting on the hips, in what someone might think of as a provocative pose. The knees bent and spread, in what could be pornographic, but also the position taken for birth. The head is tilted to the right. Mouth taped into a smile. Even the camera angle is the same. There's the ritualistic nature of the scenes, from the degrading pose of the mother, to the 'sleeping' infant with the music box." The word *sleeping* was tagged with air quotes.

"It has to be the same person," she went on to say.

"Superintendent Sinclair assures me that the public never had access to these photos. That leaves us with one conclusion. The Madonna Murderer of sixteen years ago, and the man who killed Tia Sheppard, Sachi Anderson, and their infant sons, is without a doubt the same person."

A beat went by before Irving said, "We have some additional information. That's why I've asked Dr. Glaser here today."

The toxicologist opened a manila envelope and pulled out copies of a toxicology report. He quickly dealt a sheet to everyone.

"When the coroner was performing the autopsies on the Andersons, she discovered what looked like an injection site on the left side of the infant's head," Dr. Glaser said. "The toxicology tests show that the child was injected with a lethal dose of acepromazine, an animal tranquilizer. Acepromazine was quantitated in blood and postmortem tissue, which led to the discovery of concentrations in the liver and brain. Cause of death was respiratory arrest."

"Put to sleep," Ivy said.

"In effect, yes."

"That doesn't fit his earlier MO," Abraham stated.

"MOs can change," Spence said, taking the opportunity to jump in before Cantrell did any more speaking for him. "It's the signature that stays the same."

Ivy tapped her pen against her notebook. "I think he's feeling guilty for killing the infants. He always smothered them before. Now he's putting them to sleep."

"What a kindhearted guy," Ramirez said sarcastically.

"I agree with Ivy," Cantrell said. "And this isn't a

game for him the way it is for some serial killers. This guy is doing something he thinks is right. In his mind, he's rescuing the children."

"How would he get the drugs?" Hastings asked.

"A veterinarian would be the only person licensed to handle such narcotics," the toxicologist stated. "My guess is that the drugs were stolen."

"Or the killer is a veterinarian."

"Or works for a vet."

"There have been some clinic break-ins," Irving said, "but it always comes down to druggies planning to use the stolen drugs themselves or sell them on the street."

"The question is, what does the killer want out of the crime?" Agent Spence asked. "If we can understand that, we can get a clearer picture of this guy."

"His overriding fantasy is to rid himself of his abusive mother," Ivy said. "For that reason, I would guess that his mother is still alive. He might even live with her."

"He might even take a trophy from his victim and give it to his mother," Spence said. "Like a necklace, a barrette. Something small."

"This guy is smooth," Cantrell said. "Possibly quite charming. The normal, commonsense clues we use when sizing people up don't apply when it comes to sociopaths."

"A sociopath is willing to let someone die for his own selfish purposes," Ivy said. "He doesn't value human life."

"You know what I think is significant?" Agent Scott said. "In most cases, there were no signs of struggle. Does he take them so by surprise that they don't have a chance? Or are they too terrified to move?"

"In many cases victims don't fight back because

they hope to be allowed to live if they behave," Cantrell told the group. "It's actually rare to find a victim who does fight back. Extremely rare. With the Madonna Murderer, it could partly be due to the surprise factor. I think he attacks his victims and kills them right away. Most serial killers like to toy with their victims awhile, sometimes for days. And they still don't fight, even when they have to know what is going to happen to them. The fact that the Madonna Murderer kills his victims immediately gives him a sort of conscience, for lack of a better word. He wants them dead. There is still the violence of the act—the repeated stabbing—but the goal is to kill, not to torture."

"What about this Reynolds woman?" Ramirez asked, flipping through his papers, looking for something he'd read earlier. "The one who lived for a while after the attack. Was she ever able to tell the police anything?"

"Nothing substantial," Agent Scott said.

"Too bad."

"What else do we have?" Irving said, directing the conversation in a more productive direction.

Ivy realized she'd been holding her breath. Perspiration was running down her spine. She went through a breathing exercise. *Rising, rising. Falling, falling.* Her muscles relaxed. Her heart rate slowed.

"We've entered all the information in the FBI's Violent Criminal Apprehension Program, but so far have come up with nothing." Agent Scott was talking about a computer base that allowed police officers all over the country to share information.

"Sometimes serial killers travel, committing similar crimes in other areas of the United States," Scott continued. "When that happens, a case can appear isolated when in fact it's not. It's important to stay

connected not only within Chicago and the surrounding areas, but with the whole country.''

At that point, the toxicologist excused himself.
After a flurry of distracted good-byes, the discussion
continued with hardly a pause.

"Any possible evidence found on the scene?" Cantrell asked.

"Bloodstains, prints, fibers, hair, anything?" asked
Spence.

"Nothing. The only thing he left was his usual calling card—that damn snow-globe music box," Abraham said. "They are mass-produced in some sweatshop
in Bangladesh, and sold at almost every discount store
in the nation."

"We have someone following up on that to see if any
single store has sold an unusual amount," Irving said.

"Does it always play the same song?" Spence asked.

" 'Hush Little Baby,' " Ivy murmured.

"When my granddaughter was born, somebody gave
her a stuffed bear that played that damn song," Abraham said. "I took it out and burned it."

The discussion turned to other aspects of the case:
mode of entry. How did he get into a secure building?
It was agreed that anybody could get into a secure
building if he waited by the door long enough until a
resident or visitor went in or out. Then there were the
knife wounds. He used to stab the women thirteen
times. Now he stabbed them twenty-two. The significance was lost on everyone in the room.

For two more hours they tossed ideas back and forth.

Ivy suggested they track down sales of Polaroid film.
Spence, the sale of used police cars. Sometimes of-
fenders were known to buy police cars so they could
impersonate a cop.

That led to a discussion about how he found his victims to begin with. Someone pointed out that insurance agents were privy to a client's personal history.

Insurance agents went on the list.

Another person noted that oftentimes hospitals and even police didn't put private volunteers through a background check.

Volunteers went on the list.

They would have a squad of plainclothes officers watch hospitals, especially the delivery wings.

They would cross-reference released prisoners and released mental patients with volunteer police and volunteer hospital aides.

At that point, Hastings announced that her bladder was going to bust and she needed to eat.

Everybody pretty much agreed with that too.

When she returned from the bathroom, people began bombarding her with food requests. "I'm not going to be the designated gofer," she said.

"We'll take turns," Ramirez told her, tossing a ten-dollar bill in her direction.

She grabbed it. "Damn right, we will." She took off down the nearest flight of stairs to hit the McDonald's up the street.

In the bathroom, Ivy and Mary Cantrell were both washing their hands when Mary said, "Did you write *Symbolic Death*?" She shut off the water and tore off a section of paper towel. "Are you *that* Ivy Dunlap?"

Ivy turned the tiny bent metal crank on the paper-towel machine, moving her arm like she was playing a hurdy-gurdy. "Yes."

"I thought so."

Ivy was surprised she'd heard of the book. She'd actually written it as a catharsis, a class project. Her professor had urged her to publish it. "This could be huge," he'd told her. At the time, her mind had fast-forwarded, creating a future for herself as a top-selling author with whirlwind book tours and guest spots on *Good Morning America* and *The Today Show*.

Feeling overexposed just thinking about it, she'd never sent the manuscript to New York. Instead, it had been picked up by a rather obscure university press and was released with a modest print run. It seemed Ivy Dunlap lacked the credentials to create any kind of a buzz. What a sad commentary on the United States. The same book, written by Claudia Reynolds, would have produced a media frenzy.

Mary tossed her wet towel in the wastebasket, then leaned against the tiled wall, her arms crossed just beneath her breasts. She was several years younger than Ivy, dark-haired and pretty, but carrying an air of raw intensity that was more than just her intentionally projected image of the strictly professional career woman in her navy-blue tailored suit and crisp white shirt.

Women hadn't been admitted to the FBI for all that long, even less time in the Behavioral Science Unit. The year the first woman came along was 1984 if Ivy remembered correctly. In such a male-dominated field, women had to think twice as fast, work twice as hard.

"When I was in high school," Mary said, "my best friend was murdered."

Jesus. Soon it would be like breast cancer where one in an ever-changing number of women would be touched by a killer. "I'm sorry."

"Normally I don't tell anybody that. I'm telling you because I was impressed by your insight. And I have to admit that, as I read your book, I kept expecting you to come out and say that your life had been touched by one of these madmen too. But you didn't."

"No." Ivy was suddenly unable to look Mary in the eye. "No, I didn't." She felt sick that her answer had to be so evasive.

"That's why I went into this business."

"Because of your friend's death?"

Mary nodded.

"Did they catch the killer?"

"Yeah, but he was a juvenile and the jury went easy on him." Mary dug around in her purse, pulled out a cigarette, and lit it with a pink Bic. Smoke-free building, but what the hell? "I've quit smoking three times, but I always start again." She offered a drag of the cigarette to Ivy.

Ivy shook her head. "No, thanks." She mentally calculated how many years ago it must have been that Mary's friend had died. "Is he out now? The killer?"

"He gets out soon." Mary took a few deep drags, making up for the last several hours. "Well, at least he isn't lonely in prison," she said sarcastically. "His girlfriend writes to him and goes to see him all the time."

"Killers don't change. People need to understand that. They don't suddenly grow a conscience."

Mary turned on the water faucet, doused her cigarette, and tossed it in the trash. "You want to hear something really sick? His girlfriend is my sister."

Chapter 18

Three days after their arrival, Special Agents Anthony Spence and Mary Cantrell offered their conclusions to a group of about fifty people. All the members of the task force were there, plus about a hundred various police officers and officials. No press. No cameras.

"Single white male with deep psychiatric problems that require medication," Agent Mary Cantrell said from the podium at the front of the room. "Probably lives with his mother or another female relative. Age, mid-forties."

Spence broke in, leaning into the microphone. "We would have said late twenties, except that we know it's the Madonna Murderer, and he'd have to be in his forties by now."

"It's unusual for a serial killer to be that old," Cantrell said, "but this is an exception."

She continued. "Possibly dates some, but doesn't have any real girlfriend. He might have a job that requires skill with computers. Maybe a computer programmer. The kind of job where he might work around a lot of people, but interacts with them only briefly during the day."

"Or he could possibly be a telemarketer," Spence said. "Someone who touches people from a distance, who can skillfully manipulate them. He might also be an agent, maybe an insurance agent. An insurance agent who has access to his client's medical records. He also has tremendous organizational skills. That's apparent in the way he never leaves any evidence."

"He might drive a four-door car like a Caprice, several years old," said Cantrell. "Maybe even an auctioned police car—but I think our guy might be too smart for that. But say a Caprice, or a Caprice-type car, because that's what policemen drive. He may have even tried to become an officer, but failed some part of the test. He may be a volunteer right now, directing traffic after concerts and football games."

When she was finished, Spence took over the podium to address possible tactics.

"We're going to give you some proactive measures that have worked for us in the past, plus some ideas that apply to this case only. The first suggestion is that you hold a candlelight vigil for the latest victim. Have detectives stake out the location of the vigil to see if anyone suspicious shows up. Nine times out of ten this kind of gathering will attract the killer. Another suggestion is to stake out the graves of previous victims. We know from experience that the killer almost always visits the places where his victims are buried. John Chapman was caught this way. So was Vincent Thomas. You might advertise for volunteers to help with the investigation. As Agent Cantrell said, many serial killers have tried to be policemen, and several have been known to be volunteer police. That's because these men need to dominate and need to be in control. They crave authority. Another possibility is to run a fake birth announcement in the paper, along with an address where officers will be lying in wait.

"Before closing, I want to go over some signs to watch for. These predators, as unique and individual as they appear from the outside, fall into certain patterns. Be aware that serial killers can reach a burnout stage where they get careless. Sometimes they reach a grandiose stage where they become bold, even to the point of impersonating an investigator. If the stress of everyday life gets too extreme, they may snap. Here's a little-known fact: People who are getting close to snapping sometimes start wearing the color yellow. The brighter the color, the closer they are to snapping. Lastly, when the predator can't find his victim of choice, he'll take whatever is available."

The next half hour was spent with Spence and Cantrell answering questions, then the meeting broke up. "I wish all local law enforcement could be as receptive to us as you've been," Mary said.

Detective Irving shook their hands, thanking them for their time and input.

"Keep us informed," Mary said. "Even though we're going back to Virginia, we'll remain involved in the case."

Four hours later in the task-force room, Ivy tossed her notebook aside. "I have to get some real light," she said, rubbing her temples as if she had a headache.

Max could sympathize. His own head was throbbing. It didn't look as if either of them had slept much the night before, and now they were both getting sluggish.

"There's an outdoor smoking area on the roof," he offered.

"You could probably use some fresh air yourself," Ivy said.

Max thought it a strange comment for her to make, an obvious invitation that he join her. Curious, he grabbed a bottled water from the stocked refrigerator and went along.

Outside, in a small alcove made of roofing tar, pea gravel, and a tiny picnic table, Ivy closed her eyes and tilted her face to the sun. "God, that feels good. How can something bad for you feel so good?"

Max didn't think it felt all that great. It had to be about 120 degrees out there on the roof. In the distance, he could see shimmering waves of heat rising off the nearby four-lane. He'd already had enough.

"I think the sun plays a greater role in all of this than we'll realize in our lifetime," Ivy said.

He took a long drink of water. "How's that?"

"I think it could be the root of our mental and physical well-being. Look at the deformed frogs that are being found in Minnesota. Scientists have proven that the deformities have something to do with the depletion of the ozone."

"I don't dispute that the deteriorating health of amphibians should be taken as a serious warning, but tying lack of sunlight to criminal behavior? You psychologists always go too far. If you'd just stop when you quit making sense, you could be taken a lot more seriously."

She laughed.

Lack of sleep did weird things to people. In some individuals, it slowed down certain thought processes. In others, it gave the brain a boost. One of the great crime fighters of all time, Eli Parker, cracked some of his biggest cases when he'd gone more than forty-eight hours without sleep. His theory was that it turned on the subconscious mind so that he was better able to access and understand things that hadn't been evident to him before.

"No amount of artificial light can make up for sunlight," Ivy said. "And now, with the diminishing ozone unable to filter harmful rays, making it foolish and dangerous to worship the sun—well, we're destroying what keeps us sane."

"You'd better go take a nap. My grandmother always said a fifteen-minute nap can mean the difference between sense and nonsense."

"Have you ever heard of the Griggs Light Deprivation Experiments?"

He shook his head.

"About fifteen years ago, some highly controversial natural-light studies were conducted. One of the tests required three students to live underground for six months. They would have no clocks, no TV, no radio. No outside stimulation of any kind. They could sleep when they felt like it, eat when they felt like it—and under artificial light, they could read all the books they desired. In return, they earned a tuition-free year of college."

"Quite a deal."

"Not really. Shortly after the experiment ended, the female subject killed herself. The two males were never able to return to their studies due to an inexplicable inability to concentrate.

"My question is: What effect, if any, does lack of sunlight have on the criminal mind? I propose that even in the most unsusceptible of people light deprivation can cause depression and, in some cases, seizures. In susceptible people, it can lead to neurotic behavior, even suicide. I was in the middle of applying for grant funding to determine if any correlation could be drawn when I received the call from Abraham."

"I hope you weren't going to put kids underground."

"I want to do comparison studies on the test results of adolescents who attend school in buildings with natural light and those of children who learn under artificial light. I'm hoping to prove the natural-light students do better."

"That's a fascinating theory. So fascinating that I have to again wonder what you're doing here. What is it about this case that makes it important enough to take you from your home and your work?"

He didn't expect an answer, and from the pained way she was staring at him, he didn't think he was going to get one. "Forget it." He finished his water. "I'm heading back. You can stay out here and bake if you want." He turned to leave when her next words stopped him.

"Max. Wait."

She'd never called him Max before, a clue he took to mean this could be something interesting.

When he turned back, she was looking away, in the direction of Grand Avenue.

"I have to tell you something."

She still didn't look at him, and he began to feel the heavy dread that sometimes came over him in confrontations with Ethan. It occurred to him that the last time a woman he barely knew had something important to tell him, it had been to say she was dying.

"Last night . . . I couldn't sleep."

Even though her words were unremarkable, the feeling of dread didn't leave.

"I think we're all having that problem," he said.

"No, this is different."

She wanted out, he immediately decided. Just when he was getting used to her, she wanted out.

She swung around and he could see that the blinding sunlight had turned her pupils to pinpoints surrounded by blue.

"*I'm* Claudia Reynolds."

Blue, blue, blue.

She was watching him, waiting for some kind of response, but his brain had shut down. He was afraid his mouth may have dropped open.

"I can't keep it a secret any longer and remain part of this investigation."

"*You're* Claudia Reynolds?" He was having trouble processing the information.

"Yes."

As a detective, he'd come across a lot of hard-to-believe things, but he was rarely taken by surprise.

His mind refused to go in the direction she was trying to lead. She was bullshitting him. For some reason, she was bullshitting him. Claudia Reynolds was dead. A copy of her death certificate was in the original case file.

"You don't believe me?"

"Hell no!" he shouted. "Come on. Abraham was involved in the case. He would have known—" He stopped in midsentence, midthought.

Now things were coming together, possibly making sense. Abraham. Yes. Abraham *had* known. Abraham had also made the arrangements for Ivy to come to Chicago.

She pulled up her white top so that it rested above her rib cage. Her stomach was crisscrossed with raised scars, some white, some pink, as if they'd never really healed. She began to unbutton her khaki pants.

"Don't. You don't have to do that."

"You have to believe me."

Pinning her top between her chin and chest, she unzipped her pants to reveal an abdomen with the same crisscross scarring pattern. She raised her chin to look up at him. "Do you believe me, Detective?"

He was seeing her for the first time. For the very first time—with eyes that were at once discerning and burning with pity and anguish and anger and remorse. Rage toward the man who had done this rose in his throat, almost choking him. Even though her top had dropped back into place, he could still see the scars in his mind's eye, forever etched there, crisscrossing her abdomen.

"I believe you."

With a look of satisfaction, she rebuttoned and zipped her pants. "Good."

"Abraham," Max said woodenly, his mind staggering forward, grappling, trying to piece this entirely new puzzle together.

"He did it to save my life," she explained. "It was the only way. The killer would have found me. Killed me."

"Why are you here? Why did you come back?"

She stared at him a moment, then said with quiet conviction, "I'm going to catch that son of a bitch."

If the Madonna Murderer knew she was alive . . .

His mind ran the gamut from his discovery of her dead, lifeless body somewhere, sometime, to the possibility of the killer using her as a gambling tool. "Do you understand the danger you've put yourself in?"

"I'm not afraid."

How the hell had Abraham allowed this? No, *sanctioned* this? "If the killer finds out who you are, I might not be able to protect you."

"I didn't tell you who I am so you could protect me. I told you because I want you to know how much I can help. How important I am to this case."

She appeared lighter somehow. Of course. The weight of her burden had shifted to him. It was damn heavy.

She shook back her hair, pulling herself up straighter. "And I hate lies," she added.

Was she sane?

"What are you thinking?" she asked.

"Abraham," he said, quickly shifting gears. "We have to tell him we've had this conversation. But no one else can know about you. Not even the others on the task force. It's too risky. If this were somehow leaked to the press, they would run with it and you would be the Madonna Murderer's next victim."

"Abraham could take me off the case. He could send me back to Canada."

"That might not be a bad idea."

She unbuttoned her shirt cuffs, then rolled up her sleeves.

What now?

On her upturned wrists were more scars. "These weren't done by the Madonna Murderer," she stated without emotion. "They were done by me."

She rolled her sleeves back down, looking as if she'd just finished with a sinkful of dirty dishes. "I spent two years in a Canadian mental institution. Do you know what kept me going, what made me decide that I wanted to live? Knowing he was still out there somewhere, hibernating but ready to strike again. I educated myself. I learned what I had to learn so that I could find the madman. Don't take that away from me."

"For some reason, your updated resume is failing to impress me. None of what you've told me fits the job description. Let me get this straight. Are you threatening to kill yourself if I pull you from the case?"

"Don't be absurd. If you pull me from the case I'll go to the press, tell them who I am, then sit and wait for the Madonna Murderer to show up. And when he does, I'll kill him."

Chapter 19

"Any interest in going for a drive?"

The voice at the other end of the line belonged to Max Irving. It was Sunday morning, and Ivy, who had stayed up half the night mulling over the case, was still in bed.

"A drive?" she asked, trying to sound wide awake, trying to pull her head together.

"Ethan and I are going for a drive north of Chicago. I thought you might like to come with us. Get out of your apartment for a while."

Her answer came without hesitation. "I'd love to."

It had been two days since she'd revealed her true identity to Max, and although on the surface things between them hadn't changed, she was aware of an undercurrent of mutual respect that hadn't existed before.

"We'll pick you up in an hour," Max said.

"I'll wait for you in front."

After hanging up, Ivy turned on the television, going directly to the weather channel. A cool front had moved in overnight, and the daytime temperatures weren't supposed to get above the high seventies.

She took a bath and got dressed, putting on a pair of jeans and a black top with three-quarter-length sleeves. On her feet she wore jogging shoes.

Max arrived on time. Introductions were made, and Ivy's breath was taken away by Max's son. He was beautiful, with blond hair and Scandinavian features, high cheekbones and blue eyes. He looked nothing like Max, who was as dark as Ethan was light.

"Hi," he said, getting out of the front seat of Max's two-door car. He was reserved but polite.

"I'll get in back," she said insistently.

Max, who stood near the driver's door, shot his son a look, and Ivy could see her position in the car had already been discussed.

"That's okay," Ethan told her, sliding in. "I'd rather sit in back."

She didn't want to start out by making an issue of where she should sit, so she got into the passenger seat, quickly finding her seat belt and adjusting it.

It was one of those perfect days, a day with a cloudless sky and air that was clear and remarkably pollution-free.

They drove north on Sheridan Road, following the Lake Michigan shoreline.

"Is this too windy?" Ivy asked, looking at Ethan over her shoulder. She had her window cracked a couple of inches.

He pulled off his headphones, and she repeated her question. He shook his head. From his attitude, she discerned that he didn't consider her a pain in the ass—he just didn't consider her at all.

"What are you listening to?" she asked.

"Neil Young."

"Ah, another Canadian. Canada is known for its

good musicians too," she said, shooting a glance in Max's direction in a teasing reference to their first meeting. For Max, he looked relaxed, dressed in jeans and a T-shirt.

"Do you know a lot about Canada?" Ethan asked, showing a little more interest in her.

"I live in Ontario," she said. "In a little town called St. Sebastian." She told him about the university where she taught. "It's a beautiful campus, lots of stone buildings."

"I saw Neil Young in concert. He opened for Pearl Jam."

"I saw Neil Young in concert too. Years and years ago."

"Have you ever been to Toronto?" he asked.

"Several times. It's only ninety miles from my house. A beautiful city, but I hate the traffic."

"Is it worse than Chicago?"

"Much."

"Have you been to the Hockey Hall of Fame?"

She smiled. "No, but I've heard of it. I've seen things about it on the news."

"Ethan and I are planning to go there sometime," Max said, keeping his eyes on the road.

Ethan didn't reply. Instead, he dropped back in the seat and replaced his headphones.

They stopped and bought sandwiches and drinks, taking them to a park near the Grosse Point Lighthouse. Once there, they found a picnic table overlooking the lake.

When they were finished eating, Max got a Frisbee out of the trunk and tossed it to Ethan. He caught it, but didn't toss it back.

"Come on," Max said. "You used to love to play Frisbee."

"I used to shit my diapers too, but I don't do that anymore."

Max laughed. "Throw it to me."

Ethan threw it.

Max caught it, then tossed it to Ivy, who was unprepared and missed.

Laughing, she got to her feet and ran after the Frisbee, picked it up and threw it to Ethan.

They played for about fifteen minutes.

After that, they toured the lighthouse, then walked along the beach.

"Remember the time we came here with Grandma and Grandpa Irving?" Ethan asked his dad.

In the last hour, a transformation had come over him. He was smiling and laughing and having fun. "Grandma waded out in the water, then she saw the SWIM AT YOUR OWN RISK sign that said the water had a high level of bacteria in it. She was out in half a second, running all weird. Running toward the car, yelling at grandpa to quick, get the baby wipes. There were all these people around—a lot more than today—and it looked like, you know, like she'd shit her pants."

Max was laughing too, but now he apparently had to try to rein it in. He'd let Ethan get away with the shitting his diapers comment, but now, when Ethan's grandmother was involved, Max must have felt compelled to play parent. "You shouldn't talk about your grandmother like that."

"You know it was true. You know that's what everybody was thinking. Grandma thought it was funny too.

Remember? She's probably still telling her buddies in Florida about it."

"She's your grandmother," Max reminded him.

"I know—"

Suddenly Ethan's expression changed. "Don't you mean *your* mother?" His smile vanished, and the light in his eyes was extinguished. He swung around and walked purposely down the shoreline, away from Max and Ivy.

"This parent thing is tough," Max said, "but I didn't think I could let that one go by."

"He's a nice kid," Ivy said. "I'm not just saying that. Some kids I know are absolute brats, and I have to lie and tell their parents that they're charming, because who wants to hear that their kid is spoiled and obnoxious? Like you said, parenting is tough. There are no solid answers."

"We don't get along like we used to," Max said with regret in his voice. "I know that's the way it is with teenagers, but it's hard to deal with. I'll be glad when he outgrows this phase."

"Often there's a basis for teenage angst. Teenagers have a tendency to overreact, and when something does bother them, they don't verbalize it. Even among themselves, teens rarely talk about real issues."

"He's gotten touchy lately about the fact that he's adopted."

Ethan was adopted? That explained why father and son looked nothing alike.

Max told her about Ethan's mother, and about how he'd come to adopt Ethan. It would have taken a lot of guts to do what Max had done.

"I keep wondering if we should get a dog," Max said, watching Ethan in the distance. "We used to have one, but it died last year. Old age. He was just a couple years younger than Ethan. I keep thinking we'll get a new one, that a dog would be good for Ethan, but neither of us is home enough to give a puppy the kind of care it requires. Maybe when this case is over. But then I think in another two years Ethan will be gone to college, so maybe we shouldn't get a dog at all."

"What does Ethan think about it?"

Max thought a moment. "I don't know."

"Are you sure you two live in the same house?"

"I didn't ask you along so you could psychoanalyze my relationship with my son." He was beginning to sound more irritated with her than with Ethan.

"You aren't annoyed because Ethan and I were carrying on a conversation, are you?"

"I have to admit you displayed an uncanny skill for targeting in on his obsession. It was almost scary."

"Are you talking about music?"

"Dangle music in front of him and you can lead him anywhere. For a minute, I thought we were going to get into one of those who-I've-seen-in-concert scenarios."

"Do you like music?"

"I used to. When I was young. Then I got too busy for it."

"So do you look on music as something frivolous?"

He thought about that a moment. "Maybe so."

"Music is art, and art is an integral part of the human experience."

He stopped and stared at her in a threatening way. "Does everything always have to turn into something deep? Can't it simply be that I don't like music?"

"Doesn't it seem strange that the very thing you trivialize is the very thing Ethan is crazy about?"

"You're reading too much into it."

* * *

On the way back to Chicago, Ethan was quiet. Ivy turned to look at him and saw he was asleep—or at least he appeared to be asleep, his head tipped back, eyes closed.

Half an hour later, he said, "Pull over. I have to throw up."

"There's no shoulder," Max said, sounding amazingly calm.

"I have to puke!"

There was no window in the backseat so Ivy quickly rolled down the passenger-side window. Ethan leaned forward, stuck his head out, and threw up. A car roared past, its windshield wipers going, horn blaring to finally fade into the distance.

The road widened and Max was finally able to pull to the side. As soon as the car stopped, Ethan bailed out, followed by Max and Ivy.

"Get away," Ethan said, swinging his arm behind him. "Nobody needs to watch me."

Max and Ivy looked at each other, then got back in the car.

A few minutes later, Ethan walked over to the car and got in, collapsing in the backseat, his face pale, his shirt removed and clutched in his hands.

"You okay?" Max asked.

"Yeah. Let's go."

"Do you think it was the sandwich?" Ivy asked. "I don't feel sick. Do you?" That question was directed to Max.

"It's car sickness," Ethan said, sounding embarrassed. "Let's just go. I just wanna get home."

"Why didn't you tell me you get carsick?" she

asked, while at the same time Max said, "I thought you'd outgrown that."

"Apparently not," was Ethan's dry comment.

"You have to ride in the front seat," Ivy said, opening her door.

"I'm okay now."

"Please." Then to Max, "Max, he has to ride in the front."

"Jesus," Ethan said. "If it'll make you happy."

They quickly switched places, with Ivy settling in back, behind Max.

When they arrived at her apartment, it was almost ten o'clock.

"I'm sorry you got sick," Ivy said as she got out of the car.

Ethan smiled. "That was pretty funny stuff though," he said, surprising her with direct eye contact. "I puked on that car's windshield."

Ivy nodded, smiling at the memory. "Funny stuff."

"Do you like her?" Ethan asked his father as they pulled away.

"She's my partner," Max said, for lack of a better definition.

"Is that all?"

"That's all."

Max hadn't done a whole lot of dating over the years. He'd mainly done a lot of running away from the women who pursued him. There had been a defense attorney he'd seen for two years. Another was Ethan's pediatrician, who had pursued him so relentlessly that he'd given up and gone out with her. Both women were smart and charming—but highly stressed. The mix hadn't been right. In both cases, it had produced a clash of two highly stressed individuals, with the catalyst for those stresses being such polar opposites that the relationships never had a chance.

"Why'd you ask her along today?" Ethan asked.

"She doesn't know anybody in Chicago and doesn't have a car, so I thought she might like to get out."

"Okay," Ethan said, not sounding convinced.

"I assure you, the only thing she'd want to do with me is use me for target practice. And by the way, I *am* your father, and that makes my mother your grandmother."

Ethan crossed his arms over his chest. "Whatever."

Max's strategy had always been to avoid confrontational issues, but Ivy's earlier comments came back to him, and he found himself saying, "Why are you pushing me away? Why are you deliberately trying to alienate yourself?"

"I don't want to talk about this."

"I do."

"Are you saying I have to discuss it? Is that an order? A command? Will you ground me longer, continue to not let me drive, if I don't talk to you?"

So much for Ivy's advice, Max thought, wishing he hadn't brought up the subject of Ethan's attitude. Interrogating cold-blooded killers was easier than arguing with his son.

That night, Ivy reran the day in her head. It was so strange. Whenever she thought of her baby, she thought of him as an infant—forever young. Over the years, she always had to remind herself that no, he would be six now, or he would be nine now. But no matter how often she reminded herself of what his age would be, she always saw him as an infant, his face indistinct. He always seemed so far away.

Sixteen . . . If he'd lived, her baby wouldn't be a baby, he'd be a young man. He'd be Ethan's age.

She pulled her black suitcase from under the bed and opened it. Inside was a small gift box. She wasn't sure why she'd brought it along, especially since it was something she hadn't been able to open since putting it away sixteen years ago.

When she took on her new identity, she was supposed to leave everything from her old life behind. Not just so she couldn't be traced, but so she could become a new person. But there was one item she had refused to part with.

She sat down on the bed and untied the blue ribbon. With shaking hands, she tried to make herself open the box.

She couldn't.

It would hurt too much.

It was said that time healed. For Ivy, that wasn't the case. Being a psychologist, she understood the stages of grief and knew she hadn't completely faced what had happened all those years ago. Being the mother of a murdered child, she feared she never would.

Chapter 20

Max and Ivy sat in an unmarked car in Chicago's
Graceland Cemetery. In another car, on the opposite
side of the gathering, were two plainclothes officers.
Darkness had fallen and white tapered candles with
paper shields were being lit. Two days earlier, an article announcing the candlelight vigil had run in
Wednesday's edition of the *Herald*, making the press
and the Chicago Police Department temporary allies.

Graceland Cemetery was located in Area Three, just
a block north of Wrigley Field. The famous cemetery
protected the remains of people like Marshall Field and
George Pullman. It was also said to be haunted.

In order to keep the ghosts in and the people out,
a towering redbrick wall surrounded the grounds, the
wall topped with three rows of razor wire. The massive
iron gates were locked every evening at precisely 5:00
P.M., and it was only by special permission that the
police had been allowed to stage the candlelight vigil.

"This place is supposed to be haunted," Ivy said,
her throat tight as she struggled to calm her stomach,
trying to divert herself with talk of ghosts, because it
wasn't the ghosts that unnerved her, but the possibility
of coming face-to-face with the Madonna Murderer.

"I've heard that," Max said. "What's the name of the statue that's supposed to walk around at night?"

"Eternal Silence."

"Also known as Statue of Death. Total bullshit."

"Is that thing on?" she asked, referring to the palm-sized video camera he held in his hand.

He fiddled with the focus. "Ready to roll."

He pushed a button and the camera began to hum as he unobtrusively recorded the event playing out in front of them. "Nine thirty-two p.m.," he said in a monotone voice for the sake of documentation. That was followed by the date, the case, and the two people present. "Big turnout," he commented.

"You don't believe in ghosts?" she asked.

"No, do you?" His voice had the slightly distracted quality of someone concentrating on something else while trying to carry on a conversation.

"I've never actually *see* anything that would lead me to believe ghosts exist, but I have to admit I've heard some pretty convincing stories."

"Mass hysteria. That's all. Like that school full of kids in Tennessee. Hundreds of them were admitted to surrounding hospitals. They were dropping like flies. They just had to touch somebody and they went down. Thought they were the victims of biological warfare. Tox screens came out okay. Air tested fine. Nothing was found."

"I remember hearing about that," Ivy said, beginning to relax.

"The mind can play strange tricks on a person."

"It's called psychogenic illness," Ivy said.

"Oh, Christ. No psychology lesson, please."

"Can you turn off the sound?"

"Why? Don't want the inaneness of this conversation exposed to the entire task force?"

"Exactly."

"They love that kind of thing."

"That's what I'm afraid of. How many people do you think?" Ivy asked. "Fifty? Sixty?"

"Closer to a hundred."

But then five of those hundred were officers. Twenty more were probably curiosity seekers.

"I think he's too smart to fall for this," Max commented.

"Doesn't matter. He doesn't have to fall for it. He'll know the whole thing's being enacted for his benefit. Hopefully he won't be able to keep from enjoying the attention. With nothing to tie him to the murders, he should feel somewhat safe."

"Bathing in the glory."

"That's right."

"See anybody suspicious?"

"How about the tall guy near the tree, to the right of the crowd?"

Max squinted. "Shit. That's Carpenter. I told him to blend, not lurk. He may as well be wearing a damn uniform."

"Time for me to join the party," Ivy said, picking up the bouquet of flowers from her lap and reaching for the door handle.

"Wait." Max fiddled with the dome light so it wouldn't come on when she opened the door.

Earlier, it had been decided that Max should keep a low profile, since his face might be familiar to the killer, thanks to the media. And even though Ivy's picture had appeared in the paper, she hadn't been identified: She could very well be a friend or relative.

With the light off, Ivy slipped from the car without

fear of attracting undue attention, solidly closing the door behind her.

The night air was heavy and humid. Crickets chirped and fireflies played among the tombstones. When she was little, Ivy used to lie in bed on hot nights, counting the cricket chirps outside her open window to determine how old she would be when she died. How strange that children played such dark games. So much of their play dealt with death and violence. Did anyone else think that was peculiar?

Stick a needle in my eye.
If I die before I wake.
Blackbirds baked in a pie.
Pray to God my soul to take.
Ashes, ashes, all fall down.
Three blind mice.

It had rained that morning, and the ground under her square heels sank as she made her way across the grass, moving in the direction of the shifting white lights and bowed heads, in the direction of the murmur of prayers.

At the edge of the crowd, someone offered her a lit candle. She accepted it, whispering a thank-you as she glanced up into the face of a middle-aged man.

Is it you? she silently asked, trying to memorize a face she could barely distinguish in the flickering candlelight which threw black slashes of moving shadows across his cheekbones, his forehead. Fingertips brushed hers and she looked down, prepared to see talons instead of nails.

Too dark.

He flashed her a wistful smile. As he turned to leave, firelight suddenly washed away the shadows, revealing tear-filled eyes.

Not you, she thought.

But he won't look like a monster, she reminded herself. *He'll look like anybody else.* He could be capable of tears. That's what people didn't understand. That's what the public had to be made to realize.

She moved deeper into the now singing crowd, her mouth beginning to move, her voice taking up the words of a song long forgotten, from a time when she'd gone to church and prayed like everybody else.

Silly people, she thought with sorrow-tinged affection. With your Saint Christopher medals and your rosaries and your holy water. How many of them were praying, not for Sachi and her baby, but for themselves? Thinking that if they were good enough, prayed enough, smiled enough, tithed ten percent of their income to the church, that they would be safe from the kind of horrors that had befallen Sachi Anderson? Didn't they understand that the same God who created them had also created the Madonna Murderer? Wasn't that exactly how Jeffrey Dahmer justified his killings? Saying God had made him a predator? That he was simply carrying out God's wish?

The scent of earth from the fresh graves hit her. She saw they were marked with photos and stuffed animals and hanging baskets. And she thought of another small grave, in another cemetery, in another part of town, a grave she'd never visited. . . .

Ivy bent and put her bouquet with the others, then straightened as the last verse of the song died out. Someone began to pray. Someone else began to wail with a voice that was wild and high.

Ivy lifted her head, trying to find the direction of

the wailing, but the voices rose and fell as the sound was carried from person to person, soul to soul.

A sense of evil seeped into her, a black pit of no remorse, no guilt, no blame. The surface of her arms tingled; the hair on her scalp shifted and cold air rushed down her cheeks and neck. She wanted to move, wanted to get away, go back to the car where Max Irving sat with his video camera. But her feet felt like lead, her muscles atrophied.

And she knew with utmost certainty that the man who had killed her baby, the man who had killed Sachi Anderson, was somewhere in the crowd watching. He had turned the tables on them, and suddenly something that had been devised to flush him out had instead turned into a way for him to hide in plain sight.

She forced herself to stay ten more minutes, then she made her way back to the parked car.

He watched her walk away.

Hers was a familiar face. The face from the paper. The face that was now in his scrapbook. The face that had no name.

He paid close attention to where she went, to the car she got into, to the license plate. CR 427. All numbers were significant.

When she opened the door, no dome light came on. Which meant she was a cop. She got into the passenger side. Which meant there was another cop with her. Detective Irving?

He liked to keep up with the investigators and their families. He liked to know what was happening in their lives, liked to follow them so he could keep tabs on their likes and dislikes. In that way, he could engage them in conversation if he ever so desired.

He'd attended the first communion of Sinclair's daughter, and he'd sent a stuffed bear to his granddaughter, Kiki.

He was very curious by nature, and he had to find out who the woman was.

He turned back to the vigil. It was for him. He knew that.

Stupid people. Stupid, stupid people.

They were all there for him. The cops. The candles. The people. The sad, sad people. For him. Who said one person couldn't make a difference? He'd touched them all. Every one of them.

Whores, whores, whores.

He grew hard. *Dirty boy. Dirty, dirty boy.*

Something nagged at the back of his mind. The baby. The photo of the baby someone had put on the grave.

You saved him, he told himself. *Saved him!* Comforted, he raised his voice in song.

Ivy stepped into the task-force headquarters, where members of the team were huddled around a computer screen. Irving was perched on the corner of a desk he'd staked out as his, one foot on the floor, the other dangling, making his creased gray slacks short enough to show a brown sock that appeared to have had bleach spilled on it.

It seemed she'd walked in on the task force's version of Interpretation Theater. The sound had been turned off, and Ramirez was adding his own dialogue to the videotape that had been made the previous night. The view was quite obviously from a car. Near the bottom of the screen was the top curve of the steering wheel.

"Oh, yeah," Ramirez was saying in a high, feminine voice. "Put your hand there. Right there."

Everybody laughed, and then someone else added another ad-lib. "Cemeteries turn me on."

A burst of fresh laughter.

"Cemeteries make me hot."

Another burst of laughter. Then Hastings spotted Ivy standing inside the door. Her smile dissolved. One by one, officers looked behind them to see what had changed Hastings' expression.

They were treating her like an old schoolmarm. Was she *that* stuffy? *That* serious?

Maybe. Probably. In fact, Ivy could barely recall a time when she'd laughed a laugh that wasn't tinged with sorrow. These young officers could still cut up because even though they saw evil on a regular basis, they hadn't been touched by it personally.

"Don't stop because of me," she told them.

"We were just having some fun," Hastings said, trying to fill the silence that had collected around them.

Ivy slid her backpack across one of the long, lunchroom-style tables.

"We were actually waiting for you," Max said, rewinding the tape to the beginning.

"The el was crowded. I had to wait for a second train."

She was finally getting the hang of getting around Chicago after so many years away, but she still hadn't quite figured out what now qualified as rush hour. And with metro universities making more and more downtown warehouses into student housing, the morning trains were often filled with just as many summer-session students as office workers.

Playtime over, the team quickly got down to business. It turned out that everyone involved in the vigil stakeout had taken note of the man who'd given Ivy the candle.

"A weird-ass," Hastings said.

The tech at the computer stopped the video at the very moment light met the man's face. A few key clicks and the face filled the entire screen. Another click and the image was being printed out.

"I don't think he's the one," Ivy said.

Max looked up at her.

She shrugged. "Just a feeling," she said, recalling how the black feeling of despair had washed over her *after* she'd walked away from the man on the screen.

"We'll run his face through the database," Max said. "Along with all the others."

Chapter 21

She couldn't say how many times she'd dreamed she was back in her old Chicago apartment. Hundreds. Maybe thousands. And in every one of those dreams, Ivy relived events that had actually taken place—except that in the dreamscape she always knew it was a dream . . . and she always saw the killer's face, a face she could never remember upon awakening. Dream therapists liked to say that every person in your dream is an aspect of yourself. And that the dream itself is a metaphor. But Ivy knew the dream was a mind trick, a trip back to an unthinkable event that had redirected the course of her life.

It was also said that dreams repeat themselves over and over until you "get it," until you learn the lesson your subconscious is trying to teach you.

She used to think that maybe she was supposed to see the man's face, *remember* his face. But how could she remember something she'd never seen?

"This the place?" Irving asked, maneuvering his car into position to parallel park.

Ivy looked across the street at the five-story brick building that took up half the block. Different. Very different. Maybe that was good.

The chipped white paint had been sandblasted off to reveal what it had been hiding: lovely red-orange brick. Different too was a green canvas awning that now covered the walkway to the front door. On each side of the path, perennial flower beds burst with color and greenery.

"It actually looks inviting," Ivy said in amazement, her eyes still on the building as she twisted sideways in her seat, craning her neck to see through Irving's window.

He smoothly wedged the car into a space Ivy would never have attempted. With an efficiency of motion that she was becoming accustomed to, he shut off the engine, and they got out.

Max was poised to cross the four lanes that were lined with quaint lights and divided by brightly painted yellow lines when he noted that Ivy was hanging back, both hands clutching a small coin purse.

She wore a red skirt that fit smoothly over rounded hips and fell to her knees. Her legs were bare. On her feet were the clunky shoes she almost always wore. Her top was black, knit, and slightly fitted.

He stared at her.

Then stared some more.

"Forget the meter," he said.

"No. . . . I better put in some money." She began digging around, and that's when he realized she was stalling.

He squeezed between car bumpers to join her on the sidewalk. He caught her elbow and she looked up at him with her short red bangs and lips the color of her skirt. Was she doing something different? Wearing more makeup or something?

"We don't have to do this," he told her.

She slipped a quarter in the meter. "I don't want you to get a ticket."

"Not the parking meter—and by the way, I won't have to pay the ticket. I mean *this.*" He motioned in the direction of the looming apartment complex.

She glanced at the building, then back at him, and he could see when the realization of what she was doing hit her. She smiled self-consciously, laughed a little, then snapped the small container closed and slipped it into a tiny black leather bag she wore as a kind of low-slung belt.

She turned away slightly and put a hand to her forehead, almost as if to shield her eyes from what was out there. Then she ran her fingers through her bangs and blew out a breath. "The mission's gone. It used to be right there." She pointed.

"Chicago's changed a lot in the last sixteen years."

"And the apartment. It doesn't even look like the same place."

"Maybe that's good."

"Why would they get rid of the mission?"

"They built a new one. Over on Lourdes. It can sleep a hundred people."

"Oh. Well. That's good."

"We don't have to do this," he said again.

She checked for traffic, then stepped off the curb and strode across the street with Max quickly catching up, falling into step beside her as they went up the walk.

"I *have* to do this." She paused. "Don't worry. I'm not going to fall apart on you."

He put up both hands. "Never said you were. Never even thought it."

But of course he had. Scene of the crime. Scene of

the place where a serial killer had plunged a knife into her and murdered her infant son. In that setting, a breakdown was almost a requirement.

Inside the lobby, they rang the building manager. A man's voice answered.

"CPD," Max said into the speaker.

"What?"

"Police Department. Homicide."

The buzzer went off, giving them immediate entry. The office was right inside the set of security doors. A small, worried-looking man got up from his desk as they stepped inside.

"Homicide?" he asked, his eyes round, his hands moving frantically in front of him. "Who's dead? Who's been killed?"

Max flashed his badge, then slipped it back into his pocket. "Nobody. Not recently, anyway. We just want to look at one of the apartments."

"283," Ivy added.

"283?" the man asked. "Why?"

"Police business."

"Is someone living in it?" Ivy asked.

"We use it for storage. It hasn't been rented for years." He stopped abruptly, then began to wave his finger at Max. "Those murders. That's what this is about. Those women. The babies. I'm not supposed to tell the tenants, but 283 is the room where a woman and her baby were killed years ago. After it happened, nobody would live there so it was turned into storage. Even after the remodeling project five years ago, when everybody had forgotten about the Madonna Murderer, we decided to leave it as storage."

"How long have you worked here?" Max asked.

"I started when the place was remodeled."

"Has anyone ever asked to rent that specific room?"

"Rent it?"

The man had an annoying habit of answering a question with a question. "I don't think so. Wait. The manager here before me told me that some guy wanted to rent 283. He didn't even care if it still had blood on the walls."

"Would you have the guy's name?"

"Maybe. If he filled out an application."

"Check that out for me, will you? And the name of the previous manager. I'll need that too."

"He's old. Really old. Like nursing-home old. Was losing his marbles when I started here."

"I'd like to talk to him anyway."

"Yeah, okay. I'll see what I can do."

"Thanks."

"Wanna see the apartment? Wait. I'll grab the key."

A minute later they were taking a creaky elevator up to the second floor, then the man was scurrying along the hallway toward 283.

Everything was new. New paint, new wallpaper, new red carpet, new light fixtures. But the floor under Ivy's feet was still uneven, still bowed from years and years of weight and shuffling feet. And the hallway, which went on and on, still seemed off, as if the perspective wasn't just right.

Too soon they were standing in front of room 283. The door was the same door, now painted green instead of sticky varnished brown. But with a new door handle, new lock, new discount-store metal-punched numbers.

The apartment manager unlocked the door and pushed it open. All three of them stood there, looking inside.

Ivy's heart dropped.

The remodeling project hadn't included room 283.

Irving's voice drifted in her direction from what seemed like another dimension, muffled, indistinct. "Could you leave us to look around?"

Another voice responded. "What? Oh. Oh, sure." Then came a shuffling, followed by the closing of the elevator doors.

With feet that seemed mired in mud, Ivy stepped forward into the room. Her heart was beating so rapidly that she distantly wondered if she might have a heart attack. Wouldn't that be strange? To die here? To come full circle like that?

The first thing that hit her was the smell. That creepy old-building smell, mingling with odors of all the people who had ever slept on the multitude of stained mattresses stacked against one wall, and all the people who had ever sat on the four porcelain toilets that were in various stages of decay. It smelled like stale sweat and urine and fabric that held the dust, skin sloughings, and mites of a hundred years.

Ivy edged past one of the toilets that was lying on its side like a wounded soldier.

"Quite a place," Irving commented, picking his way past a stack of linen and chenille bedspreads that looked as if they came from the fifties.

It was an efficiency, set up in much the same way as Ivy's current apartment. Directly inside the door was a kitchen and sleeping area, the rust-stained sink stacked with plumbing and electrical supplies along with long, narrow boxes that held fluorescent bulbs. There was no living room.

The bed was still there.

Next to the window the Madonna Murderer had escaped through. No sheets. No blanket. Just a stained, striped mattress. *The same mattress?*

She couldn't move any closer.

Her gaze shifted to the left of the bed, where the bassinet had stood. It was gone, thank God. The broken lamp was gone, and the shattered snow globe. But the mattress. The stained mattress. *Was* it the same one? If so, why in the hell hadn't they gotten rid of it?

Even though she'd imagined standing in this exact spot hundreds of times in both her dreams and waking hours, nothing could have prepared her for the reality of it.

Why hadn't they gutted the room? Left the way it was, it seemed almost a monument to the horrors that had gone on there. A place forever locked in time.

"Do you think he was the one who wanted to rent this room?" she asked, feeling no need to explain who "he" was.

"Maybe. Maybe not. Could have just been someone who wanted to be able to say he lived here. Like people always wanting to spend the night in the room where John Belushi died."

"I'm not anybody famous."

"Humans are morbidly curious as long as it has nothing to do with them."

She was beginning to calm down. Her heart wasn't beating so rapidly.

Seeming to sense that she'd gotten a grip on her

emotions, Irving asked, "Does this trigger any new memories? Anything you may have forgotten?"

Images flashed in her mind. A man in a dark hood bending over her baby.

"No crying," she said. "My baby wasn't crying."

She ran a tongue over her dry lips. "The killer, he was standing there. Over the bassinet. I turned on the light, and saw him."

"Did he look up when you turned on the light? Do you remember his face?"

She took a deep breath and concentrated very hard, then finally shook her head. "He would have looked up, wouldn't he have?"

Irving shrugged in a way that said he probably agreed. "You'd think so."

He seemed so out of place in the killing room. He was part of her new life, not the old. "Hypnotize me," she said.

"What?"

She could see that he thought he must have misunderstood.

"I know you're a qualified hypnotist. I know that you once caught a rapist by hypnotizing his victim."

"I didn't do it where the actual crime took place. And it was a long time ago."

"I'd think the scene of the crime might be the best place." She tipped her head, watching him closely. "Are you worried that I'll flip out? Go crazy?"

"Is this what you had in mind to begin with? And you knew I wouldn't go along with it if you told me back at Headquarters?"

He was a hundred percent correct. "Look." She held out her hands to show him that she wasn't shaking. "I'm not afraid."

"That makes one of us."

"Wow. A man who admits when he's scared. I'm impressed."

"I haven't hypnotized anybody in years."

"I trust you."

"I don't want you to have to relive your baby's death."

Ivy chewed on her lip and looked away, her eyes not staring at walls with bloodstains that looked like rust, but into the past. Her brows drew together and she rubbed her forehead with fingers that turned white from the pressure.

"You okay?"

"Yeah." She pulled in a deep breath and squared her shoulders. "Yeah." She waved her hand with a distracted, dismissive air, then sucked in another deep breath. "I have to do this."

Without waiting for his consent, fearing it might never come, she dropped to the stained mattress, then lay down, hands on her stomach, eyes closed, head where a pillow should have been.

Max had seen a lot of weird things in his days as a homicide detective, so why did the image of her pale face against its grisly backdrop give him such chills?

And how could he say no to something that might help the case, that might help catch the Madonna Murderer?

From the chaos in the room, he located a vinyl-covered kitchen chair and placed it near the bed. Then he sat and began to coax Ivy into a hypnotic state, leading her down a long flight of stairs that would take her deeper and deeper into her subconscious. They were halfway down the steps when he suddenly stopped.

With her eyes closed, she frowned, waiting for him to continue.

"You know what?" he said, putting his hands on his knees. "I'm not going to do this."

Her eyes flew open.

"Why not?"

"We'll do it the right way. In a neutral environment. With a video camera and tape recorder." He couldn't believe he'd almost let her talk him into it. "This is wrong. Too fucking creepy."

She sat up and swung her bare legs to the floor. "You're a homicide detective. You should be used to creepy by now."

"You never get used to creepy."

She put her hands over his hands and squeezed hard while staring into his eyes. "We're running out of time. It's been almost two weeks since Sachi Anderson was murdered. That means the killer could strike again soon. It's not going to matter if you don't have documentation. It's not going to matter if I freak out. It doesn't even matter if this drives me over the edge and I go insane. Which, by the way, isn't going to happen. I've lived for this moment. I've spent the last sixteen years waiting to catch this maniac. Don't make it harder. Don't put up roadblocks. Because you know as well as I do that tonight might be the night. Tonight you might get a call telling you there's been another murder. Do this," she pleaded. "You have to do this."

And so he did it.

She was a good subject and went under fairly quickly. And when he took her back to the night of sixteen years ago, it happened just the way she'd said, starting with a noise in the room and Ivy turning on the light.

"Now what are you doing?" Max asked, leaning closer.

"Screaming," she said in a chillingly monotone voice.

He swallowed. "Why? Why are you screaming?"

"There's a man in my room, standing over my baby."

"Remember, you're simply observing, not participating. The man you see—does he look up?"

"Yes."

"Can you see his face?"

She frowned in concentration.

"Ivy, can you see any of his face?"

"My name is Claudia." She continued to frown, as if looking deeply into her own mind. "A pale cheek. Pale skin. Very pale skin."

"Albino?"

"Not like that. Like someone who doesn't go outside much."

"His eyes. Can you see his eyes?"

"He's wearing a black hood. His face is in shadow."

"What's he doing now?"

"He's dropping something. A snow globe. I can hear the glass shattering. The baby isn't crying. Why isn't my baby crying? I scream and throw myself at him. But he's so strong. His hands are like claws, like bird claws. Talons. And he's *so* strong. He's throwing me back across the bed and the lamp is knocked to the floor. Now the room is dark. And the baby isn't crying." Her voice rose hysterically. "The baby isn't crying!"

"Did you see anything? Before the light went out?"

Without hesitation, she said, "Mother."

"Mother?"

"A MOTHER tattoo on his forearm. With a rose. A red rose. Mixed in with the tattoo are hairs. White skin with straight black hairs."

She let out a gasp. "He's hurting me," she said. "He's hurting me." All the terror, all the horror of the moment was evident in the shocked disbelief of her voice.

"Do you know him? Do you see his face?" he persisted.

"No . . . No . . ."

"He can't hurt you. Nobody can hurt you," Max reassured her. It would do no good to keep her under any longer.

She let out a sob.

Max grabbed her gently but firmly by both arms, speaking close to her face, to her tightly closed eyes. "You're safe, Ivy. You are safe. It's sixteen years later, and you are safe."

She pulled in a shuddering breath.

"We're going to go back up the stairs one at a time until we reach the top. When we get there, you'll wake up. When you wake up, you won't remember any of this. You will feel rested, refreshed. You won't remember any of this. Up the stairs. One, two, three. . . . You've reached the top step, full consciousness. . . . Now, slowly open your eyes. . . ."

Max sat back in the chair as Ivy slowly opened her eyes, her unfocused gaze clearing as she realized where she was. She groggily sat upright and swung her legs to the floor. With arms crossed at her waist, she sat there trying to get warm even though she knew it had to be at least eighty degrees in the small room.

"Do you remember anything?"

She touched her face. "Have I been crying?" With

the back of her hand, she wiped at the tears. "That's the last thing I wanted to do. Cry in front of you." She sniffed and wiped a little more, then said, "I remember trying to see his face, and it was like the dreams I sometimes have where it's always hidden by a black hood."

"Is the hood like an executioner's? Or Death's? Something he wears when he's killing?"

She thought a moment, then shook her head. "It's a sweatshirt. A black sweatshirt. He probably wore it into the building in case someone saw him, so they wouldn't be able to identify him. Damn," she said, pounding a fist against her leg. "I was hoping to come up with something new."

"Don't be too hard on yourself. You may not have remembered his face, but you remembered something else. A tattoo."

"Tattoo?" She gave that some thought, then her face cleared. "A tattoo that says MOTHER. It's on a banner woven through a red rose. That's good. That's something," she said.

"That's very good. More than we've ever had on him before."

"So now what?"

"We'll see if we can come up with a match on the Internet. If not, we'll get one of our sketch artists to put together an accurate image, then we'll run it through the tattoo database and also get it out to the media."

"My God. Can you imagine how many people in the country have a tattoo like that?"

"It will take an enormous amount of manpower to check up on all the false leads."

"We were right about his mother fixation," she said, getting up from the bed.

"I'm hoping good old mom is still around and recognizes her son's tattoo."

"I'm not sure she'd turn him in if she did. She might prefer to deal with him herself."

"Which could escalate the killings."

Downstairs, they returned the key while getting the name of the previous manager.

"Couldn't find the name of the guy who wanted to rent that room," the manager said. "But I've got some boxes in storage I can go through."

"Give me a call if you come up with anything," Max said.

They stepped outside.

In the short time they'd been in the apartment building, the weather had taken a turn, an east wind carrying in one of those violent summer storms that made the windows rattle and turned the sky dark as night.

Angry wind pushed at the basement window, shoving it open with a loud *thud* as the metal hinge caught, keeping it from opening more than a few inches. Raindrops sharp as knives stabbed against his arm as he struggled to reclose the window, the latch finally catching.

He used to be terrified of storms. When he was little, he used to hide under his bed. His mother would find him there, and she would laugh at him.

But now storms gave him power. They made him strong, made him more than he used to be. With each crash of lightning, his power grew. He could feel the hot blood pumping through his veins with every thunderous heartbeat, feel the oxygen saturating his brain. Man was such a complex machine, a malformed, sickening joke. If aliens landed on Earth, they would have to think humans hideously ugly with all of their guts and fluids and teeth.

He was horny.

He needed a woman.

Not a whore, but a real woman.

He stood in the basement with his hand deep in his pants, wrapped around his power. Any woman in the world would want him. Any woman in the world would gladly die to have him. Even his mother.

"Do you have a hard-on?" she'd asked him one morning when he was sixteen. She'd laughed and stuck her hand down his underpants and he'd shriveled up like a button. "Think you'll get a girl when you can't even keep it up? But don't worry. Your mamma will always love you."

That's how she was. One time she would berate him for masturbating or having girlie magazines, the next she would be putting her hands down his pants as if she owned everything about him.

His first date had been with a girl who was popular with the guys because she'd put out anytime, anywhere. But that night, when it had come time to stick it in her, he'd shriveled up just like the day his mother had put her hands down his pants. And the girl had laughed at him. Just like his mother.

Whores. They were all whores. That was the reason. Men paid his mother for sex. Not much anymore, but occasionally an old customer came around. And he would wonder, *Are you my father? You ugly son of a bitch.*

He would remind himself, reassure himself, that he couldn't have come from her.

What he needed was someone who wasn't a whore. Someone who was clean and pure and virginal.

Ivy Dunlap.

The name sprang into his mind.

He was halfway there, because she was already interested in him.

It had been easy to find out her name.

All he had to do was follow her home from police headquarters. Inside the lobby of her apartment building, he'd watched her get her mail, taking note of the box number that matched her apartment number. All he had to do was find her name on the security panel near the locked double doors.

Ivy Dunlap.

After that, he'd gone home and done a search on his computer, not expecting to find anything, thinking he'd have to use other avenues, other connections, other resources. Instead, he immediately found out that Ivy Dunlap had written a book. *Symbolic Death: Inside the Mind of a Serial Killer.*

He'd ordered the book off the Internet, wondering why he hadn't heard of it. He thought he'd read every serial-killer book that had been published. With a little more digging, he discovered that the book hadn't had a national release, and that it had been printed by an obscure press in Canada. So. Ivy Dunlap was from Canada. They had brought her in to catch him.

He found that extremely funny. Extremely satisfying.

The phone rang. He picked it up before the first ring stopped. It was Dr. Mathias.

"I've had something come up," Dr. Mathias said. "I'm going to have to reschedule this week's appointment."

"Since I'm doing so well, maybe we could just skip it."

"Are you taking your medication? You know how important that is."

"I'm taking it."

A lie. He hadn't taken it for two months. Funny that Dr. Mathias hadn't noticed anything different about him on their last visit. But then Mathias was always preoccupied, thinking about golf and his expensive girlfriend.

"Then we'll just skip this month," Dr. Mathias said as if his mind had been probed and his thoughts manipulated. The Manipulator. Maybe that's what he would call himself from now on. Gosh, but he'd always hated being called the Madonna Murderer. The Manipulator. With a capital M. He liked that. Manipulator of the Mind. M.M.

"Would you mind if we started meeting on the twenty-second of the month instead of the thirteenth?" the Manipulator asked.

"The twenty-second?" Dr. Mathias questioned in that vague way of his. "I don't see why not. I'll have Irene pencil you in."

The Manipulator picked up a snow globe and shook it. "Super," he said, watching the flakes of snow fall gently on the mother and her infant son.

Yesterday he'd driven to Max Irving's house. He'd parked his car a block away and sat there, drinking pop and waiting. Ethan Irving had finally come out and he'd followed him to a record shop in a strip mall. He'd followed him inside and taken note of the CDs he examined and the purchases he made. Now he knew what the kid liked; with the help of the Internet, he could study up on it.

An interesting kid. A nice-looking kid.

He hoped the rain stopped soon. He had a hockey game to go to.

Chapter 22

Ethan's day had started out bad and kept getting worse. First of all, someone outbid him on the *Plantations of Pale Pink* Guided by Voices seven-inch auctioned on eBay. That kind of find didn't come along that often. Shit, there were only a few thousand made. Then his dad had called to tell him he wouldn't be able to take him to his hockey game. So even though Ethan was old enough to drive, he had to bum a ride, which made him feel about twelve years old. He and his dad had been getting along pretty well lately, so why wouldn't he let him use the car? Why was he still hiding the keys?

Ethan and his team members were warming up on the ice, slapping pucks back and forth. Ethan caught a flying puck in his gloved hand, then dropped it near his feet. Using his stick, he played with it a little, moving it back and forth in front of him, then he shot it back to his teammate Ryan.

The other crappy thing that had happened was that he'd found out he'd been adopted not once, like he'd always thought, but twice. A place on the Internet said they could find a person's natural parents, so

Ethan had paid them two hundred bucks to discover that his mother—or the woman he'd always thought was his mother—had *also* adopted him. Now, if he wanted to go back any further, he had to pay another two hundred bucks.

Maybe it was a scam. Maybe the whole thing was a lie. Maybe they told everybody the same story so they could get more money out of them. His friend Jake had tried to get a fake driver's license off the Internet. He got a passport photo taken and gave the guy all the info he wanted on his card, along with a hundred bucks. Jake hadn't wanted the ID to drink. He'd wanted it to get into an over-21 concert. Why did bands do that? Play someplace where half their fans couldn't go? Maybe they didn't want teenyboppers hanging around, acting stupid. Yeah, that was probably it. But anyway, Jake got ripped off. Jake had told the guy he needed it in time to go to the concert, and the guy had told him that was cool, not to worry. Jake bought his ticket, then waited and waited, but the ID never showed up.

People could be such assholes.

Ethan figured the guy doing the scamming was some fat hillbilly with a Confederate flag hanging in the back window of his pickup, thinking it served the kid right for trying to get a fake ID. He was probably sitting around scratching his belly, laughing about it with a mouthful of rotten teeth.

Ethan signaled to Ryan that he wanted to quit with the puck and just skate. He was getting a weird edge on his right blade, but Casey, the only guy who really knew how to sharpen hockey skates, wasn't at the rink that night.

The whistle blew and everybody gathered up the scattered pucks and skated in. Ethan scanned the bleachers.

No Max.

Suddenly Ethan didn't feel like skating. He didn't feel like playing.

He knew Max was working on some headache of a case, but Max was always working on a headache of a case. His not showing up was just one more sign that he really didn't care, that Ethan was really no more than a pain in the ass. Max was just too nice to say so to his face.

No matter how you looked at it, life sucked.

Ethan's present frame of mind didn't do the game any good. He missed some easy plays, broke his best stick, and ended up in the penalty box two times for hooking and high-sticking before the coach took him out completely. That night's game was part of a summer-league tournament, not as important as school-year games, but still important. And the coach used the summer games to determine his school-season lineup.

"What's wrong with you?" Ryan asked as Ethan dropped down on the bench and pulled off his helmet. He wiped at the sweat pouring off his head. "Are you sick or something?"

"My skates are dull," Ethan said. "The blades kept slipping out from under me."

"Better get them sharpened before the next game."

"Yeah, I know."

He was just going to come out and ask Max about the adoption thing. Max would be pissed to know he'd gone behind his back, but Ethan had to know.

He got to his feet. "I'm going to change."

"Coach won't want you to leave."

Yeah, the coach liked you to stay on the bleachers whether you were playing or not. But Ethan wanted to get into dry clothes. "I gotta piss."

"Okay, bud."

Ethan neatly sidestepped Ryan's hand. "Don't hit me on the ass. You know I hate that." He was heading to the lockers when an unfamiliar voice said, "Tough game."

He looked over to see a dark-haired man of about forty standing near the locker-room entrance, his arms crossed at his chest. Was he somebody Ethan was supposed to know? Somebody's dad? Or somebody who knew or worked with Max?

"I don't know what was wrong with me," Ethan said.

"That's the way it goes. There'll be other games."

"Oh, yeah," Ethan said absentmindedly, wishing the guy would shut up. He didn't feel like making small talk with somebody he was probably supposed to know but couldn't place.

"Even Gretzky had bad nights. Says it's part of the game."

"Are you a personal friend of Wayne Gretzky?" Ethan asked sarcastically.

Wayne Gretzky was Ethan's hero. Max had promised to take Ethan to the Hockey Hall of Fame in Toronto, the city where Gretzky began his career. Ethan still wanted to go, but not with Max.

"I don't know him, but I've seen him play a few times," the guy said. "Ran into him after a game and he talked to me like we were buddies."

"Yeah, I'll bet he did." The guy was full of shit.

"Too bad your dad couldn't make it to the game tonight."

So he *was* some buddy of his dad's.

"But your dad's job is important. Really important."

"It doesn't matter if he's at the game or not."

"Need a ride home?"

"No. No thanks. I'm riding with a friend."

"Just thought I'd make the offer. Want me to throw that away for you?" he asked, indicating the broken stick Ethan held in his hand.

"Sure." Ethan handed him the hockey stick and headed into the locker room, not giving the guy another thought.

Chapter 23

Max pushed the mouse across the mousepad, clicking on a site called Tattoos, Tattoo, Tattoos. While waiting for the page to download, he took a bite of his ham and cheese on rye.

He and Ivy were sitting in his office, the wet black umbrella they'd shared propped against the wall, dripping water on the floor. Ivy had pulled up a chair near the corner of the desk. He could hear the crinkle of her sandwich wrapper and smell her almond cappuccino.

"How's your sandwich?" he asked absently while clicking on an icon labeled "traditional tattoos."

"Great," she said around a mouthful of food. "I was starving."

She'd gotten the house vegetarian with sprouts, tomatoes, black olives, mushrooms, and cranberries, hold the onions. Apparently his post-hypnotic relaxation suggestion had worked. In fact, *he* was more traumatized by the hypnosis than she was.

He typed the word *mother* in the search box. "Okay, here we go," he said as pictures began to appear.

He kept his eyes directed at the screen. "Didn't know there were so many MOTHER tattoos."

Ivy got up and moved closer, bending so she could see the screen. "There," she said, pointing a finger with the hand that held the cappuccino. "That's it."

He clicked on the small photo; an enlargement quickly filled the screen. "You sure?"

"That's it, exactly." Not a shred of doubt.

Couldn't sound more certain than that. He saved the photo to disk, then printed out a handful of copies. "We'll have the photo lab put together what we need for the media while I work on getting approval to run it in the papers and on TV. We'll also get a copy to David Scott so he can run it through the FBI's tattoo database."

"How are we going to explain the source of the information?"

She still didn't seem overly concerned. Maybe he should try hypnosis on himself.

He'd never had much faith in the power of hypnosis, but when he was in college he'd taken a course out of curiosity, then became involved in some experiments that led him to believe it could be a useful tool under the right conditions. But he'd never used it to keep his own head from exploding.

"We'll just say an eyewitness came forward, and for that eyewitness's safety we can't divulge the name," Max said.

"I think we should tell the rest of the team who I am. The secrecy is hindering the investigation."

Abraham had taken the news of Ivy's confession well. Rather than getting angry, as Max had expected, he'd seemed relieved that the secret was out.

"There are too many people involved. And people talk. It's human nature." He pulled up his address book on the screen, then put in a call to FBI Agent

Spence. When he didn't answer, Max punched in Mary Cantrell's number and quickly explained their strategy.

"You have to be aware that running the photo could trigger another killing," Agent Cantrell said. "On the other hand, I don't think you have any choice. The vigil didn't flush him out. The leads on stolen drugs were dead ends. I see the tattoo as the next step. Realizing that we have such knowledge about him could trick the killer into making a mistake. That's what we're after. A mistake. And so far he hasn't made any. But you need to protect your source. Don't let the witness's name get out, or his or her life will be in danger."

Conversation over. Max hung up and glanced at Ivy, who was sipping her coffee, staring at the tattoo printout in her hand.

Two days later the photo of the tattoo ran in the Chicago papers and made national television news. A couple of matches were found in the FBI tattoo database, but one of the guys ended up being dead, the other in prison.

Task-force members hit the streets, checking out every tattoo parlor in a six-county area.

"Seen anybody with a tattoo like this?" Ronny Ramirez stuck a five-by-seven photo under the tattoo artist's nose.

The guy was a biker, with long blond hair pulled back in a ponytail and arms covered with tattoos, some good, some bad. He shook his head. "Nobody gets those kind of tattoos anymore, man. I've never even done a tattoo like that."

Regina Hastings pulled her gaze away from a glass

display case of body-piercing jewelry. "We don't want to know if you've done one, we want to know if anybody's come in wanting you to change one into something else. You do that, don't you? Change tattoos so they look like something completely different?"

"Yeah. Sure. We even do it free sometimes for kids who want to get out of gangs. But I ain't seen one of these in years." He tried to hand the photo back.

"Keep it," Ronny said. "And if somebody does show up with that kind of tattoo, don't say anything to him. Just call this number." He handed him a card with the number of the direct line to the task-force office.

"Homicide, huh? What'd this guy do? Kill somebody?"

It was obvious the tattoo artist didn't want to rat on one of his own.

"He's killed a lot of people," Ramirez said. "He's killed babies."

"Oh, fuck me." The guy stuck the card in the pocket of his black leather vest, then patted it. "If he comes around here I'll give him a tattoo with an HIV-infected needle."

"Just give us a call instead," Hastings said dryly.

"Ten down, fifteen to go," Hastings said four hours later, crossing A Good Poke off their list. "That's just metro Chicago. I didn't know there were so many tattoo parlors around."

"You got any tattoos?" Ronny asked, shooting a glance in her direction as he pulled out of the parking lot.

"You'll never know the answer to that one. Turn right, next block."

"Tell me." He stopped at a red light. "Why'd we only go out one time? I forget."

"Because I found out you were an asshole."

"Oh. Oh, yeah."

"Are you admitting it?" she asked, amazed.

He made the right turn and they rode in silence for a couple more blocks. "I don't like to be laughed at," he finally said.

"Who does? But when something's funny, I laugh. That's the way I am."

"Guess that explains why I dumped you."

"*I* dumped *you.*"

"I dumped *you.*"

She laughed.

"Don't laugh at me."

"Asshole."

"Come on, Hastings. I just tried to apologize, and you keep calling me names."

"Okay, okay."

"How about going out again?"

"It would be a waste of our time."

"How's that?"

"As you know, I don't do it on the first date. I don't do it on the second either. Or the third."

"How about the fourth?"

"You're so full of yourself. For me, sex has to mean something. I have to feel something for the guy. I don't see it as simply recreation."

"I think the same way."

"That's bullshit. You have a reputation, Ramirez. And it ain't a good one."

"Don't say ain't."

"I was making a point. And anyway, we shouldn't be talking about this now. Not when we're on duty."

"Are you a virgin?" he asked, suddenly sounding enlightened.

"Nope."

"Sure?"

"Positive."

"Start young? With sex, I mean."

"When I was fourteen I was raped, beaten, and left for dead. So yeah, you could say I started young."

That shut him up.

Some so-called musicians were so stupid they couldn't read music. Because of their stupidity, he spent hours listening to cassettes of their songs, transcribing it to notes so other idiots could play the exact same tripe. He'd transcribed some big names. The money wasn't great, but it allowed him more time to himself, less time having to wear his social mask.

When he was little, other kids picked on him. They used to steal his lunch and steal his money—when he had any—and steal his clothes. Not because they wanted them. They weren't anything anybody would want; they did it just to be mean. His mother had tried to get him to fight back, taunting him with the same words the kids used, words like *chicken, sissy, baby*. Later, those words evolved, became more cutting. Then he was called queer and faggot and pussy. He didn't like guys.

He didn't know why everybody thought he liked guys. But he didn't like girls either. He hated everybody equally.

Above his head, he could hear his mother's snores. She was sleeping like a baby.

She was building up a tolerance to the drugs, but she should still remain asleep a couple more hours. Yesterday she'd given him a heart attack by waking up unexpectedly, so he'd upped her dosage again.

She'd sued somebody once. That's how she'd gotten

the house. She'd been drunk, coming out of a bar, when she fell and broke her leg—that time in four places. It had been a compound fracture that had required surgery and metal pins. She sued the owner of the bar, and ever since she'd just sat around watching TV all day, getting loaded.

But he had bigger things on his mind than his mother.

At exactly 6:00 P.M., he shut off the cassette player and pulled the headphones down so they rested around his neck. Then he turned on the local news. He always gave the news his undivided attention.

He always hoped to be the lead story, but unfortunately that rarely happened. Usually the reports about him were buried by the media, world happenings taking precedence over his cleansings. Gosh, but that was frustrating.

Tonight was different.

Tonight was his night.

The blond female newscaster sat at her sprawling studio desk, a fake Chicago skyline behind her. The camera moved in close so her entire face filled the screen. She was beautiful in a doll-like way, and her makeup and hair were perfect, her pearl necklace both seductive and sterile.

"The Chicago Police Department is asking citizens for help in finding the perpetrator of the two mother and son slayings that have recently occurred in the Chicago metro area. Although the killer's identity is yet unknown, he is believed to have a rose tattoo on his forearm."

The camera cut away and the newscaster's image was replaced by that of a rose tattoo with the word *mother* floating across it.

"If you know anyone with this type of tattoo, or know anyone who has had a similar tattoo in the past, please contact the Chicago Police Department. As an added note, the police request that you do not approach this person yourself. Instead, please call the number on the screen."

Adrenaline roared through his veins. A lead. After all these years, they had a lead. It was exciting. Exhilarating. He dropped to his knees and covered his mouth with both hands, trapping the sound of his laughter.

His heart was thumping erratically.

His thoughts were tangled.

How had they known about the tattoo?

How did anybody know?

Think. Think.

The only person who could possibly have connected it to the Madonna Murderer was Claudia Reynolds, the whore who'd lived long enough to talk to the police. But *if* she'd seen his tattoo, why hadn't her knowledge of it come out sixteen years ago?

No. It had to be something that had recently come to light.

Think, think.

Ivy Dunlap.

He didn't know why her name sprang into his head, but it did. Why was she involved in the case?

The answer was there somewhere. He just had to find it. He just had to figure it out. And he would. He was clever. He was smart.

He scrambled to his feet and opened the locker, quickly removing the combination lock. Then he carefully lifted a shoe box from the top shelf. Sitting back on his bed, he removed the lid. Inside was a blue baby blanket. He pulled out the blanket, then unwrapped the item inside, holding it up to the light.

He didn't know why he'd gotten the tattoo in the first place. He guessed it had been his last attempt to please the cow upstairs. But it hadn't pleased her. Not at all. She'd taken one look at him, grunted, and said she hoped he hadn't paid money for it.

It had actually felt good to cut it out, to remove it from his body. Afterwards, when the blood was pouring down his arm, dripping off his fingertips, he'd thought about chopping up the tattoo. Maybe putting it in spaghetti sauce and serving it to the bitch. But that hadn't seemed right. So he'd dropped it into a jar of formaldehyde. He didn't know what he was going to do with it, but he was sure something would come along.

Chapter 24

Max pulled into his driveway, hoping to find Ethan at home the way he was supposed to be. He didn't like thinking of his son in terms of what he might do next, but when Ethan had already pulled so many stunts it was hard not to dwell on the negative.

Using the remote, he opened the garage door, slipped inside, and parked, shutting the door behind him and cutting the engine.

It had been a week since the tattoo story and photo had run in newspapers and on TV. So far, nothing. Max was even beginning to doubt the authenticity of the tattoo. Not that he thought Ivy was lying, but maybe she was so desperate to come up with a clue that her subconscious had produced one. How had she seen a tattoo and not the killer's face? And why would his face be hidden if he'd planned to kill her?

The manager at Ivy's old apartment hadn't been able to come up with the name of the person who'd wanted to rent room 283, and while the investigation into the drug thefts had garnered them a few arrests, nothing pointed to anything other than kids wanting to get high on a very dangerous substance.

Yesterday a small group had begun to picket Police

Headquarters, carrying signs that said: PROTECT OUR CHILDREN. PROTECT OUR MOTHERS. No big surprise that they made the front page of the *Herald*. Abraham had been delighted as hell about that.

Everyone in the task force was exhausted, so Max had told them to go home early and get a good night's sleep.

A good night's sleep. He couldn't remember what that was like. He hadn't had a good night's sleep in years.

The door between the garage and kitchen was unlocked.

One of the rules was to always lock the doors. Max tossed his keys down on the kitchen table. Maybe they should order a pizza. He got a beer out of the refrigerator, unscrewed the cap, and took a long drink.

No music.

He just realized there was no music playing. Whenever Ethan was home alone, he cranked up his stereo so high that the bass rattled the windows. Max put the beer on the table, then hurried down the hall to Ethan's room. He pounded on the closed door. When there was no answer, he opened it.

Ethan was in bed.

Ethan wasn't alone.

A girl shrieked and pulled the covers over her jet-black hair.

The needle on the record player had long ago reached the end of the album and it filled the room with a metered, *tick, tick, tick*.

"What are you doing here?" Ethan demanded.

"I live here, remember?"

Even though it was still light outside, the room was dark. A red lava lamp bubbled in the corner, along with burning incense that failed to mask the smell of pot.

Max's thoughts scurried along, wondering how best to handle the situation. Things were easier when Dr. Spock could be consulted, but after a kid reached age twelve, you were on your own. You wouldn't find *pot smoking* or *sex* next to *diaper rash.*

But Ethan was a good kid, a smart kid, and Max couldn't help but take part of the blame for the problems they were having. He wasn't around enough. At a time when Ethan thought he was an adult who didn't need to answer to anybody, Max was working too many tough cases that often required late hours.

His mind went down a familiar path: He should quit Homicide. He should get another job. What? Police training? He would qualify for that. Private detective? That might give him time off between jobs, but he'd still put in long days when working a case.

"I'm going to go take a shower," he said. "And when I'm done, we're going to talk." Max stepped back and closed the door.

Ethan's rigid body relaxed. "Son of a bitch."

From beneath the covers came a stoned giggle. Heather stuck out her head. "I thought you said your dad wouldn't be home until the middle of the night. Do you think he recognized me? Will he tell my parents?"

"Last time he saw you, you had blond hair. Anyway, even if he did recognize you, he probably wouldn't say anything."

"Your dad is so cool."

"You won't think he's cool in about ten minutes.

Hurry and get your shirt on and get the hell out of here."

Ethan hated to think of her leaving, hated to think of facing Max's wrath by himself, but it wasn't any of Heather's business. This was private stuff. Family stuff. Getting-grounded-until-he-was-eighteen stuff.

With total lack of modesty, Heather stood and put on her bra and shirt.

She'd been hanging around a lot lately, and earlier that day she'd confessed that she liked him and wondered if he wanted to get stoned and make out—an offer that had both thrilled and scared him. At some point during the last hour, she'd voluntarily removed her bra and shirt. He was wondering if she expected him to go all the way, wondered if he *wanted* to go all the way, when his dad had shown up.

Ethan figured that for Heather sex was a newly discovered obsession, like someone else hearing the Pixies for the first time, then going out and getting their hands on every one of their CDs. Which was a hard thing to do, Ethan knew, because there had been so many EPs and b-sides released, not to mention all the bootlegs.

"Well, bye," Heather said.

He just realized how fucked up he was. His mind had gone off on some Pixies tangent when he should have been thinking about how to best face his dad. He thought regretfully about how good her skin had felt pressed to his, how great she'd smelled. "Yeah, bye."

"Hope you don't get in too much trouble."

Ethan thought he heard the shower shut off. He motioned for her to leave, flapping his hand in the direction of the door. "Go! Go!"

After she left, he put on his shirt and opened a window, hoping his dad hadn't been able to detect anything other than incense. Then he grabbed the Visine and put several drops in each eye, the excess running down his face. Why the hell had Max come home early tonight? It wasn't like he spent every night rolling around in his bed with Heather Green.

Thinking about his old man barging in on them, he giggled, then pressed a hand to his mouth. *Stop it.* He had to think. *Defense is the best offense. Defense is the best offense. . . .*

Max wasn't even sure Ethan would still be around when he finished his shower. But surprisingly, he was. Max found him sitting at the kitchen table. Barefoot. Wearing baggy cargo pants and a black Stereolab T-shirt. His arms were crossed, and he was the one who looked pissed.

"I hope to hell you were using a condom," Max said.

Ethan didn't answer.

"Were you?"

Ethan squirmed a little. "I would have . . . if we'd gotten to that point."

"Do you expect me to believe that's the first time this has happened?"

Now was when he was supposed to use a line like, I wasn't born yesterday.

Max was about to start in on Ethan's pot smoking when Ethan stopped him cold.

"I want to know about my mom. My real mom. And my real dad."

Max stalled. "What do you mean?"

"I mean, I found out Cecilia wasn't my real mom."

Ethan got a stricken look on his face, and when he continued talking, his lips and voice shook. But he kept going, getting all the words out. "I found out *she* adopted me. Is that true?"

So many times Max had envisioned telling Ethan about his past, his mother, but the right time had never seemed to come along. First he was too young. Then, suddenly he was too old; the lie that wasn't really a lie had gone on too long.

But somehow he'd found out.

Ethan fiddled with the Velcro of his pants' pocket. "There's this place on the Internet where they find your real parents."

Max felt an overwhelming sense of loss. *Ethan.* He loved his son. Loved him every bit as much or more than his biological father ever could. Didn't he? Because how could one's heart feel any fuller? But Max also knew that they'd been moving toward this point for thirteen years. With Max trying to hang on and Ethan trying to get loose.

When Ethan was little, one of his favorite books was *The Runaway Bunny.* He especially liked the part about the mother bunny finding her baby wherever he went, no matter how lost he was, or how far away he wandered.

Barefoot, wearing a white T-shirt and gray jogging pants, Max pulled out a chair and sat down.

"Why'd you adopt me?" Ethan asked, staring at him with bravery and a trembling lip.

"I adopted you because I wanted you."

"I don't believe you. You adopted me because Cecilia begged you to, didn't you?"

Max's heart seemed to stop beating. Who had Ethan been talking to? Who had told him such a cruel truth?

Was this what had been driving Ethan? Thinking that Max didn't want him? Didn't love him?

"I always knew you hadn't known my mother very long. And when I got older, I started wondering why you adopted me in the first place. Then Simon down the street told me that his mother told him it was because Cecilia had begged you to, that she wanted to find me a father before she died. Is that true? I can tell by your face that it is."

Simon's mother, Isabelle, baby-sat Ethan after they moved to the suburbs. It had been the perfect setup, since she was so close and also watched several other neighborhood kids. Isabelle didn't have a lot of excitement in her life, and she stirred up trouble wherever she could. She'd been guilty of planting the seed of many squabbles between adults as well as juveniles.

"When I met your mother, she was dying and didn't have anywhere to go," Max said quietly. "I only knew her a short time, but she was one of the bravest women I've ever known and I fell in love with her in an almost spiritual way. She was honest with me and told me right out that she was looking for someone to take care of you. She went shopping for a father, and I never quite understood why, but she picked me. When she told me of her plan, I ran like hell, but then I went back. She was almost out of money and she was dying with nowhere to go, so I brought you both home with me."

"Who's my real mother? *Where's* my real mother?"

"Cecilia had a friend who became pregnant. Cecilia couldn't have children of her own, so she adopted you."

"Do you know anything about my real parents?"

Real, real, real. Max wished he'd quit saying that. "Cecilia said your mother was a college student when she had you—that's all I know. She never mentioned the father."

Max could see by his eyes that he was losing him. Ethan was imagining a talented mother, a brilliant father. How could he get through to him? How could he make him see how much he meant to him? How could he possibly make him believe it?

"My whole life has been a lie."

"It hasn't. There isn't anything false about it. I'm your father. You're my son."

"Cecilia wasn't my real mother. How do you think that makes me feel, finding that out? And how do you think it makes me feel, finding out I'm just another one of your charity cases? Some orphan you dragged in and had to take care of? I don't have any brothers or sisters, I don't have a mother, and now I find out I don't really have a father either. When I was little, and you used to carry me around on your shoulder— who were you carrying? Your son? Or the kid a dying woman made you take? When I was little and you bought me a cop costume and took me trick-or-treating—who did you take? Your son? Or a welfare case? And when you taught me to skate—who were you teaching? Your son? Or the kid you felt duty-bound to take in? Can't you see what I mean? My whole fucking life has been a lie!"

He ran from the room, into his bedroom, slamming the door.

Max followed and found him facedown on the bed, sobbing into a pillow. A man, and a child. Suddenly Max recalled a scene of ten years ago, when Ethan had come home crying because an older child had stolen his Scooby-Doo backpack on the first day of school.

Ten years . . .

So much could change in ten years. Ethan had been a child then, crying a child's tears. Now he was almost a man. In two more years, he would be old enough to vote and go to war. In two more years, he would be old enough to leave if he wanted to.

Max knew Ethan didn't want to be seen crying, and Max wanted to respect his privacy, but he couldn't let the evening end like this, not without telling his son one final thing, the unabashed, unvarnished truth.

"I adopted you because Cecilia begged me to," Max said from the doorway. "But sometimes fortune falls on those who least expect it. I'm one of those people. You brought something into my life that had been lacking. You are my son. I love you more than I can ever say. And I can't begin to comprehend how empty my life would be without you in it."

Chapter 25

Ivy often dreamed of the night she was attacked. But now, ever since visiting her old apartment, she relived that attack two, often three times a night. And every time the dream was the same, and every time it was different. Always painful, always brutal and smothering and real.

Every night, she told herself it was a dream. Only a dream.

But the music. It sounds so real. Right outside the door.

It's only the people downstairs.

And the sound of someone breathing, right beside my ear?

Only Jinx.

The smells.

Just this old place.

But the music. It sounds so real.

Right outside the door.

Open your eyes. Open your eyes and the dream will end.

In the dream, she opened her eyes. And discovered she was still dreaming.

Open your eyes, and you'll see that it's just a dream.

Like a swimmer surfacing from a deep dive, she kicked her feet and swam up, up, up to the top.

She opened her eyes.

Slices of light from the street cut in around the window shade, creating geometric patterns of light and dark that fell across walls and floor.

With one foot still firmly in the dreamscape, she thought, *Something here is strange. Something is not quite right.*

The music.

The music was still playing. Tinny notes. Just the melody, sounding as if it were coming from a miniature music box.

Hush little baby, don't say a word.
Mamma's gonna buy you a mockingbird,
If that mockingbird don't sing,
Mamma's gonna buy you a diamond ring.

Gasping, Ivy shot upright, fully awake now.

Jesus. She put a hand to her chest, grasping for a cross that wasn't there.

Who was doing that? Where was it coming from?

Outside her room.

She tossed back the covers and got to her feet. Without turning on a light, her eyes accustomed to the dark, she moved in the direction of the now fading notes. Through the kitchen, to the locked door.

Abruptly, the music stopped.

She looked at the doorknob. Jinx's collar was still there where she'd hung it.

She wrapped her hand around the bell so it wouldn't make any noise. Carefully, slowly, she unlocked the dead bolt, pulling open the door until the chain caught.

Nothing. Nobody.

She waited.

She listened.

Then she silently undid the chain . . . and opened the door several more inches.

Nobody.

No one.

She let out a gasping breath, aware of the frantic *lub, lub, lub* of her heart. Behind her, Jinx meowed a question.

She was beginning to think she'd imagined the whole thing when a final crystal-clear note rang out. She sucked in a new breath, her gaze pulled from the winding flight of stairs to drop to the floor in front of her.

There, just outside her door, was a snow-globe music box.

A multitude of possibilities collided in her brain. Was this a sick joke?

Had the Madonna Murderer left it?

If so, why had he singled her out?

Did he know who she really was?

Was he still in the building?

The last thought had her slamming the door, locking the locks, appalled at herself for having opened the door in the first place. Then she rushed to the phone and called Max.

He answered on the second ring, his voice groggy. "Irving," he mumbled.

Gripping the receiver in both hands, Ivy's words tumbled out. "Max. The Madonna Murderer may have just been here. You need to set up a perimeter around my apartment building."

"Tell me what happened." Now his voice was clear, alert. "Slowly."

She told him about the snow globe.

"Did you see anyone? Hear anyone?"

"No. Just the music playing."

"Are you calling from your apartment now?" A cautious question, containing components of his immediate concern mixed with a need to keep her calm.

"Yes."

"Are you sure he's not in there?"

"In my apartment?"

She looked over at Jinx, who was washing his face. Jinx would be acting weird if anyone else were there. "He's not here . . . but I don't know about the rest of the building."

"Lock the door and stay where you are. I'll be there as soon as I can."

He hung up.

Ivy gazed around her.

What if the person who'd left the box *was* still in the building? What if he came back and retrieved his "gift"? Then there would be no evidence.

You have to go out there.

You have to go out and get it.

No. Wait for Max. I'll wait for Max.

It might be gone by then. He might come back and get it, and the evidence will be gone.

Ivy flipped on the kitchen light. From a drawer, she dug out a package of yellow cleaning gloves. She ripped open the package and put on the gloves. Then she unlocked the door again.

The globe was still there.

The hallway was still empty.

Shaking, her heart thundering so loudly in her ears that she could hear nothing else, she picked up the globe, careful to touch it in only two small places with a fingertip and a thumb. Back inside, she quickly relocked the door and leaned weakly against it, her chest heaving. Finally, when she'd calmed down enough, she looked at the object in her hands. With the illumination of the kitchen light, she could now see the interior of the globe.

What the—?

She frowned and lifted it closer to her face.

Inside with the swirling snow floated a thick piece of something tan in color.

What the—?

The object was water-saturated, the edges ragged and fluttering. She could see holes. Then she realized there were straight black hairs poking out from the holes, which weren't holes at all; they were *pores*.

She let out a little yelp and almost dropped the globe.

Pores.

Across the surface was a rose, and a banner that said MOTHER.

Chapter 26

By the time Max reached Ivy's, the perimeter had been established; there were two squad cars at the scene plus the crime technician's van. Outside the apartment building things were quiet, but inside was pandemonium. People in all stages of undress clogged the hallways, demanding to know what was happening while the police tried to calm them.

The apartment manager ran up to Max. "What's going on here?" He wore boxer shorts and a white tank top stretched across his belly. "I don't want to lose my job over this. You vouched for that woman. I wouldn't have leased the place to her if I knew she was going to be trouble. My tenants expect to be safe here."

"Mr. . . ." Max searched his brain for a name.

"Hoffman."

"Mr. Hoffman, let's try to stay focused on our main concern. Who else might have access to this building other than the tenants?"

"Nobody."

"What about newspaper delivery?"

"The papers are left in the lobby and a guy on the first floor delivers them."

"What about painters? Repairmen? Exterminators?"

"Well. Yeah, sometimes I give people like that a key."

"Get me a list of names." Then to a nearby officer, Max said, "Get a team to make a sweep of the building, make sure nobody's hiding anywhere." The officer nodded, then Max was moving through the crowd, hurrying up the stairs to Ivy's apartment.

When he got there, Ivy was standing near the kitchen sink holding her cat in her arms. Two technicians, white masks around their necks, were staring at an object on the table.

A snow globe.

"You gotta see this," said one of the techs.

"Oh, yeah," his partner agreed, nodding as he kept his gaze locked on the globe.

Max moved closer. Then closer, for a better look. Finally he straightened. "Is that real?"

"We don't know. Have to get it to the crime lab."

"Is that formaldehyde I smell?"

"Oh, yeah."

Max shook his head. "Do you mean to tell me that crazy son of a bitch cut a chunk out of his own arm?"

"A little present for me," Ivy said.

He stared at her for a moment. She didn't look too shaken, all things considered. When their eyes met, their thoughts collided somewhere in the center of the room, asking a question they couldn't speak aloud.

Why did he single me out?

Why did he single you out?

Max forced his gaze away from hers. "Prints?" he asked.

"Nothing on the globe. We're going to do the door

and hallway, but with so many people living in this building it'll be tough to come up with anything. But if the tattoo is real, there's a remote chance the lab might be able to extract DNA."

"Guess we got his attention," Ivy said.

Her cat meowed and squirmed, then jumped from her arms, its feet thudding on the floor, and ran to hide under the bed. "Now we know he reads the paper or watches the news."

What were they going to do with Ivy Dunlap? he wondered. And what did this mean? Had the killer figured out who she was? Or had he singled her out simply because she was involved in the investigation? He had an old habit of leaving small gifts for people involved in the case.

Five minutes later, the crime technicians slid the globe into a paper bag and left the apartment. Ivy closed the door behind them.

Max ran his fingers through his hair. "This has certainly gone in a direction I wasn't expecting."

"I can already tell what you're thinking," she said, crossing her arms and leaning a hip against the kitchen counter. She wore a long T-shirt kind of thing—maybe something she slept in—with jeans pulled on underneath. Her feet were bare. A window air conditioner blasted tepid, stale air in his direction. "You're wondering how quickly you can get me on a plane out of here. No, we don't know why he singled me out. It could be he saw the picture in the paper. With a little investigating, he could have found out where I live."

Max was fried. Burnt-out. Exhausted to the point of stupor. He dropped down on one of the stools. Elbows on the table, he buried his face in his hands. "Shit. I can't pull my head together." He was beginning to understand why Abraham had aged so quickly while working on the Madonna Murderer case. Max was standing in quicksand and the sky was falling, all at the same time.

He felt her hand on his shoulder.

He looked up, startled by the contact.

"Want some coffee?" she asked, slowly pulling her hand away from what he now understood was merely a gesture of sympathy. Brothers in arms.

"What time is it?"

"A little after four."

He should call Ethan. He would in a minute. "Do you have a gun?"

"I asked if you wanted coffee."

He looked up at her. "Do you have a gun?"

"No."

"Do you know how to use a gun?"

"I learned several years ago."

"We'll get you a gun. What about a mobile phone? Do you have a mobile phone?"

"No."

"We'll get you a phone too."

She poured a cup of coffee and placed it in front of him.

He took a drink. "We'll put twenty-four-hour sur-veillance on the building. Maybe a cop in your apartment."

"I don't want this to be about protecting me. I want it to be about catching him."

"We can do both at the same time."

"Thanks."

"For what?"

"For not immediately telling me you're going to send me home."

"You can fight with Abraham about that. And besides, whatever the Madonna Murderer knows about you—whether you're Ivy Dunlap to him or Claudia Reynolds—you're still our best chance to catch this guy. Tonight proves that." He was quiet a minute. "How did he get into the building?"

"Anybody can get in the building if they wait at the door long enough. I have people let me in all the time."

"At three in the morning?"

"Could he be a tenant? That would be a helluva coincidence."

"We'll get Mr. Hoffman downstairs to give us the tenant list. I think that'll prove to be a dead end."

"Maybe he got in the building earlier in the day, then waited."

"Hid in a stairwell or something."

"Yeah."

"That seems the most likely scenario. We'll have to interview everyone in the building."

"There are a hundred apartments in this building."

"Have a better idea?"

"No."

Max pulled out his mobile phone and called Ethan. "I'm not going to be home until tonight," he told him.

"What about my game?"

"You have a game? Where?"

"Home. At Cascade."

"Catch a ride with somebody. I'll try to get there, but I can't promise you anything." Max knew he probably wouldn't make it, but at least he'd know where Ethan was.

"What about finding my real parents? You said you'd help me with that."

The kid was breaking his heart and didn't even know it. "I will."

"When?"

"Soon." Max told him good-bye and hung up, slipping the phone back in his pocket. "You were right about Ethan's problems being more than simple teenage angst," he told Ivy.

"You talked to him?"

"Yeah." Max let out a sigh. "He's suddenly decided that I don't love him, and wants to find his real parents." He elaborated on what he'd already told her about Cecilia, about Ethan being adopted not once, but twice.

"Do you know anything about his real parents?"

"Only that the mother was a friend of Cecilia's who had an unwanted pregnancy. I don't know anything about the father."

"You must have contacts the average person wouldn't have."

"What if his birth mother doesn't want anything to do with Ethan? I don't want him getting hurt. On the other hand—and I know I'm being selfish about this—what if she wants to see him?"

"Some children have an overwhelming need to know where they come from. I can understand your concern, but his birth mother could never replace you. You're his father. You're the one who has been there for him all these years. *You* are his past. *You* are his memories."

"What if his mother was a victim of rape? That happens more than you know. I wouldn't want Ethan to find out something like that."

She crossed her arms at her waist. "My grandmother would have said you're oversteering your headlights."

He looked up at her, and she could suddenly tell that he'd remembered her son, her murdered son.

"Christ, Ivy. I'm sorry. I shouldn't be talking to you about this."

"It's okay."

"I don't know what I was thinking."

"Do you know how nice it is that you *know* about my son? I've spent the last sixteen years lying to people about my past. Do you know how wonderful it is to hear about Ethan, to be able to say, I had a son too? And if he had lived, he would have been tall and strong, weak and wise. He would have needed me, and he would have pushed me away. Ever since he died, I've had to deny his existence. When people would ask me if I had children, I couldn't say I used to have a son. I had to say no. That hurt so much, to say no. And it created a wall between me and every single person I met. If I liked someone—male or female—I knew we could never be more than casual acquaintances, because my secret was too big. It was too much a part of everything I am, and I knew they would never be able to begin to know me without the knowledge of my past. I love to hear about Ethan. Because when you talk about him, when you tell me about the hardships of being a parent, I feel closer to the son I lost. So don't ever stop talking about him." Her voice caught, and she paused to collect herself. "Don't ever stop talking about him," she whispered.

He put his coffee cup aside and got to his feet. She thought he was leaving when he pulled her into his arms and held her close. Just held her, held her, held her.

Chapter 27

Darby Nichols tied her running shoes and headed out the door. She liked jogging early on Sunday mornings because everybody was still in bed. There wasn't much traffic, and there weren't many people cluttering the sidewalks, getting in the way, slowing her down. Come fall, Darby was going to be a high school senior, and she hoped to do well enough in track to get at least a partial sports scholarship. Her strength was distance running, and today it was her plan to go twelve miles.

The course she'd mapped out took her through several Chicago neighborhoods, shopping areas, a forest preserve, and two parks. A half-mile from her home, she hit Crocus Hill Park, one of her favorite areas. Pigeons fluttered out of her way, then settled again on the wide sidewalk with clucks of mild complaint. The air was thick with morning dew, and the sun was just beginning to warm her skin. She was young. She was healthy. She had her whole life ahead of her.

The sidewalk forked. She took the left path leading to a stone bridge that spanned a small pond where people gathered to feed the ducks. As she approached the bridge, her feet slapped a steady rhythm that seemed to coincide with her breathing and her heartbeat, a sound that put her in that slightly meditative state it took for her to make it the whole twelve miles.

Without conscious thought, her gaze locked on something in the distance. A splash of color against the more muted shades of nature.

Slap, slap, slap.

Her brain registered printed fabric. A discarded shirt? Dress? People could be such pigs.

As she drew nearer, she asked: A person? Sleeping in the park? A homeless person?

In Chicago, you saw a lot of homeless people. She'd learned not to look at them, not to make eye contact. Because even though she pitied them, and wished something could be done so they didn't have to live on the street, they also scared her. With their bold stares and the weird things they said that made her feel she should respond out of simple politeness. It was better not to look.

Finally she was upon the brightly colored fabric. Her legs slowed . . . and slowed . . . and slowed, until she was walking. Until she stopped dead.

She put a hand to her mouth. *"Oh my God."*

She turned and ran, her feet pounding against the sidewalk, her legs and arms and heart pumping madly. The park was a blur. Streets flashed by, the colors streaked like images caught in time lapse.

It seemed as though it took hours, but finally she was home. She pulled open the door to her house, her sanctuary, shouting for her mother, her voice wobbly and choked.

In an instant, her mother appeared at the top of the stairs wearing her sleep shirt with the pictures of stuffed bears, her processed hair sticking out all over, her mouth hanging open in fear. She and Darby had fought last night, arguing about something stupid. That was forgotten.

"Mom," Darby managed to gasp, her chest rising and falling. Her legs, legs that were used to running twelve miles, could hardly support her. "You have to call the police."

Her mother floated toward her, one hand on the railing, her mouth still open, her face a panic-filled question of wanting to know and not wanting to know. "W-what's wrong? Are you hurt? Did something happen?"

"Oh my God!" Darby burst into tears. "I think I found a dead person!"

She had purple butterfly barrettes in her hair.

That was what Ivy focused on. The butterfly barrettes, catching and reflecting the morning sunlight. All of the murders were horrendous acts of grotesque brutality, but why did it seem so much worse when they were staged in such an idyllic setting? The previous, more recent murders hadn't taken place in such a public place. More unusual was the fact that this baby was close to a year old.

The mother was beginning to draw flies.

Not houseflies. These were the heavy-bodied flies that laid eggs in dead things. Bloat flies. Maggots. One of the flies crawled across the victim's cheek, to the corner of one bulging eye, and stayed there awhile. For the fly, the body was simply a meal, simply a place to lay eggs that would turn into larvae, that would also feed until there was nothing left but fabric and bone, perhaps some hair. Perhaps some teeth. Everything had a purpose.

Another fly settled in the dried blood near the woman's nostril, then it took off and began to circle her mouth, which was taped into a smile, her swollen tongue protruding.

One arm was bent, a hand on her hip in that "come hither" pose the Madonna Murderer liked so much. Making a mockery of his victims. Her print dress had been cut almost completely off, her blood-soaked bra pulled down around her waist. Her panties were wrapped around one ankle, her spread knees bent, her vagina exposed to anyone who dared to look in her direction. Jammed deep inside her was the handle of a broken hockey stick. Across her abdomen were the usual multitude of knife wounds.

The police had cordoned off the area. Five squad cars were strategically placed, their lights flashing, dispatch radios squawking. An ambulance was parked at an angle, on a rolling incline, its back doors open while two attendants stood holding a gurney, waiting for the coroner and crime technicians to finish so they could bag the body and take it to the morgue.

Everybody had a purpose.

Outside the yellow crime-scene tape the press was accumulating, shutters whirring and video cameras rolling. The cover of tomorrow's *Herald* would most likely feature the body bag being wheeled into the ambulance. The headline would be something like, MADONNA MURDERER CLAIMS TWO MORE VICTIMS. And people would buy more weapons. They would put additional locks on their doors, and check them several times throughout the night. If they could afford it, they would have a security system installed.

And they would quit going for walks. And they would quit smiling and nodding at strangers. Because they would know that behind one of those responding smiles, a killer lurked.

People would talk about moving away, getting out of Chicago. But then they would read about a random murder in some small town of 350 people, and they would know that no place was safe. And so they would live their continuously more withdrawn, insulated lives, but they would not feel secure, not even in their own homes. And if they went somewhere—to a movie, out to eat—they would always be looking, always wondering. . . .

Max's mind must have been heading up the same path, because he said, "Even if we catch this guy, there will be another one out there. And another."

"You can't think about that," Ivy said.

He'd just finished taking Darby Nichols's statement, and during the entire procedure, he'd been cold and distant. When it was over, he'd handed her a card, saying, "There's a number of a psychologist you can call if you need to talk to anybody. It's free." He kind of smirked, mocking the fact that Chicago had hired a full-time psychologist whose only job was to deal with innocent people who'd come upon murder scenes.

Ivy had felt compelled to say something to the poor girl and her mother, offer them some measure of comfort. But what was there to say? In the end, she thanked them for their statements and finished with, "I'm so sorry this had to happen."

They stared at her with shocked faces, nodding mutely, and Ivy felt so incredibly sorry for them, because she knew they didn't yet know how this one incident would impact the rest of their lives. At the moment, it was still something that had happened that they needed to distance themselves from, something they thought they could forget, or at least put behind them. They didn't yet know that would never happen. They would never be able to distance themselves, to forget or put it behind them.

The baby had been found a few yards away, under the shelter of the stone bridge, his body wrapped in a baby blanket as blue as his face. On the blanket were pictures of frolicking lambs. Little lamb. Little innocent lamb. Not a mark on him. Next to him, on the ground, was the signature snow globe.

The technicians finished collecting site evidence. The gurney was brought in, the bodies tucked into black body bags. Soon there would be no sign of what had happened there. Soon children would be running, laughing, screaming, down the hill to the pond to feed the ducks.

Max was staring at the ambulance attendants, watching as one of them carried the baby to the ambulance, no need for a gurney.

"Let's go," Ivy said.

At first, he didn't seem to hear her. He just kept staring in the direction they'd taken the baby.

"Max?"

He seemed to come out of it, shaking off a trance. "Yeah, let's get the hell out of here."

It wasn't that simple. As soon as they reached the security tape, the press attacked. Cameras clicked. Microphones were jammed in his face. Fifteen questions were thrown at him at once, over and over.

"Who are the victims?"

"Was it the Madonna Murderer?"

"What are you doing to protect the citizens of Chicago?"

"What leads do you have?"

"Is the FBI involved?"

"If not, why not? Shouldn't they be?"

Without saying a word, Max pushed past them, parting the sea of people, Ivy following as the wave closed in behind her.

"A press release will be issued later today," Ivy said.

Five microphones were immediately shoved in her face. "Who are you, and what is your official involvement in this case?"

Chaos. Everybody was speaking at once. Ivy repeated her statement, then jumped in Max's car. He was already behind the wheel.

"You shouldn't have said anything," Max said, honking his horn as he slowly pulled away. Cameras were still clicking.

"Somebody had to say something. Of course, it should have been you rather than me. . . . That will make nice front-page fodder. You and I fleeing the scene."

"They know they're supposed to wait for a press conference or press release. Is nothing sacred? Jesus. They're like a bunch of tabloid paparazzi."

"Are you okay?"

"I don't know." He wrenched the steering wheel to the right. "What does a nervous breakdown feel like?"

"Maybe you should see somebody, talk to somebody."

"I'll be fine just as soon as we catch this son of a bitch."

The weight of the case was on his shoulders. He had the task force, he had the FBI, but he was in charge; he made the decisions.

"We're moving too slowly," he said.

"We have to move slowly, otherwise we might miss something."

He suddenly pulled over and stopped the car. He wiped his face, then stared straight ahead through the windshield. "It was the hockey stick," he finally said.

"He's never done that before. Do you think it has some significance, or was it simply the right tool for the job?"

He was quiet a moment, his breathing uneven, a little ragged, as if he were struggling for control. "Ethan plays hockey."

Christ. "Okay, let's suppose for a minute that there is a connection somehow. What's the message he's sending?"

"He's playing with our heads, that's what he's doing."

"He's also communicating in his own twisted way. He's letting us know that he's watching us. The hockey stick could be purely coincidence, but say it isn't. Then he's telling you he knows enough about you and your family to know that Ethan plays hockey."

Max pulled out his mobile phone and dialed. Moments later, he was speaking to his son. "Ethan? Yeah, I know it's early. Do you have practice today? A game? No, nothing's wrong. Okay, I'll pick you up when you get off work. Nine o'clock." He disconnected. "No practice, no game," he said, sounding relieved.

"I don't think he'd go after Ethan. It's not what he's about. Ethan is practically an adult, and he's

really after the mothers anyway. The children are
secondary."

"Logically, I know that. But I have this pain in my
chest and throat, and I just realized what it is. Fear.
In all the years I've been in this business, I've never
felt fear."

She could offer him no words of comfort. There was
no greater fear than the fear of a parent for a child.

Chapter 28

"Looks good, don't you think?"

Alex Martin sat at his desk, admiring his byline on page three of the *Chicago Herald*.

"Not bad," Maude agreed.

Was that a grudging agreement? Alex wondered. Was she toying with him? Maybe even teasing him a little? With Maude, it was hard to tell. She always had a hint of a smirk about her.

Alex had had a hard time convincing her to even run it past editorial, but she'd finally relented and once she made up her mind about something you were pretty much in. She'd been around so long, and her track record was so good, that no one argued when she pushed a piece, even one as unusual as Alex's.

Maude left, and he concentrated on the paper in his hands, reading his article for the third time. . . .

The newspaper was almost ripped from Ivy's hands as the Green Line train roared into the underground station, the noise deafening as the back draft tried to suck her closer to the narrow ledge.

The double doors opened and she stepped inside. There were two tone-dead *dings* before a prerecorded monotone male voice announced, "Doors closing. Next stop is Pulaski. Doors open on the right."

Ivy dropped into the nearest empty seat, quickly continuing with the newspaper article.

MADONNA MURDERER STRIKES AGAIN

Early Sunday morning the bodies of April and Joshua Rodrigez, a young mother and her one-year-old son, were found in Crocus Hill Park. When asked about the progress of the case, police refused comment. Investigators involved in the slayings include Ivy Dunlap, a Canadian academic with a degree in criminal psychology, and Detective Maxwell Irving, who heads the case. Detective Irving has an impressive list of solved cases to his credit, the most famous being the Roth Family Slayings, and the Child Welfare Poisonings.

An accompanying piece was titled: THE CHICAGO POLICE DEPARTMENT—HOW MUCH DO CITIZENS HAVE THE RIGHT TO KNOW?

If police had issued a warning to young mothers, would April Rodrigez and her baby still be alive?

That was followed by comments taken on the street. *"I'm scared,"* said one young mother of two children. *"I'd just stay home with my doors locked, but I have to work. I have to take my babies to the sitter."*

"I don't think the cops are doing enough. Why can't they catch this guy?"

"I heard the police don't care, because the victims are unwed mothers."

"I'm thinking about moving. I hate to quit my job, but my son's safety is more important."

"They don't care. The cops don't care. They see so much of this. They've become desensitized. They're just punching the clock, putting in their time like every-body else."

Then came an interview with Darby Nichols, the girl who had found the body.

Ivy had seen enough.

Alex Martin. That little shit. And she'd thought Irving was too rude to him. Now she knew he hadn't been rude enough. But the newspaper articles had given her an idea, one she wanted to run by Irving. . . .

She glanced up in time to see the redbrick building with the tar-paper roofs and JESUS SAVES sign warning that her Central stop was coming up. She tucked the paper under her arm, grabbed a handrail, and got to her feet along with about ten other people. Above the opening double doors was a sign that said: MOVE TO ANOTHER CAR IF YOUR IMMEDIATE SAFETY IS THREATENED.

Ivy was living in a fishbowl. The Police Department had relocated her neighbor tenant so they could set up shop in the apartment next to hers. Two officers were stationed there at all times, keeping their eyes on monitors feeding back images of every outside door in the building, the hallways, and stairwells, plus the door to her apartment. Ivy couldn't pee without someone knowing about it.

She stepped off the el, aware of the weight of the fourteen-ounce Chief's Special revolver and mobile phone Max had insisted upon in the message bag that lay snuggly against her, the strap crisscrossing from right shoulder to left hip. She took paint-peeled metal steps to street level, where she sidestepped a dead, flattened rat, then hurried to catch her connecting bus to Area Five.

"Anybody seen Irving?" she asked when she reached the task-force room. She wanted to run her idea past him.

It looked like they were holding a telethon. Phones were ringing and the new recruits Max had ordered weren't enough to keep up. They would have a lot of bullshit to sort through, and now, with the new articles written by their buddy, Alex Martin, they would also have to waste time dealing with the outraged public.

Ramirez, a phone to his ear, called to her, "He was here a while ago, but left, saying he was going to see Superintendent Sinclair."

Max dropped into the leather chair with a sense of defeat. "Nothing like having the press on your side," he said sarcastically.

Abraham was semireclined in his office chair, balancing a pen between the fingertips of both hands. Spread out on top of the desk was the article by Alex Martin. "I knew that little runt would be trouble. But you didn't come here to talk about him, did you?"

Max rubbed his face and distantly noticed that he'd forgotten to shave again. "Ethan found out about Cecilia."

"Oh." Abraham let the information sink in. "That has to be tough."

"And now he wants to find his birth parents. I told him I'd help him."

"Haven't you tried before?"

"Yeah. I thought it would be wise to have the medical history of his parents. Ran into a dead end."

"I know a guy who's really good." Abraham flipped through his Rolodex, quickly copied down a name and number, and handed the paper to Max.

"Thanks." Max pocketed the slip. "I'll give him a call. But that isn't what I came to talk about either." He got straight to the point. "I don't know if I can do this anymore, Abraham."

"What do you mean? You want *out of Homicide*?" Abraham asked, clearly stunned. "What else would you do? It's not that easy to walk away from."

"There was a hockey stick left at the crime scene yesterday."

"Oh, shit." With Abraham, there was no need for Max to explain his anxiety.

"I can't put Ethan's life in danger."

"He's just messing with your head."

"It's working."

Abraham leaned forward, elbows on his desk. "Have you talked to anybody down in Stress Management? They turned Detective Blackwell around."

"I don't need a shrink. And Blackwell . . . He's still going to snap. Haven't you seen that weird gleam he gets in his eyes? The man's hanging by a thread. The only difference is that now he doesn't know it."

"How about if we put you down for a temporary leave of absence once this case is over? A sabbatical, if you will."

"I don't know if that will do the trick." Max got to his feet and Abraham followed.

"Think about it, will you?" Abraham asked.

"Yeah. Sure."

"I quit once," Abraham told him. "It didn't do me

any good. In fact, I got worse. Started drinking more. Had some pretty good blackouts. I had to pass my unsolved cases on to CHESS. The problem is, there's no closure when you quit. You're left with an open wound of what-ifs."

"We're all victims," Max said. "You, me, Sachi Anderson and her baby. Darby Nichols, even Ethan indirectly. All victims. All touched by the hand of a murderer."

Max's phone rang.

It was Ivy.

"A technician from the crime lab is on his way here," she told him. "He has some results for us."

"I'll be there in twenty minutes."

When Max reached Area Five, the technician was already there.

"Tox screen on the baby is back," the technician said. "Our guy used the same stuff as before."

"Anything else?" Max asked.

"The tattoo is real."

That announcement brought about a mixed reaction. Some people laughed, some cheered, and some just shook their heads.

"That's not all," the crime-lab technician said, apparently saving his best for last. "The tattoo isn't new."

"What do you mean, 'isn't new'?" Ivy asked, getting up from her desk and moving closer.

"I mean it's been soaking in formaldehyde for a long time. Possibly years. We won't have a definitive answer until we run more tests."

"Care to make an educated guess?" Max asked.

"Ten years old at least."

Somebody whistled.

"So this guy cut off his tattoo years ago and put it in formaldehyde," Ramirez said. "Why?"

"Because he's crazy," Hastings said.

Everybody moaned at her lame joke.

"He could have cut it off because he decided he didn't like his mother anymore," Ramirez volunteered.

"Or he could have cut it off because someone saw it and he was afraid that person would use it to identify him."

That observation came from Hastings.

"We were looking for a guy with a tattoo. Guess now we're looking for a guy with a scar," Ivy said.

"What about DNA in the tattoo?"

"We put an urgent priority on it. It's unlikely we'll get anything, but we should have an answer for you in a few days."

"Even if DNA can be extracted, it probably won't do us any good," Max said. "I'm guessing we won't find a match in any of the databases."

"He's getting more daring," Ivy said. "I'm afraid this might be a sign of escalation."

"I agree," Max said. "He's getting bold. He's gotten away with it so many times that he now thinks he's invincible. He may be escalating, but he may also get sloppy and do something stupid. We have to be vigilant."

Regina Hastings stood up and stretched, motioning to the ringing telephone. "Be my guest. Somebody. Anybody."

Ivy sat down and began taking calls.

Evening rolled around, and Ivy still hadn't run her idea past Irving. She finally caught up with him at Sully's, a local bar where a lot of the cops went after their shift instead of going home. At Sully's, they could be with people who knew what it meant to be a cop in Chicago.

She found Irving there, playing pool.

His jacket and tie and dress shirt had been discarded, so that all he wore was a white T-shirt, silver watch, and dark dress pants. He chalked his pool cue and bent down to make a bank shot. Yellow striped nine ball in the corner pocket. Under the rectangular beer light that hung from chains above the green felt of the table, cigarette smoke collected. The darkly paneled room was enveloped in an eye-burning fog.

He made the shot, missed by a fraction of an inch, and laughed. While his opponent moved in with his stick, Max perched back on his bar stool as if he and the stool were old friends.

Ivy moved through the haze of smoke and took the seat beside him. "I've been looking for you," she said.

In front of him were three empty shot glasses and three beer bottles.

"Can I get you something?" the bartender asked. She was one of those hard, tough women who looked older than she probably was. Someone who wouldn't take anything from anybody.

"Coke."

Max's opponent landed the eight ball in the side pocket. He picked up the pile of wrinkled bills from the edge of the table, asking, " 'Nother game?" He was small and wiry. Probably somebody who made a living playing pool.

Before Max could answer, Ivy did it for him. "No. Not now."

"This your wife?" the man said with a grin. "You in a shitload of trouble?"

"No, she isn't my wife," Max said, turning his back on the pool table and motioning for the bartender to give him another drink.

The bartender placed Ivy's Coke on a square napkin and poured Max a shot of gin. Then she fished in the pile of bills in front of Max and pulled out what she needed.

"Take her Coke out of that."

He downed the gin as if it were medicine, then grabbed the beer for a chaser. "In the South," he said, "they call everything a Coke. So if you say you want a Coke, you then have to specify if you want a Pepsi Coke, or a Coke Coke."

"What about Sprite?" Ivy asked. "Or Mountain Dew?"

"No, I think it's just the dark soda. All the dark soda is Coke."

"Oh." She took a sip from her glass, then carefully placed it back on the napkin. Behind her, someone dropped some money in the jukebox and the voice of Billie Holiday took over the room.

Ivy fiddled with the corner of her napkin. "What are you doing here?" she finally asked.

"I'm tired," he said without hesitation, his voice weighted down with the burdens he carried. "I'm tired of this shit, this ugly, terrible shit invading my life." He laughed bitterly.

Now that he'd started talking, it seemed he couldn't stop. Alcohol did that to a person. Made them say and confess things they would normally keep locked inside.

"What life?" he said, their conversation blanketed by the music. "I have no life. I can't *have* a normal life. How do you talk to someone about their favorite

TV show, or a current movie, when babies are being murdered? And it's not going to end. If this fucking case is ever solved, there will be another one to replace it. Because the maniacs are everywhere."

"It just seems that way because you're in the middle of it."

He shook his head. "Do you know how many unsolved homicides I have on file? Over five hundred. There's no escape. I've tried becoming an alcoholic like half the people in Homicide, but it didn't work out. How do they do it? Getting wasted every night? I wanted to, but I couldn't function the next day."

The conversation shifted. "How do *you* do it?" he asked. "You almost seem to be thriving on this case. Is it because you got away from him? Does that give you some kind of strength? A feeling of power instead of this . . . this stinking despair? This hopelessness?"

She let him talk. If she said anything, she doubted he would listen anyway.

"When I got into this, I'll admit I was idealistic. And also this machismo thing was driving me." He paused and focused on something that was farther away than the walls of a tavern in metro Chicago. "I don't suppose anything is what it really is when you're on the outside looking in. But you"—he shook a finger at her, emphasizing his point—"you have personal reasons. A purpose in being here, doing what you're doing. I understand that. It makes sense. While me—" He brought the spread fingers of both hands to his chest, suddenly a man of gestures, a man who talked with his hands, possibly the biggest hint that he was drunk off his ass. "I—I just invite this crap into my life."

He helped himself to a swallow of her Coke, putting

the glass back down while crunching on an ice cube.
"I should get the hell out of here," he told her with
conviction, as if this were something he'd been thinking about for longer than just the last few hours. "I
should take my son and go someplace far away. Someplace where this kind of insanity doesn't happen. Oh.
I forgot," he said with the same sarcasm she'd noted
yesterday morning in the park. "There isn't any place
like that. I'm contaminated. And when I go home, I
take that contamination with me. I take it home to
my son."

He finished off his beer, drinking from the bottle
instead of using the glass, then turned to Ivy. His
blood alcohol had to be near the legal limit, but he
didn't seem that drunk. There was clarity in his dark
eyes, purpose. "I'm thinking of leaving Homicide
when this is over."

"You need to go home and get some sleep," she
said. "I'll get you a cab."

"You think I'll go home and sleep? Sleep. What the
hell's that?" he asked, his thoughts veering off course,
down another tangent. But he quickly remembered
his original trajectory. He grabbed both of her hands,
turning them palms up. With his thumbs, he caressed
the ridges on her wrists. Not taking his eyes from hers,
he said, "We'll catch the bastard, won't we?"

"Yeah." She had to believe it.

He was too sensitive for this business. She could see
it in eyes that were fringed with black lashes. Funny,
she'd never noticed sensitivity there before. But all his
defenses were down. He would hate her tomorrow for
seeing him like this.

But if a detective was too hard . . . that could be
bad too, she thought to herself. Because it took a cer-

tain amount of sensitivity to understand another human being. It even took a certain amount of sensitivity to put yourself in the mind of a serial killer.

Max gave her hands a squeeze, then dropped them. "Is it time, Julia?" he asked, swinging around.

The bartender checked the clock above the cash register. "Fifteen more minutes."

"My son has a hockey game," Max explained. "And I'm not going to miss it."

Ivy drove him there.

They took his car, and he told her where to turn, and when to get in this lane or that so she could exit, while he sat in the passenger seat, shaving with a battery-operated shaver.

They ended up northwest of Chicago, in suburbs that looked brand-new.

"Welcome to my world," Max said with a flourish of one arm.

It wouldn't have gotten him any points with his son if he'd arrived at the hockey game drunk, so Ivy had first taken him to a diner where he'd ordered a steak burger and French fries. Ivy got the special of stuffed acorn squash and chocolate cream pie because she loved chocolate cream pie. The squash was simply a way of relieving guilt over the pie. Occasionally, Max would take a bite of something on her plate without even asking, as if it were his right.

Ivy leaned forward and told him the idea that had come to her as she'd read Alex Martin's commentary. "We'll have the paper print a letter written to the killer from an infant he's murdered. In the letter, the baby would be talking directly to the Madonna Murderer, telling him what he'll miss out on now that he's dead, telling him how sad and lonely he is. We know that the killer loves these babies in a twisted way, so we use the letter to make him feel remorse, make him feel guilty. If he's put in a state of anxiety, then maybe he'll make a mistake."

"The idea's good," Max said, "but it's too risky. We're dealing with a psychopath here."

"You're the one who said we weren't moving quickly enough. It's risky, but we have to try, don't you think? So far, he's the one in control. We tried the candlelight vigil. We exposed the tattoo. We need something bigger."

"He responded to the tattoo. At this point, a letter from the baby he killed could send him over the edge."

"I think we need to push him now, while he's feeling pressured. Sending him over the edge might be the only way he's going to make a mistake that's big enough for us to catch him."

"I'll run the idea past Agents Cantrell and Spence."

She smiled. "Good. In the meantime, I'll put a letter together."

They fought briefly over the bill, with Ivy winning. She paid, leaving a nice tip for a waitress who she'd calculated was a single mom probably working two jobs. Then they continued on their way to the hockey game, pulling into the arena parking lot with fifteen minutes to spare.

Having arrived, Max shut off the shaver and tossed it in the glove compartment. Outside the car, he stood in front of Ivy and asked, "How do I look?"

He'd put his jacket back on, but had left the tie in the car. She rebuttoned two buttons of his shirt, then gave his chest a pat. "There."

"Thanks." He grasped her lightly by both arms and planted a quick kiss . . . on her forehead. Probably because it was closer than her lips, Ivy reasoned, feeling a twinge of disappointment. It was the second time in a matter of days that he'd pulled her near; she decided that, as unusual as it was in a man, Max was simply demonstrative—and possibly still a little drunk.

The game was exciting, giving her a hint of what it was that drove all those sports moms. Ivy screamed and cheered, then immediately booed loudly when Ethan was put in the penalty box for high-sticking. She didn't believe in violence in competition, but the other team was high-sticking like crazy and the referees just ignored it.

Ethan's team won by one point, a goal scored after the game went into overtime.

When it was done, she and Max hurried down the bleachers to congratulate Ethan.

His face was red from exertion, and he loomed over Ivy in his skates, seeming eight feet tall and four feet wide, all padded under his green jersey. When he pulled off his helmet, his blond hair was dark with sweat. She could tell he was glad to see his father, giving him a look that was tinged with confusion. That confusion bled over to her. He must be wondering what she was doing there.

Mothers and fathers filed out, telling him good game as they passed. Ethan had played well, making three of his team's four goals. One woman stopped and grabbed Ivy by the arm, leaned close and said, "That son of yours will be playing pro hockey."

She was gone before Ivy could correct her. She looked at Ethan, ready to make some light comment, when he spun away, heading for the locker rooms.

Before ducking inside, he stopped and said something to a dark-haired, middle-aged man waiting at the locker-room entrance. The man turned and waved in their direction.

That night, Ivy couldn't sleep. She kept thinking about Ethan, about the way the woman had thought he was her son.

Sometimes she dreamed that her son was still alive. But she knew it was just a dream, a mother's fantasy. In her imaginings, his face was always out of focus. She could never quite see what he looked like. But now she knew that if her son had lived he would have looked like Ethan.

She lay in bed thinking about the letter from the dead baby. It would be hard to write, but she would do it, she *must* do it. And while she was doing it, she would think of another baby, her baby. . . .

She rolled over, disturbing Jinx, who meowed with faint reproach. What a good cat. He'd taken to the tiny apartment better than she ever thought he would. Then again, maybe he was simply biding his time, waiting to go home.

"Here's the letter I want you to run." Ivy pushed an eight-by-ten sheet of typed paper across the diner table. On top of it was a diskette.

Alex Martin pulled it closer, avoiding the puddle of coffee that had spilled when he'd poured too much cream.

They were sitting in a back booth of a greasy grill where a bored waitress with big hair brought them coffee in stained white cups that were probably as old as the building itself. Definitely not a place Alex would have chosen.

He hadn't been surprised to get Ivy Dunlap's phone call. He hadn't even been surprised to find that she wanted to meet with him. He knew the article in the Monday *Herald* would have ignited some rage within the police department. That's what it was supposed to do. But what *had* surprised him was finding out that she wanted him to work with them to help catch the Madonna Murderer.

"It's a good idea," he said after reading the piece she wanted him to put in the paper.

"It's been okayed by the department and the FBI. But then I doubt that's something you'd be worried about."

The first dig. That didn't bother him.

She was an attractive woman, although she had a directness about her that was a little disconcerting, even for him.

"I suppose you want to know what's in it for you."

He laughed, and said, "You've got me all wrong."

"Oh, come on. I don't have time for any diversionary tactics. This isn't a game to me. It has nothing to do with making any kind of name for myself. But for you . . . that's what it's all about, isn't it?"

"Not at the expense of the truth. That's all I'm after. The truth."

He leaned against the back of the booth, angry now, coffee forgotten. He resented her implications and accusations. He wasn't a tabloid reporter after some grisly crime for the sake of shock value. "I think you'd better find another reporter. Maybe someone from the *Sun Times*."

She didn't even pretend to be interested in her coffee. "It's pretty much common knowledge that behind most newspaper reporters is a frustrated fiction writer."

Ouch. That hurt. But it wasn't really true. He was the only frustrated fiction writer he knew. Everybody else at the *Herald* seemed to like his or her job just fine.

"If you run this, if you help me, I promise to give you a story. An exclusive story."

He perked up. "About the investigation?"

"About me."

Intrigued once more, he leaned forward. "About you?"

"I have a story to tell. One I think you'll be interested in."

After meeting with Ivy Dunlap, Alex caught the Red Line back to the paper.

"This is great stuff," Maude said after she had read Dunlap's piece. "I don't mean the writing," she quickly corrected, catching Alex's frown. "The idea that the paper is going to be involved—that's great. There's been concern over the growing conflict between the media and the CPD. We've needed something like this to soften the hostility."

"So we'll run it?"

"I have to get final approval, but I don't think I'm getting ahead of myself by telling you this will get you the attention you deserve—both in-house and out."

Alex almost hugged her, but stopped himself at the last minute. She was his superior, and he didn't think a hug or maybe even a twirl would go over that well. But he wasn't worried about approval. Maude hadn't had a submission turned down in years.

"Wanna go for coffee?" he asked. "My treat." He'd never made such a daring offer before, and was surprised when she said yes.

At a table in the basement cafeteria, she pulled a flask from the giant canvas bag that never left her side, and added an ample amount of brown liquid to her coffee. She offered the flask to Alex. Suddenly they were almost equals. He shook his head and she stuffed it back in her purse.

"How far would you go for a story?" she asked.

"I'm not sure. It would depend on the situation."

"You gotta have guts," she said. "Did I ever tell you about the time I posed as a hooker to get a story?"

Looking at her now, he couldn't imagine. He would have shuddered, but he was too polite to do so.

That evening, Alex called his mother. "Did you get the copy of my article?" he asked, even though he knew she had to have gotten it since he'd sent it by overnight courier.

"I'm so proud of you!" his mother said. Sometimes she would spout a mouthful of shit just to build his confidence, but he and his mother were close and he knew her enthusiasm for his article was genuine. He told her about the new piece they'd be running.

"It isn't dangerous, is it?"

She would never quit worrying about him. He smiled at her small-town naiveté. "No, not dangerous at all."

Chapter 29

Psychiatrists had labeled him obsessive-compulsive, but he just liked things done in a certain way, a certain order. Nothing wrong with that. If a particular order wasn't followed, he couldn't concentrate on anything else because there was always a chaos shouting and shouting and shouting at him, making a clutter in his head. The only way he could make the clutter go away was to go over everything again, doing it right. And then he had to do it more than once. Like when you wrote the wrong letter, and then you had to print over it to correct it. You had to print over it again and again and again, so the right letter became dominant.

At 8:05 every Monday, Wednesday, and Friday, he caught the 427 bus at the corner of Winslow and Hughes to head to his part-time job at the computer-software company Astral Plain. Just before boarding, at precisely eight o'clock, he bought a copy of the *Chicago Herald* and *Chicago Sun Times*. He didn't read them until he got on the bus. He couldn't even peek at the front page when he picked it up. Instead, he'd make the print and the photo all blurry, so he couldn't cheat, so he couldn't see it before it was time.

As the bus pulled laboriously away from the curb, he would sit down and open the *Chicago Herald*.

He was making the paper all the time now.

Several days ago, he'd read about the deaths of April and Joshua Rodrigez. He loved to read about himself while he was sitting right in the middle of the world. In plain sight. He was smart. And they were stupid. So stupid.

Today there was no picture of attendants lifting a gurney with a black body bag into the back of an ambulance. Instead, there was a huge photo—it took up the entire top half of the page—of a stuffed bear. A baseball glove. A graduation cap. A telescope. A Beatles album. *Sgt. Pepper.* Which was the album that marked a turning point in their career. It had songs like "Lucy in the Sky with Diamonds," and "Lovely Rita."

His eyes tracked down.

Dear Madonna Murderer,

A letter. A letter to him.

Excited, intrigued, he lowered the paper and looked around.

There was the smelly old bitch who rode the bus all the time. Some college students with their backpacks and weird hair, their pierced faces. They didn't smell, but they bothered him almost as much as the stinking ones. Then there was a girl in an orange fast-food uniform with white cuffs and a yellow smiley button on her collar below her ugly, frowning face that said, Have I told you about today's special? Nobody was looking at him. Nobody noticed him.

He was invisible. The invisible man, able to move freely among the masses without danger of being seen. His gaze dropped back to the paper.

Dear Madonna Murderer,

I'm writing to you from the cemetery. Why the cemetery? Because I'm the baby you killed three days ago. It's lonely out here. And dark. It's always dark. When they were throwing the dirt on top of me, I was so scared. I cried and cried, but nobody heard me. Why did you kill me? Wait. Don't tell me. I think I understand. I think you may have done it because you love me. Is that it? Do you love me? And you didn't want me to have to suffer through life the way you have suffered. Am I right?

I know how hard you've had it. I know that your mother hasn't always been good to you. But I'm lonely. And sad. I'll never have a chance to do any of the things children do. You've taken that from me. I wish you hadn't done that, I wish you hadn't killed me. I wish I could have made up my own mind about life, you know?

It was signed *Joshua.*

He stared and stared at the name.

How stupid did they think he was?

He sat there and *pick, picked* at himself, pulling and picking, pulling and picking until all of his eyelashes were gone.

The bus lurched to a halt. People got off. People got on. And suddenly he realized this was his stop.

He folded the paper and jumped to his feet, hurrying down the rubber walkway, diving through the back doors just before they closed, the rubber seals brushing his shoulders.

Standing on the sidewalk in a furious rage, he attacked the paper, tearing it and tearing it into smaller and smaller pieces, finally shoving it deep inside a trash container. When he looked up through a red haze of anger, people were staring at him.

"Fuck you!" he screamed, spit flying. "Fuck you!"

Responses to the dead-baby letter began arriving the following day. Most showed up as letters to the editor, a few were sent directly to Alex. Suddenly he was a pseudostar. Upon receiving the day's mail, he would put the letters in a sealed plastic bag and take them directly to Homicide. At the front desk, he was issued a temporary pass and allowed to venture where no Alex Martin had gone before.

The majority of the letters they'd received so far were from outraged readers, full of accusations of exploitation and sensationalized journalism. But others were clearly written by someone who was disturbed. It would be the job of the police department's certified document examiner and forensic linguist to come up with a description of the disturbed writer.

Alex had done his homework, and he knew that document examinations could be one of the most effective ways to link a suspect to a crime. One of the earliest cases in which a document examiner played a key role was the Lindbergh kidnapping. But it would take the skill of a forensic linguist to come up with an even more telling profile. By examining the order of the words, the usage, the patterns of speech, the linguist could determine gender, education, and ethnic background. A good examiner could often pinpoint

the area of the city in which the suspect had been
raised.

In the second floor Madonna case room, the letters
were carefully sorted and examined, three of them
raising hopes of legitimacy. Then they were sent to
the crime lab, where the letters and envelopes would
be photographed and examined for any microscopic
fibers. From there, they would go downstairs to the
document examiner.

Other proactive measures were also being taken.
The cemetery where the latest victims had been buried
was being staked out, and expectations among the task
force were high. They needed this break.

Harold Doyle had been a certified document examiner with the Chicago Police Department for nine
years. He'd worked on kidnapping cases, and poison-
ing cases, bank robberies, counterfeiting, and embez-
zlement. He was good, but not cocky. As soon as he
received the letters from the crime lab, he faxed copies
to the FBI office in Quantico, and to Patty Hund,
the Chicago-based linguist. Then he began his own
careful examination.

He would study the letters with a high-powered mi-
croscope, then begin the tedious search to see if a
match could be found in the questioned documents.
The paper would be run through an ESDA, Electro
Static Detection Apparatus, which filled in indenta-
tions with graphite, and copies would be sent to every
government office where signatures were on file.

It wasn't his job to dissect the contents of the letters,
but he read them all the same. The first was handwrit-
ten using black ink. The characters were small, the
indention left on the paper deep.

It's bad enough that you allow scenes of violence to dominate front-page news, but now you have descended to a level that could only be called trash journalism. Do you think these kinds of tactics will gain more readers? Do you think it will make the killer feel so bad that he'll come forward and confess? Don't insult his intelligence.

The next letter was written in a more feminine hand, small and cramped, with a slant to the right. A cursory glance told Doyle that in all likelihood it had been written by a woman in her sixties. But he would examine it anyway, and file a report.

Letter to the editor.
Shame on you. How do you think the families of the victims feel, seeing a letter "written" from their dead grandson, or nephew? How do you think that made them feel, to open the paper and see that? I am canceling my subscription. Shame on you.

The last letter had been printed on an ink-jet printer and was similar to the first except that it was addressed to the Police Department.

CPD.
The letter in yesterday's paper is an open admission of your lack of expertise. Anyone reading it will see it as the desperate plea it is, an admission of your total bafflement. Why not simply run headlines that read, WE HAVEN'T GOT A CLUE?
Have you no pride? Have you no shame? Re-

sorting to such juvenile tactics. Why don't you get out your junior-detective kit?

Doyle suspected that the first and last letter had been written by the same person, but it would be up to Patty Hund to make that determination.

The sound of the ringing phone woke her.

Heart pounding, Ivy lifted the receiver to her ear, fully expecting to hear that there had been another murder.

"In your profile you said he may have intended to major in math. Well, *everything* is numbers."

"Max?"

Ivy pressed the button that illuminated the green light on her travel clock. 2:50 A.M.

"All of it. The thirteen stab wounds. Then the twenty-two stab wounds. Even the number of your old apartment, although that was probably a very strange coincidence. But someone who deals in numerology might argue that there are no coincidences."

The brain fog began to lift, and she remembered that Max had left Headquarters a few hours early to take Ethan to a hockey game miles away in Michigan. "Where are you calling from?"

"My car."

"I thought you weren't heading back until tomorrow."

"I decided to drive straight through after the game. I didn't want to be away any longer than I had to. Ethan's asleep in the passenger seat, and I've been listening to one of those weird programs you sometimes pick up in the middle of the night. It's about numerology."

She scooted higher in bed. "My old apartment was 283. That doesn't go along with your theory."

"Yeah, but in numerology, you add all the numbers together."

"And that makes thirteen. . . ."

"Exactly. Everything he was doing sixteen years ago was based on the number thirteen, even down to the thirteenth victim, Claudia Reynolds."

"Is that why he stopped? I was number thirteen?"

"Possibly."

"But the babies . . ."

"For some reason, he doesn't count them. Probably because he doesn't think of their passing as punishment. He's always rationalizing his role in their death. He's playing God, sending them someplace where he thinks they'll be better off. Thirteen symbolizes death and birth, the end and the beginning. Change and transition. For some reason, his number has now changed from thirteen to twenty-two."

"But two and two is four."

"Twenty-two is a master number," he explained. "It doesn't break down. And get this—twenty-two means 'mastery on all planes.' 'Supreme power.' 'Special abilities.' "

She turned on the bedside lamp and reached for the tablet and pen she kept within arm's reach in order to jot down any ideas that might come to her in the middle of the night. "I think you might be onto something." Her heart was beginning to beat a little faster. "If you're right about this, then that would mean he plans to kill a total of twenty-two mothers. Where is this knowledge going to take us? How can it help?"

"Considering the killer's fascination with numbers, I think it's only reasonable to surmise that he might also work with numbers. Like a math teacher, or an accountant maybe. Numbers would be his life. We need to go back and check with the area mental hospitals to find out if any patients were math teachers or accountants.''

"I agree."

"Sorry to wake you up, but I had to run this by somebody. Sometimes things that seem so rational in the middle of the night make no sense the next day. I had to know."

"I'm glad you called."

"Go back to sleep," he said, the signal breaking up. "I'll see you in the morning."

"We got a few results back while you were gone. Nothing breaking."

"I'll pick you up on the way so you can fill me in."

Chapter 30

"Could you—" Max motioned to his coffee as he turned the car onto Grand, heading in the direction of Area Five. On the way to Ivy's, he'd stopped and picked up a half-dozen bagels and two cups of coffee from Bagels, Bagels, and now he ate as he drove.

In the passenger seat, Ivy pulled the plastic drink tab from the lid, and passed the coffee to him.

"Anything come of the DNA testing?" he asked.

"It was too degraded for the lab to get anything from it."

"He's too smart to give us something that easy. How about the drugs? Any leads on the drugs used in the babies?"

"Brought in a couple of kids who were caught selling it on the street. I guess it's a new kind of high, but they hadn't sold any to anybody who fit our profile."

"What about the last crime scene?"

"Nothing."

"Your apartment? Anything happening there?"

"I think he must know the building is under surveillance. Maybe we should make a big show of moving the cops out."

Max shook his head, checked the rearview mirror,

then over his right shoulder before executing a lane change. "If he figures out who you are, you'll be the next target."

"Which would make me the perfect bait."

"Not a good idea. What about responses to the letter from the infant? Documents or Forensics come up with anything yet?"

"No, but Linguistics came up with a character analysis that closely matches our profiles."

"Good for us. Any leads from the envelopes, paper, or ink?"

"Not yet. Every public-document office in Chicago is trying to come up with a possible match, but that could take weeks. We're going to run another letter soon."

"That's not a good idea."

"Why not? We're hoping to keep up an ongoing conversation. The responses have stopped, and the longer we can keep him talking, the better chance we have of catching him."

"You don't even know if any of the responses are actually from him. You might be putting energy into a strategy that will simply be a waste of our time, time that could be better spent elsewhere."

"Is that your only concern?" she asked, trying to imply that it was a damn lame one.

"I'm afraid it might backfire. I'm afraid the killer might overreact. That it could actually accelerate the murders."

"What are you basing that on? We already know he feels guilty about killing the babies. Why not use that to our advantage?" She was dismayed to find them arguing again, but she wasn't going to back down in order to avoid a confrontation.

"I don't know what I'm basing it on. There is nothing to base it on. There's been no other case like this in the history of serial killings. That's what I'm basing it on. This guy doesn't fit the pattern, and he might not react the way we want him to."

"So we don't run the new letter?"

"This isn't a dictatorship. I'm not going to tell you not to run it, I'm just saying it's against my better judgement."

"Really? There wasn't one other person who thought it was a bad idea, that's including three experts on serial killers."

Unable to finish her bagel, Ivy wrapped the remaining half and tossed it back in the brown bag, rolling the top down with a loud, angry rustle of paper. They continued in silence through two lights. "Why did you okay the first letter then?"

"I thought it was worth a try. We've done it, but we don't want to push it."

"I think you're being too cautious."

"You don't know what you're doing."

"Oh, so we're back to that."

"I don't want to fight."

"Neither do I."

They pulled into the parking lot. Max found a spot in the shade under the overhead ramp. They got out and walked toward Headquarters in silent hostility.

Chapter 31

He was having trouble staying focused. Random thoughts would jump into his brain, then jump out before he could fully explore them.

Something eating away at him. Eating, eating, knocking on his head, trying to get in, trying to get out.

Go away.

Babies, babies, babies. Little baby boys smelling like powder and cream. Take their breath away, take their breath away. . . . Hush, hush, sweet little boy, Momma's here. Momma's right here.

"Last call," someone said.

He looked up, his hand gripping an empty drink glass, the short kind that was used for whiskey on the rocks. His brain crash-landed, putting him back in the here and now, a crappy neighborhood bar a half-mile from his home. His mother had sent him out—he looked up at the clock—hours ago to get her a six-pack of beer. Instead, he'd bought drinks for himself. And when her money ran out, he started using his own.

The bartender, a thin, world-weary man with deep creases in his cheeks, was still waiting. "Somebody should put you out of your misery," he told the bartender.

"What?"

It was always fun to throw things like that at people. They never knew how to react. How easy it was to disturb someone with just a few words, words that didn't fit the protocol. Humans came with a manual, a set of rules, a code that saturated every waking moment of their pitiful lives. But if you stepped outside that code, it threw people off because there was nothing in the manual about seriously fucking with somebody's head.

"I said, Somebody should put you out of your misery. Wouldn't you like that? Think about it."

He usually didn't drink. His mother drank, and he didn't want to do anything she did. And drinking made things he could normally suppress rise to the surface. But there was such a feeling of release to it, such a sense of freedom.

"No more bartending," he said. "No more moving between crummy sets. Your home. The bar. Home. Bar. See what I mean?"

"Get the hell out of here."

"I want another drink."

"You ain't gettin' another drink, now get the hell out before I call the cops."

He wagged a finger at him. "You don't know who you're talking to." He leaned closer. "I have power."

The bartender laughed in his face. "Get out of here, psycho. You don't scare me. You're just another loser." He picked up a cordless phone and began dialing.

The murderer of infants, the murderer of mothers,

got to his feet knowing he possessed the power of God in his hands. "I'm leaving."

He lurched from the building, then dropped into his car, which was parked a block away. He sat there in the dark, watching the last of the customers leave the bar. Engine idling, he watched as the lights went out, one by one. Finally, the bartender emerged from the building, locked the door, then began walking down the sidewalk in his direction.

He tromped down on the accelerator. The engine roared, the car flying forward. With a heavy thud, the left front fender struck the bartender, tossing him over the hood where he landed in a crumpled heap in the street near the curb.

What had he done?

What was happening?

Out of control. Out of control.

Now what? The man would talk. He would turn him in.

He executed a U-turn and came back for the pathetic, worthless life-form that was trying to crawl away. He ran over him again, bones crunching. Then again, and again, finally leaving the scene.

He looked in his rearview mirror. It was late; the streets were deserted.

He got on the interstate and drove a full fifteen miles north of where he lived and pulled into a self-service car wash, closing the door behind him. Quickly, he fed money into the meter, turning the dial to *hot/soapy*. With the wand, he directed the high-power washer toward the car, knocking off chunks of flesh, the water running pink around his feet. After that he drove home, silently entering the house through the side door that led directly to the basement. He kicked off his bloody shoes, then crawled into bed, rocking himself to sleep, sucking his thumb, his mind chanting, *Out of control. Out of control.*

Pounding on the floor above woke him. He looked at the clock: 11:45 A.M. He jumped out of bed, his heart racing while the pounding kept on and on. He lost his balance and fell to the floor, to the cement, holding his thick head. Confused. He was so confused. *Can't remember. Can't remember.*

Last night. He remembered being sent out for beer. Instead of coming back, he'd spent her money. He'd gotten drunk. No wonder his head hurt so much, no wonder he couldn't think. No wonder he couldn't remember anything else.

And now she was awake and furious. Unsedated, yet confined to bed, she'd want to know what he'd done with her money. She would yell at him, scream at him.

Dirty boy, dirty, dirty boy.

Chapter 32

Regina Hastings loved Chicago—she'd lived there all her life, but the heat was smothering. They should let cops wear shorts the way they did in Florida.

She'd grown up south of Chinatown in what was referred to as one of Chicago's bungalow belts. The houses were small, the lots were small, and most people didn't have air conditioners. But when you're little, you don't notice things like that.

She rechecked the address in her notebook, slowing her Corolla in order to spot the house numbers. She was on the south side of the Twenty-fifth District, an area of town she wasn't that familiar with. Her beat had always been north of Grand. She spotted Hanks, the tavern where a brutal murder had taken place a few days earlier.

She was sick of the Madonna Murderer case. When she was initially "chosen" to be a part of the investigation, she'd found it flattering. And she thought it would be fun, interesting, a break from rapid-response patrol, not to mention more hours and more money. But damn. She was always assigned the boring jobs. If she'd wanted to do this kind of door-to-door shit, she'd have become an Avon lady. And if she'd wanted to work on a project that required long-term commitment with possibly no chance of fulfillment or success, she'd have become a cancer researcher.

And she had to admit to herself that she missed being able to torment Ronny all day.

The fucking house numbers. Wasn't it a law that residents of Chicago had to have visible numbers on all the houses? If it wasn't, it should be.

Counting back from the corner, she finally hit pay dirt.

The place she was looking for was in a run-down area that the revitalization project hadn't yet found—or had purposefully overlooked. It was rust-stained stucco, with pale green shutters and matching trim. Weeds grew in the chain-link fence that surrounded an adequate yard. She could hear downshifting semis from one of the nearby interstates.

This was about the twentieth stop she'd made today. A month earlier, they'd investigated everyone they could find in the Chicago area who'd been released from a mental hospital within the last five years. *Now* they'd decided to go back *ten* years, which gave them a head count of literally hundreds of ex-patients to wade through. This time they were looking for patients who had a connection to math. And guess who had to do the footwork? Give it to Regina. Regina will do it.

The task had seemed insurmountable, but thank God they'd pulled officers from other sections who were now having as much fun as she was. What really burned her butt was that Ramirez was lounging around at Headquarters, soaking up air conditioning, faxing handwriting samples to offices, schools, public agencies, basically any place that kept documents on file. Maybe she should give him a break. He'd actually been going out of his way to be nice, but she was scared shitless of becoming just another notch in his belt. Instead of driving him off as it did most guys, her rape revelation seemed to have increased his interest. Almost every day he invited her over to his place for dinner, but she always declined, mostly because she knew that a little wine, a little candlelight, could send her over the edge and pretty soon he'd know the what and where of her tattoo.

She stepped from the little green Toyota she'd recently purchased. She'd never had a new car before, and she couldn't help but admire it on a daily basis, looking it over for door dings every time she got out. Two days ago, someone in the parking lot at Headquarters had put a tiny dent in it. She'd flipped out when she'd seen it.

Dressed in her blue uniform, her badge in place, clipboard in hand, Regina approached the fenced yard looking for signs of a dog. There were none. The gate wasn't locked, so she lifted the metal latch.

At the front door, she knocked, then stepped back to wait, grateful that the porch was at least shaded. To her right, a window air conditioner hummed. The shades were pulled down tight to keep out the hot sun. She knocked a second time. Finally a middle-aged man answered, drying his hands on the red-and-white-checked apron that was tied casually around his waist.

"I was canning spaghetti sauce," the man said with a friendly, almost bashful smile. He was of average height, dark hair, dark eyes.

A man who cooked. For Regina, it was almost love at first sight.

"Just wondered if I could ask you a few questions," she said. "It'll only take a minute."

"Sure." He opened the screen door wider. "Why don't you come in? It's too hot to stand outside."

Regina didn't hesitate. "Thanks," she said, stepping inside the cool darkness. As her eyes adjusted, she noted that the living room was neat and tidy even though the furniture was old. From the back of the house, a television blared loudly.

He closed the door to keep the cool air from escaping, then took a seat on the couch while she sat in a chair nearest the door.

"That smells good," she said, her stomach growling in a Pavlovian reflex.

"It's an old family recipe," he said, bobbing his head. "Lots of garlic and oregano."

She got back on track and established that his name matched the one on her list. She asked her first question on the standardized form Detective Irving had drawn up to simplify her job. "Were you a patient at the Elgin Mental Hospital?"

"That's right." His affirmative got the ball rolling.

That was followed by several more seemingly harmless questions. "What do you do for a living?" she asked. "Chef, maybe?" Good to joke around, lighten the mood a little. Everybody was intimidated by the uniform.

He rubbed his hands together. "I do like to cook, that's true, but when I'm not cooking I transcribe music."

She made a note of that, balancing the clipboard against her leg. "What does that mean exactly?"

"Say, would you like something to drink? Iced tea? Pepsi? Water?"

"No thanks, but that's nice of you to ask. What do you mean by transcribing music?" she repeated.

"I listen to music and transcribe it into notes."

"Oh, wow. So you're a musician?"

"More into music theory."

She had no idea what that meant, but she plowed on. "Anything else? Do you do anything else?"

"I write code part time for a place called Astral Plain."

"Code?"

"For computer programs."

"That must be tough. I don't know anything about computers. I mean, I know how to read and send E-mail and that's it. I keep thinking I should take a class. I think the department even offers them for free."

"Yeah, you really should."

"So you design programs?"

"No, I write the code. Code. You know. The system of numbers that gives the computer the commands."

Red flag.

But the connection with numbers didn't really mean all that much. She'd had a lot of red flags that day. In fact, one of her interviews was with a math teacher, another an accountant. It seemed like the mathematics field went hand in hand with mental instability. Good thing she hated math.

He stared at her, trying to read her mind, but couldn't.

She was one of those tacky kind of women with huge bleached hair, big boobs, and a cocky, almost mannish way of carrying herself. When she wasn't working, she probably spent a lot of time in bars or at home laughing along with a sitcom soundtrack.

"Do you like foreign films?" he asked, noticing that she wore no wedding band.

She waved his words away. "When I see a movie, I don't want to have to read the print at the bottom of the screen—"

"Subtitles. They're called subtitles."

"Well, I don't want to have to read anything, and I want the actor's voices to move with their mouths." That said, she got back to the questions. "How long have you worked at your present occupation?"

Sweat was rolling down her face, taking cream-colored makeup with it. Her shirt was wet at her armpits, and she was beginning to smell up his house.

"Are you married?" he asked.

"Can we please stick to the question? And no, I'm not married."

"Five years," he said. "I've been with Astral Plain five years. I've been transcribing music a lot longer. It's kind of an off and on thing, you know."

She jotted that down. "Well, that's it. Told you this wouldn't take long." She got to her feet and held out her hand toward him, obviously expecting him to shake it.

He didn't want to touch her, but he forced himself to take her hand—and immediately knew he'd made a mistake.

The handshake was the final part of the interrogation.

"That's quite a scar you have there," she said, turning his arm so she could get a better look. "Did you get it cooking?"

He laughed nervously.

"It's a burn from a car accident I was in years ago. Doctors tried doing a graft, but it didn't take." His mind raced.

"Hey," he said as smoothly as possible. "Would you like to take a jar of spaghetti sauce with you?"

At first he feared she was going to refuse. But then she smiled with those big yellow horse teeth of hers and said, "Sure. I'd like that."

He hurried to the kitchen, his eyes rapidly moving from place to place, looking for something, something—

He opened one drawer, then another.

There. A heavy wooden meat tenderizer.

He picked up a quart jar of spaghetti sauce, wrapping a big kitchen towel around the base, hiding the wooden mallet, then scurried back out to the living room.

"Careful," he said, extending the spaghetti sauce to her. "It's still hot."

"That smells great." She reached for the jar with both hands.

He pulled the meat tenderizer from under the wrapped towel. Swinging high and swiftly, he brought it down against her temple, the blow dropping her to her knees, the spaghetti sauce falling with her, breaking, the sound muted by the towel and the thick red contents of the jar. Dazed, she moved her sauce-covered hand to her gun. Before she could make contact, he stepped hard on her hand, her fingers snapping. He struck again, and again, and again until she lay on the floor unmoving.

He stopped his ragged breath and listened for any sound from the bedroom. Nothing but the television blaring away. She hadn't heard a thing. Why did drugs get such a bad rap? If he had his choice, he'd keep his mother medicated for the rest of her life.

"Are these all the reports from today's canvass?" Max asked, thumbing through a stack of papers. He stood in front of the wall of fame—the wall loaded down with an ever-growing array of crime-scene photos, the metro map with the yellow-headed marking pins denoting every Madonna Murderer crime scene since the very first eighteen years ago. In the center of the wall someone with a sense of humor had enlarged a color photo of the formaldehyde globe with its floating tattoo so it was now the size of four eight-by-tens.

It was 7:00 P.M. and most of the superficial members of the task force had gone home two hours ago. The only people left were Ramirez, Ivy, and Max. Any phone messages would be handled at the main switchboard.

"Wait a minute, Detective." Ramirez dug through a stack of papers. "Hastings faxed these to us about an hour ago." He handed them to Max.

"Why didn't she bring them in?"

"Says she got sick when she was out doing her canvassing," Ramirez said, leaning so far back in his office chair Max thought he might tip over. "Heatstroke, maybe." Ramirez shrugged, pulled another sheet of paper from the desk and handed it to Max. It was a faxed note from Regina.

"Anything stand out in the interviews?" Ivy asked.

She sat at a table in the corner of the room, a half-eaten sandwich at her elbow, along with a cold cup of coffee. She'd spent the entire day reading and rereading crime-scene interviews, trying to find anything that may have been missed the first, second, and third times through, something that might tie in with Max's number theory.

Max handed her half the stack, then dropped down on the sofa.

"An amazing percentage of mental patients have some kind of math background," Ivy commented.

"I have three right here," Max said.

"That seems odd. Doesn't that strike you as odd?"

"What are you saying? That the answers aren't accurate?"

Ivy rubbed her temples. She'd been sitting under fluorescent light for too long. All the numbers and letters on the page in front of her were jumping around. "I don't know. I'm not thinking straight. So where do we go from here?"

"We'll pull the patients with a mathematical background and you and I will interview them starting early tomorrow."

Ivy nodded dully. She needed to close her eyes for a while. Maybe she would lie down on the couch. Take a little nap before going home to feed Jinx. . . .

The sound of a plastic receiver clattering into the cradle jarred her, and she realized she'd been sleeping while sitting at the table. She'd been *dreaming* about lying down.

"She doesn't answer her phone."

"Who?" The question came from Max.

"Regina."

"If I were sick," Ivy said, talking with her eyes closed, "I wouldn't answer the phone. Half the time it's just a telemarketer anyway."

"Yeah. Yeah, I guess you're right." Ramirez got to his feet, gathering up his take-out trays, wrappings, and cups. "Maybe I'll swing by her place in the morning, see if she's feeling any better."

"Let's all call it a night," Max said. "I promised Ethan I'd be home early." He checked his watch and realized it was already too late for that.

The next morning, Ronny Ramirez went by Regina's place even though it was a whole forty-five minutes out of his way and would mean fighting rush-hour traffic on the way back to Headquarters. She had an apartment in a suburb north of Area Five. It wasn't a great place, not like Ramirez's warehouse apartment, but it was okay. The building was a huge brick thing that looked like a hospital—and maybe had been a hospital at one time. A lot of old people lived there, and a lot of crying kids. When you walked down the dark hallway, you could smell the gross stuff they were cooking. At his place, they didn't allow kids. His place was geared toward single people in their twenties, with a lap pool and a great workout room.

Her car wasn't in the parking lot. She'd just gotten it two weeks ago, having him come out and look at it when they were taking a break. Like a kid with a new toy, he thought, smiling to himself.

She must already be at work, he decided.

He pulled out his cell phone and dialed Headquarters. "Extension 280."

A woman answered, but it wasn't Regina. "Regina there?" he asked.

Whoever was manning the phone must have been new—she had to ask, and then she came back on the line with a negative.

Ronny pushed the end-call button, then sat there drumming his fingers on the steering wheel. She should have been at work by now. Thirty seconds later, he parked his black Lexus and went into the building.

He buzzed her room, but there was no answer—not unexpected. So he buzzed the office manager and asked to be let in to check on the welfare of a friend.

The female manager accompanied him to Regina's room, knocking. When there was no answer, she unlocked the door.

He'd been to her place several times in the past two weeks but still hadn't been able to get her to soften toward him. She thought he just wanted in her pants. He *did* want in her pants, but he'd been forced to grudgingly admit to himself that he liked her. Hell, he couldn't quit thinking about her. He'd always been physically attracted to her, but something happened the day she told him about being raped and almost dying. He began seeing her as a multidimensional person with feelings and a past. And he suddenly wanted to prove to her that he could treat her with the respect and admiration she deserved.

The only pet Regina had was a fish she'd told him was called a betta. He wasn't a pet person—pets were a pain in the ass. Anytime anybody in his building left for a few days, they always had to find somebody to take care of Muffy, or Fluffy, or Foo Foo. At the time she'd told him about the fish, he'd wondered why anyone would want a damn fish, but later he'd caught himself looking at it, admiring the colors.

"Regina!"

Silence.

It didn't take but a minute to see that she wasn't there—the apartment consisting of a combined kitchen-living area, a bedroom, and a bathroom. The bed was a mess, but the other times he'd been there it had been unmade. The bathroom didn't have that humid, recently used feeling. The sink was dry, and when he pulled back the pink shower curtain, so was the tub.

He went back to the bedroom, where her computer was set up against the wall opposite the bed. Neatly stacked near the monitor were the inquiries she'd faxed him.

"She's not here," said the manager, a young black woman who seemed nervous now that she'd allowed him access to the room.

She'd been there, that much was obvious.

He suddenly felt like an idiot. It wasn't like him to overreact, and he didn't quite know how to deal with it.

Yesterday she'd been really pissed about being given the street assignment while he got to sit in air-conditioning all day. So, knowing Regina, she'd gone out, gotten more pissed with each growing minute, and finally decided to play hooky—since she'd also been complaining about needing a day or two off.

She'd come home, faxed the questionnaires, then gone to visit a friend. Probably a guy, Ronny figured, a jealous knot forming in his stomach. She was most likely at the guy's place right now, laughing about how she'd duped everybody.

Well, he wouldn't squeal on her. He might need her to cover for him sometime.

"Thanks for letting me in," he told the manager, as they both headed for the door.

Chapter 33

"I have some information for you," the voice whispered in Alex Martin's ear. Alex gripped the receiver tighter and glanced up from his desk to see if anyone was within hearing distance. Heads were bowed, workers pecking away at their computer terminals.

"What kind of information?" Alex whispered back into the telephone.

"About the Madonna Murderer."

"Who is this?"

"I can't say."

Thrilled, his heart racing, Alex said, "I'd never divulge a source."

"I can't risk it. If I tell you, if he finds out I called you, I'll be killed. Can you meet with me someplace where we won't be seen?" The man's voice was of medium timbre, static, and trembly. He was scared shitless.

"Where?"

"A cemetery. I'll give you directions."

"Why a cemetery? Why not a coffee shop?"

"Because people know who you are. I can't be seen with you." He gave Alex directions, then said, "I have to go. I hear him coming. You'll be there, won't you? Please be there." The caller hung up.

A lead. A real honest-to-God lead.

Alex quickly found Maude, who was sitting in front of her computer, huge green bifocals on her face.

"I'm heading to the Daley Center to do a little research," he told her.

"On the Madonna Murder case?" she asked.

"Yeah."

He hated lying to her, but he was afraid if he told her the truth she might insist on his calling the cops, and he wanted this to be his story. He could almost smell a Pulitzer. The cops were already taking credit for the dead-baby letter, when he knew damn well it was something he could have come up with if given a chance.

"What about the police logs?" she asked, leaning back in her seat so she could stare at him.

"I'll pick them up on the way back."

"That'll be cutting it close."

"I'll call them in if I have to."

"Police logs? Nobody wants to take police logs over the phone."

"I'll be back in time. Don't worry."

Two weeks ago, she would have told him to get his ass over to Area Five. Today she just smiled and told him to have fun, then settled back in front of her computer.

In his car, Alex thought about how his life had changed—all because of a murdering psycho. He hated to think of it like that, but there it was. The senior editor of the *Chicago Herald* actually knew his name now, and he was being given real assignments—

real, actual, satisfying assignments. And Maude was almost treating him as an equal rather than a pain in the ass.

He slowed his little red Protegé for the tollbooth, tossed in the coins, and floored it, not waiting for the light to turn green. The only people who waited for a green light were geezers traveling through on their way to Michigan.

Everybody else might be running red lights, but not me. I'm no lawbreaker. No, sirree.

The Protegé was a nice car, but it was the cheapest model offered; the windows had to be hand-cranked, and he could hardly hear the stereo because of road noise. Before long, he'd be able to trade up, get a car with power windows, a good sound system, and a lot more insulation.

They said the Madonna Murderer was driven by an intense hatred for his mother. Mother and son. He and his mother got along really well, but some of his friends weren't so lucky. They had weird relationships that could only be described as volatile. Oedipus. Now, there was a kinky concept, but maybe not so far-fetched. Maybe he would do a piece on that. Yeah. He'd run that by Maude. See what she thought.

Faint music drifted to him from beneath the noise of the engine and the roaring of the semis that surrounded him. His roommates made fun of him because they said he liked to listen to bad music. He turned up the radio all the way. Van Halen. Guy music. Cock rock. Sure it was stupid. Sure it was loud, but it was primal, empowering.

He sang along, pounding a hand against the steering wheel.

Yeah, his life had turned around.

The cemetery ended up being one of those hidden, deserted places you sometimes came upon in the heart of the city. Following the directions he'd been given over the phone, Alex turned off the street and took a dirt road overgrown with grass. He drove beneath dense foliage, past toppled tombstones, until he reached the far south edge of the cemetery. He sat there a moment, wondering if he should turn around and get the hell out of there, when a man stepped out from behind a large stone. He waved and smiled.

The guy was pale and thin, a little geeky, Alex supposed. Totally harmless. Alex shut off the car engine and got out.

"Alex Martin?" the man asked, smiling, then casting a nervous glance over his shoulder.

"The same."

Alex pulled a pen and reporter's tablet from the breast pocket of his shirt while approaching the man, who still stood nervously near the tombstone. "Thanks for calling me," he said. "I want you to know I won't divulge anything about you. Not what you look like, or where we met. Nothing."

"I know," the man said, nodding and smiling.

"You can tell me as much as you feel comfortable with."

"I wanted to ask you something."

"Shoot."

"About the dead-baby letter."

A flicker of irritation passed through Alex. Always the dead-baby letter. Was he never going to get the credit he deserved?

"It was a lie, wasn't it?"

"What do you mean?"

"The baby didn't write the letter, did he?"

"I don't follow you."

"The baby didn't write the letter," the man repeated, more insistently this time. "Somebody else wrote the letter, didn't they?"

"Yeah . . ." Alex said, nodding slowly, wondering what the hell was going on. He'd gotten himself a real head case here.

"*You* wrote the letter, didn't you?"

"I had some help."

"From the police?"

"I can't tell you that."

"From Detective Irving? Did he help you write the letter?"

"I said, I can't tell you that."

This was a total bust, just like so many of the letters they'd received in reply to the dead-baby piece. There were a lot of nuts out there, and Chicago seemed to have a surfeit of them. Looked like he'd be back in time to get the police logs posted after all. Goodbye, Pulitzer. "Did you have something you wanted to tell me?"

"I don't want you to print any more letters."

"That's not up to me. I'm just a small cog in a big wheel."

"You're a traitor, Alex Martin. That's what you are."

"To who?"

"To the babies."

"The babies?" Alex had had enough. He turned and began walking toward his car.

"I'm talking to you!"

"Go fuck yourself." The words were tossed angrily over his shoulder.

From behind him came a rustling sound, a scurrying.

Alex turned in time to see something sparkle in a small shaft of sunlight that cut through the trees above his head. An axe. *He must have had it hidden behind the tombstone,* he thought in detached disbelief. A fucking axe.

Chapter 34

Ivy gave Jinx a full fifteen minutes of lavish attention to make up for leaving him in what amounted to day after day of solitary confinement. She petted him and brushed him and talked to him in the high voice that made him smile at her with his eyes.

It was a good thing cats didn't have the ability to anticipate tomorrow, or next week, or next month. Otherwise he might revolt, especially since he hadn't grown up in such confined quarters. At one time he'd been wild and free, walking leisurely through tall grass, sniffing at dandelions. He'd climbed trees and rolled in the dirt. He'd dozed in the shade of a lilac bush while blue jays screamed at him from above.

Ivy and Max had spent the previous day going door-to-door, following up on former patients of the Elgin Mental Hospital who had backgrounds in math. The statements were much more in-depth than the original questionnaire. Two men had seemed promising, but they'd both come up with solid alibis for the nights of the murders. And none of them had triggered anything in Ivy.

But would he? If she came face-to-face with the man who'd savagely and grotesquely attacked her in the middle of the night, would she know he was the one? Or would she smile and nod and go her own way? It was highly probable she'd seen him already, maybe even made eye contact, maybe even spoken to him.

Because that's the way it was with many serial killers. They blended. They moved among the masses, changing color to match their background.

Ivy locked her apartment, all the while aware of the camera directed at her door as she inserted the key. He wasn't coming back, not to her building anyway. He'd made the statement he'd wanted to make and was too smart to allow himself to be videotaped. That assumption didn't keep her from watching hour upon hour of tapes of people coming and going from the building.

They'd caught a couple of drug deals going down, and a prostitute working out of her apartment, another guy stealing welfare checks from tenants' mailboxes. The few suspicious men who'd slipped in without keys had checked out as being friends and relatives of tenants.

He wasn't coming back.

"Hear about your buddy?" the officer at the front desk asked when Ivy arrived at Area Five.

"Who's that?"

"Alex Martin. A body with his driver's license and press ID was found somewhere on the north side of Area Five in a Catholic cemetery."

Her breath caught. "Has he been positively identified?"

"No, but his car was there too."

The room took on a haze of unreality.

If the officer continued to elaborate, Ivy didn't hear it because there was too much noise in her head. Alex Martin? *Dead?*

Carrying the fog with her, she moved blindly through the checkpoint to take the stairs to the second floor. She burst into the task-force office, almost crashing into Max. "What's this about Alex Martin?"

He grabbed her arm and turned her back around. "I tried to call, but you must have had your phone off. Come on. Let's go check it out."

Once they were in his car racing toward the crime scene, Max filled her in on what he knew. "Last month we had a body turn up that appeared to be the victim of some kind of ritualistic sacrifice. That body was found in a cemetery."

"Any leads?"

"A few of circumstantial evidence, but nothing solid. The circumstantial points to a gang of teenagers or young adults who may have taken up Satan worshipping."

"And you think this is another sacrificial murder? Why Alex Martin? And why did you want me to come along?"

"When the cops got there this morning, they found a broken snow globe a few feet from the body."

When he'd told her about the possible sacrificial murder, Ivy had actually felt relief run through her. It had nothing to do with the Madonna Murder case. She was in no way to blame. Now she felt overwhelmed by horror, guilt, remorse.

"It's because of the letter," she said in a low voice.

"We don't know that. It may have nothing to do with the Madonna Murders. It could be someone using it as a sick trick, or using it to throw us off. That's what we're going to have to find out."

Of course, she reasoned. Of course the presence of a globe didn't mean it had been left by the Madonna Murderer. Everybody knew he left a snow globe at every scene. Any maniac could copy him.

The cemetery was deep and narrow, no wider than the domestic lots that flanked either side of it. A place forgotten, with many of the tombstones knocked to the ground years ago by kids committing their first crimes. After cutting their criminal teeth there, the delinquents had moved on to bigger offenses. If they didn't respect the dead, who did they respect?

The grass hadn't been mowed all summer, and not last summer either from the feel and look of the fallen branches hiding under tangles of dead grass, ready to trip an unsuspecting visitor.

"It doesn't look as if anybody's been buried here for years," Ivy said.

"A lot of these little cemeteries have been forgotten," Max told her, picking his way between fallen stones. "This is probably owned by a church that died out years ago."

The crime scene was at the back of the cemetery where trees towered over the ambulance and crime technician van, washing everything in a dense darkness. At the border of the grounds, undergrowth grew as thick and secretive as a jungle.

There was an altar a few feet from where the tangled jungle began, a place where Easter mass must have been said at one time.

Side by side, Ivy and Max approached the scene,

walking in the paths created by tires of the vehicles on location. A little red car was being loaded onto the back of a wrecker so it could be hauled to the crime lab. The local FBI was there, along with a couple of homicide detectives Ivy had met briefly at Headquarters.

Shutters were clicking while another technician ran a video camera.

One of the detectives spotted them and broke away from the group. "As soon as we found the broken snow globe I gave you a call," he said as he approached.

"Does it match the others?" Max asked.

"Hard to say. The thing's shattered. Even the figurines inside. The victim's body has been here awhile—it looks like crows have been making a meal out of him. My guess is, the globe was placed next to the body, on the altar, but something—probably a bird—knocked it down."

"Any idea what the victim was doing here?"

"Not yet. After we get a positive ID, Homicide will be procuring statements from fellow employees, friends, and relatives."

"Get copies to me as soon as you can."

"The grass around the altar has already been vacuumed, so you can walk on it. We aren't done with the body and the altar itself." He glanced at Ivy, then back to Max. "It's pretty bad. Hacked up with an ax is my guess. A couple of our guys got sick. I haven't seen that happen in a long time."

Max suddenly wished he hadn't waited for Ivy to show up. Now he realized it might have been a little insensitive on his part. She'd become so much a part of everything that he hadn't stopped to think. For a moment, he'd forgotten that she wasn't used to seeing dead bodies on a weekly basis.

As the detective walked away, Max turned to Ivy. "You can hang back if you want."

That, of course, was taken as a challenge. Her chin went up, the line of her lips straightened.

She came along.

It was bad. Really bad.

The body was lying faceup on the altar, its severed arms not far away in the grass. The eyes were gone, most likely ravaged by birds, leaving two black holes staring up at the sky. The face was bloated. Blowflies and maggots churned in every opening, giving the body a strange sense of life.

"It's Alex Martin," Ivy said numbly, able to make out enough of his features to confirm his identity.

"This can't be the work of the Madonna Murderer," Max said in a low voice, so only Ivy could hear. "Killing an adult male?"

"I don't think you should eliminate the possibility so readily. There are exceptions to every rule of human behavior."

"We can't afford to spend time going in the wrong direction."

The Madonna Murderer hadn't struck in more than two weeks. Everyone was expecting a new murder any day now, and they couldn't afford to waste time on false leads or clues.

"What about Jonas Sandberg, of Sweden?" Ivy asked. "When he was finally captured for the murder of twelve teenage girls, he was put in a mental institute. Sweden is lax when it comes to incarceration. At night he would sneak out and murder young men, then be back in bed by morning. Nobody thought it could be him because he'd never killed men before, and the method he used was completely different from the murders of the young women. It wasn't until emphysema kept him tethered to an oxygen tank that the murders finally stopped. He sadly voiced his inability to continue killing to another patient, who turned him in."

"For chrissake, Ivy," Max said with a touch of humor. "I was just stating my opinion and my concerns. I'll keep my eye on this case, but I'm also not going to let it distract me—and I don't want it to distract you either."

She was crouched on the ground near the shattered snow globe, already distracted. "It's the same kind." She pointed. "There's part of the baby's blue blanket. There's part of the mother's head."

"The lab will be able to determine whether or not it's an exact match."

She let out a deep breath and stood up. He could tell she'd already decided this was her fault, and that Alex Martin had been killed by the hand of the Madonna Murderer.

They got in the car and headed toward Headquarters.

"Your instincts were right about the letter," Ivy said. "I should have listened to you. That's why he killed him. Because of the letter. Because he knew Alex was behind the dead-baby letter. He probably thought Alex wrote it. He killed him to make sure there would be no more letters."

It was possible, Max thought, yet he was unwilling to commit vocally. "It's so outside his MO."

"This was a crime of anger. Maybe he's taken on

another persona to deal with people like Alex, a persona who is even more hate- and revenge-driven."

"If that's the case—and I'm not conceding anything here—was there anyone else he could perceive as being involved in the letter writing?"

"I suppose he could suspect other employees of the paper, all the way from the editor to the people in the print room."

"That's strictly supposition. We need hard facts. I'm still not sure this was the Madonna Murderer at all."

"What if we discovered that one of the Madonna Murderer's victims has been buried at that cemetery? Would that give us enough of a connection?"

He picked up his cell phone and pushed speed dial. "This is Detective Irving. Get in touch with Records and find out if any of the Madonna Murderer's victims were buried at St. Anthony's Catholic Cemetery." That was followed by a long pause. "What's the address? Okay. Got it." He ended the call. "Write this down," he said to Ivy. She dug into her bag and pulled out pen and paper, quickly jotting down the address.

"What's going on?"

"Regina Hastings. She's been reported missing."

Chapter 35

"Grab that map out of the glove compartment, will you?" Ivy found it, quickly locating the street Max had given her. "Tuesday was the last time anybody saw her," Max said.

"The day she canvassed. You're going to have to get in the right lane to take exit 12B. Didn't Ramirez go by her place?"

"Yeah, but there was nobody there. Said he just figured she'd spent the night somewhere else."

"What about the forms she faxed?"

"Maybe she didn't fax them."

He grabbed the mobile phone again, punching a single digit for speed dial. When someone answered, he said, "Get the forms that were faxed from Officer Hastings's place. First make sure there's a questionnaire for every name on the printout sheet. Then take the faxes down to Documents. Have them determine whether or not they were all written by the same person. My hunch is that one of the printout names won't have a matching answer sheet, or one of the sheets will have been written by someone other than Hastings."

He ended the call and focused on the road and the

traffic, edging his way in between two semis to finally hit the right lane just as the exit came up.

Ivy continued to guide him through several turns. "There it is. Spring Green Apartment Complex."

A black-and-white patrol car was wedged in at an angle near the doors.

Max pulled in and stopped in a no-parking area. Inside the double doors, he flashed his badge, which quickly granted them access to the heart of the building. The manager spewed out directions to Hastings's room, as if she'd already done it several times in the last few days. "There's already people up there!" she shouted after them as Max and Ivy took to the stairs.

Up three flights and down the hall to the right. Apartment 324.

The door was open; they could hear voices long before they got there.

Inside were two women, one close to fifty, the other about twenty-five. They were speaking to a uniformed officer who was taking down notes.

Max introduced himself and Ivy.

The women turned out to be Regina's mother and sister.

"Regina always calls me every two or three days," the older woman said. "Never goes any longer than three, ever. I called her several times, leaving messages, but she never returned my calls. I have a key to her apartment, so I came over. Her car was here, but she wasn't. But she doesn't always drive, so I tell myself she's probably at the police station. I know how she's been working with you, Detective, and I know she's been putting in long hours. So I told myself not to worry, even though I was worried, even though I couldn't help it because that's the way mothers are, isn't that right?" she asked, directing the question to Ivy.

Ivy smiled and agreed.

"My daughter tells me I'm worrying for nothing, but she'll put my mind at ease. She calls the number Gina gave us, the emergency number of the task-force office, and they say she hasn't been there for three days.

"Something's wrong. I can feel it. Something's very wrong."

She began to cry, and her daughter put her arm around her, trying to comfort her.

"If that Madonna Murderer got her, I don't think I can live. I don't think I can live with that in my mind every single day of my life. It's the first thing I'll think of when I get up, and the last thing before I go to bed at night." She broke down completely and her daughter led her away to a couch in the corner.

"What about contamination?" Max asked the officer.

"They told me they've both been in and out of here since yesterday. Probably touched almost everything." He lowered his voice so the women couldn't hear. "Even though they called to report her disappearance, it seemed like the sight of me and the uniform made everything that much more real. She's been going off like this every few minutes."

Max nodded and pulled out his phone. "We need the mobile crime unit," he said into the receiver. He gave them the address. "We'll need them to comb the place for fibers and possible bloodstains, plus dust every surface for prints. Also tell them they'll be examining and transporting a car."

As soon as he disconnected, his phone rang. It was the third time Ramirez had called in an hour. "We don't know anything new," Max told him. "But when we do, I'll call you." He disconnected and slipped the phone into his pocket.

"Don't touch anything else until the crime lab is done," Max said as he and Ivy left the officer to finish questioning Regina Hastings's mother and sister.

From the description they'd been given, they found Regina's car—a little green Toyota—in the parking lot, under the shade of a corrugated-steel-covered carport.

"It looks brand-new," Ivy said as they approached.

Without touching anything, they peered in the windows. Nothing. Not a piece of trash, a gum wrapper, nothing. Using the remote and extra set of keys Regina's mother had given them, Max popped the trunk. The lid flew open, and they stepped closer.

"Oh my God," Ivy said, bringing a hand to her mouth.

There was Regina, or what used to be Regina. She'd been badly beaten, her face bruised and grossly swollen.

Ivy leaned closer. "My God, Max. She's still alive."

Chapter 36

"You can't get these refilled," the pharmacist said, trying to give back the empty brown containers. "Not for another week."

"But my mother's out of her medicine. She's in pain. What if I pay out of pocket?"

"I'm sorry. These are both controlled substances. If she's been taking them as directed, she should have enough for another two weeks. She hasn't been giving her medicine to anyone else, has she?"

"Of course not."

He was sweating, and acting suspicious, but he didn't care. It took all of his willpower to keep from jumping across the counter and wrapping his hands around the guy's throat, choking him, then taking the drugs he needed. "She can't see very well, and she dropped some down the sink. She's not supposed to stop these things cold turkey. You know that."

"I can't refill them."

Was the guy smirking at him? It looked like he was smirking. It looked like he was *glad* he couldn't refill the prescriptions. "Let me use your phone," he demanded. "To call her doctor."

The pharmacist dragged the phone across the counter,

dialed the number on the prescription container, and handed him the receiver.

"Dr. Paragus is out of town," the receptionist said. "You'll have to call back Monday."

"This is an emergency," he said through gritted teeth. "An *emergency*. Do you understand the meaning of that word?"

"If it's an emergency, you should go to the emergency room," the female voice at the other end of the line said coolly. "Otherwise call back on Monday."

He slammed down the receiver.

Kill the bitch.

Kill them all.

You don't know me. You don't know who I am. You don't know what I've done, and what I can do.

"Wait!" The pharmacist yelled from behind the counter. "You forgot your containers."

Without turning around, the muscles in his neck as taut as piano wire, he lifted one arm and threw the finger. He strode out of the pharmacy, only slightly aware that people were staring at him. *Fuck you*, he thought. *Fuck you, ugly old man. Fuck you, ugly old lady. Fuck you.*

He walked, with no thought of his direction. Angry, angry, angry. Shit, shit, shit. He ducked into the first bar he came to and ordered a shot of tequila and a beer.

Shit, shit, shit. What was he going to do? She was waiting for him. Waiting for him to return with her pills. Things had been going so well, they'd been getting along so well.

He couldn't go back.

How could he go back empty-handed?

He could tell her they couldn't refill the prescription. But then she would wonder why. And maybe she would figure out that he had upped her dosage.

For a few days, he'd actually *liked* her. One night, he'd even sat next to her bed and read to her from *Reader's Digest.*

He couldn't go back.

He had to go back.

He ordered another tequila and beer.

An hour later, he was coming out of his slump. What was he afraid of?

Baby.

She was a crippled old woman. What could she do to him? Nothing. *He* was the one in charge, *he* was the one with the strength, the power.

Shouldn't drink, a voice in his head said. *Remember what happened last time?*

Nothing.

Nothing happened.

Are you sure, the voice taunted. *Are you absolutely sure?*

YES! YES! I'm sure. I'm absolutely sure. So shut up. Just shut up!

He ordered another drink.

Time became nonexistent. Occasionally, he would look at the hands on the clock above the bar, but they meant nothing.

"Closing in five minutes," a voice announced. A voice that seemed to come from the end of a long tunnel. "Want me to call you a cab?"

You talking to me?

"Hey buddy. You need a cab?"

"No," he said clearly, straightening away from the bar.

He turned and left the seedy building, stepping out

into a confusing collage of rain and darkness and reflected neon.

He walked, the rain falling down on him, plastering
his hair to his head, but he couldn't feel it. He stopped
and raised his face to the sky, his eyes wide open,
droplets hitting him, blinding him, but still he couldn't
feel it.

He continued walking.

Suddenly he was beside his car. Correction: his
mother's car. He tore the parking ticket from the
wiper and tossed it to the street. Then he got inside
and stuck the key in the ignition.

Autopilot. The car seemed to be on autopilot, making all the correct turns, going the correct speed, staying in the correct lanes, finally taking him home,
finally parking, not in the garage, where he'd hidden
that bitch cop's car for a while, but in the alley behind
his house. Correction: his mother's house.

Lights were on upstairs, but he tried to ignore them.
He let himself in the side door that led directly downstairs, to the basement. He moved quietly, each
wooden step creaking, telling on him.

"Is that you?" she shrieked from upstairs.

He froze.

"Get your ass up here!"

He stood there trembling.

"Get up here! NOW!"

Something warm and wet ran down one leg, filling
his shoe and spilling over. The overpowering smell of
urine hit him in the face.

Slowly, because she was his mother and he was a
good boy, he went up the steps. He walked through
the kitchen.

He found her in the living room. She hadn't left her

bedroom in weeks, but somehow she'd managed to drag herself to the couch. She shoved herself to her feet and stood there, tottering, trying to balance on her good leg.

She was the only person who had power over him. She was the only person who could still make him tremble in fear, still make him wet his pants.

"I . . . was in an accident," he said. Anything to keep her calm, to keep her from yelling at him. "I mean, I saw an accident, and had to stay there and talk to the police."

"You're lying."

"No. No, it's the truth. It was a hit-and-run. This guy was hit and left in the street to die."

Light from the kitchen reflected from the metal chain around her neck, the necklace taken from the whore Sachi Anderson. It was there, caught in the sweaty folds of her skin, winking at him, beckoning.

"You're a worthless piece of shit. I should have drowned you when you were born. I should have tied a concrete block to you and tossed you into Lake Michigan."

"That would have been murder," he said woodenly.

He could feel himself retreating, and suddenly he was watching the scene with the detachment of a non-biased observer. It was safe here. The power was still within him, but it had gone into sleep mode, ready to be called forward when he needed it.

"It ain't murder when you don't even qualify as a human."

"Qualify." That wasn't a word she would normally use. "Have you been watching *People's Court* again?"

He could see that his question baffled her, just as his question had baffled the bartender. He picked up a lamp and began walking slowly toward her, jerking the cord from the receptacle as he moved.

The fear in her face!

It was glorious!

Glorious!

He would like to have a photograph of it, but this wasn't the time. And anyway, he would never forget her expression. It would be etched deeply into his memory, beside all of his other memories of her.

"Put that down."

Never taking her eyes off him, she took a step back. She tried to fall into her mother-bitch role, tried to scare him into obeying her, but this time it didn't work. And even when she was yelling at him, he could see the fear in her eyes, the terror.

He didn't want the moment to end. He wanted to embrace it, savor it, draw it out for as long as he could.

"Who's your sweet cakes?" he asked.

"Y-you are."

"Who do you love more than Elvis?"

"Y-you."

"Who do you love more than that dumb-ass on that stupid soap opera?"

"You! You! You know it's you! S-so p-put d-down the lamp," she pleaded, reaching imploringly toward him, then pulling back her hands to clasp them together in front of her.

He smashed the lamp down on the table. It shattered, and he pulled the cord free of the broken ceramic. "Say the words," he commanded, wrapping both ends of the cord tightly around his hands. "Say the words."

"I love you!" She was sobbing now. Tears of fear running down her cheeks, her jowls shaking.

"Again!"

"I LOVE YOU!"

With one swift movement, he wrapped the cord around her neck and pulled tightly, his muscles bunching from his power, his incredible power.

Across his mind flashed a picture.

A boy and a woman.

Mother and son.

Mother and son.

He watched as her face turned purple. Watched as her eyes bugged out. He pulled and pulled and pulled. When he finally let go, she fell heavily to the floor, air escaping her lungs, rushing past her lips in a *hiss*.

There.

Finally.

Now she was quiet. Finally she was quiet.

Now she was the good mother. The mother he loved.

"Time for bed," he told her. "You've been staying up much too late."

He unwrapped the cord from her neck and dragged her across the floor to the bedroom. *Deadweight,* a voice in his head taunted. *Deadweight. The bitch is dead, now go to bed. The bitch is dead, now go to bed.*

It took an enormous amount of strength, an enormous amount of time. He shoved and lifted, shoved and lifted, finally getting her into bed. He tugged at her arms, tugged at her legs, trying to achieve a natural arrangement, but nothing worked. He jerked the sheet from under her weight and covered her with it. He was walking away when he thought he heard her say something.

"What?" he asked, turning around.

Dirty boy. Dirty, dirty boy.

"Shut up!"

He found a blanket on the floor and tossed it over her face so she'd quit staring at him.

Dirty boy, dirty, dirty boy.

"I'm a good boy," he whispered, backing away while not taking his eyes off the bump in the bed. "I'm a good boy." He reached blindly behind him, found the wall switch, and turned off the light, dousing the room in darkness.

Goodnight, sweetheart.

"Goodnight, Mommy."

The next morning he woke up late. He jumped out of bed and ran upstairs, quickly putting together some juice and oatmeal. He placed it on a tray, wishing he had a flower, then he carried it into his mother's room.

"Time for breakfast," he announced, his heart thudding heavily in his chest. "Rise and shine."

She didn't move.

"Rise and shine," he repeated.

She didn't move.

Grasping the tray with one hand, he slowly approached the bed, then carefully lifted the edge of the blanket with his free hand.

He dropped the blanket and jumped away.

His mother stared back at him, her face grotesquely swollen, eyes bulging, tongue protruding. The tray slid from his fingers and fell, the glass shattering, juice and oatmeal splashing his pants. He dropped to the floor, shards of glass embedding in his knees. He put a hand to his mouth and emitted a choking sound. A gasp. A gag.

She was dead.

His mother was dead.

Tears poured from his eyes. He could feel them falling over the back of his hand, hot and burning.

She's dead.

The bitch is dead.

His mouth was hanging open. His breath came in short, quick gasps, and he made a sound that was a cross between a sob and a laugh.

Something sparked in his brain. A recent memory. A blond-haired boy in a hockey uniform standing next to a red-haired woman. If you took away the hair, they looked remarkably alike.

Mother and son.

Mother and son.

Chapter 37

"If you had to choose between having a big head or a little one, what would it be?"

Preoccupied with the CD in his hand, Ethan didn't answer at first. "Huh? Oh. I don't know. A big one, I guess. People with big heads are smart. If you had a little tiny head, then you'd be a moron."

Ryan's constant chatter was getting on Ethan's nerves. He'd asked him to come along to the record show at Navy Pier for purely selfish reasons: Ryan had a car. Ethan had justified it by telling himself Ryan would get off on the show as much as Ethan. He thought that once Ryan actually got there, he'd enjoy it.

Vendors were there from all over the country, all over the *world*. If you were looking for some obscure album from a short-lived group nobody had ever heard of, chances were you'd find it there.

They'd both purchased three-day passes, but now, only five hours into the first day, Ryan was already bored. He'd hit the first heavy-metal tables he'd seen. Then, without bothering to do any comparison shopping, without bothering to go any deeper into the myriad of tables and people, he'd spent all of his money in the first hour.

"How much for the Cocteau Twins box set?" Ethan asked the sleepy-looking guy with a nose ring and pony-tail who stood at a long display table. Behind him hung a black Stereolab T-shirt. Next to that was a long-sleeved Radiohead shirt.

"Eighty bucks."

"I order it through Cheapo for sixty-five."

The guy took a long sip of soda. "If you can get it. They might tell you they can order it, but it'll never come in. Been out of print for years."

Ethan knew that. "How about this Guided by Voices?"

"Twenty-five."

Guided by Voices were amazing, but this was live, recorded at somebody's birthday party, which meant Robert Pollard had probably been wasted. You don't want to listen to Guided by Voices when they're wasted. *You* can be wasted, but they can't. Music that was normally floaty and haunting turned into harsh punk rock, and the vocals turned to shouting, not singing. Shouting was okay in the right place, take the Clash, for instance. It just didn't work for Guided by Voices stuff.

"Thanks." He put the CD back.

"How about *Under the Bushes, Under the Stars*?" the vendor asked.

"Got it."

"*Alien Lanes?*"

"Got it." Ethan picked up a My Bloody Valentine album. *Loveless.* He had the CD, but didn't know they'd put *Loveless* out on vinyl. He'd never seen it on vinyl before—and that amazed him.

"Is this a reissue?" he asked.

To his right, just off his shoulder, Ryan continued his prattle. "Ever noticed how it's hard to tell the difference between a punk and a scurve?"

"No. That's really rare. They only pressed a couple thousand."

Vendors always told you that crap. Ethan wasn't stupid. And yet, it was really weird that he hadn't known about it. Could it be a bootleg?

"It's because punks have that 'haven't washed my hair in two weeks, just got out of bed thing' going— and it took them hours to look like that. Where scurves, on the other hand, really *haven't* washed or combed their hair in two weeks. There's no shine to it, and they have a real bed-head thing going in the back."

Ethan slid the album back into place and turned to his friend. "Do you wanna leave?"

Ryan looked around, as if trying to find a reason to stay. "This is boring," he said, apparently not finding anything interesting.

"What would you be doing if you weren't here?"

Hands deep in the front pockets of his cargo pants, Ryan shrugged. "I don't know. Playing video games. That's more interesting than this."

Ryan was addicted to video games. A lot of Ethan's friends were addicted to video games.

"I'm not ready to leave," Ethan said. "I won't be ready for a long time. Why don't you go on home?"

"Are you still spending the night at my house?"

It seemed pointless now. "Nah. I'll go home after I'm done here."

"How will you get there?"

"I'll figure something out. Maybe I'll take the el to

the police station and catch a ride with my dad. Or
I'll call him and he can pick me up."

It was always such a downer when you tried to draw
someone into your infatuation, thinking all they had
to do was listen to Galaxy 500's cover of Yoko Ono's
"Listen, the Snow Is Falling," or Spiritualized's *Ladies
and Gentlemen We Are Floating in Space,* Grant Hart's
Good News for Modern Man, to see that music was
art in its most multilayered form, a combination of
lyrics and notes that could create a unique, cinematic
wonder in your head.

But they never got it. They didn't want to get it.
Ryan would rather sit in front of the TV playing Killing Time with heavy metal blasting in the background
than listen to something with any depth.

"I'll find a way home," Ethan said. "Don't worry.
And hey, thanks for the ride."

"No sweat."

Ethan watched as Ryan bobbed away, moving
through the crowd to finally disappear.

He expected too much from people, that was the
problem, Ethan thought. He expected too much from
life. In a way, he wished he could be like Ryan, so
easy to please, satisfied to sit in front of the TV all
day, killing imaginary people and sometimes getting
killed himself. Lyrics from a Kurt Cobain song played
in his head, the ones about wishing he could be easily
amused like everybody else.

After Ryan had gone, Ethan continued to wander
among the people and tables. He had a hundred dollars to spend, and he was going to have a hard time
deciding how to get the most mileage out of his
money. He had to take into account the rarity of his
purchases. If it was something he could get somewhere

down the road, then he should wait. But if finding a
treasure was a one-time deal, he should act now.

But eighty bucks for the Cocteau Twins box set?
Damn. That was a lot of money. He didn't know. He
just didn't know. Then there was the Velvet Underground box set with outtakes from the *Loaded*
sessions—

Somebody bumped into him, turned around,
grabbed him by the arm with a clawlike grip, and apol-
ogized. "Sorry. Really sorry."

"That's okay," Ethan said, shaking him off, even
though he didn't think it was okay. Why didn't the
jerk look where he was going?

The guy was staring at him as if he expected Ethan
to say something else.

"You don't know who I am, do you?" the guy
asked.

Now Ethan remembered where he'd seen him before. The hockey game. "You're my dad's friend,
uh . . . Mr. . . . Mr. . . ." Ethan didn't have a clue,
but he was hoping Mr. Whoever He Was would fill in
the big blank space floating between them.

"Grant."

"Mr. Grant."

He laughed in a good-natured way that Ethan found
irritating. "Grant's my first name. Grant Ruby. So,
you're taking in the big show, huh? Looks like we
have some of the same interests."

Ethan looked down and saw that in the guy's hand
was the burgundy, fabric-covered Cocteau Twins box
set. What the hell? Guess he could mark that one off
his list. "You know somebody who likes the Cocteau
Twins?" Ethan asked, thinking it couldn't be anybody
at his school.

"It's for me. Rather an indulgence at seventy bucks, but I've been looking for it for a long time, and it's getting rarer and rarer."

Ethan didn't know what was more amazing, that he'd been able to talk the vendor down to seventy bucks, or that here was somebody else who liked the Cocteau Twins, and the guy was a middle-aged fucking nerd.

He asked Ethan what he was looking for. Side by side, they began walking through the crowd, past tables, as Ethan ran through his list, expecting the geek's eyes to glaze over the way everyone else's did whenever he talked about his obsession.

But they didn't. He jumped right in and kept up. He knew all about Portishead, and Stereolab. He knew that Doug Yule sang vocals on "New Age," not Lou Reed. He knew about the history of groups and artists. He knew how Morrissey used to be in the Smiths, and how he was a strict vegan, and how he wouldn't let anybody eat pork rinds at his concerts.

"Are you hungry?" the guy asked. "I am. Wanna grab a piece of pizza at one of these places?"

In front of them were the food vendors. Ethan said, "Sure."

Ruby offered to pay for Ethan's, but Ethan wouldn't let him. They found a table that was away from the main traffic flow and sat down across from each other.

"That just blows me away that you know so much about music," Ethan said, picking up his slice of pizza.

"I majored in music theory," Ruby said.

"Cool. What do you do now?"

"A lot of self-taught musicians can't read music. So

they record something, then send it to me to transcribe."

"Then how do you know my dad? I figured you worked with him."

"We're practically neighbors. I live on Davern Circle and I've run into your dad a few times. I used to have a nephew who played hockey. He graduated a few years ago, so you wouldn't know him. But I kept going to the games. I dig hockey almost as much as music."

When they were done eating, they sat there, continuing to talk. They talked about record labels, about how the majority of labels didn't care anything about the music, they just wanted a pretty face they could saturate the media with. The people who were doing the good stuff weren't being signed.

"Same with radio," Ruby said. "It has nothing to do with music. For the station, music is just the noise in between the ads."

"No shit. It's even hard to tell the songs *from* the ads."

"I know. It's like solid ads."

"And nobody cares. Nobody cares that they're being spoon-fed shit. They just think, I like this shit because everybody else likes this shit."

"I know, I know!"

They both laughed.

And Ethan suddenly began telling Ruby everything, about how Max had adopted him, and about how Ethan had tried to find his birth father, only to find out that the woman he'd always thought of as his birth *mother* had actually adopted him. It all came pouring out.

It was because of the music. That's why it happened. It had unlocked a door, and left Ethan thinking that here, finally, was somebody who understood him, somebody he could talk to.

They wandered around some more, Ruby saying that he'd better not spend any more money.

Ethan wondered if he should get the My Bloody Valentine album. "The guy said there were only a couple thousand pressed, but I don't know if I believe him."

"It's true," Ruby said. "You'd better get it."

So Ethan bought the album for twelve bucks, and walked around with it under his arm, the bloodred cover protected with a plastic sleeve. He bought a couple of other CDs that he'd been looking for, then decided he'd try to come back tomorrow. The vendors always dropped their prices as the days progressed.

"How you getting home?" Ruby asked.

"I don't know. I thought I'd stop by my dad's office, see if he's around."

"I can give you a ride. I only live a couple of streets away."

"You wouldn't care?"

"I'd like the company. And we can listen to the Cocteau Twins on the way."

"Cool."

Ten minutes later, they were in Ruby's car.

One of the things that was so great about the Cocteau Twins was the way the vocals sounded like another instrument, not like words at all but sounds, melody. There was a part in "Iceblink Luck," from *Heaven or Las Vegas,* where you could actually make out a few words—something about burning a madhouse down.

Around there was when Ethan began to wonder about Ruby. That was when everything his dad had drilled into him from the time he was little came rushing back. Stuff about never getting into a car with a stranger. But Ruby wasn't a stranger. Was he?

Maybe he lied. Maybe he doesn't really even know my dad.

But Ethan had seen him wave to his dad at the hockey game, the one he'd brought Ivy to.

But had his dad waved back?

As far as Ethan could tell, they were heading in the right direction, northwest out of metro Chicago.

It was late, after nine o'clock, and it was dark.

His new buddy's car was one of those big jobs that old lady losers or rich people drove. The bigger the better, they must think. But Ruby's was old, and the shocks weren't good, because whenever they hit a bump, the front end would start to bob, bob, bob, gradually stopping, only to start again as soon as they hit another bump.

Ethan wanted him to shut off the music. This kind of music, the kind that should be worshipped, didn't belong in a crappy, creepy car like this, coming out of little speakers. The music didn't go with a man who, when you took away his interest in music, was just a little weird. He didn't actually *look* weird, but now that they were together in his claustrophobic car, Ethan was picking up an uncomfortable vibe.

"This your car?" Ethan asked.

You'd think somebody who liked music so much would have a good stereo. This one sounded like shit.

"It belongs to my mother," Ruby said.

No explanation of where *his* car might be. In the shop, probably, Ethan told himself. People were always getting into fender benders in Chicago, that's one of the reasons his old man refused to get a new car. He said it would just get run into, so why bother? And some people had crappy cars they kept just to drive downtown. Maybe that was the deal with Ruby.

If Ruby was his real name.

Where had that come from? Why wouldn't Ruby be his real name?

"Do you mind if we shut this off?" he asked, motioning toward the CD player even though the interior of the car was dark and Ruby couldn't see him.

"I thought you wanted to hear it."

"Not through those crappy speakers. There's no high or low end. Can't you tell?"

"I know this car's a piece of junk. I'm going to trade it in for something else."

"I thought it was your mother's."

"It is, but she can't drive anymore."

"Why? Too old?"

"I don't want to talk about her," he said, his voice rising in obvious irritation. "Let's talk about you. What would you say if I told you I could hook you up with your real mother?"

Leeriness briefly forgotten, Ethan twisted in the seat so he could get a better look at Ruby's silhouette. "You could do that? How?"

"I know some people."

"Wow. That would be great. More than great."

Ruby cut across two lanes to the exit ramp.

"Wrong exit," Ethan said.

"I know, but my oil light's on, see?"

Ethan leaned over and saw that, indeed, the red light was on. "Oh, man." Why'd he ever get in the car with this loser?

Ruby pulled off onto a dark side street. "Got extra oil in the back."

He got out and went around to the trunk. Ethan heard him banging things together that sounded like tire irons or something. Then he lost track of him until he knocked on the passenger window, almost sending Ethan through the roof.

"You scared the crap out of me," Ethan complained.

Ruby shouted through the rolled-up window. "Come out and hold the flashlight for me, will you?"

What a joke.

Ethan had one foot on the ground when something unseen, something powerful, hit him full on top of the head, the force bringing him to his knees. Pain radiated through his skull, all the way to his teeth. Behind his eyelids, star bursts flashed, then the world turned black.

Chapter 38

"Her condition is critical," the doctor told Max, Ivy, and Ronny Ramirez as they stood in the hallway outside Intensive Care.

"How can she even be alive?" Ivy asked. "How could anyone survive that long locked in a trunk?"

"She couldn't have been there over eight to twelve hours—and only if most of those hours were overnight," Dr. Montoya said.

"You're sure?" Max asked.

"The temperature inside the trunk would have steadily increased throughout the morning," the doctor explained. "An *uninjured* person wouldn't have been able to withstand more than a few hours in the heat of the day."

"I'm putting a twenty-four-hour guard on her," Max said. "She's the only one who can identify the person who did this to her. And it's extremely important that we catch him, because if we don't, more lives are in danger."

"Well, you'd better hope to find another eyewitness, because Regina Hastings is a long shot. If she does come around she'll most likely be brain damaged."

Ramirez made an anguished sound, and Ivy squeezed his arm in sympathy.

Max's mobile phone rang. The doctor took the opportunity to excuse himself to speak to Regina's family.

The call was from Harold Doyle of Documents. "You know those faxes you sent down?" he asked. "Half of them were written by someone other than Regina Hastings."

"You sure?"

"Positive."

"Do any of them match the letters written to the paper?"

"Haven't gotten that far, but I'm working on it."

"Call me when you have something."

Max disconnected, then dialed home. Nobody answered, but that didn't surprise him. Ethan had gone to a music show and was staying the night at Ryan's.

"He must have gone to her apartment and faxed the questionnaires," Ivy said as soon as Max hung up. "Then, after putting her body in the trunk of her own car, he went back in the middle of the night to leave her in the parking area."

"You're probably right."

"I wonder if he thought she was dead, or if he put her there to finish her off."

"He's playing with us again, that's what he's doing," Max said.

"I had the feeling something was wrong that first night," Ronny said. "Why didn't I go by her place then?"

"You couldn't have been sure," Ivy said, trying to reassure him. "Regina's independent."

"Yeah, but she takes her job seriously. I should have known. I should have known."

Max's phone rang again.

The call was from Raymond Lira, Vice Squad. "We just arrested a guy for dealing acepromazine," he told Max. "Offered him a break if he worked with us, told us who he sold to. One of his clients sounds like it might be our man."

"Get a sketch artist down there."

"Now? It's late."

"I don't care. Get someone down there."

"Should they use the Identi-Kit?" he asked, referring to a kit that contained interchangeable paper features.

"No, get Barbara Ainsworth if you can—she's the best. If we're lucky, we might be able to make tomorrow's paper."

He contacted the task-force office. "Call the papers," Max said. "Tell them to save us a spot. Find out how long they can wait to go to press. And get in touch with taxi companies and metro transit to see if anybody recently picked up a male passenger near the Spring Green Apartment Complex."

Using the right bait was everything.

The Manipulator was cruising down Interstate 90, heading in the direction of his house, feeling calm, feeling in control. Everything was falling into place. Everything would be all right.

The streets of Chicago were spread out before him—strings of twinkling lights. Beautiful. Really beautiful.

He'd agonized over how he was going to get the kid to come with him. But in the end, it had been so easy. He'd been following him off and on for a couple of weeks. He knew the way he hung out at music stores. He'd even taken note of his purchases. That was all it took. The record and CD show—that was a gift. The perfect gift.

And now little Adrian was in the trunk of his car, waiting to be reunited with his mother.

They were still alive. Both of them. Their deaths had been faked in order to trick him. *That's* what had screwed everything up. They were supposed to have been the thirteenth victims. But because neither of them had really died, everything was wrong. *That's* why he'd always felt there was something missing. Some big hole that was always there, in the back of his brain. And whenever he turned his thoughts toward it, trying to look at it, trying to see what was whispering to him, annoying him, he could never turn his head fast enough. He could never see it.

But now everything made sense.

He wasn't crazy.

"He was more like . . . I don't know . . . skinny. He was one of those skinny white guys."

"So, he had a thin face?" asked the sketch artist.

"Yeah."

"How about the forehead?"

"Big. He had a big forehead."

"Eyes? Were they big, small, average?"

"Average."

"Facial hair?"

"Did he have any? No, but he had these little dark lines above his mouth that he needed to shave."

"Mouth. Big? Little? Average?"

"Big."

They went on and on.

The sketch artist deftly filled in short dark hair. She changed the shape of the jaw a couple of times until the drug dealer was finally satisfied. "Yeah, that's the guy."

Max, who'd been sitting quietly at a desk in the corner of the room, now came forward. "Was there anything else about him that stood out? The way he talked? The way he dressed? Mannerisms?"

"He had no sense of style."

"What do you mean?"

"His clothes were dull. He had no sense of style, man."

"Anything else?"

"He talked like a college-educated white guy."

"How's that?"

"I don't know. He didn't use any street language."

"What about tone of voice? Was his voice deep? High?"

"He had a soft voice. Talked like this: 'How much do I owe you?' " the informant said in a smooth, low voice. Then he laughed. "Yeah, that was it. Just like that. *'How much do I owe you?'* " He laughed again.

Ivy pushed the print button at the computer where she'd been sitting, taking notes. The printer spewed out a copy of the description, which they put with the composite, faxing and e-mailing both to the papers.

Ivy and Max followed up the faxes with phone calls to make sure they would make the morning editions. While she had the assistant editor of the *Herald* on the phone, she got home phone numbers of coworkers who might have information on Alex Martin.

"Maude Cunningham would be your best bet," the editor told her. "She was his desk advisor."

After hanging up, Ivy gave Maude a call. "Can I come by and talk to you?" Ivy asked. "I know it's late, but——"

"Come over," Maude cut in. "I won't be doing any sleeping tonight."

While Max tied up loose ends at the task-force office, Ivy caught a cab to Maude's Lincoln Park address.

Maude reminded Ivy of Bette Davis toward the end of her career. Tough, dignified, and a little scary. She smelled like whiskey and cigarette smoke.

"Come on in," Maude said, standing in the doorway of her apartment, the ceiling light casting a yellow glow above her head. Behind her, a cat meowed. "I don't want Miss Kitty to get out."

Ivy stepped inside, and the woman closed the door behind her. The entryway walls were covered with framed newspaper photos and articles. "Is this you?" Ivy asked, pointing to a beautiful young woman standing next to the Queen of England.

"Yeah, believe it or not, I used to be good-looking. She used to be good-looking too." She let out a cackle.

Ivy didn't even attempt a response. "What can you tell me about Alex Martin? Do you know why he went to the cemetery? Was he meeting someone?"

"He didn't mention the cemetery to me at all." Maude shook out a filterless cigarette and lit it, blowing out a cloud of smoke. "I think he thought he was going to get a scoop, and didn't want me to butt in. If he'd told me it had to do with the Madonna Murderer, I wouldn't have let him go." She pulled a piece of tobacco off her tongue, then examined the lit end of her cigarette. "I'd been bragging to him about getting the story, no matter what. It was kind of exciting having somebody that young around who looked up to me and wanted to listen to my bullshit. Alex was a nice kid, but I had to edit the hell out of his stuff. He'd go off on tangents that had nothing to do with the subject matter. But he was good. Just needed some restraining, that's all. He was after a Pulitzer, you know that?" She let out a sad laugh and shook her head. "Poor kid."

Chapter 39

The *Chicago Herald* and the *Chicago Sun Times* ran the sketch along with the identifying characteristics of the Madonna Murderer on the front page, right under an article about international terrorists. The fact that the Madonna Murderer's first victim had been buried in the Catholic cemetery where Alex Martin's body was found had quickly gotten out, and that knowledge now figured prominently in all media coverage.

When the paper hit the stands, task-force members were waiting to read it and pass it around. Some had come in early. Others, like Max and Ivy, had stayed the night in their second-floor home away from home.

Shortly past daybreak officers hit the streets in pairs, recanvassing all the former patients Regina Hastings had visited, beginning with the interviews that had been written by someone else's hand.

A brief lull gave Max the opportunity to call Ryan Harrison's house to check on Ethan.

"He isn't here," Judy Harrison said. "Wait. Let me see. Maybe he came over after I went to sleep."

The receiver clattered in Max's ear. He heard her walk away, then heard her come back and pick up the phone. "He's not here," she said firmly. "He and

Ryan went to the music show downtown yesterday. Ryan came home in the afternoon, but Ethan stayed. He decided not to spend the night here, and said he'd catch a ride home with you."

"Thanks." Max hung up, then immediately dialed home.

There was no answer.

"Did anybody take a call from my son yesterday?" he asked the room of burnt-out, half-asleep people.

That question was followed by a lot of head shaking.

"I'll check the books." Ivy uncurled stiffly from the couch where she'd spent the last hour with her feet tucked under her, trying to stay awake. Two others jumped up to help.

Every phone call was entered into a logbook, with the time, subject, and caller ID. In a matter of minutes, they were done.

"Nothing here."

Max tried calling home again. Again there was no answer. He called Ethan's hockey coach. He called the homes of several of Ethan's buddies. He called the bagel shop, hoping to find that Ethan was filling in for a sick coworker at the last minute.

Nobody had seen or heard from him.

Feeling sick to his stomach, Max put in a call to the crime lab's fingerprint expert, Joel Runyan. "Get any prints off that hockey stick?" he asked.

"Three different ones," Joel said, "but so far we haven't found any matches in our database."

"I've got a print I'm going to fax you. I want you to see if it matches anything you lifted from the stick. And Joel, I need those results immediately. Drop whatever else you're doing." After hanging up, Max hurried to his office and pulled a set of fingerprints from his desk. He enlarged them on his copy machine, then faxed them to the lab. He was heading out the door when Ivy caught up with him.

"I'm going home," he told her without stopping.

She fell into step beside him. "Is something wrong?"

"I can't get in touch with Ethan."

"I'll come with you."

Traffic wasn't bad, and they made it to Max's in less than forty minutes.

At the house, there was no sign of Ethan. "I don't think he's been here since yesterday," Max said, panic beginning to grab him by the throat. He called Ryan's house again. They hadn't heard from him.

"Let me talk to Ryan," Max said.

Ryan was put on the phone. "I'm sorry, Mr. Irving. I tried to talk him into coming home with me, but he wanted to stay."

"Did he say where he planned to go, what he planned to do after he left Navy Pier?"

"He was going to call you, or catch the subway to your office. That's what he told me, I swear. I *swear*."

"I believe you." Max hung up, then quickly gathered some recent photos of Ethan. "Come on."

They ran outside and dove into the car. Max took off, tires squealing as he made a U-turn, heading back in the direction they'd come.

"Maybe I should drive," Ivy said, clinging to the door as he swerved in and out of traffic.

"I'm okay."

"Are you thinking Ethan's disappearance has something to do with the Madonna Murderer case?"

"I didn't want to hear those word spoken out loud."

He pulled sharply into the right lane, cutting off

a white Taurus. The driver honked and threw him the finger.

"You're jumping to conclusions," Ivy reasoned. "Ethan was probably hanging out with some friends, maybe got drunk, and was afraid to come home. Didn't you tell me he's done that before? Didn't you say he's under probation for drinking?"

"Yeah, but he's been doing so well."

Max rubbed his forehead. Sweat trickled down the side of his face. "You're probably right. My brain is foggy. Too many sleepless nights. I'm overreacting, that's all." But he didn't stop sweating, and he didn't stop cutting people off.

Max's phone rang, and he quickly answered it. It was Joel Runyan from the crime lab.

"The set of prints you faxed matched one of the prints found on the hockey stick," Joel said.

Max's throat tightened and his stomach knotted. "Are you sure?" Max asked, his voice strained. "How many points?"

"Fourteen."

A fourteen-point match was nothing to dispute.

"Who do the prints belong to?" Joel asked.

Max swallowed. When Ethan was little, he used to like to have his prints taken. Max had a drawer full of them. "My son," he said. "They belong to my son."

"Have you seen this kid?"

"Have you seen this kid?"

Separately, Max and Ivy moved quickly from one vendor to the next, showing Ethan's school photo as they went.

There were hundreds of vendors, and as they

worked their way forward with no results, Max's panic grew.

Finally a guy with a nose ring grabbed the picture from Ivy and stared at it. "Yeah, I saw him. He bought a My Bloody Valentine album from me."

"Max!" Ivy could feel her heart thudding in her stomach.

Let him be okay. Let Max's son be okay.

Max turned toward her. Walking sideways, he backtracked, cutting through the mob to reach her side. "You've seen him?" Max asked. "When?"

"Yesterday. I saw him a couple a times yesterday."

"Have you seen him today?"

The vendor shook his head. A woman showed up and slipped behind the table, dropping a copy of the *Chicago Herald* on top of some boxed and sorted CDs. "Here's your paper, hon."

"He was with a guy who looked kinda like that," the vendor said, pointing to the sketched face looking up at them from the paper.

Ivy thought Max was going to pass out.

He swayed a little. He squeezed his eyes shut. He pulled in a shuddering breath, then brought a closed fist up hard against his mouth, as if to keep an anguished sob from escaping. And he just stood there, for the longest time.

Ivy grabbed his arm. "Come on, Max," she said softly. He didn't move, so she grabbed him by both arms, shaking him firmly, saying, "Max. Don't fall apart. Not now. You can't fall apart now."

He let his fist drop away from his face. Bloodshot eyes stared hard at her, as if trying to figure out who she was, and what she was doing there. Then she saw the recognition, saw the detective taking over for the father who couldn't function. He straightened. Side by side, they hurried from the building, heading for his car and Area Five Headquarters.

His dad would find him, Ethan told himself. His dad would find him, and when he did, he would beat the holy shit out of the guy who'd done this to him.

Panic flooded through him, and a sob would have escaped if his mouth hadn't been covered with duct tape. He couldn't feel his hands or arms anymore; they were bound tightly behind him. He couldn't feel his feet, which were tied at the ankles. His hair was stuck to his head, and he knew he'd been bleeding.

He was lying on the floor in a dark room. He had no idea how long he'd been there, because he'd been unconscious. The son of a bitch had hammered him, knocking him out.

The smell.

The smell was so bad that he kept gagging against the tape. And what terrified him so much was that it smelled the way Max sometimes smelled underneath the lemon shampoo.

He tried to pray, but kept forgetting the words. He kept thinking about all the horrible stories he'd heard, not from his dad, but from some of the officers at the police station. Ethan used to go down there when he was little. He even had a cop uniform. Different officers would sit him on their desks where he would swing his legs back and forth and fiddle with his pretend badge, thinking it looked real, thinking it *was* real. And if he asked an innocent question, the officers would tell him the answers with stories he hoped were made up. He would go home and have nightmares, worrying that someone might come in and steal him during the night, or cut out his liver and eat it. He used to become so terrified that he made his dad keep the hall light on all night.

He couldn't quit thinking about those stories he thought he'd put away along with his pretend police uniform, his pretend badge. Stories about predators, about evil people who had no conscience, who enjoyed making people suffer before finally killing them by strangulation, or bludgeoning, or cutting off piece after piece until the victim bled to death or died of shock or both.

He whimpered in terror. If he was going to die, he wanted it to be fast, to be over as quickly as possible. He didn't want to be tortured. *Don't torture me. Please don't torture me.*

He wanted to just close his eyes and disappear. Just close his eyes and no longer exist.

Where was his dad? Was he looking for him? No. Probably not. He thought he was at Ryan's. Max probably didn't even know he was gone.

Please come. Please find me. Don't let him cut me up. Don't let him hurt me anymore.

He wished he could shut off his brain, but he couldn't, and his thoughts just kept moving forward. His breath was coming in short little puffs. In his panic, he began to hyperventilate.

After he was dead, Ruby would peel off his skin and use it to make lamp shades. He would cut him up and put him in a suitcase. He would dump the suitcase in the water somewhere, weighting it down with cement blocks. And Ethan would sink down, down, down. . . .

*   *   *

"Music," Ivy said from behind the wheel of Max's car, driving as fast as she felt was safe. "What if it's not mathematics, but *music*?"

Her words finally sunk in, with Max slowly responding from another realm. "Music?"

"We've been looking for someone who deals with numbers, but what about music? Pythagoras was one of the first to point out the close relationship between math and music." She sensed that Max was listening, so she continued with her theory. "He also believed in what he called the table of opposites. Light and dark. Good and evil. He went so far as to say that math and music have connections internally and externally, affecting the currents of our souls and the structure of the universe. I think it's significant that Ethan may have been picked up at a music show. Is Ethan the type to just hop in the car with a stranger?"

"No."

"So he had to use bait. What's bait for Ethan?"

"Music."

Max was sounding better, stronger.

Ivy cut into the Area Five parking lot, and Max jumped out and ran inside the building. He took the stairs up two flights and down the hall where he burst into the task-force room.

"Go through the reports again," he said, gasping for breath.

Phones were ringing, but no one was answering. Mouths hung open. All eyes were on Max.

"Run cross-references on our databases. Go through the canvassing reports again, but look for a man who's involved in the music field."

He turned to Ramirez. "Any matches yet?" he asked, unable to keep the desperation from his voice.

Records was doing a nationwide search, trying to match the face to someone who had a criminal record.

"No, nothing," Ramirez said. "But it can take a long time. Days maybe."

"We don't have days," Max said. "He's got my son."

Chapter 40

"Okay," Ramirez said from his computer terminal. "Got a couple of matches. One guy was a music major at Chicago School of Music, but never graduated. The other has been in a band off and on. Both have spent time in mental hospitals." He pushed print, then handed the two addresses to Max.

The task-force room was chaos. Every phone was ringing, most of the calls from people who'd seen the composite in the paper.

In the last year Chicago had expanded its SWAT team, hiring twenty additional officers, most of them deputized so that they could follow a maneuver to the end. The increased manpower and broader scope of skills gave them the advantage of splitting up if necessary. Max put in a call to Commander Richard Miller, ordering the deployment of two teams. They would be in position in thirty minutes.

Max hung up, continuing to bark out orders. He sent one pair of detectives to the Elgin Mental Hospital, another to South Side Chicago Mental Hospital.

"Ramirez and I will take the address west of Pulaski. Cartier—you take the Delaware Park address."

Ivy got to her feet, prepared to go. Max stopped

her. "Stay here and answer phones. And don't do anything else. You've done enough already."

"What are you talking about?"

He grabbed her by the arm. "The dead-baby letter set him off," he said harshly. "Now he's after everybody involved in the case. He knows I'm in charge, so how can he hurt me the most? By hurting my son."

Max was almost out the door when a breathless Harold Doyle from Documents caught up with him. "I think we may have a handwriting match from the Human Services office. He applied for welfare back in '93. The name's Grant Ruby."

Max immediately recontacted the SWAT team leader. "We've got a positive ID," he said. Using police code, he instructed them to converge on the Delaware Park address. They would station themselves three blocks away and wait for further instructions. He radioed air patrol and ordered two units to rendezvous at the target site.

Ivy sat down at the desk, the ringing phone near her elbow going unanswered.

Grant Ruby.

He had a name. Finally, he had a name.

Grant Ruby.

Ethan was missing, kidnapped by the Madonna Murderer, a murderer who now had a name.

Max hated her, but that wasn't important, that didn't matter.

Ethan.

Had he taken Ethan because of the letter? Or because of Max? Or was there more to it than that?

Think, think.

Max. He's heading for the killer's house right now.

Ethan might already be dead.
And Max will find him there, his dead son.
Oh, God.
Think, think.
Was there more? Something she was missing?
Something all of them were missing?

The target rendezvous was in a part of town most
officers had never seen, located at the end of a cul-
de-sac with a chain-link fence around a yard that was
overgrown with weeds. The one-story house was
shoved under an interstate on-ramp, all of the shades
pulled down tight, hiding dark secrets.

Max and Ronny Ramirez got out of the unmarked
car and approached the house, the gate creaking as
they passed through. One block away the SWAT team
waited for instructions. One block in the other direction were four squad cars ready to cordon off the area
and follow the SWAT team in if necessary. A mile
away, police air-patrol helicopters hovered.

Max knocked on the door while Ramirez stayed to
one side, his magnum drawn and ready. When no one
answered the knock, the men picked their way around
the house, but already Max's heart was sinking at the
air of abandonment.

The garage was empty.

There was a wide, dark stain across the floor where
it looked as if a body had been dragged, the trail
stopping abruptly near the garage door. Regina's
blood? Or Ethan's?

"They're not here," Max said, straightening from
where he'd been examining the floor.

Max radioed the SWAT team commander, sending
one group away. The remaining team converged on

the house, shields in front of them, guns drawn. With one shot, they blasted through the front door and hurried through the house, their boots echoing on the floorboards. Within five minutes, they confirmed what Max had feared: Nobody was there.

The smell in the house was so bad that some of the men gagged, others held their hands over their noses and mouths.

Death.

Max knew that smell.

He sent the SWAT team away. He sent the choppers away, then radioed for the crime lab.

Ramirez and another police officer took the basement, where the foul odor seemed to originate from.

The room was illuminated by a line of fluorescent bulbs down the center of the ceiling. The cement floor was shiny, almost black, as if it had been scrubbed again and again. Along one wall was a desk and computer, the Microsoft logo twirling and bouncing from one edge of the screen to the other. Not far from the computer was a single bed, neatly made, one white pillow fluffed and in place, waiting to welcome a weary head. Along another wall, under the small basement window that had been covered with cloudy plastic, were wooden shelves full of neatly labeled canning jars. The glass jars had been lined up with precision, the exact same distance between each jar, the exact same distance from the shelf edge.

Ramirez trained his flashlight on the jars. "Big fan of spaghetti," he commented, feeling the hairs on his arms stand erect. All the jars were labeled "spaghetti sauce." He shifted the light to train it on the floor where a small puddle had formed near a gym-size locker.

"Think we found the source of the stink," he said loudly, for the benefit of the officers waiting upstairs. "We're gonna need a hacksaw."

The shudder of boots on the stairs announced the arrival of an officer with the hacksaw. By the time the lock was removed, a crowd of cops had gathered.

Ramirez opened the door. Out poured sawdust and lime, along with a mutilated, rotting body with no head.

A call came in from Ramirez, letting the remaining members of the task force who'd stayed behind know that the shakedown had been unsuccessful. "But they found a decapitated body," announced the female officer taking the call.

Ivy sat down heavily. "Ethan?" she asked, all of her attention focused on the officer. Oh, God, oh, God. Not Ethan.

The officer slowly hung up, and just as slowly said, "They don't know yet."

"And the killer?"

"He wasn't there."

Ivy had to get away. She had to get some air.

Moving in a haze, she left the room.

She ran up the stairs, bursting through the heavy metal door into the blazing sunlight on the rooftop where she and Max had gone the day she told him who she really was. Even though the sun was boiling the tar under her feet, the heat of it felt *real,* reminding her that she was alive.

While Ethan wasn't.

No! No! She couldn't accept that.

Oh, Max. *Max.* What was he doing now? Saying now? Feeling now?

The Madonna Murderer, still out there. Still out here.

Somewhere.

Where?

Where would he go?

Where would he go?

Max sat on the front step of the porch of the house that belonged to the Madonna Murderer. As soon as they said they'd found a body, he suddenly couldn't breathe. His chest hurt so much he'd wondered if he was having a heart attack, not really caring, considering it in a purely detached way.

Snatches of conversation crept to him, echoing hollowly in his mind like a dream. Somebody said the body was leaking, and fluid was running all over the place.

And there was no head.

The body had no head.

Max let out a choked sob and covered his face, praying it wasn't his son.

He should have gotten out years ago. This day, this moment was the future he'd felt hanging over him for the last ten years. This was the destiny he'd been moving toward.

Ivy pulled Max's car to a stop across from the brick building, near the spot where Max had parked the day they'd come there. Not even thinking about the meter this time, she hurried across the street, dodging traffic.

She pushed the manager's button, but nobody answered. She pressed her face close to the glass door and peered inside. The office was dark. Saturday. It was Saturday. She began jabbing buttons at random, begging someone to let her in.

The security door buzzed.

She jumped on it, yanking it open.

She walked past the elevator to take the stairs to the second floor. The dimly lit hallway smelled like incense and something else she couldn't place. She reached under her jacket and unsnapped the leather holster, slipping the solid, heavy revolver free.

When Max gave her the gun, she never thought she would use it. She'd hoped that she wouldn't. Now she prayed she would. Over the years, she'd imagined helping to catch the Madonna Murderer, helping to bring him in, picking him out of a lineup, identifying his voice. . . .

The woman who cried when Jinx killed a rabbit, the woman who took in baby robins that had fallen from their nests, now imagined the way it would feel to pull the trigger, to put a bullet through the center of Grant Ruby's forehead.

He had made her want to kill with ten times the passion and hatred he felt toward his own victims. He had made her want to kill with the fervor and single-minded intensity that only a person steps away from madness could feel.

She moved silently down the empty hall until she reached the door of her old apartment. 283.

Cool, detached, she raised her fist and knocked.

Chapter 41

He wouldn't stand out in a crowd. You probably wouldn't even notice him unless you looked directly into his black, hollow eyes.

"Say something," Ivy commanded with a two-arm stance, never blinking, never taking her eyes from his. A snapshot image flashed in her brain. He was the man from the hockey game, the man who'd talked to Ethan and waved to Max.

He stepped back and she moved forward. The door swung closed behind her. Inside the apartment, candles and incense burned. Lots of candles, with flames that danced and bobbed against red glass.

That smell. What's that horrible smell?

The hand with the gun began to tremble. Ivy shifted her support arm, readjusted her stance. "Say something! Say something, you son of a bitch! Say something so I know it's you!"

He smiled a sweet, awful, empty smile that implied everything was working out. Then he spoke one word: "Claudia."

In her mind, Ivy tumbled backward, falling into the deep, dark, stagnant pool that was her subconscious. In there were all the things she'd never wanted to remember, all the things she couldn't face. Memories of that night.

That smell. My God. What is that smell?

With the gun still aimed at his face, she fumbled in her pocket for the mobile phone Max had insisted she carry.

Max walked blindly toward the front door.

A hand reached out, stopping him.

Abraham. When had he gotten there?

Max pushed Abraham's hand aside. "I've got to see the body. I've got to know if it's Ethan."

"It's in bad shape, Max. I'm not sure you'd even be able to tell. Dr. Bernard's on her way here. She'll let you know what she finds out."

"I'd know," Max said. "I'd know my own son."

Abraham stared at him for a few moments, compassion and pain in his eyes. "You stay here," he finally said. "I'll look."

Abraham left Max waiting on the porch. As soon as he opened the door, the stench hit him. He lifted his tie to his nose and mouth, pressing tightly, willing himself not to gag as he made his way downstairs.

The smell in the basement was so bad that the officers had cleared out, waiting for the specialists to arrive.

When the locker was opened, sawdust and lime had spilled to the floor, the mutilated body following so that now it lay on top, a congealed tangle of coagulated blood and rotting tissue.

Jesus. Oh, Jesus. It can't be Ethan. Don't let it be Ethan, Abraham prayed as he approached. Standing directly over the body, he bent closer, his gaze moving over butchered limbs, picking out landmarks that proved the carcass was human. Fat. A lot of fat, and Ethan was slim.

He needed more information.

He looked around the room and spotted a broom. He shouldn't touch the body, not until the crime techs and coroner were done with it, but Max was waiting. Abraham had to give his friend an answer, one way or the other.

Using the broom handle as a lever, he shifted the body, stirring up a fetid wave of odor. The entire mess rolled, then stopped, exposing a sawdust-covered pubic area where a black X had been drawn with Magic Marker.

A woman.

The body belonged to a woman.

Max heard Abraham shout his name. Then the front door flew open and Abraham burst out into the fresh air and sunlight. Gasping, he grabbed Max by the arms, saying, "It's not Ethan. The body belongs to a woman. It's not Ethan."

Max's legs went weak and he dropped to the steps, burying his face in his hands. *Thank God. Thank God.*

His phone rang.

Automatically, he reached into his pocket and pulled out the phone, his mind disconnected from a response that was second nature. "Irving."

"Max."

The breathless, tension-filled voice belonged to Ivy.

"Max, I'm at my old apartment on Division. The Madonna Murderer is here. Max? Did you hear me? I've got a fucking gun pointed at his head right now so you might want to get somebody over here."

Dial tone.

End of call.

"Here she is," Ruby said, his voice rising.

It was the voice of Ivy's nightmares, the voice of her horrors.

"Here she is!"

It took her a moment to realize he wasn't talking to her. With her heart hammering, her breathing coming in short gasps, she pulled her gaze from him for a fraction of a second—long enough to look in the direction he was speaking.

Against one wall of the kitchen was a refrigerator—probably the same white, rounded refrigerator that had been there when Ivy had rented the apartment. The door hung open, light spilling on the floor, cold air seeping out, curling around her feet. On the center metal rack was a human head.

Her gaze shot back to Ruby, her mind refusing to believe what she'd seen. Ruby was still there. *That's a good psycho, don't go anywhere. Don't try to move.*

A head. A goddamn head in the refrigerator.

No.

Yes.

Look again. You have to look again. Quickly now. Be fast. Now! Look now!

The eyeballs were swollen, almost ready to pop. Straggly, blood-encrusted gray hair framed the face.

Gray hair. Not Ethan. Not Ethan.

Then who?

The mouth was taped into the Madonna Murderer's hideous signature grin.

"Here she is, Mother. She came. Just like I said

she would." His voice suddenly changed, becoming cheerful and childlike. "Watch me! Watch me!"

Ivy stared at the head—she couldn't seem to pull herself away—it was so mesmerizingly horrible.

When you see something you don't understand, your unconscious forces you to keep looking until you figure it out. Ivy kept looking, looking. . . .

"Watch me! Watch me!"

She dragged her gaze away from the decapitated, grinning head to see candlelight reflecting off something Ruby held in his hand, something he swung at her in a long, sweeping motion.

It struck her wrist. The gun clattered to the floor like a toy. Ruby kicked it, and it spun away into the fetid darkness.

A knife. He had a knife. Where had it come from? Had he had it all along?

A sensation of heat enveloped her arm, and she realized she couldn't feel her fingers.

Something splashed down her leg. She thought she'd wet herself, but then distantly realized it was blood.

Her hand. Had he cut off her hand?

No. It was still there. Covered with blood, but still there. Blood dripping off the fingertips, falling *plop, plop, plop* to the floor.

She looked up in time to see the knife coming at her again. She sidestepped, the blade just nicking her arm.

It was a reenactment.

Or maybe her life had gotten caught in some kind of weird time loop. But here she was, reliving the same nightmare of sixteen years ago.

Her will to survive kicked in. Somehow she grabbed his arm—but he was strong, so strong, his hands like talons, his muscles like taut, sinewy rope. As the woman in the refrigerator watched, never blinking, grinning in pride, the Madonna Murderer plunged the knife again and again, some thrusts hitting their mark, some deflected by Ivy's struggles.

They tumbled to the floor, falling near the bed, Ruby on top.

As Ivy lay there, feeling the stickiness of her own blood on her hands, she sensed the futility of it all, felt her strength and will to live draining away. This was her destiny, and destiny couldn't be changed. She'd tried. Hadn't she tried?

She just wanted it all to stop. Wanted her life to stop.

Socrates said the perfect society would be based on a great lie. People would be told that lie from the cradle, and they would believe it, because human beings need to make order out of chaos.

Ivy had told herself a great lie, a lie she'd lived with and believed. She'd thought she could make a difference. She'd thought if she studied hard enough, if she learned everything she could learn about men like Ruby, then she could catch him.

But her baby was dead. Nothing would bring him back.

Her baby was dead.

She had been able to save herself, but not her baby.

She was alive; her baby was dead.

If only she'd been more careful. If only she'd been stronger, faster. If only she hadn't gone to the store that night. If only she'd put her baby up for adoption the way everyone had begged, suggested, cajoled, he'd still be alive.

She hadn't been able to live with the full memory

of that night, so her mind had grown a protective skin around that memory and put it away.

Her baby was dead.

Whenever she thought of him, his face was a blur. But she could see him now, in her mind, blue lips, blue fingers. Dead. Dead. Dead.

She let out a sob. *Let him kill me.* Let him finish. A beginning, a middle, an end.

Ivy turned her face away so she couldn't see the madman hovering over her.

Across the expanse of hardwood, lying on his stomach on the floor almost beneath the bed, was Ethan.

Ethan. Oh my God. Ethan.

Are you alive? Please be alive.

His mouth was sealed with duct tape. His hands were taped behind his back, his cheek pressed to the floor, his pupils large and glassy.

Are you alive? Please be alive.

He blinked.

Thank God.

His eyes reflected all the horror he'd seen, and all the fear he felt. And now someone was finally there who wasn't the Madonna Murderer. With his eyes, he reached out to Ivy, begging her for help, begging her to make this stop, make it all go away.

How can I save you, she thought, *when I couldn't save my own child? How can I save you?*

She turned in time to see the knife come down. She twisted away. He missed, the blade becoming embedded in the floor. With her last bit of strength, she jumped to her feet and ran for the kitchen, for the refrigerator. While Ruby struggled to pull the knife from the floor, she grabbed the head by fistfuls of gray hair, pulling it from the metal rack. Her hands spread over the cold ears, she held the face away from her, her arms outstretched, shrieking at Ruby.

"STOP!"

He looked up—the color drained from his face. His mouth dropped open.

The head was heavy, and her arms were shaking. A weakness was building in her.

"Put the knife down!" Ivy shouted. "PUT IT DOWN!"

He looked guilty, as if his mother had caught him doing something he shouldn't.

Behind her, Ivy heard the layered thud of heavy footfalls. Help was coming. A lot of help. Outside, sirens screamed. The door crashed open and she heard Max's voice calling her name.

Max would never forget the image that met him when he broke open the apartment door—Ivy holding a human head in her hands as if it were a cross held up to ward off Dracula. A man—the Madonna Murderer—stood there, staring at the head in horror, looking as if he'd just come face-to-face with his own private version of hell.

And then Ruby moved. He came at Ivy with a gleaming knife raised high, screaming, "I hate you! I hate you!"

All of Ruby's hatred for his mother was directed into that scream, that attack. He would strike a deathblow.

In his years as a detective, Max had never shot anybody. But now he pulled the trigger. Once, twice, three times—because Max had the feeling a single bullet wasn't going to stop Grant Ruby. Sick animals were the hardest to kill.

Ruby's mask of hatred crumpled, to be replaced by one of idiotic surprise, total and utter surprise that his life's work had been cut short in his very moment of triumph.

He was dead before he hit the floor.

Time became weird the way it always did when adrenaline flooded your veins. The third bullet had barely left the chamber when Max thought, *What have I done?*

Ethan.

Ruby was the only person who knew if Ethan was alive or dead, the only person who knew where Max would find him.

In the very second he had that thought, Ivy spoke his son's name.

He was distantly aware of Abraham and the other officers behind him, but they were a peripheral blur, not important.

He slid his revolver back in the shoulder holster as he ran the few steps through the kitchen into the main room. He was afraid he'd misunderstood Ivy's communication, but then he spotted Ethan on the floor, on the other side of the bed.

He dropped to his knees beside him, his hands shaking. Ethan's eyes were open and locked with his. Max pulled off the duct tape. As soon as his mouth was uncovered, Ethan began to sob.

"Here—"

An officer handed Max a pocketknife, blade open. Max cut through the bindings on Ethan's wrists and legs, then he sat on the floor and pulled his son into his arms, hugging him, kissing his blood-matted hair, rocking him, tears spilling.

*   *   *

Someone must have taken the head from her hands. Ivy had a vague awareness of Abraham being there, of a tourniquet being tightened around her arm, of two ambulance attendants putting her on a gurney.

I'm not dead, she thought she whispered, but they didn't seem to hear her. Perhaps the words had only been unvocalized thoughts. Would they put her in a body bag? For some reason, that idea gave her no anxiety.

Outside, cameras flashed and reporters shouted questions, trying to put microphones in her face. And then she was rushed away, sirens wailing, the ambulance rocking her to sleep.

Chapter 42

The story of how Claudia Reynolds reemerged as Ivy Dunlap hit newsstands, and Ivy became an overnight celebrity. People she didn't even know sent flowers to her hospital room. Reporters posed as long-lost relatives trying to get a story. Every national morning show wanted to book her, and two publishers had already contacted her about writing an autobiography.

She'd almost bled to death. By the time the ambulance reached Blessings Hospital, her blood pressure was almost nonexistent. It took four pints of blood to get it back up. One specialist worked on her wrist and hand while another repaired her other injuries—three wounds that had miraculously missed all major organs. There were five less-severe cuts to her arms, cuts that had required a total of twenty-two stitches. If Ivy had been conscious when they were working on her, she would have insisted on twenty-three, or twenty-one. Twenty-two allowed the Madonna Murderer one final statement.

Abraham came to see her, and he had one thing on his mind: He wanted her to stay and work for the Chicago Police Department.

"We haven't yet decided what your exact position

would be," Abraham explained. "It would be up to
you. You could join Homicide as our expert in the
field of criminal psychology. Or if that feels too con-
strictive, you could be a hired freelancer. We're
flexible."

Two minutes earlier, she'd pushed the button on
her morphine pump. Now all she could do was lie
there, trying to absorb his chatter.

"By the way, Max is staying on," Abraham added.

She wasn't surprised. She hadn't been able to picture him anywhere else.

"Naturally, he's concerned about Ethan's safety, so
until Ethan's older, Max is going to keep a lower,
more administrative profile while retaining his position
as Chief of Homicide. I think it can be done if we
work at it."

"That's good," she said, struggling to keep her
eyes open.

"I'll leave you alone," Abraham said, seeing that
she was having trouble staying awake. "But think
about staying. You'll think about it, won't you?"

She nodded.

On the third day of Ivy's hospitalization, the needle
was taken out of her hand and her supply of morphine
cut off. She was wheeled into a sitting area with a
huge window where she could see a bit of Lake Michigan in the distance, and maybe a couple of sailboats
if she were lucky.

That's where Max found her, in a wheelchair, staring out the window.

She immediately asked about Ethan.

"Still shaken up, but glad to be alive," Max said,
sitting down in one of the vinyl-covered chairs.

Ivy knew Ethan had spent one night in the hospital, then had been sent home.

How long would it take for him to recover, to forget and be able to live again as a teenager?

Sadly, Ivy knew that would never happen. He, like so many others, had been touched by the hand of a madman, and that kind of touch left latent prints that would never, ever go away. Ethan would return home and find that he'd lost the foolishness it took to hang out with his old friends. They wouldn't understand, and with the impatience of youth, they wouldn't want to understand. He was a drag, that's all they would know. And when somebody's a drag, you don't hang around with them.

Maybe Ethan would meet new people, people who were a few years older, who had more life experience. But even then, no matter what they'd gone through— loss of a parent, loss of a sibling—they wouldn't be able to understand the darkness and fear that came upon Ethan at odd times.

"The tire tracks at the murder scene of Alex Martin matched the tire tread on Ruby's car. Or rather, his mother's car."

She nodded, not surprised.

"He canned her."

"What?"

"Part of her, anyway. There were thirty jars of spaghetti sauce in the basement. DNA in some of the sauce matched the mother's. A meat grinder was also found to contain her DNA."

"Oh, Christ. I could have done without knowing that. I'll never be able to eat spaghetti again."

"Sorry. Thought you might find it interesting.

Here's another bit of information. In his high school yearbook, Ruby said that he hoped somebody wrote a book about him and hoped that book was made into a movie. Unfortunately, that will probably happen."

He got up from the chair and walked over to the window. He looked out for a moment, then turned back to Ivy. "I'm sorry I blamed you the other day. If you hadn't come up with the letter idea, the Madonna Murderer would still be out there."

A man who could say he was sorry. He had her attention. But Ivy believed in taking responsibility for her own actions. "You had every right to blame me. The letter drove Ruby over the edge. It got Alex Martin killed and Ethan kidnapped."

"There was no way we could have predicted the outcome. And we had to do something."

"I became too confident," she said truthfully. "We should have approached with more caution."

"Ruby may have come after Ethan anyway, eventually. The hockey stick proves he'd been following him for a long time. He wanted you both. Our knowledge of the tattoo was the first piece of the puzzle for him, leading him to the possibility that Claudia Reynolds, the only person who could link the tattoo to the Madonna Murderer, was still alive. At that same time, he was trying to find out who Ivy Dunlap was, and what she was doing here. We found a well-thumbed copy of your book, *Symbolic Death,* at his house. One theory is that he figured out that you and Claudia Reynolds were the same person. Then he saw you with Ethan that night at the hockey game. Because of the similarity of your features, he drew the same conclusion others who saw you together did. He thought you were Ethan's mother. And he thought if your death had been faked, then so had your baby's. Another theory is that he wanted to harm Ethan simply because he is my son."

She nodded. "It would have been a thrill for him to know you were called to the crime scene to find your own son's body."

"He may have even wanted me to be the one to track them to your old apartment."

"What did you find out about the sixteen years of no murders?"

"Shortly after you were attacked, he checked himself into a state mental hospital where he was evaluated as paranoid schizophrenic with obsessive-compulsive tendencies. He was put on heavy medication, stayed there several years until the mental hospital did some housecleaning and ejected over a hundred patients. In all that time, he'd never been diagnosed as dangerous. I'll see that you get a copy of his file. It seems his favorite pastime was sculpting figures out of chewed-up bread. Most of the figures were of the Madonna and Child."

"And nobody picked up on that?"

"Apparently not. As a child, he suffered severe abuse at the hands of his mother."

"Which will most likely spark a fresh debate on whether or not people are simply born bad or shaped by outside influences."

"If he'd been taken out of that environment when he was an infant, would he have gone on to murder?"

"It's media attention like this that stigmatizes mental patients," she said with feeling. "The schizophrenia didn't make him kill. That, combined with an abusive childhood, created a lethal cocktail."

"As you can probably guess, he quit taking his medication several months ago."

"Wasn't anyone monitoring him?"

"He was under psychiatric care, but he was able to convince his doctor that he was doing remarkably well and still taking his medication."

"I'm sure he could be quite persuasive," she said. "What about Regina?"

"No change. The doctors said if she hasn't regained consciousness by now, she probably won't."

"They don't know who they're dealing with."

He agreed. "I chose her for the task force because I liked her tough, straightforward attitude. By the way, your cat's fine," he said, examining a scratch on the back of his hand. "He hates me, but he's fine."

"It's not you. Jinx doesn't like anybody. He's really half-wild, poor guy."

"I heard a rumor that you're leaving the hospital soon."

"They're releasing me day after tomorrow."

"Can I give you a ride to your apartment?"

"That would be nice."

Once she got there, once she'd given Jinx all the attention he could stand, she would open the box she hadn't been able to open for sixteen years. Inside she'd find a tiny white gown. It had been an extravagance, something she couldn't afford, but she'd bought it anyway. Recalling its softness, she imagined raising it to her cheek. It would smell like the attic of her house, but maybe, just maybe, the brushed cotton would still hold the faint scent of a baby. *Her* baby.

"I know Abraham's been to see you. I know he asked you to join Homicide. Have you come to any kind of decision?"

"Not yet."

She thought about her future. For sixteen years,

she'd lived for one thing and one thing only, and now her life seemed superfluous.

What would she do?

Take care of Jinx.

And every day she would go over questions that had haunted man since the beginning of time. What am I doing here? Who am I? What's my purpose?

Those deeper, more reflective questions often came with middle age, but with Ivy it was more than that. "I know this seems weird, but now that Ruby is gone, now that he's dead, I feel . . . I don't know, empty. I used to be able to see into my future, but now I look and there's nothing there."

"That's understandable. He occupied a big space in your head for a long time. You'll have to find something else to fill that with."

"I don't know if moving here is the answer. If I move, there will be no going back. If I move, I'll have to sell my house in St. Sebastian, a house that's been a refuge for me." Could she and Jinx live where there were no fields piled high with round stones shaped by glaciers?

"Maybe you'll find a new refuge."

It was strange, but in her mind, she'd already given up her world where the only death she saw was an occasional dead mouse or baby bunny that Jinx had caught. "It's safe in St. Sebastian."

But it was also a world that had never seemed quite real. Because of the secret she carried, she'd never been able to open up to people, never been able to move beyond a certain level of intimacy. But how could she leave the security of St. Sebastian to embrace a world of murder and chaos?

What about her research?

Maybe she could continue with it in Chicago. In Chicago, she could visit her baby's grave, because she was ready to do that now.

"What about you?" she asked. "I heard you decided to stay in Homicide."

"We can't go back," he said quietly. "None of us can go back."

He'd been faced with the same decision she was facing, and had chosen the harsh reality of Homicide. And while such a world hadn't broken him, it had left him scarred. Left his son scarred.

He was silent. She knew he was thinking about what was ahead for her. "I won't beg you to stay," he said. "You're the only one who can make that decision, but Abraham was right when he said that you can't close the door on this kind of thing and expect it to remain closed. I really wish you could go back to Canada and forget all of this happened. But you know it won't be like that. And personally, I hate to think of you so far away."

"It's not that far. Two hours by plane."

"It wouldn't be the same."

"What are you trying to say?"

She could tell by his expression that he was struggling over how much of himself to reveal. "I'm saying I'll miss you," he admitted. "But I want what's best for you, not for me."

He was her friend, she realized, and she'd needed such a friend for a long time. "I know," she said softly. There were only two people in the world who knew her and understood her: Max and Abraham.

He moved away from the window. "I've got to be

going soon. Don't want to leave Ethan alone too long."

"Tell him I said thanks for the roses. They're beautiful."

"He'd like to see you, like to talk to you, but not right now. It's all too fresh. He cries a lot, and he has no control over it. I think he's embarrassed about that."

"It's good that he's showing emotion."

"That's what I told him. Cry like hell if you want to."

"If he ever needs to talk, I'm available—day or night. Please tell him that."

"I will."

He picked up her uninjured hand, cupping it between both of his as if it were a fragile bird. "You saved my son's life. Take comfort in that."

She knew they were both thinking of a son she hadn't been able to save. And even though her loss had been so long ago, the horrific experience in her old apartment had finally brought her memories to the forefront. "The mind is such an amazing universe," she said, feeling something lift from her heart—a heaviness. Saving Ethan had absolved her of the guilt she'd carried with her for so long.

A nurse appeared from around the corner. "There you are. We've been looking for you. Time for your meds." She extended a paper cup containing a codeine tablet that Ivy swallowed with gratitude. Her hand was beginning to throb. The doctors had been able to reconnect nerves and tendons, but she would probably never regain total mobility. And in a few years, they'd warned, arthritis would likely set in.

The nurse wheeled Ivy back to her room and helped her get settled in bed.

"Is the pain bad?" Max asked when the nurse had left.

Ivy opened her eyes. "Sometimes it hurts like hell," she admitted. "But I'll be okay. It'll just take some time."

"You're an incredibly strong person, Ivy Dunlap."

She smiled, grateful not only for the compliment, but because he'd called her by her real name. Because she *was* Ivy now. She'd been Ivy for a long time.

She was beginning to drift to sleep when he leaned over and pressed his lips to her forehead. "I left something on the table next to your bed," he whispered. "Something that might help you come to a decision."

Shit.

Oh, Shit.

Regina felt like shit.

Like a thick cement blanket was crushing her, keeping her from taking a deep breath.

Sleep. Just sleep.

But she couldn't sleep. She felt too shitty to sleep. Her head hurt. Her eyes hurt. Her joints hurt.

And the pain just kept increasing. It wouldn't go away. Just kept knocking, knocking on her brain until she had to force her eyes open.

Bright, blinding light.

A weight against her thigh.

Someone with dark hair, a forehead pressed against her leg.

Get off.

She tried to move, tried to shift the person away,

but all she managed was a little twitch and a moan that was not much more than an exhalation. With her hand, she tried to bop whoever it was on the head, but there was all this crap on her arm, which was attached to a board.

The movement was enough to get his attention, though. He stirred and looked up at her. Ronny Ramirez.

Ramirez?

She felt a sweetness blossom somewhere deep inside her, and managed to croak out a single word, spoken with tender affection. "Asshole."

He turned his head to look at her, and the joy in his face was remarkable to behold.

Ethan hadn't been able to listen to music since the night the Madonna Murderer had coaxed him into his car and Ethan had fallen for it so easily.

Piece of candy, little boy?

The psycho had taken away Ethan's soul by using something he loved to trick him, trap him, draw him into his sick, macabre world.

A knock sounded on his bedroom door. Ethan quickly wiped the tears away and propped himself up on his elbows. "It's unlocked."

The door opened far enough for Heather to peek in. Today her hair was red. "Can I come in?"

He sat up, wondering if she could tell he'd been crying. "Yeah. Sure."

So far, none of his other friends had been over, and even though that didn't surprise him, it still hurt.

She held up a CD jewel case, her bracelets jingling. His stomach took a dive.

"You won't believe what I found. An outtake of

Velvet Underground's 'Ocean.' I remembered how
you were looking for it once. Did you ever find it?"

"No," he said numbly. "Look, I don't feel like listening to music, okay?"

"Just one song," she pleaded. "You have to hear
this."

She slipped the CD in the player. Without waiting
for an invitation, she plopped down on the bed beside
him so they were sitting side by side, feet on the floor.
When the music started, she fell back, eyes closed.

At first Ethan tried not to listen, tried to block it
out, but the song was so compelling, so haunting, that
it kept coming to him and coming to him, and he
couldn't push it away.

Wow.

Oh, wow.

He fell back against a mattress that had not so many
years ago been covered with Winnie-the-Pooh sheets,
next to Heather, and closed his eyes. He was deep
within the song when he felt her strong fingers against
the back of his hand, wrapping around, latching on.

Ivy picked up the red cloth journal Max had left on
the table beside her bed. The title? *Death as the Re-
ward, a Manifesto* by Grant Ruby.

The book contained pages of notes Ruby had put
together over the years. But it was the final entry that
solidified her decision to move to Chicago as nothing
else could have. Max knew her so well.

It was written with intricate precision, in small,
neatly printed letters of black ink. The lines were as
straight and exact as if the paper had been ruled.

*Medication is always the suggestion. Medication?
I don't need medication. Why do I need medication to keep me from seeing the truth? To paint my
eyes with false hope and false reality?*

*People dressing nicely, talking nicely, saying good
morning, saying excuse me. A lie! A lie!*

*People are stupid. They create false worlds, false
realities, in order to deny the purposelessness of
their lives. They construct houses and have children
in order to control the chaos, to fool themselves
into thinking life has meaning. They are able to say,
Look! I'm mowing the yard! Look, I'm feeding
the dog! Look, my kids have a happy childhood!
See, life is more than suffering and pain.*

*People are stupid. They don't understand that
death is the prize! They don't understand that I'm
simply a creature of the world who is able to see
things the way they really are. If I want to kill,
there's nothing wrong with that. I'm just more advanced than you, a few generations ahead of you.
So when you are alone in your house, when you are
alone in your car, when you are traveling, when
you are running out for a gallon of milk, BE
AWARE. BE VERY AWARE.*

I'm out there.
I'm not alone.

Turn the page for an excerpt from
a new blockbuster novel of suspense
coming from Anne Frasier
in March 2003

He hovered over the prone, unmoving girl, deftly drawing a thick black line on her eyelids, curving it upward at the corners. That was followed by a smidgen of rouge to her colorless cheeks. Next came the lipstick. Bloodred in a gold metal tube.

He could hear his own rasping breath as he carefully applied it to lips that had been soft and full but were now chapped and cracked. As carefully as a mortician he worked, and as he did he could feel his heart beating in his head.

He had the desire to kiss her, and leaned closer.

Wake up, my princess. My little princess . . .

Like a baby bird, her cracked lips opened under his. He felt her deep inhalation sucking the air from his lungs—a cat, trying to steal his breath. He pulled back to see her staring silently at him, her pupils dilated and glassy from drugs and the dark, windowless basement where she'd spent the last two weeks. Had she learned her lesson? Would she finally act like a lady now? Would she ask him how his day had been? Would she ask him what he'd like for supper? And later, would she sit on the living room floor near his feet while he listened to Kurt Weil records? Would she rub his temples until his headache stopped, saying in the most soothing of voices, "There, there"?

Her throat rattled.

Splat—something wet hit his cheek. It took him a moment to realize it was spit.

The thankless bitch! The thankless little bitch!

Heat roared through his veins until he thought his skin would split, until he thought his eyeballs might pop from his head. Enraged, he grabbed her by both arms and jerked her to her feet. "I've been working my ass off every day, out punching the clock, and this is the thanks I get?" He wrapped his hands around her neck. "I slave over you, trying to teach you basic etiquette! You bitch!" He shook her. "You spoiled, spoiled bitch!"

He squeezed and he squeezed, and when she went limp he kept on squeezing until he was certain she would never insult him again.

She continued to stare at him with accusation in her eyes long after she was dead.